I0779533

THE HEALER ACADEMY

book one

MARINDA MISRA

To Papaya
- my first and biggest fan

PART ONE

CHAPTER

ONE

Ｉ couldn't look away from the light. The flame flickered and the wax crackled, making the light dance across the words on the page in front of me. Only when my eyes started to water did I look down again at the book on the kitchen table.

Hagsfoot is a large root that has...that has...that...has...

Bark rot.

The page went out of focus as my chest constricted ever so slightly, as if a string was tied around my heart and someone, somewhere, was gently tugging on the other end. The skin around my mouth tightened into a frown. I had managed to keep the *pull* at bay for a whole four pages and had started to hope it had gone away.

The *pull* shouldn't have been happening now anyway. I wasn't praying, and I definitely wasn't anywhere near the Holy Forest. There was no reason it should have bothered me tonight....

The exam. I needed to focus on preparing for the exam.

I put my elbows on the table and propped my head up on

3

my hands, determined not to lose focus again. Earlier that day I had seen the Examiners to the Healer Academy arrive, riding past my aunt's cottage on their way to the village green, three imposing figures in their wagon with their armed guards. Not far behind was another wagon of poorly dressed fifteen-year-olds—the lucky ones who had already earned their scholarships.

That would be me.

The *pull* tightened.

"Focus," I muttered. "Whatever this is, it isn't real. Tomorrow's exam is." I closed my eyes as I ran a hand down my face, then opened them, finding my place on the page again.

Hagsfoot, found in the desert plateaus of south Tamerin, is a large root that has a very small, dead-looking stem. The extended drought season makes most of the plant grow downward to avoid having its moisture evaporate. Use gloves when digging it up, as the outer layer can cause a painful rash, which is ironic since the inner part, when properly prepared, can soothe almost any skin irritation.

I smiled to myself as the tightening in my chest lessened. I was alone again. Normal again. Well, as normal as I could be.

My finger moved to the next page, tracing the outline of a beautifully sketched flower. It had a slim stem with two blades growing up from the ground at the root, and at the top a perfectly circular yellow and orange flower made up of a thousand little petals.

Butterlace is found in the meadows of Northwest Tamerin, in the fertile hills of—

I screamed as our front door was suddenly attacked by a pounding outside that threatened to knock down the thin wall of our cottage.

"BEREDITH!" A man yelled from outside, rapping again. I jumped to my feet and ran from the kitchen through the open doorframe, across our small front room, hopping over the baskets and boxes I knew were there in the dark. I threw open the front door and shrank back at the dark shape of a man. He was tall, with limbs that always looked like they weren't attached to his body right. I recognized him as Theo, a farmer in our small village. For a moment he looked relieved, until he saw it was me and not my aunt.

He took a step back.

They always did.

"Kailin! Where's your aunt?!"

"She's, um…" I stammered. Something was off about him, and it wasn't just that he was here in the middle of the night. Something about how he smelled.

"She's right here," my aunt grumbled, appearing behind me in her sleeping smock and pushing me aside. I gladly let her. If I could keep my interactions with other members of our village to somewhere near zero, I considered it a good day.

"Now what do you want?" my aunt asked. "By the Great One, you better have a good reason—"

"It's the Grouses' cottage!" Theo interrupted, bouncing from one foot to the other. "It's burning to the ground!"

That's when I recognized the smell.

Smoke. And a lot of it.

My aunt wasted no time, turning back into the dark room and making her way to the kitchen where all her healing satchels were kept, stocked and ready.

"Has anyone been hurt?" she called back, her voice calm, yet still sharp.

"Only Marily was badly burned," Theo said, referring to Kert Grouse's wife. I stepped back into the shadows when he tried to follow her, but she had blown out the candle and he tripped, spilling a whole box of rags waiting to be stripped into bandages. My aunt was back in a moment, pulling on her boots, satchel strung over her healer apron. She helped Theo to his feet and the two of them turned to the door.

"What should I do?" I asked. Theo nearly jumped out of his skin, having forgotten I was there. I had become good at being forgotten. It was better than the alternative.

"Don't let that girl anywhere near the family!" Theo snapped at Aunt Beredith. "She'll bring her bad luck, and the Grouses have suffered enough tonight!"

I took a step back further into the shadows.

Not far enough to escape my aunt as she locked eyes with mine.

She was as tall as Theo, but built more sturdily. From a distance, when she was wearing her gray healer apron, she could have been mistaken for a blacksmith, except no blacksmith had ever been so intimidating.

"Stay here," my aunt said, shoving Theo out the door. Turning back to me, she added in a quieter voice, "I might need some other supplies, in which case I'll send a runner back. You're the only one who knows where anything is in this mess."

I nodded, but the sound of her running feet was already disappearing. I waited a moment longer to be sure they were gone, then I peeked out the door into the night.

It was almost exactly as it should have been. A bright moon overhead illuminated the strip of thatch-roofed cottages and plowed fields surrounded by a sea of forest now black in the night. What was not as it should be was the lights aglow in the buildings of the village center a half mile to my left, and the men and women shouting at each other and running down the road toward where a blaze was brightening the sky. The villagers were close enough and the moon was bright enough that I could guess who each of them was, and I found myself sinking back into the shadows again.

I shouldn't be afraid of them. Aunt Beredith wasn't afraid. When someone in the village would bring up my history, like Theo just did, she would glare flint at them until they sulked away or changed the topic.

But I wasn't her. I was just me, and I knew deep down I could never fight back. Maybe I had thought differently once, but that had been a long time ago, before I learned better. All I allowed within myself anymore was the unwavering hope of escape.

No, not just a hope. A reality that hadn't happened yet. It was that real to me.

A loud crash from down the road made me venture out, horrified and fascinated to see that the sky had turned orange. I could hear the shouts from the Grouses' farm even from here.

I took a step out onto the dirt path leading from our door to the road. The air was still chill, the stars out like any other night, but the blaze, the voices, all those things seemed to be pulling me forward.

I froze, not even daring to breathe.

No, it wasn't the *emergency* that was calling me, the fascination and novelty of the disaster.

It was calling me. The *pull* wasn't strong, but that feeling in my chest, now that I was paying attention, was definitely there.

I took a step back toward the safety of my shadows and the *pull* became stronger.

The thumping of feet on the road made me turn my head. Dural appeared in the moonlight. He hadn't seen me yet, so I stayed where I was to watch him run past. He was almost to the end of our path when his eyes caught mine. He nearly tripped, but saved himself by making it look as though he had been reaching down on purpose to grab something.

I ducked behind the doorframe just as the rock hit the side of the house.

He was gone again when I poked my head out again, the shape of his silhouette black against the glow he was running toward.

A part of me wanted to shut the door and stay away from everything that breathed, but my hands were balling into fists instead.

My chest began to hurt from the strain now in it, as if another heart, stronger than mine, was locked behind my ribs, making my blood pump faster and bolder.

I'm going to be a Healer.

My next steps were unconscious as I ran back into the kitchen to grab the other healing satchel and my boots. Then I was on the road, running toward the fire. I had no idea if there would be anything for me to do; Theo said only Marily was hurt, but I didn't stop running. My aunt had said to stay home, and every self-preservation instinct said to stay hidden from the other villagers, but my heart was beating with a new rhythm of purpose and I longed to follow it. A feeling like fire suddenly burst inside me, and for a moment all my fears were burned away.

My pace picked up to a sprint.

I stopped at the edge of the Grouses' property, breathing heavily from the exertion and coughing from the smoke and ash that filled my lungs and stung my eyes. It was almost a sweet smell, earthy and warm and deadly. Men and women had formed a bucket line leading from the stream that ran along the forest's edge, too desperate and distracted with putting out the flames to notice my arrival, their yells barely audible against the roar of the flames and the cracking of solid wood beams now falling apart. It was clear there would be little left of the cottage. The insides were almost gone with only a skeleton of rafters and outer walls left. Now it was just a fight to get it under control so it wouldn't spread to their crops, or worse, the grove of the Grouses' Family and Memory Trees only yards away. My head jerked around as I heard a scream and saw my aunt bent over a body on the ground, working furiously on Marily with Kert holding her down.

I looked back at the fray, and my heart sank as I realized there really wasn't anything for me to do. If I tried to join the bucket line I would be turned away at best, and if I helped my aunt she would give me a good tongue lashing for disobeying her.

The *pull* had been wrong. I should have stayed at home, hidden and safe.

A loud crack from a collapsing piece of roof drew my attention to the other side of the house, away from the line of people with their buckets. That's when I saw him: the Grouses' ten-year-old boy, Alexi, had a long stick in his hand, and instead of being terrified, the fool was actually poking the flames! My fury at his stupidity was only outmatched by my terror.

I started to run toward him, just as the walls crumbled.

"ALEXI!" I screamed, but it was too late. I got just close enough to see the boy's eyes widen as the wall fell toward him.

I threw my hands up to cover my face as sparks and cinder exploded in front of me, but I forgot about the stinging of my singed skin when Alexi cried out again. I squinted through the blazing flames and saw him lying five feet away under a smoldering board. I didn't hesitate as I grabbed him and pulled him out, only to hear him scream even louder as I moved him to safety.

"I got you." I looked him over. His burns weren't as bad as I feared, thank The Great One. "You're safe now."

"Kailin?" he asked, coughing through the smoke.

"Yes, it's me."

"You pushed the wall on me!"

"Of all the—" I started, and that alive, fiery feeling I had felt while running flared again.

"Get away from me!" He made as if to get up and run, but instead screamed and collapsed to the ground. I tried to get another look, to find what was wrong, but he kept smacking me away.

"Stop moving and let me—"

"HELP!" He screamed. "Kailin's trying to damn me!"

I slapped him. He looked at me, his eyes wide with shock. I was in shock as well, but I was too angry to let it show. I had never fought back before, but tonight was different.

I was different.

"Now tell me where it hurts!" I yelled in his face. "Or by the Great One I will plant the Memory Tree over your grave myself!"

He burst out crying. "My leg," he sobbed.

And that's when I saw the dark stickiness seeping out of his trouser leg. Mechanically, I reached into my satchel and got out a pair of scissors. I cut open his trousers, then swallowed back the bile that boiled in the back of my throat. There was a six-inch-long nail pushed all the way through his calf. The tip just barely poked out the other side.

Then the *pull* was back, but this time it seemed to be calming me, clearing my mind.

I'm a Healer.

Not yet. I had learned everything I could from my aunt, and helped when the villagers let me near them, but I hadn't attended the Healer Academy. I hadn't even passed the entrance exam yet.

You are a Healer.

The words came to my mind like a voice. I looked up, but no one was nearby. In all the chaos, no one had noticed us, and I doubted anyone would hear me if I called out.

I was on my own.

I pulled out a stick and put it in Alexi's mouth.

"Bite down on this if the pain gets to be too much," I said. Alexi nodded his head, suddenly trusting me. That shocked me more than anything else I had seen tonight.

I looked back at the wound. The nail was stopping most of the blood from pouring out, but a good amount was still soaking the grass. Was one of the main arteries hit? Aunt Beredith had explained the concept to me after I saw her make what she called a tourniquet when Kafli, at the farm just up the road, had impaled his leg on some farm equipment. She said if one of the main arteries was hit, you needed to do more than just patch up the bleeding; you needed to stop the flow of blood to the whole leg before the person bled out.

But how was I supposed to know if that was what was happening, or if he was just bleeding because he had a nail through his leg?

My hand began to shake as I realized I had no idea what to do next.

Think think THINK! What would Aunt Beredith do?

I looked up again, but I couldn't even see her.

Then the *pull* was back stronger than ever and I couldn't pay attention to anything else.

I closed my eyes and took a breath, trying not to cough in the smoke, instead absorbing the air, the grass, and the rusty smell of blood under my hands. I could see in perfect detail Alexi's leg in my mind, as if I were looking at it. The torn, Peasant-brown pants covered in dirt and ash. The exact placement of the nail, the angle, the way the blood was seeping out. What it would look like if I could see beneath the skin, the muscles connected by tendons to bones and—

Completely full of blue light.

All right, my eyes were shut, so I wasn't actually hallucinating, I was just visualizing.

I looked closer at this visualization and could see now instead of there being just one light there were actually thousands upon thousands of smaller lights, like mini stars moving around and against each other in one direction or another. These movements seemed random except for in a few cases where it formed into rivulets that either took in or emptied out into the area around them.

Actually, those larger movements looked a lot like—

I snapped my eyes open, but the little blue lights were still there.

I felt my heart stop and my head grow dizzy.

What in the world was happening to me?!

Alexi whimpered and I pushed my concerns for my sanity to the side and focused back on what I was doing.

I looked at the lights, trying to find what I felt they were telling me.

I traced them along his leg until—

There was a shaft of darkness, something that made the light stop.

And it was cut through one of the rivulets close to the bone, the light pooling out of him, losing its glow as it went.

The artery had been cut.

In one movement I grabbed the scissors and cut away the rest of his pant leg. Throwing the scissors back in my satchel, I took out the leather strap and held it in my hands.

Where to put it...

As if in answer the lights brightened about two inches above the cut.

Not questioning, I wrapped it around his leg and tightened, just like I had seen Aunt Beredith do.

Alexi screamed, but I kept tightening as hard as I could. I counted to ten before I let myself look. When I did, I almost let go of his leg.

It had stopped bleeding.

The lights were gone.

And I had no idea where I was.

That's when I noticed the shadow rushing up behind me.

I wanted to run, but I was holding something in my hands I knew I needed to keep holding.

"I heard a scream." A woman knelt next to me. I had never seen her before, but she was analyzing the leg in front of me as if she knew what she was doing.

The Academy.

She must be one of the Healers from the Academy here for the exam.

Because I was going to be taking the exam tomorrow.

I was shocked at my lapse of memory; my visualization must have disoriented me more than I thought.

"His leg has been punctured," I said, still holding on to the leather strap for dear life—or really his life.

"Yes, I can see that." She turned to look at me and I froze. She was easily the most beautiful woman I had ever seen. Her hair and eyes were dark in the shadows of the now-dying flames, but her features were fine and strong in a way that could only be described as regal. Her mouth was turned down in a frown as she took me in, and I became horribly aware of how I must have looked in my sleeping smock, with my dull lavender eyes and frizzed black hair. Not silky raven-black that changed colors at night like some of the other girls in the village. No, mine just looked as if I had rolled around in the fireplace.

I bit my lip, waiting for her to pass judgment on me.

"But he most likely didn't need a tourniquet," she said with disapproval. That changed, though, when she examined the leg better. She touched the top of his foot. She pulled away and looked at me, confused but also pleased. "I didn't know such advanced techniques were part of the examinee training."

"It's not," I replied, pulling my eyes away. "I just knew I needed to stop the bleeding before removing the nail. I'm not sure how I knew where to put it..."

How *did* I know where to wrap it?

I looked down again at Alexi's leg, but the vision of the lights was gone.

"I just did what felt right."

I looked back at her, and her eyebrows were raised slightly as she studied me.

"Instinct combined with skill is always a useful combination in a Healer," she said. I must have looked as dumb as I suddenly felt because a small smile crossed her lips. "What's your name?"

"Kailin."

"My name is Healer Cathrina." Her smile broadened and I felt as if I were I was floating. No one had ever smiled at me like that before, not even my aunt. "Is that a healing satchel? May I borrow it?"

I was saying yes when man came running up behind her. He was tall with black hair to match his short beard. If there had been any doubt in my mind that she was from the Academy, it was now gone. I would have known Healer Arios anywhere. He had been coming to our village to run the exam for the last five years.

"There you are," he said. "I see you've found a patient to work on, even out here in the backwoods."

The smile disappeared from the beautiful Healer's face.

"Are you offering to make yourself useful or are you just here to watch?" she snapped.

The relief that had been on his face was replaced with a dark mask. He bent over next to me and deftly took the tourniquet out of my hands.

"I'm Healer Arios," he said, turning to smile at me. "Forgive my grumpy companion, she doesn't like me stepping in and showing her up."

"I know," I said, dumbfounded by his smile at me.

"Really?" He looked amused. "I thought I was the only one who knew how much I annoyed her."

"No, I mean I know who you are."

"Am I going to die?" Alexi whined through his stick.

"Not a chance," Healer Arios said, his voice perking up. "We'll have you up and running in no time!"

"But she touched my leg!" Alexi moaned, draping an arm over his face. "Can you take the evil out of it?"

"Evil?" Healer Arios said, looking at me. I wanted to bury myself in a hole when I saw recognition dawn on him and, though his eyes were still kind, the smile was gone. "Oh," he said. "You're the bastard girl, aren't you?"

The fire that had driven me to action was instantly put out.

I was just Kailin again.

The orphan girl with the whore mother.

"I don't think you have to worry about evil," Healer Cathrina said. "If it weren't for this young woman's quick thinking, you might have lost your life. You should be grateful she was here."

"But my mother said she is a taint to the world." Alexi said the words, but I heard something I had never heard before in his voice. It almost sounded like doubt. I turned to the woman, and she was looking at me again, her eyes kind and strong and believing.

And for the moment I felt like believing as well.

"We'll see you tomorrow, Kailin," she said. "Go try and get some rest. I look forward to teaching a girl with such amazing instincts."

I could only nod as I stood and headed for home.

Deep inside, the fire was back, burning quietly, fueled by the beautiful stranger's belief in me.

Tomorrow.

Tomorrow my life was going to change.

CHAPTER

TWO

The kitchen door slammed open, drawing my head off my folded arms where it had been resting on the table. The sky was gray with morning light, and my aunt's silhouette was muted and blurred. She entered quickly without pausing, shutting the door and the cold behind her.

I watched her as she made her way to the Blessing Tree on the wall across the room, gently touching the roots, then her heart, then the worn metal leaves. She stood staring at it a moment, and when she finally spoke I jumped.

"Wake up that fire."

I got to my feet as she made her way to the other side of the table, setting down her healer's satchel as I threw another pile of kindling onto the fire, poking and blowing on it until the flying sparks began to eat away at the wood as hungry as the inferno last night.

"How's Marily holding up?" I asked, blowing on the blaze one last time.

"She'll live," she said. "The burns were widespread, but

there won't be any permanent damage other than scar tissue, if she changes her bandages and keeps putting ointment on."

I threw a larger stick onto the fire before turning around.

My aunt had already emptied out her satchel. What I saw made my heart sink. There was only a scrap of bandage, a broken metal needle, a dirty mixing bowl, and four empty white cloth herb bags.

"That was the last of the bandages," I whispered, walking up to the table.

"We can make more out of that box of rags." My aunt stared at the pile, then she looked up at me, her eyes hardening. "Don't you dare start feeling sorry for yourself. We have those bandages to heal, and they were used exactly how they were meant to be used."

She shoved the wooden bowl into my hand, and I turned around to the sink under the window next to the fireplace, ladling water from a large pot I had boiled the night before, knowing we would need clean water when she got home.

"Was anyone else hurt?" I asked as I poured some of the disinfectant powder into the bowl, trying to sound innocent.

"Alexi's leg got impaled when a wall fell on him." I could hear the rushing of her taking down a bundle of herbs that had been hanging from the ceiling, then her hands as she stripped the leaves. "He has kindling for a brain for being so close to the flames."

I started scrubbing, putting my entire body into pushing the hard brush into the wood. "Is he going to be ok?"

"Yes." She sounded sour. "The Examiners got to him. He'll be fine."

"Oh." I paused in my work. "Did you talk to them..."

"Healer Arios came over and spoke to me once Marily was stable. He explained Alexi's injury and what he and the other Healer had done."

"Is that all he said?" I asked as I started scrubbing again.

"Yes. Why? Did someone stop by the cottage?"

"No...just wondering." I should be happy. Somehow they had known not to mention me. Probably Healer Arios knew my presence there would have only caused more problems, and honestly, if Aunt Beredith knew I disobeyed her I would get in trouble. But still, I had done a good job, on my own, and maybe a part of me had hoped...

No. No hoping. At least not until my escape.

My eyes lifted to the window and the morning light just turning golden outside. The view was perfect, with the sun barely above the trees of the forest and warming off the chill of last night, lighting the spreading branches of our grove of Family Trees with a touch of gold to their full, green leaves. I could see our nearest neighbors through the grove, coming out of their homes to begin their own morning chores at their farms and vegetable gardens. The road snaked its way out as far as I could see all the way to the now-destroyed Grouses' farm just barely out of view—the limit of how much of this world I had ever seen.

At least for now.

"Are you planning on scrubbing out the bottom of that bowl?" My aunt was now across the room having just finished retying the bundle of herbs she'd pulled down.

"I'm sorry," I said without a trace of repentance. "I was just thinking about how wonderful it will be once I leave in a few days."

"Feeling confident now, aren't we?"

"And why shouldn't I be?" I snapped, turning on her, the same fire as last night in my voice. I guess some of the sparks hadn't completely been smothered. "I'm the best student in your class, I help you with every case, whether those shrubs know it or not, and after last night I think I'm more than quali-fied to get into the Healer Academy!"

I realized my mistake too late and turned back to the sink, attacking the poor wooden bowl as if I could somehow scrub out what I had just said.

"And what happened last night?" my aunt asked, her voice sharp.

"I didn't mean last night," I said quickly. "I meant last week, when I helped you with Corlina's baby."

Silence stretched between us, and I was sure she was going to call me out. I could feel her eyes on the back of my head, and it took everything I had not to turn around and confess that I had disobeyed her.

"Kailin," she said, her voice now tired. I relaxed a little and trusted myself to look at her. "When did I ever tell you that getting into the Academy was about being qualified?" With a sharp movement she snagged the herb bundle back onto its hook hanging on the ceiling. "You get into the Academy by being careful and focused. When I was tested there was a girl who failed because she didn't clear out the stray wood shav-ings they had left in her mixing bowl. Made a complete mess of her tonic."

My face froze, and for a moment I could see the same horrid fate happening to me. "They wouldn't—that's not fair!"

"Kailin." My aunt's voice had become hard again. "If your life hasn't taught you that nothing in this world is fair, then I don't know how you will ever learn."

I turned away from her, from the harshness of her words.

Fairness. But in order for something to be fair there needs to be a set of rules, and who got to decide those rules? I took a quick glance out the window again at our neighbors, who were oblivious to me watching them.

It's the others. Other people, in other lives than my own,

who would decide what I'm worth, who were free to mete out their justice for the crime of my birth. That same crime that had lost my brilliant aunt her own scholarship to the Healer Academy, dooming her to a life as a Peasant, all because I was born.

The Healers in Divlan dictated her destiny just because she was needed at home, and those outside our small window dictated mine every day with their hate and sneers.

But not after today. After today I would get to make my own destiny.

I stepped out of my aunt's cottage, trying not to spill the small bowl of balm that was to be my offering. It was only a short walk down the road to the entrance of The Holy Forest, but balancing my too-full bowl of murky liquid even for so short a trip made me stressed. It had taken three days to steep it just right, but I felt like running to the Altar anyway, the pressure to not be late almost more than any religious devotion I might have been feeling.

I followed my aunt around the bend in the road, and I could see the path leading to the village center, with its cluster of buildings and the hidden village green in the center. I could hear the crowd that had gathered, but otherwise we were alone on the road. But instead of following it to the village green, my aunt turned off on another small path leading into the underbrush. I held my breath as I followed her to the small clearing of low-lying bushes and the ancient Arbor and Altar.

I stopped at the edge, my feet unwilling to move forward as my stomach sank into my knees. It wasn't just my fears of tardiness that made me want to hurry from the sight of the Holy Forest's entrance. Though it was probably blasphemous of me, over the years I had grown to hate this place. Or maybe it wasn't hate I was feeling—maybe it was just fear.

I thought about asking Aunt Beredith if we could just drop off the offering and forgo the prayer, but I knew that would be foolish. If ever there was a day I needed divine help, it was this one.

The Altar was a rectangular stone block, worn by time and weathered into a rough texture and shape. Images might have once been carved into the gray stone, but they had long since disappeared.

The Arbor above it was a beautiful piece of work that the previous generation had lovingly labored over. There were leaves and flowers carved into the pillars, with a massive tree reaching out its branches along the top. The Blessing Tree, the symbol of The Great One, was a familiar image in every home, but here, marking the path The Great One supposedly took when He retreated back into the shadows of the Holy Forest, all the stories seemed more real.

A glare from Aunt Beredith got my feet moving again and, keeping my eyes on the dark green of the forest beyond the Arbor, I knelt next to her and placed my offering next to the other ones on the Altar's surface. There were three other bowls with their own balms or tonics along with a plate of honeyed sweet bread, and even a small carving of a bird. Offerings from the other students most likely.

I placed my hands on my heart and bowed my head.

Hello Great One, it is me, Kailin again...

My chest tightened in the familiar way it always did when I prayed, but today the *pull* seemed stronger than usual, even worse than last night.

I'm taking the exam in a few hours, which you already know, because you know everything.

Ugh, how could I believe He would really hear my prayer? I was just a nobody in the middle of nowhere that no one cared about. Why should He listen to me?

I squinted my eyes tight, pushing out a stray tear that had escaped.

"If you are listening," I whispered, "please let me leave this place."

My ribs screamed, the *pull* no longer a gentle tug but a force strong enough to wrench my torso forward. My eyes flew open as I gasped for air, my hands falling on the edge of the Altar, pushing back as I stared in horror at the forest only yards in front of me.

Because instead of the peaceful foliage it had been only a moment earlier, it was now a hole of darkness, with the trees pulled back and a path leading into its depths.

Not again! I prayed and tried my hardest to tear my eyes away, to escape the call to that blackest of nightmares.

Because the *pull* was not the only secret I had been carrying with me for as long as I could remember. Every time our village had gathered at the Arbor and Altar for the sacred rituals, this same dark path would appear, calling me.

But it had never called me this strongly before.

As if sensing my thoughts, the *pull* became almost unbearable, and I could feel the worn grain of the stone digging into my palms.

I can't!

You can.

And the sun disappeared from the sky.

I blinked.

I was standing at the top of an impossibly tall building, looking out at a world of empty, unfamiliar streets and structures—and it was all burning.

I wanted to run, to hide, to get away from wherever I now was, but my body would not move.

The air was silent, as if I had never been able to hear, and other than the flames, perfectly still. I struggled against my invisible bonds again, and at last I was able to turn and walk away, finding myself in a beautifully decorated hallway made of carved stone. The fire was here as well and I was afraid, even though I could feel no heat. Then I noticed the way the flames moved between the carvings on the stone, and my breath caught at their intricate dance. One pillar was decorated with climbing vines carved into the stone, and I reached my hand out to the flames, but there was no pain. Only a faint tickle, like a butterfly landing on my skin.

I turned a corner and the walls around me were no longer stone. They were now large, ancient trees.

Trees I knew.

And I was filled with panic.

I ran, knowing instinctively where I was, for the hallway was gone and I was surrounded by dense undergrowth from beyond the safety of the Holy Forest's edge. I ran, and as I did so I started to feel something that had been missing before—heat.

The flames began to feel warm against my face, growing hotter as my terror soared and my legs ran faster. With each step the heat intensified until I wanted to scream from the pain, knowing beyond a doubt that I was going to be roasted alive.

Right when I was sure I wouldn't be able to take it anymore, I burst through the trees into a large clearing. The perimeter was on fire. Giant shafts of red and orange flames reached up into an invisible sky, but the grass was soft and cool beneath my bare feet.

Exhausted, I fell to my knees and stared straight ahead, afraid to look down and see the blackened and blistering flesh I was sure now encompassed me.

That's when I saw him.

Standing in the center of the clearing was a man.

From the light of the fire I could make out that he was tall and strong, with eyes held in a shadowed face. He was looking straight at me, but I couldn't make out whether he was angry or pleased I was there.

All I could see was the reflection of fire dancing in his eyes.

"Come on, Kailin, we need to get going."

I blinked and the light turned back to normal and the trees were as they had always been. Aunt Beredith was using the Altar as a support as she got back onto her feet.

My hands were gripping the edge of the Altar as I stared at the greenness of the forest. There was no sign of the darkened path. In fact, everything looked infuriatingly normal.

"Kailin? Are you?"

"Yes," I croaked out, then coughed. "Yes," I said again. "I'm coming." I looked down at my hands and commanded them to let go. With stiff joints I peeled them off the Altar, my palms red and pocked by the rough stone they had been holding on to so tightly. I closed my eyes, forced my breathing to become normal, and stood. I didn't open them again until I had my back to the Holy Forest.

My aunt was at the edge of the clearing, waiting for me, her head tilted to the side.

"Sorry," I muttered, and walked past her down the path as fast as I could.

THREE

I let myself breathe only when I was back on the familiar packed dirt of the road, arms crossed tight around my chest as I hurried toward the village center. No, if I was honest with myself I wasn't hurrying toward anything, but I was definitely running away from something. From whatever that was back at the Altar. I shuddered again at the memory, still so fresh I was afraid to close my eyes even to blink and find myself back in that burning world once more.

I was hallucinating. That was the only logical explanation. I didn't think I was insane, so it must have been the stress of the exam and not sleeping last night that finally collected its toll on my system. A cloud must have moved over the sun for a minute, changing the shadows of the trees, and then I just thought I saw something...

I had to be hallucinating, because the other option, that I really saw something, that I really saw...No. There was nothing back there except genuine faith and questionable old stories.

So why was my heart racing?

Voices ahead drew my attention to the cluster of buildings only yards away, catching laughter as a group of boys came around the corner of one.

I forgot about dark trees and burning buildings when I saw that one of them was Dural. I tensed again when he saw me. He had been in Aunt's Beredith's class since we were both five, and he had tortured me with pebbles thrown at my head when my aunt's back was turned. Because of my curse he never actually touched me but as we got older the rocks got bigger.

The other boys stopped laughing when they saw me, and they all whispered at Dural while pointing at me. Dural bent down to grab another rock, but then he noticed Aunt Beredith coming up behind me and stood back up. He instead gave me a smile that made my blood turn cold before leading the other village boys to join the crowd.

He was taking the exam today as well, and I could easily see him knocking over whatever salve or tonic they asked us to make, extinguishing all my dreams.

I thought I would be sick.

We entered the darkened space between the outer ring of buildings. I slowed as the noise from the gathered crowd grew louder, and stopped at the corner. I found myself unable to leave the comfort of the shadows. I peeked around the corner, my hands still tight against my chest. There must have been over a hundred people on the green, not just from Valehaven but from the small, lone farms on the outskirts of the Holy Forest, whose children would also be taking the exam this year.

A large green-and-yellow tent was in the center with the crowd mingling around its closed entrance. I could name every face I saw, which meant that everyone out there would know who I was as well.

Aunt Beredith moved past me a few feet before she saw I hadn't followed her. She turned back and glared, and I drew a breath before stepping out into the light.

At first, nothing changed. No one noticed. I kept my head down and tried to make myself as small as possible, hiding in Aunt Beredith's shadow as much as I could.

It didn't last. Before I was ready, the conversation around us paused and then took on a new tone.

"Is she really going to take the Exam? Aren't there rules about that?"

"It's bad luck, no one will make it into the Academy this year if she's here."

"We used up all the honey we had left making that sweet bread for an offering, anything to quash her curse."

I scooted closer to my aunt.

"Stand up, Kailin," she hissed.

I looked up at her, hoping to convey how crazy I thought her suggestion was.

Her eyes narrowed, and I straightened my spine.

"Move faster, Avonly! We want to get you the best spot in front!" The voice made my eyes dart up in search of the black-smith's daughter. Ignoring the glares, I strained my neck to see above those in front of us, and caught a glimpse of blond curls piled on top of a thin frame.

Avonly was between her parents, a balding man and a small woman with a face that resembled a toad most of the time. Avonly was in her orange-brown Peasant dress, just on this side of having too much color for our ring. It was also the nicest thing anyone in the village owned.

Avonly's parents were pushing her to the front of the spectators and despite the jostling, her eyes found mine. She paused in her step and gave me a shy smile. I felt the edges of my own mouth form into a smile back, grateful for one friendly face amid all the glares. Her mother froze a few steps in front of her and turned to see why her daughter was no longer attached to her hip. When she saw me her face transformed the rest of the way into an amphibian. She grabbed Avonly's arm and dragged her away.

The sun suddenly felt too warm on my face and I looked down. It wasn't this hot in the shadows of the building.

Then there was an arm around me, strong and steady.

"Look up, Kailin." This time my aunt's voice was missing its hard edge, and I slowly raised my eyes again, letting Aunt Beredith steer me forward. "They're just worried," she whispered. "They're blaming their made-up curse, but really they are just afraid of you."

"Afraid?" I snorted.

"Yes," she said, her voice getting hard again. "Today, for the first time, you are competition."

Competition. I looked up again at the back of Avonly's mother's head and wondered if she really did see me as a threat to her daughter's future.

"Well, Beredith." A stout older woman with red cheeks, wispy blond-gray hair and beady, excited eyes grabbed Aunt Beredith's shoulder. Nolina, the baker's wife, was the only person in Valehaven with the guts to touch Aunt Beredith. "You've been waiting for this day for quite a while."

"Yes." My aunt's tone remained even as she glanced toward Nolina's hand. When the woman didn't remove it my aunt stiffened. "Kailin and I have been preparing for today for a long time."

"Don't get me wrong," Nolina continued, leaning in as if she and my aunt were good friends. "It would take a miracle for her to earn a scholarship, but to think that if she did, you would finally be rid of this runt left in your charitable hands! I would say that would be worth all the work you put into her."

Nolina smiled at me, as you would smile at a chicken before wringing its neck. "To have to give up your spot at the Academy," she sighed dramatically as she turned back to Aunt Beredith. "And with only one year left before graduating! All because your whore of a sister died after disgracing us all and giving herself to that passing tramp." She was shaking her head at this point, as if she were chastening my long-dead mother. "No one deserves to have the responsibility of raising a bastard child, you least of all with all you already had to give up."

"She's a good girl most of the time," my aunt said, finally shaking off Nolina's hand. "Not nearly as much trouble as some of the children in this village—"

"We all know you did the best you could," the annoying woman continued, as if Aunt Beredith hadn't replied. "But honestly, there isn't much to work with when a child is born like that. I just wanted to let you know no one will judge you for how she turns out, even if she ends up following in her mother's footsteps. As The Great One said, 'You can tell what type of fruit it will be from the tree it fell from.'"

I shrank at her words. Every time I would see them walking toward me, every time their cruel eyes would turn my way, I would tell myself it wouldn't bother me this time; this was the time I would be strong.

But then I wasn't. I was just Kailin.

I felt Aunt Beredith place a hand on my shoulder, and I began to breathe again. "As you know," the obnoxious woman continued in her boisterous voice, "It was too bad *my* son Esac never had a chance to study with you. *He* would have easily passed the exam, he's so bright, but we needed him to stay here and help his father." She then leaned in again, as if letting my aunt in on a secret. "We all know some children aren't so needed."

A smile crossed her lips in her self-importance, and I wondered how much more hate this woman could possibly have for me. The monstrous lump in my stomach turned a somersault, and if Aunt Beredith hadn't been holding my shoulder with an iron grip, I'm sure I would have run home and tried to forget about ever wanting to attempt the Exam.

"You're absolutely right," Aunt Beredith said with false enthusiasm, bringing the baker's wife's eyes back to her. "I mean, my girl is so small. Your son, however, will make a wonderful addition to the army when we go to war with Richark. We are all so lucky such a useful boy is available for the king's service."

The Nolina gave a look of surprise and almost fear, then her eyes turned hard. With a huff she turned and went off, probably to find someone else to praise her son to.

"Is Esac really going to fight in a war?" I asked.

"We don't know if there is even going to be a war," Aunt Beredith said, letting out a breath. "Let's get to the front with the other examinees."

Just then the talking died down and we could see movement at the door of the large tent. I caught my breath as three stately figures emerged, led by one old, bent man. My pulse pounded in my head, making me feel lightheaded and nauseous.

This was real. It was really happening.

Father Gant, leaning heavily on his walking staff, was standing in a small circle with the Examiners, his soft face and feathery white hair accented with his smile as he laughed at something one of them had said. Valehaven couldn't afford an actual Priest, but Father Gant did his best to fill the role. I couldn't imagine a real Priest doing a better job than him anyway.

He did look slightly ridiculous in his simple Peasant-brown shirt and trousers while standing next to the immaculate and colorfully dressed Examiners. It made me grateful our village never attracted any rings more inside than the passing Tradesman to make me feel how outside we were.

The Healers were the innermost ring I had ever seen. That just went to show how little of the world I had seen; Healers were only two rings inside us. Aunt Beredith had told me I should be grateful because the next two rings, the Merchants and the Lesser Nobles, were unbearable. When I would ask her if she had ever seen a Noble, the innermost ring outside the royal family, she would always look hard at me. "Those are the worst. If you see one coming, always walk the other way."

It was a chilling thought that when I entered the Academy I would be mingling with the other rings. But then again it couldn't be that bad. Healer Arios and the other Examiner I met last night, Healer Cathrina, seemed nice.

Healer Arios was up there now, in black trousers and a light-green shirt with a matching darker-green vest modestly edged with a simple line of yellow embroidery, respectfully cut at the waist to show his ring as a Healer. Staring at it, I couldn't help but look around even though I knew what I would see. We were Peasants. None of our men wore vests.

I looked back at him just in time to see him look my way. When his eyes met mine he gave me a smile. Inner ring or not, he was easily the most handsome man I had ever seen, with his black hair, light-tan skin and dashing close-cropped beard. He looked to be around my aunt's age, and I wondered if she thought he was handsome too.

Healer Arios's eyes continued to scan the crowd before he

leaned toward the other male Examiner, who was new to me, and said something to him I couldn't hear.

This Examiner was shorter, with long, silky black hair tied in back, a clean face, and a glare that made it clear he would rather be anywhere than surrounded by Peasants in a backwoods village. His shirt was a light red with a darker red vest, edged in a more elaborately designed embroidery. Aunt Beredith had told me it was an inner ring thing: you could always tell how important a man thought himself by how elaborately decorated his vest was. He must have thought very highly of himself.

The last Examiner was the woman from the night before. Healer Cathrina was just as beautiful in daylight as she had been in the dark, with her dark-brown hair draped around her shoulders with just a hint of it pulled back into a small bun at the nape of her neck, held in place with two beaded sticks, the beads dangling off the end only an inch or so—a proper length for a Healer. Her gown was a soft violet, the color going nicely with her skin, just a shade darker than my caramel. There was a matching braided belt across her waist with a pouch hanging from it.

As her eyes swept over us I felt something different than when the other Examiners looked at us. Her gaze showed an interest the others lacked, as if she were looking at more than just our vestless men or the plain hair sticks most of the women wore. Her eyes were also the most striking shade of violet I had ever seen.

She turned her head just then and caught my eye. She smiled in recognition. I couldn't help but smile back.

Then I heard my aunt gasp.

Healer Cathrina's eyes left my face, and I could see them widen as she looked beyond me. Her face went pale. She looked back at me, and her hands clasped in front of her started to shake.

I didn't understand; only a moment earlier she was so friendly and kind. Now she looked at me like everyone else I had ever known.

She looked afraid.

"We need to go," my aunt whispered in my ear. Her hand was tight on my shoulder as she turned me away from the tent.

"*What!?*" I said pulling back. "But it's about to begin!"

"Now!" She hissed, but when she tried to move the crowd pushed her forward, the nearest ones glaring at her.

"What's wrong?"

"Nothing," she snapped. "I just think this is a bad idea. We need to get home."

Aunt Beredith didn't want me to take the exam?! What happened?! Was that woman dangerous? No. She was kind. And she believed in me last night. And so did my aunt until a moment ago!

"Please," I begged when she started to push me. "Whatever you're afraid of, it can't be worse than my life will be if I *don't* take the exam."

My aunt held my eyes and I saw a softness there I had never seen in her before. But there was also fear. So much fear I didn't understand.

She looked over my shoulder, and I turned my head.

Healer Cathrina wasn't looking at us anymore. She had turned back to the other Examiners, talking to them in a low voice, her face calm and relaxed.

As if the terror I had seen there had never happened.

My aunt didn't say anything, but she turned back to the front, holding me in front of her, her fingers digging into my shoulder.

After another laugh from the group at the front, Father

Gant placed a hand on Healer Arios's shoulder before stepping forward.

Father Gant smiled warmly and made an effort to straighten his aged back. "Friends and family. It is that time of year again, when representatives come from the great Healer Academy to try and test our children. Ever since the late King Tarien II, may he rest eternally with The Great One, saw fit a hundred years ago to offer scholarships so even those of our lowly position may learn the sacred arts of healing, our small village has had an unprecedented number of young men and women who have left our humble home to do us honor in Tamerin's capital of Divlan and beyond."

I sucked in my breath at the excitement his words breathed into me. By "honor" we all knew he meant the elevation in ring. The scholarships were one of the only ways you could advance in the rigid social structure of the world, skipping completely Tradesman and becoming automatically, through acceptance and graduation of the Academy, that of Healer. You had to serve for ten years in villages throughout the kingdom, affectionately referred to as your "rural duty" to pay back the cost of educating you, but you were no longer a Peasant.

It was the dream every Peasant and Tradesman wished for their children, and why we all had been studying so hard for so long.

But I wanted more than just a ring advancement.

I wanted a new life.

"You have all been studying for years with Beredith, our own scholarship winner," he continued, kindly leaving out that my aunt had never actually graduated and hence was still a Peasant. "You have learned and prayed beneath the shadows of The Great One's Holy Forest all your lives, and I know His pleasure in your strivings will grant you success."

At the mention of the forest my eyes automatically turned

to the line of trees behind him and I thought of what I had seen, or thought I had seen, only a half hour before. I stifled a shiver and looked back.

"And now," Father Gant continued, "I'm happy to introduce this year's Examiners."

He stepped a little to the side so everyone could see the richly clad group. "Our long-time friend Healer Arios has come once again." The tall bearded man nodded toward the crowd. His green eyes sparkled with his easy smile. "And this year he is joined by Healer Steverno, who, I've been told, is a new instructor at the Academy and eager to meet his new students." Instead of looking eager or even acknowledging us, the man merely shifted his gaze at the mention of his name.

"This year we also welcome to our home another great Healer from the Academy." He paused, and his face showed strain for the first time. "It is my extreme pleasure to welcome to our humble village the illustrious Lady Cathrina."

A gasp was heard throughout the crowd, and everyone fell on their faces. I had frozen solid, staring in shock and horror at the woman I had thought was only a Healer!

My aunt grabbed my arm and yanked me down so I fell forward as a Peasant should before the Nobility, but instead of staying down, my head popped back up. Lady Cathrina had her hand over her eyes. Healer Steverno was rolling his eyes while Healer Arios looked as if he was trying not to laugh.

I looked at the back of her head again, and yes, the beads were only an inch long! How were we supposed to know!?

"Please!" Father Gant was saying when I could pay attention again. "Lady Cathrina has asked, for the sake of efficiency with the exam, that the usual show of respect to her be restricted to merely a polite bow when addressing her. Please get up so we might continue with the Exam!"

At first no one moved, but then, one by one, the people got

to their feet again. Lady Cathrina tried to smile at the crowd, but she looked uncomfortable.

A Noble? A Healer? An *Examiner*?

"I know you will all show them every possible courtesy during their stay." Father Gant's eyes scanned the crowd again, as if to hold my gaze and that of my fellow applicants. "Now, will those wishing to present themselves for examination please come forward."

CHAPTER
FOUR

Aunt Beredith let go of me and I almost fell on my face before getting my feet underneath me again. Dural was already in the clearing before the Examiners. The others were moving in, standing together in line. There were four of us: Dural, Avonly, and me from our village of Valehaven, along with Baylie, an outskirts girl who had made the trek every week for our class in my aunt's cottage. We were now fifteen years old and eligible to take the exam, knowing this was our one and only chance to change our lives. I hurried forward and found my place on the end next to Avonly.

I felt a hundred pairs of eyes on the back of my head. I had lived my entire life in the shadows, but here I was, out in front for everyone to see.

As if in an answer to my unspoken prayer, I felt a brief squeeze on my hand.

I squeezed Avonly's back before letting go.

"Oh Great One!" Father Gant suddenly shouted, his arms lifted. "Please hear our prayer!"

"Please hear our prayer," I repeated, my head now bowed, my hands crossed over my heart.

"Hundreds of years have passed since our forebears landed on these shores. Fear, hunger, and disease came, not only for our bodies but also for our hearts. But You came to us, You brought us under the shade of your great branches of compassion to shield us from the scorching rays of pain, death, and sorrow. You gave us the path, and taught us the ways of those who would heal. You led us, and then in Your wisdom You departed into the Holy Forest, under whose shadow we now pray. As You rest, we will continue Your work."

"We will continue Your work," we all said in unison.

One by one Father Gant placed his hands upon our heads.

Then bowing his head like the rest of us, Father Gant's hands moved to his heart.

"As I have placed my hands and will upon these, Your followers, place Your hand of protection and guidance on them as they embark upon this new road they seek to follow. Oh Great One, please hear our prayer!"

"Please hear our prayer," I said again with the chorus behind me.

I chanced a glance next to me and saw tears in Avonly's eyes. She always became emotional during Father Gant's prayers, lending her conviction to strengthen mine.

Father Gant stepped to the side and Healer Arios pulled back the flap of the tent, motioning us forward with his hand. Hardly noticing the others around me, my heart beating frantically with anticipation, I stepped forward.

My eyes adjusted in only seconds to the dimmer light of the interior. It was larger than it appeared from the outside, but smaller than I had hoped. There was a table in the center scattered with several unmarked ceramic jars. Around the table were small workstations spaced out, each with its own table and chair, a knife, a mortar and pestle, and a pen. A *real* pen, one with the ink on the inside! Next to each table was a water bucket and a kettle sat next to the tables along with a portable fire brazier that somehow burned without smoke. The rest of the tent was bare.

The other students were hovering near the entrance like me, not sure where we should go. Once we were all inside, the Examiners entered, circling around us until we were again facing them, only in here there were no witnesses.

I was standing to the far right and hoped Lady Cathrina would stand near me and give me another confidence-inspiring smile. She moved to the other side and never once looked my way.

"Good afternoon," Healer Arios began, "we are excited to see what you all have learned during your studies. As you know, the exam for entrance into the Healer Academy is twofold. A written exam will test your literacy, arithmetic skills, and geographical knowledge. The second part will be the practical-skills portion. If you are found to be qualified, you will be awarded a scholarship, a ring advancement to that of Healer, and a ride to Divlan and the Healer Academy to begin your training."

The other students shifted in excitement, casting knowing smiles at one another.

I didn't smile. It was too soon for that.

"Now," Healer Arios said, his smile turning even friendlier, "If you would all take a workstation, we shall begin."

For a moment all we did was stare, waiting for one of us to move forward. Dural was the first to move, again, and as I followed I silently wished I had the initiative he did. I chose the workstation farthest from the tent door, hoping it would give me some sense of privacy while I worked. However, when

Healer Steverno, disgusted face and all, came over to stand right next to my station, I began to sweat.

"Everyone comfortable?" Healer Arios asked. "Lady Cathrina will now pass out the exam." I stared at my hands in the silence that followed, Lady Cathrina moving among the tables. I didn't look up when she came to me; all I could do was stare at the stack of paper she set down in front of me.

"You have two hours," Healer Arios announced, his voice resonating in my bones. "Begin."

The rustle of paper and the scratching of pens filled my ears, making my head feel light. Mechanically I turned the stack over and wrote my name on the front, the pen feeling surprisingly natural in my hand.

Then I turned to the first page.

Can you read this?

I glanced around the room, sure this was a joke. No one was looking up, and none of the Healers would meet my eyes. I looked down and scribbled a simple "Yes."

I looked at the next question.

Good, now we've determined you can read, let's try something a bit harder.

What followed were various passages, some familiar from Aunt Beredith's books, others random selections from what must have been longer articles. Each was followed up with questions about what the text said, at first just asking for simple facts but the later ones asking me to argue my answers.

Next was the arithmetic section, beginning with simple addition and subtraction, then continuing through multiplication, division, and algebra. I finished that section and moved on.

"Twenty minutes!" Healer Arios boomed, making me jump. Next to me, Baylie actually let out a squeak in surprise.

Taking a breath, I turned the page to the last section.

A blank map of Tamerin.

Label as much as you can.

That was the only thing it said.

So I began, bringing before my eyes the map I had stared at every day for as long as I could remember. I could almost see the scratches of mountains to the north, the flat plains along the center, the sun-baked hills and the forests—so many forests.

The island Tamerin.

And stretched across it all, the names I knew better than my own.

I finished before Healer Arios called to set my pen down, having run out of space on the page.

Lady Cathrina came around the room again and collected the pages.

"Now that you're thoroughly exhausted," Healer Arios said, chuckling at his own joke, "We will begin the practical-skills portion of the exam." He moved toward the center table, raising his hands toward the mess of jars. "Here are all the ingredients you will need to create a topical salve to numb the pain when placed on a swollen muscle or joint, such as a twisted ankle. But beware, along with what you need are several ingredients you will not need. Do not trust what you see your fellow applicants use, for they may lead you astray."

The tension in my shoulders released, and I could feel a confident smile building on my lips. I had learned this recipe when I was seven and could repeat the procedure backwards and upside down if I wanted to.

"Trust the training you've received and I'm sure you'll all do just fine. You have one hour."

The trap. This had to be it, the trickiness Aunt Beredith warned me about.

I looked around and could see the panic and confusion on everyone else's faces.

We all knew this recipe.

We also all knew it took a minimum of two hours.

Baylie at the station next to mine started to visibly shake.

Healer Arios walked over to stand near the door. His smile was gone, and the gravity in his eyes sank my heart.

"Begin."

Dural almost tripped in his effort to get to the table. I looked over my workstation first. I found that my knife was not as sharp as I would have liked, and with a little looking around found a sharpening stone under the cutting table. I caught out of the corner of my eye Healer Arios looking my way and I thought I saw him smile.

That was encouraging.

I chanced a glance at the brooding Examiner stationed near me. He wasn't looking at any of the students, but was staring at the ceiling as if incredibly bored.

That was not encouraging.

Swallowing my uneasiness, I moved over to the table where the other examinees were scrambling for ingredients.

There must have been about twenty nondescript ceramic jars about as tall as my hand with no way to differentiate them from the outside. I reached for one, only to have Dural snatch it out of my hands. He gave me a smirk, showing off his crooked front tooth.

And I snatched it back out of his hands.

I didn't know who was more shocked, me or him as his mouth hung open. Then his eyes narrowed.

"That's not yours," he hissed.

"I picked it up first." My hands on the jar tightened and my own eyes narrowed back at him in a glare.

"You're not even supposed to be here!"

"No talking!" Healer Arios shouted from across the tent. Dural gave me another glare before grabbing a random jar and disappearing to his station. I felt eyes on me and turned my head toward the entrance. Lady Cathrina quickly turned her head away.

I belong here, I thought to myself. *For once, I belong here as much as the rest of them.*

I took a breath and opened the jar in my hands. In it was flakes of a greenish purple leaf. Dried starshade, an ingredient needed for this salve, but it had to be fresh. I opened another jar and in it was dried starshade again. Confused, I opened the previous one, and this time pulled out a pinch to taste on my tongue. Willow weed. It looked like starshade when both were dried, but definitely tasted different. Understanding now how difficult this test was going to be, I carefully tested all my ingredients with every method I knew until I was sure I had what I was looking for, and the hour began to slip away.

I carefully checked my salve and was glad to see the only thing left was for it to simmer down. I allowed myself a small smile. Maybe I was good enough to actually finish this recipe in half the time.

"Ten minutes!" Healer Arios's voice boomed across the tent.

My heart started racing. I knew I was close, but the salve still needed twice that time to get the right consistency, and my kettle was starting to lose its simmer. If I could keep it at a high enough temperature there was a chance it would be done in ten minutes, but that would require feeding the fire. Looking around the tent, I saw no additional wood. Then I remembered that dried willow weed was great for increasing the heat of a fire. I mean, I had never done it myself, but Aunt Beredith had mentioned it once. I ran to the table and grabbed the jar with the willow weed, only to pause. I didn't know how much to add.

"Eight Minutes!"

I poured out a handful, rushed back to my station and threw it on the blaze.

With a shattering crack the flames exploded, sending me flying backwards, smacking my head into Baylie's cutting table and knocking over her kettle. When my vision cleared, all I could see was Healer Steverno's pants in flames.

He screamed and began beating at the flames. I grabbed my water bucket and threw it at him, but my fingers slipped and the bucket went flying into his legs, causing him to fall backwards right onto the table of jars. The other examinees were on their feet screaming as well, while Healer Arios had taken off his vest and was smoothing the flames. Then there was silence and everyone's eyes turned toward me.

I ran out the door before they could tell me what I already knew.

I sat on my bed, my face hidden in my arms resting on my bent knees, shunning the light from the fireplace. My bed was little more than a nook in the wall of our front room, at one time a place to sit, but it had become mine when I began sleeping on my own as a child. It had fit me then, it had stopped fitting me years before, but at the moment I was glad for its smallness.

It made it easier to hide.

I stared at nothing, wishing I were dead. My eyes were glued open because every time I closed them, all I would see was their faces. The furious expression of Healer Steverno, Avonly's helpless and pity-filled eyes, every single villager turning away as I left the tent....

The last face was the worst of all, and yet keeping my eyes open did nothing to hide it from me. Sitting close to the fire, ripping rags into bandages, my aunt's face was a blank sheet.

Avonly had tried to visit, her voice pleading through the door to let her in, but I had vacantly ignored her. She shouldn't be around people like me.

People who were cursed.

A knock came at the door, stirring neither one of us. The knock came again, this time accompanied by a soft voice.

"Beredith?"

My aunt stopped ripping. Raising my head, I could see she had frozen, and I wondered if she was even still breathing.

"Beredith, open the door. I know you're in there."

After a moment, she put the basket of rags off to the side and walked the small distance to the door.

"Good evening, my Lady," she said, opening the door and dipping her head forward. Now it was my turn to freeze solid, too shocked to stand and bow. In all the confusion of my fatal mistake and running from the tent, I had forgotten about the beautiful Noble. Why in the world was she at my door? I already knew I had lost my chance at the Academy, so what did she want?

"That's kind of formal for you, wouldn't you say?" Lady Cathrina asked, a small smile hinting on her lips. My aunt didn't smile back. "May I come in?"

Aunt Beredith stood aside and Lady Cathrina moved over the threshold. Humorously out of place in her fine clothes and regal bearing, she gave a quick look about the room, stopping when her gaze reached me. I quickly hid my face again.

"It's been a long time," Lady Cathrina said. I peeked out, and was so shocked I raised my head the rest of the way.

My aunt was smiling.

"Honestly, I thought I would never see you again," my aunt said back, no formality in her tone at all. "To say I was surprised to see you today would be the biggest understatement in history."

They *knew* each other? How did a Peasant get to become acquainted with a Noble?

Both shared a nervous laugh, then stood awkwardly in the light of the fire, looking away from each other. Lady Cathrina was the first to break the heavy silence.

"I missed you after you left," Lady Cathrina continued, her voice small. "It was never the same. Classes became dull, and you know how terrible I was at making friends."

"Yes," Aunt Beredith agreed, "but you seem to have turned out all right after...what happened. Getting your title and becoming a Healer and everything."

"You seem to be doing all right for yourself as well," Lady Cathrina said too quickly. "Village Healer, and having raised such a lovely young woman."

Aunt Beredith's eyes never flickered to my nook, but I saw the ends of her mouth drop.

"It's her, isn't it?" Lady Cathrina asked, no longer smiling herself.

My aunt only nodded once, but it was enough to make Lady Cathrina take a small breath, letting it out slowly.

"You should have said good-bye," Aunt Beredith said, once the silence had become too much.

"I couldn't."

My aunt nodded again. Lady Cathrina looked up at me, and there was a horrible pain there.

Was I the cause of it?

No, how could I be?

"I didn't just come by to say hello," Lady Cathrina said, pulling something off her shoulder. I gasped as I recognized the healing satchel I had given her the night before. I had forgotten all about it.

"Where did you get this?" My aunt said, taking it from her. I knew she wanted to yell at me as the pieces came together, her mouth only forming a hard line. It was almost worse than if she had thrown the satchel at me.

"She really is talented," Lady Cathrina said. "I saw her work firsthand last night, and she easily scored high enough on the written portion for admittance." Her words burned me, but it settled the question of how I had done on the first half of the exam. I felt as if I should be grateful for the knowledge, but I wasn't. "I'm truly sorry about this afternoon, but I'm just one voice and the others are quite firm in their decision. Rules are rules, I'm afraid."

My aunt closed her eyes, and I thought she was finally going to explode, to scream at me for my failure, of all the years and hours she wasted on teaching me. Instead, she opened them again, and I stifled a gasp.

I have never seen her look so helpless.

"Isn't there anything you can do?"

"You know there isn't," Lady Cathrina said. "I just wanted to let you know she's worth it, even if it wasn't meant to be."

She gave one last smile in my direction before turning toward the door. As she reached for the handle, Aunt Beredith suddenly shoved herself between Lady Cathrina and the door, pushing her back into the room.

"Cathrina." Her voice was low, her eyes as hard as steel. I gasped at the casual drop of the Noblewoman's title, but neither of them seemed to even remember I was there. "You *owe* me."

Lady Cathrina may have been a Noble, but in that moment I feared my aunt more.

Neither woman moved; Aunt Beredith's gaze was locked on Lady Cathrina, while the Noblewoman stared down at the door handle, lips pressed into a thin line. Finally, she closed her eyes.

"There is a way, but you're not going to like it."

"Anything would be better than having her trapped here!"

"Are you so sure?" she asked, her own gaze turning to stone as she met my aunt's gaze. "She can come, but as my *servant*. It will get her into the Academy's walls, but I can't promise anything other than that I'll look after her."

Aunt Beredith's face was unreadable. Finally, she nodded. Then, for the first time since I had run out of the tent, she turned her eyes on me.

In that one gaze was reflected back all the fear that was suddenly pulsing through my veins. A fear of leaving home, of leaving my aunt—but most of all, of the beautiful Noble I would now serve.

The fire was coming from inside me. It was blue in its intensity and so bright I could hardly look at the threads streaking out from my chest. They touched everything: the trees, the grass, the houses of my village. It seemed as if the very sky was a victim to my pyromania. Then my aunt stepped out of her cottage, and before I could shout a warning the brightest rope of all shot through the air toward her.

I jerked awake so quickly I banged my head against the crate I had been leaning against. Disoriented by the sudden pain and blinding light of the mid-morning sun, I twisted my body around, trying to get my bearings, and nearly fell out of the back of the wagon.

The wagon.

Memories of the past two days crashed down on me, hurting worse than the bump forming on the back of my head. With a welcoming breath I allowed myself to be filled with the comfortable numbness that had been keeping me from thinking about what had happened and where I was going.

Laughter floated over my head from one of the wagons ahead of mine. There were other voices as well, but these could only be heard when I closed my eyes.

"A SERVANT," one woman said to Nolina before she noticed I had come into the bakery. *"Beredith is so disappointed, she sold her into servitude."*

"Sold?" Nolina asked, "did she get any money for her?"

"Oh no," the snarky woman replied, "She's just glad to get rid of the girl, and honestly who can blame her. Nobody wants her."

I STOOD up to get a better view of my surroundings. Nothing had changed since I had dozed off. A dusty dirt road stretched in front of us to the southwest between slightly raised hills, stretching off in every direction covered in grain.

Having never left my village, I was startled at how quickly the landscape had become unfamiliar since we rolled south out beyond the familiar farms.

My memorized maps had not prepared me at all.

For years the thought of leaving and seeing the world had filled me with excitement, but now that I was living it the strangeness was overwhelming, and I felt as though each new rock, tree, and view were mocking me for never having realized how big the world was. Did it really take only a couple of hours for the extent of my worldly experience to be exhausted?

The other servants said we would be stopping for lunch when the small road we were on crossed with an even smaller road leading up north, but if that was so, we were not within sight of it yet. The only thing I could see were the three wagons ahead of mine, the seven guards on their mounts.

As if sensing my eyes on them, Healer Arios turned back to look at me from the first wagon. I quickly looked down, returning to my seat between crates at the back of the last wagon I had claimed as my own that morning.

I HAD JUST THROWN my small bag of belongings into the back of the wagon I'd been told I would be traveling in. There were four wagons altogether: one for the examiners, one for the students to ride in, one for the Examiners' luggage, and one with supplies for the journey with one small corner between crates for me. There were also guards from the Academy to protect the caravan, but they were already ahead on the road. I could see Lady Cathrina a few yards away climbing the steps to her wagon.

She didn't look in my direction.

I was startled as sudden shouts came from the blacksmith's house as Valehaven's first scholarship student in twenty years was paraded to her spot in the second wagon. Avonly looked shy as she took her first step to mount the wagon, but as she reached the top and turned toward the adoring eyes of her well-wishers, I could see a light in her eyes I had never seen before.

Leaving my assigned seat, I moved closer, hoping to maybe catch a moment with her, when I saw her mother gesturing for her to lean over.

I wasn't close enough to hear what she said, but Avonly's eyes opened wide as she visibly paled. She looked as though she would say something back, but her mother turned to receive the praise of her neighbors for having raised such a brilliant girl.

Avonly slowly turned away, stopping when her eyes found mine. There was fear in them, so much fear and hurt and heartbreak—but then they changed. She changed, and with a look I had never seen from her before, she sat down and began chatting with a lanky boy next to her with a fervor I hadn't known she had.

Quietly I moved back to my seat.

PULLING my knees up to my chest, I rested my chin on them and stared out at the cloud of dust following our caravan.

After another hour I heard shouts from up ahead. I stood again and saw what I hadn't realized I had been praying for.

Trees.

Tall, glorious trees gathered in a miniature forest up ahead surrounding a road that stretched away from ours. These plains were always known as "The Desolates," which I had always thought was a bit melodramatic. But then I had always been swallowed up in a forest of ancient trees, so I hadn't understood, hadn't known...

Now I thought the name was perfect.

There were a few buildings up ahead as well, an inn most likely to take advantage of the increased traffic such an intersection would bring, but our wagons instead were pulling off into a grove of trees at the side of the road.

Before my wagon came to a halt I jumped down, strangely desperate to say a prayer thanking The Great One for the very existence of His symbol and beg forgiveness for never appreciating His gift's shade before.

But I would also be lying if my haste to get down wasn't also motivated by more temporal desires. I was starving and looking forward to lunch.

"Hey you, lend a hand!" My driver was at the back of our wagon lifting down the boxes that had been my seat only moments before. "Lunch isn't going to spread itself!"

The other servants were leading the horses to a stream that must have fed these trees, leaving the man to set up lunch all by himself. I walked over and helped him lift down the boxes he pointed out and brought them over to the side of the road where Examiners were standing chatting in the shade of the trees. The students were over there as well, and I was annoyed they weren't helping. It wasn't as if they didn't know how. They were all dressed as Tradesmen and from their hands had obviously been living a life of work as well.

When I was close enough, I glared at the lanky one who had been sitting next to Avonly, while setting down a box in front of him. He turned his head away. I turned to Avonly to ask what his problem was, but she was looking at the ground far away from me as well. My chest went tight, not letting myself comprehend her reaction. I reached out to her as we had done since we were children, but she moved away.

I WAS STANDING in front of the spot between crates I was told would be mine, but I couldn't bring myself to climb up into it yet. I turned and saw Aunt Beredith standing off to the side with the other villagers, listening to their hurtful congratulations on finally getting rid of me.

My eyes began to sting and I looked away, not wanting her last memory of me to be of the scared, worthless orphan who couldn't hold it together.

Then I felt the familiar arm around me and turned to bury myself into her chest.

"Oh little one," Aunt Beredith whispered. "You don't have to be afraid. I'll always be here."

"How can you want me when I'm such a disappointment?"

"Disappointment?" Aunt Beredith laughed softly. "It is more luck than skill that gets you into the Academy, and I could never hold a lack of luck against anyone."

· · ·

I HEARD A SNEER BEHIND ME. Turning, I saw Healer Steverno whisper something to Healer Arios, a wicked grin on his face. Then I realized what he was snickering at.

I was no longer one of them, and the fact that it hadn't registered until now was apparently funny. My driver hadn't asked me to help because he thought I would be nice enough to assist him, but because it was now who I was.

My friend whom I had known since birth was now two rings inside me.

My eyes burning, I turned back to the wagon. There were still boxes that needed unloading, and my driver was glaring my way. Each step was purposefully placed in front of the other, knowing I would never be able to go back to the way things were.

"YOU ARE MY GREATEST ACHIEVEMENT," Aunt Beredith had said, staring into my eyes. "Not because of what you do or fail to do, but because you are mine. Now, you may not have had luck, but it seems that I have. Lady Cathrina will be kind to you, for my sake if nothing else."

"I love you," I blubbered, speaking the words we knew but never said. They felt strange on my tongue, but I knew I would regret it always if I had never said them to her.

"I love you too," Aunt Beredith whispered, then using her strong arms she lifted me up to my seat in the wagon and stepped back.

From my seat in the back of the wagon, I started to notice a pattern to the lands we passed through. Fields, trees, village, trees, and then back to fields.

But that wasn't the biggest difference. On our second day we passed a huge house with a wall around it.

Because these villages were all owned by Merchants.

And I learned quickly what that meant.

Starting that morning there was an almost constant stream of Peasants moving in the opposite direction from us. I stared at them and the rags they were dressed in, wondering what could have happened to make them look so desolate.

"Hey you," my driver called out to one of the guards plodding alongside us. "Is there some sort of trouble ahead?"

"Nothing for us to worry about," the guard replied. "Something bad happened to the water in a village up ahead. We won't be stopping there."

"Then what's with all the traffic?" The old man almost accused, casting an unfriendly eye at a woman bent over a wheelbarrow carrying too few possessions.

"The Merchant who owned the village died and his family moved to Divlan," the soldier shrugged. "Peasants can't survive on their own, they aren't smart enough, so I guess they're out looking for a new Merchant to take care of them."

That wasn't true! Everyone is leaving probably because the water supply was bad!

I wanted to tell the guard all this, but instead I watched a girl my age walking by, her dress so thin I could see the shadow of her legs through the fabric, holes not sewn but bunched up and tied with scraps of cloth.

She didn't look stupid to me.

If this was how the local Merchant took care of the Peasants living on his land, then I was doubly grateful Valehaven had never had to deal with them.

That afternoon we came to the abandoned village, or what

was left of it. It was another large one, but no one was to be seen. As we passed the small shrine to The Great One in what must have once been the village center, I saw small offerings that were days if not weeks old. I didn't want to think it, but it came to my mind anyway.

He really must be sleeping.

The only people we saw on our way out of town was a man with his young daughter, putting what must have been their few possessions into a small handcart. It was impossible not to notice how much the mother was missing.

Well, I knew what it was like to not have a mother too.

I reached in my bag for the half loaf I had saved from lunch and jumped down off the back of the wagon. My driver yelled at me, but I ran to the little girl and shoved the bread in her hands, then ran back to the wagon, catching up to it and climbing back to my spot.

I waited for my driver to yell at me, but he didn't say anything.

Neither did the guards.

But the father watched me as his daughter ate the bread.

As we rolled past the last building and the landscape became wild once more, I let out a breath I hadn't realized I had been holding.

I was no stranger to sorrow—but not like this. Before it had always been a death here, a crop destroyed there, but never something that consumed a whole community. I could see now what Aunt Beredith had been trying to teach me for years: sickness and healing weren't just about individual tragedy but connected all of us together, for better or worse.

But I also saw something else, something that sent shivers up my spine more than the newly planted grove of Memory Trees just beyond the village boundaries. I saw that illness could do more than just kill the living—it could also take the life of those left behind.

When we arrived at the inn that night, I could hear singing and laughter flooding out the open windows. My hands clenched into fists, and it took everything I had not to march into that room and yell at all of them! That only a short day's drive from them was plenty of reason to never sing again!

I was so angry that it wasn't until I finished unloading my wagon that I realized what the songs were about.

> *Bring the light, light the torch,*
> *The one that crosses the sky!*
> *For life is light and light is life,*
> *So raise your voices high!*

I let my tension go.

No matter my anger, everyone had the right to celebrate the Summer Solstice. As I listened to the rest of the song, promising the conquest of day over night and other such images of good vanquishing evil, I felt ashamed of my anger.

Yes, there was death in the world—and sorrow and sickness and heart-crippling despair like I had witnessed that afternoon—but that was only half the story. The world also had its moments of joy. Like how the Winter Solstice, with its cold winds and long dark nights, had its opposite in this day that refused to let go of the brightness in the sky.

Moments like what the lucky new students were sharing in the common room of the inn.

Moments I would have to share alone tonight.

Taking my dinner of bread and stew out to the stables, I watched in silence as the sky finally let go of the sun.

"Another year," I whispered while stroking one of the mares that pulled my wagon. "Fifteen wasn't as great as it was supposed to be." The horse nuzzled my hand, and for a moment I could imagine she was wishing me a happy birthday.

But that was silly.

A sixteen-year-old couldn't afford to believe in silly tales, like if you worked hard enough then you could make your dreams come true.

I certainly never would again.

SIX

Over the next few days we saw no more refugees, but the traffic increased hour by hour as we drew closer to Divlan. That wasn't the only thing to change. Soon we were driving under a shallow canopy of skinny trees. The villages were larger, the Tradesmen on the road were better dressed, and the Peasants wouldn't even meet each other's eyes.

Then we came to the first real town. I was expecting a larger version of the villages we had been passing through, with a few more buildings and maybe even a paved street.

I was wrong.

I couldn't stop gaping at the towering stone buildings with slate roofs all smashed against each other on the smoothly paved road. Many of them were as tall as three stories, with windows so high it made me dizzy even imagining looking out of one. And even though I knew it made me seem like a sapling, I couldn't help gawking at the swarm of street vendors, shoppers, and just plain people running around from side streets and shops, dodging between trees growing out of small patches of brick-lined earth and calling out for customers so loudly I had to cover my ears when we passed by them.

All my life I had lived around the same hundred or so people, each with a face I could recognize and a name I could give. But here, I couldn't even imagine how daily life functioned! How did you know which blacksmith to go to? Who to talk to on the street? Who your neighbors even were?

We stopped around noon at an inn with a paved curving path leading off the street to the front door. Across from that door, between the inn and the street, was a perfectly laid flower bed surrounding a fountain.

It was the most incredible thing I had ever seen. Rather than helping the other servants unload the wagons I ran around to the front to gawk.

The fountain was shaped like a Family Tree, with sweeping branches reaching out from a thick trunk. It was half as tall as a real tree, made of some smooth white stone with gray flecks throughout it, with leaves of metal that were gleaming against the bright sunshine and water that was flowing from strategic spouts along its branches to trickle and fall into the pool surrounding its roots.

I was admiring the brass birds resting in the branches next to an actual bird, when I felt someone walk up next to me.

When I glanced over, Avonly's eyes were just as wide with amazement as mine.

"How do they get the water to jump out like that?" I asked.

"Some sort of engineering, I think," Avonly replied without looking over at me. "Remember how your aunt taught us about it and how almost all the buildings in Divlan have running water? It must be based on the same idea."

I smiled, glad to hear her voice again. She must have just been putting on a show because everyone was watching, but now that we were alone she could let down her facade.

I laughed.

"I can't wait to see what sort of things they have in Divlan if this small town has something this amazing!"

Avonly stiffened. When she turned, her sweet face turned sour. Her eyes became cold as if my very existence offended her, and with a glare she turned to join the other students in the inn.

The fountain didn't seem so wonderful anymore.

"Don't let it bother you too much; it is simply the way things are now."

Someone else had come up next to me on my other side, and when I turned, Healer Arios was looking at the fountain.

Throughout this whole journey I hadn't even so much as made eye contact with him, let alone talked to him. I remembered what Lady Cathrina had said, that the "others" were firm in my failing the exam, which meant he had thought me unworthy as well. I must have looked really pathetic if he felt the need to talk to me.

"How could I not be bothered by my best friend treating me like I don't exist?"

"I'm just saying to have some patience. You're not the only one struggling to adjust. Once she has figured out what her new ring means, she'll be more bearable."

"And how would you know what she is going through?" I glared at him and wiped my face on my sleeve. Water from the fountain was obviously splashing farther than I thought it was.

"Well," he said with a disarmingly friendly smile. "Much like your self-righteous friend, I wasn't always of an inner ring."

He paused to let the meaning of that sink in. "You mean," I started, my glare melting into surprise, "you were a scholarship student too?"

"Yes, I was, though the jump was a little shorter for me.

Most—well, pretty much all—scholarship students come from the Tradesmen ring, as I was. Avonly is something of a rarity." He turned back to the fountain, but the friendliness didn't leave his face. "What your friend is going through is as much a culture shock to her as it is to you. She isn't sure how much she is expected to change—or more importantly, she doesn't really know how much she wants to change."

I was about to ask more when a short, hooded man came up to Healer Arios and touched his arm, handing him a folded piece of paper. Healer Arios looked surprised at first, and then annoyed. After a brief glance at the note, he handed it back to the man.

"No," was all he said. It must have been enough of an answer because the hooded man disappeared back into the crowd.

I looked at him expectantly, and for a moment I thought he might have forgotten me. But before I could wonder too much about what I had just witnessed, Healer Arios looked at me with the same friendly smile he had been wearing moments ago.

"I believe we are missing our lunch! Even as a servant, you won't be disappointed by what the Fountain Tree Inn has to offer." Then he leaned in. "You didn't hear it from me, but the cook's cousin spent some time in Richark and brought back a few secrets."

My eyes opened even wider than they had at the fountain.

Before I could ask if we were about to be poisoned he winked at me and walked back to the inn.

We stayed there for a few days so the future students could get more ring-appropriate clothes made for them now that we were in civilization. The other six girls seemed shy with their lovely new gowns in bright colors, but Avonly moved as if she had always belonged to this life and had been unfairly denied it until now.

It made me both angry and empty at the same time.

Before I knew it I was back in my wagon passing by the last of the town's buildings with a large grove of Family Trees on my left and fields of Memory Trees on my right. I was shocked I hadn't thought earlier how all those people crammed on top of each other could honor their families with no land of their own to plant. It made me curious to see what they did in Divlan if the stories of its size were even half true.

Divlan was not the only city in Tamerin, but was by far the largest. According to Aunt Beredith, it originally was inland only two miles along the Ural River, but over time the city stretched to and surrounded Pearl Bay. I knew it had a palace where the king and his family lived and ruled Tamerin along with the Nobles in the Royal Senate. There were also academies, including the Healer Academy.

Aunt Beredith also told me most of the business of both Tamerin and other parts of the world were performed there. The Tradesmen who would come to our village to buy our grain at harvest time would always brag about having connections to the main storehouses in Divlan.

I remembered when Dural's older brother went there as a hired hand with one of those Tradesmen. He was only supposed to have gone to the nearest Merchant manor but he was gone for almost two months. He had apparently signed on with other Tradesmen who were going to Divlan and came back not only with a substantial amount of money but also with ridiculous tales of buildings made of stone polished so brightly you could see your face in them. He also said the shortest building he found was five stories high, while most were over seven! If that wasn't enough fantasy for you, he also said there were so many people living within the walls you could walk around outside for two weeks without seeing the same person twice.

I thought he was just making it up to sound important, but when I asked Aunt Beredith she just grunted and said I would see for myself if I passed the exam. I had started memorizing her books that night.

We came to another town the next day, larger than the one before, and another even larger the day after that.

I was in the back of my wagon, wrapped in my cloak trying to hide from the late morning sun, when my stomach suddenly went tight.

And I knew before I heard the first student shout, "Look!"

My chest constricted ever so slightly.

No...

A sharp pain shot straight through my heart, yanking me from my seat and around to see the road ahead.

We were on a bluff looking down on a sloping plain cut through by a bright line that led to a brighter line on the horizon. The river Ural leading to Pearl Bay and the sea beyond. Along that line, spanning either side, were buildings.

Thousands of buildings.

They seemed to never end.

But they did at what must have been the city walls, and on the other side...

Trees. Hundreds of thousands of Family and Memory Trees.

I wondered if even the Holy Forest was this big.

The stories Dural's brother brought back were not exaggerated at all.

If anything they were too tame.

My driver was yelling at me to sit back down, but I couldn't hear him. I couldn't hear anything except my heart beating wildly in my chest, fighting between excitement and terror. The fear won.

Then I caught Lady Cathrina looking back at me. I stared at her, just as I had that first day before I ruined my life, and as she had then, she smiled at me. I thought I should smile back, but all I could do was stare.

End of Part One

PART TWO

SEVEN

By the time we made it through the forest to the city walls, the sun had almost set, and large, blazing lanterns housed in glass had been lit atop poles along the road and on either side of the cavernous entrance. I was on my knees looking over the crates, my eyes just making it over the edge. Lady Cathrina had pulled her hood down as we passed by the soldiers on either side of the gates, but the other Examiners kept their heads up, eyes straight ahead. The students all bowed their heads and looked down, as if afraid they would be caught and punished for impersonating someone more inner than their ring.

All except Avonly.

She kept her head up and eyes fixed on the road ahead as well.

The gates themselves were set in a large arch, carved with an inscription I couldn't make out. My eyes went up and up as I tried to find the top of the city walls in the darkness, disbelieving that the lights I saw already lit along the top really were where the stone stopped and the sky began. It had to be twice as tall as the tallest building I had seen in the towns, if not more!

My eyes came crashing down as someone grabbed my shoulder, pulling me off the wagon.

"Hey you!" A soldier whose armor looked too big for him loomed over me. "You think you can just catch a ride hiding on the back of an official wagon? Get down and walk just like the rest of the rot-covered—"

"Ease off, son," one of the Academy guards said, taking the soldier's hand off me.

"This one yours?"

"Yeah," the guard replied. "She belongs to Lady Cathrina, so don't injure her or anything."

"Lady Cathrina!" The soldier stumbled back away from me, his eyes wide as if he were afraid, though I had no idea why. I ran to catch up to the wagon and climbed back into my seat on the back, no longer on my knees looking around, but crouched down to make myself as inconspicuous as possible.

It darkened instantly once we moved into the city walls, the remaining light from the sun blocked by the stone monstrosities rising up around me. I couldn't help but look around again, but all I could see was walls. It was instantly suffocating, as if I might be crushed at any moment. The buildings to either side just kept rising higher and higher, their windows and doorways lit with lanterns glowing from poles in the ground between the trees.

Because even here it was still Tamerin. The trees were smaller than even the ones in the towns, growing out of raised enclosed plots of dirt as large as wagons. Their presence gave me enough courage to ignore the walls that were going to fall on me, and I sat up and looked around.

We had turned off the main road coming out of the gates

and the people didn't look that bad, all dressed nicely on their way home probably after an honest day's work. Women were in long-sleeved gowns like Lady Cathrina and men in muted-toned short coats with brightly colored vests buttoned down to their waists, then flaring off to the sides as it reached their hips and a few a little longer. Some rode on horses, others walked, and I even saw a carriage turn down a street.

So many people. It felt like there had been hundreds waiting to come in through the gates, and here inside the city... I didn't know there were this many people in the whole world. I began to feel dizzy and looked down again.

After what felt like forever, there was yelling and a creaking of wood, and I risked raising my head. We were passing through a large, arched gate, not nearly as large as the city entrance but still imposing. Then the wagon stopped and I was suddenly swarmed by people.

"Get out of the way!" A shadowed man said as he grabbed the crate next to me. I hopped down from my perch, nearly falling over as my safe haven was unceremoniously dismantled by a mass of human bodies pulling it apart. I had only a moment to grab my bag before it was carted away too.

I was now in the center of a large courtyard, and the boisterous sounds of the city were dimmed by a large wall and gate. Our horses were being unhitched and led to a stable large enough to fit my aunt's cottage four times over, and next to it was a massive door cut into the side of a cliff with servants moving crates, trunks, and boxes to its entrance. Only when I looked up did I realize the cliff was actually the side of a building.

The Healer Academy.

That's when I realized there were only two wagons in the courtyard. The Healers and students were nowhere to be seen. My driver had disappeared as well, and I was lost in the eye of a storm of people, running to unpack the wagons. I spun in a circle, panic gripping me when I bumped into a dark-skinned young man with a large crate in his arms.

"Careful there," he said, using one free arm to steady me again. I looked up at him, confused at what I'd heard. It wasn't his words but how they sounded, as though they were being meshed together, the first sound brighter than the rest.

But just as quickly as it came, the observation was lost in my own panic.

"Where are the others!?" I shouted. Though she hadn't spoken to me in days, finding myself separated from Lady Cathrina in this new place sent a fresh wave of panic through me.

"Others?" He asked, his eyebrows coming together.

"The students and Examiners!"

"They went through the main entrance, of course," he said, pointing at another gate I hadn't noticed before. It opened and several servants walked through, leading the now-empty wagons. Beyond them I could see the excited students being ushered in through the grand front doors. "I'm Robert, by the way. I take it you're new, am I right? Picked up somewhere along the road?"

I nodded, my eyes still on the now-closing gate.

"I'm to serve Lady Cathrina."

"Really!" he said, eyeing me carefully. "She's never wanted a personal servant before."

I turned back to him and glared.

"I guess she changed her mind."

He looked at me for a moment more before shrugging.

"If you're lying, you'll be found out soon enough, and if you're telling the truth, then I don't want to get on the bad side of one of my girl's lackeys." He hefted the crate in his arms to get a grip on it again and turned toward the door in the wall.

"Grab your bag and follow me inside. I'll make sure you get turned around all right."

Grateful at having found someone somewhat friendly, I did as he said and put my small bag over my shoulder, following him through the door with the stream of other servants.

So, I wouldn't be seeing the grand front entrance. Aunt Beredith had always made it sound like the entrance to Heaven itself. I knew I should feel disappointed, but I was beyond that by this point. My stomach ached and I no longer had any desire to see the finery that wouldn't be mine to enjoy. All I wanted was to see a bed and maybe a bowl of stew.

It was better lit inside from the glow of dozens of lanterns attached to the walls. It must have been a headache lighting them all every night, but from the bodies that kept pushing me out of the way, the Academy had plenty of help. About ten yards down the hall, Robert brought me to a round room with several hallways and staircases leading in every direction.

"Holly!" Robert shouted at a passing middle-aged woman just coming down one of the staircases. She was about my height with fuzzy reddish-blond hair, and she clearly looked annoyed that her progress had been interrupted.

"What do you want now, Robert? I don't have time for your nonsense, or did you forget that we're swamped with saplings tonight?"

Saplings. New students. Because tomorrow was the first day of classes. I tried harder to think about stew.

"You can spare a twig. This here is a new servant girl. I brought her, now do something with her." Then he leaned closer to me. "I'll tell Markly that you're here. She'll come get you tomorrow morning."

Before I could ask who Markly was, he disappeared into the mass of servants moving around us.

Holly sized me up, tried to make a friendly smile, failed,

then motioned her head for me to follow. She took me down some stairs and down some halls and finally, after what felt like forever, stopped in front of a door she pushed open.

"We got some spare beds in this room. Like I said, we have a lot to do tonight and I don't have time to figure out where to put you and you'll just get in the way if I try and make you help, so just sit tight and someone will come in the morning to put you where you're supposed to go." Before I could ask about dinner, she was down the hall and gone. With nothing left to do, I stepped inside and shut the door.

The room was small and square, with four bunks not much different than what I left behind. Two of them had blankets on them and a trunk underneath. There was a table and wash basin next to the wall between two of the beds, and a single lantern glowing by the door. Near the ceiling above the beds was a rectangular window with real glass in it, letting in a little light from the streets outside. I realized then I must have been nearly underground.

Like I would be someday, before a Memory Tree was planted above me...

I quickly turned to touch the room's Blessing Tree. Then I turned around the whole room again.

Then again.

There was no Blessing Tree.

I picked one of the unmade beds and dropped my bag, kicked it beneath, then lay down. I tried to stretch out my arms and legs, but a loud crash from outside the window made me jump.

I had finally made it to the Academy, just as I had always dreamed. And just like everything else I had ever dreamed, it had turned into a disaster.

How many nights had I prayed I would pass the exam and come here! So many hours studying, and for what?

Everything in me suddenly went still as I remembered my very last prayer before the exam.

If you are listening, please let me leave this place.

The Great One had answered my prayer.

My sobs soaked my borrowed mattress.

CHAPTER
EIGHT

I had a headache when the door to my room was banged open.

The other girls had come in late last night, muttering and complaining about having another girl added to their room, but I hadn't heard them get up this morning. There was light streaming in through the window. I hadn't slept past sunrise in years, but even with the extra sleep I had trouble focusing on the face leaning over me.

It was of a girl a few years older than me with mousy brown eyes and hair to match tied in a stiff knot on the top of her head, with four hair sticks dyed green and yellow with a big fat bead on each. She also had a nose just a little too large for her face.

"Are you Kailin? Lady Cathrina's new servant girl?" she asked, her voice clear and crisp, but with that same cadence to her speech I had heard last night from Robert and Holly. It wasn't strong enough that I couldn't understand her, but it did make this place seem even more alien.

"Yes..."

"Grab whatever you brought with you and follow me." She turned and started to walk away, leaving me less than a moment to snatch up my bag before I lost her in the halls. Once I caught up with her I could see she was a few inches taller than me in a slate-gray dress. A Tradesman's dress made from thick, sturdy fabric, but not as brilliant as those of the inner rings.

"My name is Markly," she said over her shoulder. "I'm in charge of all the servant girls assigned to the female Healer dormitories, including you. You may be Lady Cathrina's personal servant and your first duty is to her, but in your free time you're to report to me."

She was in charge of the servants who served the Healers? I would have thought someone would have been more mature. She must have been really good at her job to have gotten so many promotions when she was so young.

"Yes ma'am," I said, and she laughed.

"I'm your superior, not a Noble!" She smiled at me and I relaxed a little. "Now, have you had something to eat?"

"They sort of forgot about me, I guess." Then, with too much bitterness I added, "I haven't eaten since lunch yesterday."

"Shrubs," she muttered. "You won't believe how angry I was when I found out about you only this morning. I don't have much say, but I do make sure those under me are taken care of." She stopped before going up a set of stairs and looked me up and down. "At least they remembered to get you some decent clothes. Peasant or no, servants at the Academy have a standard to uphold."

"No..." I said looking down at my brown dress, confused. "These are mine."

"What?!" She leaned closer before pinching my sleeve. "But it's so thick!"

"Everyone in my village dresses like this," I said. What was wrong with my dress? Was I in trouble for some reason?

"But Lady Cathrina told me you were a *Peasant*," she said, "and Peasants don't wear cloth this nice. Who was your Merchant to allow such a thing?"

"I didn't have a Merchant."

"Don't be ridiculous, all Peasants have a Merchant." She looked at me more closely, and seemed to notice for the first time the scraps of cloth sewn together in large swatches. Even though they were made of the same thick material, this hint at shabbiness seemed to appease her. She let go of my dress.

"At least I don't have to go through the pain of getting you a proper dress. Peasant or not, I will not have those under me wandering around the halls dressed like they should be shoveling rot."

She turned and kept walking, briskly navigating a narrow stairwell full of basket-carrying men and women. They were calling out to each other to watch where they were going, but amazingly never actually colliding. It was all I could do to keep track of the bouncing brown head of hair.

"So what sort of mystical hovel doesn't have a Merchant over it?" Markly called back over her shoulder as she turned down a hallway jutting off to the left and began to climb yet another set of stairs.

"Valehaven."

"Valehaven? That definitely sounds like a made-up place."

I felt more than annoyed. "It's in central Tamerin," I said with a strange sort of pride my village most definitely did not deserve. "In the middle of the Holy Forest."

"Holy Forest!?" Markly laughed. When I didn't laugh back she slowed down again. "Wait," she said, turning. "Are you saying there really is a Holy Forest? With The Great One and everything?"

"Of course there is," I said, narrowing my eyes. "With The Great One and *everything*. We perform His rituals at the Arbor and Altar every Solstice."

"Wow," she said, her smile not exactly mean, but not friendly anymore either. "You really are a rot-covered Peasant."

I gaped at her, not believing my ears. I had heard that phrase only once before. Dural had called me that when we were ten. His mother had washed his mouth out and his father gave him a frightful beating, though I was sure the punishment wasn't about me as much as it was about him.

Suddenly I was back home, and everyone and everything knew I was worthless. I deserved being called that. I shrank in front of her, lowering my eyes. Why did I think I could have raised them in the first place? A week or so of solitude in the wagon, a few kind words from a woman infinitely more rings inside mine, and I start to fall into my habit of believing I should fight? To demand respect? To *deserve* respect?

"Oh, don't be such a sapling," Markly said rolling her eyes. "You're not in the country anymore, you'll be called worse before the day's out. We have thicker skin here in Divlan."

I didn't respond, and she grabbed a roll from the basket of a passing girl and handed it to me.

"All right, that may have been a bit harsh," she amended. "I just have never met someone who actually would, well, fit that description. Believing and rituals and actually from the Holy Forest? Don't tell the other girls, they'll call you that as well."

"Thanks for the warning," I said, moving the roll from one hand to another, contemplating chucking it back at her face.

I slipped the roll into my pocket.

"You're just so rural!" she added, turning again to continue our climb. I wondered how many more flights of stairs she was going to lead me up. "Is that actual dirt under your fingernails? You know what, it doesn't matter. You can be from a colony of magic moles living at the bottom of Pearl Bay as long as you work hard and follow the rules."

"Rules?"

She stopped again and threw up her arms, looking actually angry this time. "They didn't tell you the rules before coming here? Who was your driver? I'm going to have to complain to someone about this. Ugh!" She started walking again, faster this time. She turned another corner and almost collided with an older man carrying a box full of tools. I could hear them rattle as I followed Markly, ducking under his arm.

"There aren't that many of them," she continued. "Do whatever servants above you, like me, tell you to do. Don't start fights with the other servants. Be invisible to everyone who lives here, and do not go wandering where you're not supposed to, and by that," she said looking over her shoulder with a grin, "I mean the boy students' dormitories. There are manservants for that floor. If you so much as look down that hall from the stairs you will be thrown out on the streets faster than you can say 'no! please! I'll die out there!' You're here to wash floors, not young men."

My face turned warm and Markly's grin turned smug, confident that her speech had hit its mark.

"And which floor is that?" I asked.

"Eight."

"Eight?!" I shouted, all thoughts of boys and washing gone. "How many floors are there?!"

"Ten," Markly said, her eyebrows drawing together at my outburst.

"Ten?!"

"Didn't they tell you ANYTHING before bringing you here?" She was really angry now. Clearly she wasn't used to playing tour guide. "The Academy is ten stories tall and is built around a central garden." She had started walking again and I had to run to catch up.

"The bottom floor is half underground and has the servant's halls, the kitchens, laundry, workshops, and everything else you need to keep everyone here alive. The great foyer through the front entrance has a staircase that leads to the second floor where the dining hall and study rooms for the students are. Floors three and four are the lecture halls for the first-, second-, and third-year students, then the fifth floor is the library, and after that the sixth and seventh floors are the lecture halls for the fourth- and fifth-year students along with the offices for the Healers. After that the boy students' dormitories are on the eighth floor, then the girl students' dormitories on the ninth floor. And finally, at the very top are the Healers' Chambers."

Ten floors. Ten stories above the ground. The most I had ever climbed before today was one story to a neighbor's loft using a ladder. I had to stop as my hand moved to a wall, gripping it as vertigo threatened to take me.

"So," I swallowed. "The Healers have to walk nine flights of stairs for every meal?"

"Yes," Markly said, looking over her shoulder at me with a strange look. "Why wouldn't they?"

Markly jabbered some more about my duties with cleaning and mending and serving, but I hardly heard her. The walls were too close, the air too thin. I was considering the possibility of being sick when Markly halted in front of a small door at the top of a short flight of steps. With her hand on the knob, she met my eyes, making sure I was giving her my full attention.

"We are about to go out into the halls." Her face was completely expressionless, serious in the words she wished to burn inside of me. "Lady Cathrina warned me that you didn't have much experience mixing with the inner rings, and I need to know that I can trust you in the halls, so this is how it's going to go. When we go through this door, you are not to say a word. You are not to look at anyone. *Everyone* on the other side of this door is of a ring inside yours. They know it and you had better know it too."

My heart took three quick beats, then we were through the door. I stared down at the edge of Markly's skirt, mimicking her bowed head. Though I couldn't see their faces, I could smell the students' perfume and saw glimpses of brightly colored gowns and perfectly hemmed trousers. There weren't many of them, but their voices and laughter were the sounds of carefree young people on their first day of classes.

The tightening in my stomach loosened and I had a new, bitter taste in my mouth.

This was supposed to be my first day.

"We're almost in the clear," Markly whispered back at me. I felt relieved. My neck was beginning to cramp.

Just then an insanely loud sound rang through the walls and every door in the hallway swung open. A surge of students materialized all around me. Markly never lost pace, bobbing and weaving without so much as brushing against them.

I couldn't breathe, my self-pity gone and self-preservation taking over. My blood roared in my ears as I attempted not to touch anyone.

Markly was already ahead of me, standing in front of a door just before the hallway turned, head down but eyes cast my way watching me. The flood of bodies thinned and I shot forward, trying to run the last few yards before more students cut off my escape.

Which, of course, was when he knocked me over.

The next thing I knew I was on the ground with a teenage boy on top of me.

"Watch where you're going, you shrub!" I yelled, pushing him off me.

"I'm sorry," the older boy said, rolling into a crouch, barely freed from our tangle of limbs, when his eyes met mine. I was giving him my best death stare. I instantly regretted it when I saw his face.

It was smooth as if it had been handcrafted, with a straight nose and strong cheekbones. He had a slight tan with dark hair gently waving off to one side. His deep blue eyes were open wide with shock, which only made them more stunning. Without my permission the tension in my body disappeared, my mouth going slack.

I had seen boys before—there were plenty of boys in my village—but this one looked like a different species altogether.

And he was.

Because over his spotless black trousers and a lightweight blue shirt was a deep green patterned vest with gold embroidery on the hem, unbuttoned and draping on the floor—it was that long.

He was an inner-ring young man, and I had just insulted him.

Self-preservation was screaming in my head, but I couldn't get past my strange mix of anger and adoration. The thought of looking away from those eyes seemed impossible.

And he didn't look away either.

In fact, the only movement I saw was the ripple of skin on his neck as he swallowed.

"Are you just going to let her talk to you like that?" Suddenly the world crashed back to reality, with the boy and me in the center of a crowd of students, all eyes on me and the inner-ring boy.

"I bet you could demand repercussions for her knocking you over," another boy replied. "She's pretty enough if you hold your nose!"

The blue eyes narrowed, whatever I had seen in them gone.

I finally listened to that screaming self-preservation and pressed my forehead to the cold stone floor.

"Technically, I believe I was the one who knocked her over." I knew instantly it was the boy talking. His voice was as rich as his clothes, with a cadence to it that made you excited and eager to hear more. "Planting her would be overkill, I believe." The other boys laughed and I ground my jaw to the side.

His eyes weren't that stunning anymore.

"You can't just let what she said go, though!" A girl whined. "And she's a Peasant! Can't we have a little fun?"

Fun? My eyes rose slightly, just enough to see my reflection in his impeccably polished boots. Strangely though, they were also caked with mud on the bottom edges.

He wasn't as perfect as he first appeared. He could get dirty just like me.

"If we had 'fun' with every Peasant who was kindle brained," the boy replied, "then the labor force of Tamerin would be severely disrupted."

Kindle brain!?

My jaw started to hurt, so I forced my teeth apart and shoved my tongue to the side between my teeth until it hurt to keep my mouth shut and keep all thoughts of all the ways I could show him how kindle-brained I really was—mostly with a sharp stick.

"Well, my lady," shrub boy said, and with a start I realized he was speaking to me. "I'm so sorry to have delayed you on what must be a very important errand. I'm sure there are many floors that need to be scrubbed at this very moment. Be sure to give them my apologies."

I was in agony. Any feelings of attraction were gone and instead every fiber of my being wanted to throw myself at him and distort that perfect little face of his. Instead, I jumped to my feet and ran after Markly, trying hard to ignore the laughter and perfect blue eyes following me down the hall.

NINE

Markly didn't say anything as I approached, but once we were through the door she turned and smacked me on the back of the head.

"Do you have any idea how lucky you are?" she yelled. "I told you to be invisible! To not draw attention to yourself, because if you do, *bad things will happen!*"

"He's the one who knocked me over! And nothing happened!"

"Like I said, you were very, very lucky! He could have, would have..." She trailed off, shaking her head.

"Could have what?" I asked, grabbing her arm as my panic rose. "Had me dismissed? But I don't work for him, I work for Lady Cathrina!"

Markly gave me a look that could only be described as pity. I bit my bottom lip, my frustration and fear growing.

"It doesn't matter," she said, turning to the stairs. "Just don't do it again."

"He was a shrub, anyway," I muttered under my breath. Markly shot me a glare and I shut my mouth.

If it wasn't dismissal it was probably the "repercussion" the other students said he could have "collected" from me. But I knew that he wouldn't have been able to touch me even if he had wanted to.

Because Lady Cathrina would have protected me, no matter how inner-ring he was.

Markly resumed her fast pace, and after several more leg-killing flights of stairs we came out on the top floor of the Academy. I had always been in good shape, but muscles I didn't even know I had were screaming at me now. I felt a surge of panic when Markly entered the main hallways once more, but it was deserted except for one easily avoidable Healer locking her door.

About halfway down the hall we stopped in front of an imposing solid wood door. Markly took out a key and turned it in the lock.

"This key lets you into Lady Cathrina's chambers," Markly explained, handing me the small piece of metal. My aunt's cottage didn't have a lock, but it didn't seem too difficult to use. "You must never use it unless you know she won't be here. Actually, you should never be up here unless you know that she isn't going to be there. Invisible, remember?"

She gave me another meaningful look in case I had forgotten our conversation five minutes earlier. I nodded my understanding, and followed her through the door.

The room on the other side was a little smaller than the size of my aunt's cottage back home, which wasn't surprising since this was a room for a Noble. What did startle me, however, was how simply decorated it was.

It was comfortable, with two cushioned armchairs in front of a fireplace in the center of the right wall with a painting of a city hanging above it. Against the left wall was a long, thin table that held nicely stacked books and a vase of flowers beneath a large arched window opening onto a breathtaking view of the city. Bookcases lined every other free space of wall between mounted lanterns, with more volumes than I had ever dreamed of seeing in my entire life. A stairway took up the bulk of the far side of the room, leading up into what must have been her bedchamber. For a Noble's room I would have thought there would be more gold or jewels or fur-lined rugs, but there was none of that here. It almost gave me the feeling of being back home with its warmth.

And thankfully there was a Blessing Tree on the wall by the door. Some of the tension released from my shoulders.

"This room is beautiful—"

"This is the Lady's sitting room." Markly said. She was already across it and standing in front of a door under the stairs I had not noticed before. "The stairs lead up to her bedchamber and washroom. And this door," she added, pulling on the handle, "will take you to her storage room."

Inside was a room filled with boxes, trunks, wardrobes, and shelves filled with everything a Noble would need to live comfortably. There was also a bed pallet in the corner.

"Gowns over there, linens and jewelry over there, shoes and other whatnots over there," Markly said while vaguely waving her arms to random parts of the room. Before I could ask for clarification she had turned and gone back out the door.

I couldn't look away from the bed. She hadn't said it, but it really didn't need to be said.

I guess I was to be kept with her other things in this room when I wasn't needed. I walked over and dropped my bag and cloak on top of the blanket.

When I got to the main room, Markly was already in the hallway standing by the door, one hand on her hip. I took one more look around the room.

"Will I have to clean all this by myself?" I asked. "I mean, it is a Noble's room, so it is probably more work than the other Healers' chambers—"

Markly burst out laughing.

"Oh you're funny! Now come on, I have other things to do this morning than tend you."

I moved to follow her out, but at the door I paused. Even though Markly was giving me a look that made my cheeks feel warm, I touched the Blessing Tree's roots, my heart, and then the leaves. Thankfully she didn't say anything as I followed her out into the hall.

"Come on," she said. With bowed heads we walked down the hall and around the corner of a giant stairwell, stopping at a door on the right not nearly as nice as the one we had just left. Behind it was a narrow landing with a stairwell like the ones we had been traveling through all morning in the center, only this one didn't go up any further. On either side of it were two doors opposite each other.

"Where does this stairwell lead?" I asked, pointing down.

"Eventually down to the first floor," Markly said, walking to the door on the left.

"Wait," I said, my fists clenching. "If we could have taken the servant stairs the whole way, why did you take me out there?!"

"Because I wanted to see how you would do," she said. Her hand was on the doorknob, but she turned and glared at me. "And I'm officially banning you to the servant halls until you learn to control yourself."

"What?!"

"And this," Markly said, ignoring my outburst while opening the door, "is your new home."

The room was rectangular and ran along the length of wall parallel to the main hallway and what must have been the

Academy's inner wall. In the center of the room was a long table covered in baskets and half-finished projects, though a space had been cleared for a girl who was sitting there with a book open and a notebook next to it that she was writing in. The walls were a chaotic mess of cupboards and shelves, and a very haphazard corner of brooms, mops, and buckets that reminded me fondly of my Aunt's common room back home, only instead of an open fireplace there was a stove in the corner with a full stack of wood. The sight was broken by an arched window in the center of the wall facing outside, letting in the morning sun and lighting up another girl asleep on a smaller bench beneath it.

"Up, you two, I brought Lady Cathrina's new hobby." When neither girl stirred Markly put her hands on her hips. "And you're both supposed to be working, or have you forgotten that little detail?"

"How could we forget?" yawned the girl on the bench sitting up. "It's all you ever talk about." She looked younger than the other two, more around my age, and was more than a little portly, though it worked to her advantage in some areas. Her red hair was falling in a mess out of her bun, her nose short and slightly turned up, reminding me of a pig. "At least you've brought a little entertainment; I've been bored out of my mind."

"Gabell," said the girl at the table, not looking up from her book. "She said a new girl, not a performing donkey." Her face was serious and in a lot of ways reminded me of a very purpose-bound lizard, with brownish-blond hair pulled tight into a bun with green beaded hair sticks.

"Very observant, Lancy," Markly said, walking over to Gabell and smacking her. Gabell gave her a glare, but did move to the worktable, pulling toward her a basket of underdresses that were in various states of destruction and a tin of needles and thread. Markly then walked next to Lancy, picking up another basket full of undergarments and slamming it down on the table. Lancy had just enough time to snatch her notebook away before it was smashed underneath the basket. She gave Markly her own glare but still stood up, put away her books, and pulled down a closed box. When she sat down again and flipped open the lid, I saw it full of needles and thread much nicer than what Gabell was using. Without looking up again she took out the first garment and began sewing. Satisfied, Markly sat down herself and started her own work.

"So," said Gabell, looking up at me. "What's your name?" Then she smiled. "And where are your hair sticks?"

"Kailin," I said. Then I self-consciously pulled on the end of my braid. "And I don't really wear hair sticks that often." And by *often* I meant ever. It wasn't mandatory or anything.

Besides, Aunt Beredith never wore a pair.

"What are you, some kind of Peasant?" She smirked. When I didn't reply she started laughing. "Stick in a hole, you *are* a Peasant, aren't you! With a brown dress and everything! Oh this is going to be fun!" Then she turned to Markly, "Did you give her her initiation?"

"Initiation?"

"Yes, I did," Markly said without looking up.

"And how did she do?"

"She's not to go out until she's had some practice." Gabell groaned and Lancy shot me a glare.

"But we got a *Peasant*!" Gabell groaned again. "She's perfect for scrubbing washrooms! What's the point of having her if she's stuck behind walls?!"

Lancy shot me another glare, and I wished she had kept on ignoring me. "What did she do? Make eye contact with a second-year Merchant?" Gabell snickered and I felt my face turn red.

"No," Markly said, her voice going quiet. "She got noticed by Lord Aiden."

Lancy dropped her needle. Gabell's face went pale.

But not as pale as mine must have been.

Lord Aiden?

That boy was a NOBLE?!

Then I remembered his face, his fancy clothes, his long vest.

It seemed so obvious now.

"But what is she doing here?" Gabell whispered.

"Because Markly brought me—"

"What Gabell is wondering," Markly said, slamming down her work and standing up, looking at me with so much anger I stepped back into the hallway, "is how you got out of being punished! Our invisibility isn't just because the inner rings don't want to be bothered by our existence, it is also for all of our safety!" She looked away and sat back down, picking up her work again. "Especially from Nobles."

"Especially *that* Noble!" Lancy chimed in again, picking up her needle again.

"I guess," I said quietly, "that he had more important things to do."

"Ha!" Gabell said, without any humor.

"Just keep her behind doors for a few weeks," Markly said, glaring at her; then, turning to me she added, "And for you, Kailin, before you think you're safe because he didn't do anything right now, I saw him watch you as you ran down the hall. He now knows you exist and might recognize you if he saw you again. Even after I allow you out, you'll need to avoid him. He might decide later to take out a bad grade on you if you run into him again."

I started to laugh, but stopped when I saw none of them were laughing either. "Really? A bad grade?"

"I'm serious Kailin," Markly said.

She didn't stop looking at me until I nodded.

"I'll be careful," I said, still not understanding. So he was a Noble; well, so was Lady Cathrina! It wasn't as if I had just narrowly escaped with my life from some great natural calamity!

Then I remembered his eyes, his voice, the way his body was frozen only inches from mine as his look held my face.

Maybe I had.

"Don't worry," Markly said, her voice softening at what must have been my terrified face. "We'll teach you how to do better out in the main halls, and you're safe behind the servant doors. We don't make it a habit of biting each other."

"At least not on their first day," Gabell grumbled.

"Don't mind her," Markly said, sewing again. "She's just cross that she's locked up in here all day mending Healer Jakson's underdresses instead of ogling the new students."

"I rode with some of the scholarship students for the past two weeks," I said, moving to sit down at the table next to Markly on the side away from Lancy. "You're not missing anything."

"It's not scholarship students I'm interested in," Gabell said, making a face as if I had offered her some moldy cheese. "But at this point I would welcome any boy. I'm bored out my mind working on these stupid stitches."

"You're only bored because you are slothful by nature," Lancy said with a dull voice. Markly scooted the tin of needles and thread my way and I picked out an underdress from the basket.

"Yes, if only we were as accomplished as you," Gabell giggled. "Then we would all be great Ladies!"

Lancy leapt from her chair around the table and flew at Gabell, sending the two of them to the ground in mutual screams and curses. So much for the rule about not fighting.

Markly moved like lightning and tore the two apart, throwing Lancy back toward the table, making me jump up with a yelp, and Gabell toward a shelf-lined wall by the window, knocking half its contents onto the floor. Gabell was frightening in her own way, but I couldn't take my eyes off the girl who up to a minute ago was the most lifeless creature I could imagine. Now Lancy was breathing heavily, her hands clutching the edge of the table behind her as her eyes shot flames at Gabell.

"I study for my own will and pleasure, and you are fat and lazy for the same reason!"

"Fat?!" Gabell made a move to start the fight again when Markly stepped between them.

"Gabell! Lancy!" Markly snapped. "You will behave your-selves or I will reassign you both to scullery duty again! "

After a few more glares, Gabell gave a last huff, but instead of coming back to the table she lay back down on the bench she had been on when I first saw her. Lancy turned her face to stone again, and quietly sat back down, pushing aside her mending to make room for her books again. Markly moved back to her seat as well, giving me a small smile as if to say "welcome to the family!"

I felt as if I should have been grateful for that smile.

I wasn't.

CHAPTER
TEN

The rest of the day was spent learning my new duties from Markly and the other girls. In the course of a few hours they expected me to become the expert on Lady Cathrina's wardrobe, library, menu, and bathing habits. I had to know when she woke up and when she went to bed. I had to learn which biscuits she preferred at what time of the day and how many tea leaves in each cup of tea I made. They spent nearly an hour giving me a crash course in which of all the seemingly identically fancy gowns were appropriate for what events and then another on the only way to polish the jewels they told me she never wore.

By the time evening came I felt like I had been at the Academy a month and my feet felt like it had been a year.

It had been the dullest day of my life. No reading, no medicine making, no memorizing different plants and their properties.

Now there was only organizing and dusting, scrubbing and mending.

The life of a servant.

My life now.

Lunch, then dinner, came and went, having been brought up to our workroom by the kitchen staff. Markly and Lancy had left a few minutes earlier to go "tending," whatever that meant, and I was picking at my roll alone at one end of the worktable.

"Are you going to eat that?"

I looked up at Gabell in what I was learning was her normal place.

"Yes," I shoved half of it in my mouth, because if I had learned anything today it was that I was at the bottom of the pecking order here.

Actually...

"Can I ask you a question?" I said swallowing.

"You can for the other half of that roll."

I hesitated. These rolls were really good.

I tossed it to her.

"What do you want to know?" she asked, shoving the rest in her mouth.

"How do you do it? Live each day like this?"

"Don't worry," she said with her mouth full. "You'll get used to it soon enough."

"Are you used to it?"

"I'm not *trying* to get used to it," she said, giving me a suggestive smile. "I'm on my way out and in."

I thought of how much I hated my servant life and I had only been living it for a few hours.

"How?" I asked, leaning forward. "How can someone get a ring advancement other than through a scholarship?"

"I'm not talking about an official ring advancement," she said. "I'm just talking about not having to work anymore—at least not scrubbing floors."

When I just stared at her in confusion she laughed.

"You're not half bad looking. I bet I could get you on your own path to advancement through one of the Merchant boys."

My face paled again as I slowly leaned back and away from her, knowing with certainty I didn't want whatever she was offering.

Gabell responded by leaning in closer. I could see something green stuck in her teeth "The secret is just to become vitally important to someone's *needs* so they'll take you along when they graduate. Because, you see, there are many inner-ring boys who need some extra tutoring at night—especially in anatomy."

My eyes snapped back to my empty plate.

"Markly said we weren't allowed on that floor," I muttered.

"Of course she would say that!" Gabell laughed, and I hated the sound of it. It was throaty and forced, as if she didn't know how to do it naturally, and just like that she was inhuman again. "But let me tell you how life works here in Divlan. People say and threaten what they believe is *supposed* to be right, but at the end of the day they don't let it get in the way of what they want. If you can learn to live by that and use it to your advantage, you'll do all right."

"No thank you," I whispered.

"Suit yourself," she laughed again, moving back over to her bench.

I jumped as the clock chimed nine o'clock through the walls, as I had every hour that day. It was unbearably loud even though the sound was muffled through who knew how many layers of stone.

Markly opened the door as the eighth chime rang. When she didn't move I looked up to find her glaring at me.

"Why aren't you tending to Lady Cathrina?" she asked.

"Why aren't I *what?*"

"Tending! You know, bringing her her nightly tea and seeing if there is anything else she needs before retiring?"

She had been doing this to me all day, expecting me to know things before she'd told me about them. It wasn't a very effective teaching style.

"I thought you said I wasn't supposed to be in there when she was."

"Great One, help me." Markly marched over to the shelf of beautifully painted tea sets, pulling down a lovely miniature pot with matching cup and saucer from its shelf. She sprinkled some tea leaves from another specially marked jar into the pot, then reached for an already hot teakettle on the stove and poured water into it. All these she placed on an equally lovely tray, which she then turned and set in front of me.

"Fine," I said standing up, and I swore I could hear my legs creak. "And when am I supposed to be doing this 'tending' thing?"

"Oh, about five minutes ago."

Gabell burst out laughing as I snatched up the tray and tried to balance it while running out the door.

I raced through the hallways, not caring to lower my head as I passed two separate Healers, and slammed open the door to Lady Cathrina's sitting room completely out of breath.

Lady Cathrina turned her head at my entrance, already tucked into one of her comfy armchairs facing a warm, cheerful fire glowing in the hearth. Her hair was down, and though she looked tired, she smiled when she saw me.

"There you are," she said, her voice bright and animated. "I was wondering if you got lost in that maze they call the servant stairs."

"I'm so sorry, my Lady!" I stuttered through uneven breathing, hobbling inside and closing the door with the back of my foot. I looked down and breathed a prayer of thanks that

I hadn't spilled. "Markly just told me and…" Breathless from my fright and flight, I couldn't go on. I dropped, more than set, the tray on the table under the window and doubled over my knees. Bark-stripping stairs! I was in good shape. I shouldn't be dying like this!

When I looked up again, Lady Cathrina was laughing, a high, sweet sound that resembled a bird singing. I loved it instantly.

"You don't need to worry about tonight; it was your first day, after all. Bring that tray over here and—oh, you brought only one cup." She looked visibly uncomfortable.

I hated to see her smile gone and blurted, "I don't like tea before bed!"

She gave me a look saying very clearly she didn't believe me, but she smiled again. "Then bring the tray and yourself over. I want to hear how your first day went."

I set the tray on the small table between the two armchairs, then stepped back at what I thought was her reaching for the teapot, but instead she gestured at the other armchair.

I stared at her, not sure what she was asking of me. Did she want me to puff the pillow?

"Won't you please sit with me for a while?"

"Oh, but, I couldn't—"

"Kailin?"

"Yes?"

"Sit."

Tentatively, I moved over to the other armchair and took a seat on the tip of the cushion.

"You can sit back if you'd like," Lady Cathrina said, leaning back herself. "It is very comfortable, I assure you."

I obeyed and a shock ran through my system. I had never felt anything so soft and cozy. I was torn between loving it and being very afraid of breaking it somehow.

"That's better," Lady Cathrina said. "Now, tell me, how was your first day?"

"Well," I started, not sure what a Noble would want to hear. "I got here all right, as you can see...and I found my room, or Markly showed it to me, and you have a lot of nice things, which I'll take very good care of!" I paused, not sure what to say next. Her violet eyes were soft, yet focused, as if she were trying to pull something out of me.

"And the other girls are nice, sort of..."

I tried to bring to memory every lesson I had ever learned about interacting with the inner rings, but most of them involved putting your face to the ground and groveling. Lady Cathrina's kind and welcoming face seemed to defy all the expectations I associated with her ring. Though they looked nothing alike, she reminded me of Aunt Beredith. The comparison crumbled a wall I hadn't known was there.

"There are so many stairs!" I finally wailed, hating how pathetic I sounded. "And there is no sky, and even if there were, I wouldn't see it because I have to stare at the ground wherever I go, and I spend all day cleaning floors I don't get to walk on and mending clothes I don't get to wear. And when I do get a glimpse of outside, there are no trees, only dead, hard stone buildings. And when I tried to talk to the other girls about where I came from, they called me..." I looked down at my hands.

I closed my eyes when the first tear fell.

"I always felt alone back in Valehaven," I continued, "because everyone hated me. Now I'm here, where no one knows I'm a bastard. So why do I feel more alone than I ever did before?"

I shouldn't be telling her how much I hated it here. I should be telling her how much I loved it, how grateful I was she took me from Valehaven—but I couldn't bring myself to say the words. My legs burned, my hands were chapped, and I could feel something very close to loathing for this woman who tore me away from the open skies I had taken for granted. I felt bad instantly when I looked up and saw guilt on her face.

When I met her eyes she turned toward the flames.

"I'm sorry," she said. Then she kicked off her shoes and pulled her feet up onto the chair beneath her gown, hugging her knees. My eyes opened wide, but she wasn't looking at me. "I knew that it was going to be difficult for you to adjust to the life of a servant, but I hadn't thought about how stifled—how suffocated you would feel. You are used to a freedom that most in Divlan do not understand. They will not have pity for your loss. They've never felt the independence you've had your whole life."

I wondered how she could possibly know what I was going through, yet her words rang true with my broken heart. She was a Noble, rings inside me, but looking at her with her hair down, her knees pulled up and the enchanted way the golden light gave her eyes a life of their own, I felt for a moment she might have been just as lost in this game of rings as I was.

"It's one of life's lessons." Lady Cathrina continued meeting my eyes again. "Don't go looking for healing where there is no understanding."

I tried to let that sink in. The other servants were at the bottom of the social ladder too—if they couldn't understand what I was going through, then who would?

I took a chance, and slipped off my shoes and pulled my legs up too. I looked questioningly at her, but she just smiled.

"Lady Cathrina, I wanted to thank you for bringing me here, for changing my life."

"Your life!" She laughed. "Yes, Beredith believed I could change your life, and I guess in a way I have. But no," she turned fully to me now, letting her bare feet fall onto the soft rug as she leaned toward me, taking my small hands into hers. They felt soft and worn at the same time. "I may have moved your body from one part of the world to another, but you haven't changed since you left home. I am powerless to change your life. You are the only one who can."

She held my hands and I let her. For the first time since I'd left home I felt safe. I returned her smile and let myself believe that as long as I could end each day here with her, maybe I could survive here.

Then something changed in her eyes, and her face took that same look of fear she had given me from across the village green the day of the exam.

Then it was gone and she was smiling again.

"I think that is enough of my preaching for one night," she said, dropping my hands and standing up. I jumped up from my seat as well, my heart racing.

What did I do wrong?

"I'm glad that you're doing all right," she continued, already on the stairs up to her bedchamber. "And I know it's hard, but I'm sure that something good will come from this."

Before I could reply she closed her door and I was left standing alone in the firelight, wondering what in the world had just happened.

Hours later, lying on my new bed, I found that I could not sleep. Try as I might, whenever I closed my eyes I could not escape her words, her voice, and the firelit stare she had given me.

Both of them.

ELEVEN

My legs were burning.

I laughed at the word, thinking of my nightmares of strange blue fire and wondered if this was where those dreams were coming from. Each step seared a new understanding of endless torture and solidified my belief that the people in this city were, in fact, insane.

As I hauled the basket of sewing supplies up the last few steps to the tenth floor, I conceded that though they were in agony, my legs were not in danger of giving out like they had those first few days. After two months I could go longer without having to rest, but I seriously doubted I would ever get to the point where I could just fly up and down several stories like everyone else at the Academy—servant or student.

"There you are!" Gabell yelled as I stumbled through the workroom door. The table was still covered with the dishes from dinner, with her on the bench under the window as always, not even pretending to be cleaning up. I shot her a glare before putting the thousand-pound basket on one of the supply shelves behind where Markly was sitting.

Every day I was learning something new. Today's lesson: don't be the first one to finish eating. I hadn't thought it a potential problem, until Lancy logically suggested that since I was already done I should be the one to quickly run down to the storage rooms on the first floor on some errands that just had to be done tonight.

"Now that you're back," Gabell continued, waving her hand toward the pile of dishes, "you can take down the dinner stuff."

My face went cold.

"Aren't you going downstairs tonight anyway?"

"Yes, but I'm further up the food chain than you."

"Gabell!" Markly snapped, coming to my rescue from her seat at the other end of the table.

For once.

"Lay off her," Markly continued. "Can't you see that she's about to collapse? After you tend to your Healers, you will take down the dishes, and don't you dare complain!"

"Weak rot-covered Peasant," Gabell muttered as she stalked past me out the door. Maybe Markly stepping in wasn't so great after all—Gabell had all night to think of new tortures for me.

Even so, I sighed in relief as I walked over to the stove, bringing down the now-familiar tea set that was probably worth more than my entire village. It was a little before nine o'clock and I needed to get Lady Cathrina's evening tea ready.

"Not so fast, Kailin," Markly said standing up. "I said that I didn't want you walking all the way to the first floor again, but that doesn't mean that you're done for the night, either."

"But I have to—"

"Yes, yes, I know, but when you're done with Lady Cathrina you need to scrub the steps between the eighth and ninth floors on the east stairwell. There was a spill earlier today of something sticky."

Sticky?

"What spilled?" I asked.

Markly gave me a look the meaning of which had been an earlier lesson.

"Never mind, I'll take care of it."

A few minutes later I was pushing open the door to Lady Cathrina's chambers, carrying a tray with her tea things on it as the first chime of nine o'clock rang. I was only half surprised to see she was already there, curled up in one of her armchairs with a book, her fire merrily burning behind the grate.

"Good evening, my Lady," I said, balancing the tray while closing the door behind me.

"Good evening, Kailin," she said, giving me a smile before returning to her book.

"Are you sure you don't want me to come earlier in the evening to make your fire?" I asked, nodding toward the already glowing blaze. "None of the other Healers make their own."

"No," she said without looking up, "I know you're busy and I like to do things for myself every once in a while." I wondered about that as I placed the tray on the table under the window and poured her a cup, something I was pretty sure she could do herself.

"Just set it down," Lady Cathrina said, when I offered her the steaming cup. I placed it on the small side table by her chair, and then stepped back and waited.

"That will be all, thank you, Kailin."

I nodded my head as I had been taught to do when dismissed, and then quietly went back out into the hallway.

I had been with her less than five minutes.

When the door shut with a click, I leaned against it and let out a sigh of disappointment. Lady Cathrina had been polite and more than patient the past two months as I learned how to serve her, but the closeness I had felt that first night was never repeated.

It left me empty and aching.

I went back to the workroom and grabbed a bucket and brush from the pile in the corner. The room was empty now and felt large and cold without the other girls. Silently I took the bucket to the spigot by the stove and gave myself a moment to find the courage to turn the lever. My breath caught, as it had every time before, at the wonder that water could flow up through the walls ten stories so I wouldn't have to haul it up the stairs. I shuddered at the thought and made a mental note to say a prayer of thanks to The Great One for whoever it was that invented this miracle.

If I remembered to pray tonight.

Putting in a bit of soap powder, I took the bucket out into the hallway and made my way to the sticky stairwell, enjoying the empty halls and my raised face. For a moment I could forget that I was just a servant and enjoy the marvels around me.

Because the Academy was beautiful.

There was no other way to describe it. The walls were covered with tapestries and paintings of famous healers bringing what looked like the dead back to life, or vast land-scapes that made me almost believe that if I looked out a window I would see mountains and valleys instead of the dead stone of endless buildings. The columns and arches were intricately carved with the peaceful faces of believers looking upward as they were fed life-saving nectar pouring from the swirling branches of trees carved into the ceiling.

But my favorite part of my new home was the large windows on every floor in each of the four corner stairwells.

These were designed with stained glass in amazingly detailed images of forests, mountains, deserts, and seasides. It made the world seem huge, knowing Tamerin had so many different parts to it, and that students from all of them came here to learn. When there weren't any students on these upper floors during the day, I could stand in the light coming through them, surrounded by the tints of green and blue and almost feel as if I were back home beneath the filtered light coming through the trees.

But now the windows were dark.

I found the spill easily, as the sticky substance was a sickly shade of pink that stood out against the cream-colored stone.

I knelt down, splashing the water in the bucket as I dunked my brush.

Then I scrubbed.

Back and forth.

Gone was the gross spill.

Back and forth.

Gone was the dirt, the footprints, the filth the students and Healers had left in their wake.

Back and forth.

Gone were my ambitions, hope, and dreams.

Back and forth.

Gone was Kailin, leaving only a perfectly uniformed servant, numbed to her life, and in that numbness, free from the pain.

So why was I crying?

The stain was almost out when I heard footsteps coming from the floor below. There wasn't any curfew as I had expected in a school with two hundred or so unsupervised teenagers, but most seemed to retire to their rooms early to study. Annoyed at my solitude being interrupted, I put my head down and only caught a glimpse of a colorful skirt hem.

Whoever it was had made it up two steps when she stopped.

Great, what does this little shrub want?

"Kailin?"

I scrubbed more vigorously.

"Kailin!" I tried to ignore her, but in a moment her notebooks were cascading down the steps and she was down on the ground next to me.

"It's really you!"

I stopped scrubbing, but I still kept my eyes down, only this time it wasn't because of any rules.

"Kailin, it's me!" She grabbed my face and forced me to look at her.

She was different and the same. The same curly blond hair, now held up by colorful hair sticks with dangling beads. The same large, light-blue eyes, now lined with makeup. The same smile, now painted red.

"Hello Avonly." I had spent the past two months imagining this moment and all the horrible things I would say to her, but now I found I couldn't get my mouth to move.

"Oh, Kailin!" she said, throwing her arms around me. "I looked everywhere for you! Not obviously, because I'm a Healer now, but I did!" I hadn't moved, and she pulled back.

"I still can't talk to you." I hoped she could hear the venom in my voice.

"You're right, not here at least," she said standing.

Was she deaf and blind? By The Great One, it was too much. I needed to get away before I got hurt again. I reached for my bucket, but she snatched it up first.

"We can go to my room, it isn't far!"

I stared at her, uncomprehending as she gathered up her notebooks, then raced up the stairs, not even looking back to see if I would follow.

I didn't want to. I wanted to let her go off by herself, to shun her as she had shunned me.

But she had my bucket.

I got to my feet, brush still in hand, and followed her.

She was waiting on the landing above, a smug look on her face when I turned around the bend in the stairs. I glared at her, but she had already looked away toward the girls' dormitory floor.

Our footsteps echoed off the walls of the abandoned hallway, the lights having been dimmed an hour before.

We stopped in front of a door that was noticeably different from the others. It was in a section of the hall where the doors were closer together, the wood obviously duller and cheaper.

A scholarship room.

Then she opened the door, and I stepped into paradise.

The bed had a real mattress with thick, shiny blankets. It sat between a massive wardrobe and a large window. Though the curtains were drawn, I knew it would be an incredible view of the city below. A fireplace, the hearth already lit, filled the room with warmth and light, the nearby cushioned armchair and thick rug inviting one to sit and read by the fire. Opposite the bed was a desk covered in notebooks, their pages laid open. Beside the desk stood a bookcase with no less than five volumes, the titles on the spines entreating me to open then and soak in all the knowledge they held.

And it was all hers.

Avonly dumped her armload of books and notebooks next to the mess already on the desk.

Books. Notebooks.

Class notes.

I couldn't feel my face.

"Sit here," Avonly said, drawing my eyes back to her as she shut the door behind me. It took me a moment to register that she was pointing to the bed. "You won't believe how comfortable it is!"

I didn't move, only stood there and stared at her.

Her smile froze, then fell off her face.

"Please, let me try to explain."

My numbness thawed slightly, and I tried to channel Aunt Beredith into my glare. After a few moments more of punishing her, and honestly enjoying it, I sat on the bed.

Avonly pulled up the wooden chair behind her desk and sat in front of me. I waited, studying this girl who was once my friend.

She wore a bright-yellow gown, the color an almost perfect match for her hair. The gown had delicate embroidered ribbons crissscrossing her chest, while the ties in the back were tightened in what I thought was a little too tight. Her hair had no fewer than six hair sticks that were each painted a different color, with matching beads I had noted earlier, each the length that would be appropriate for a Healer. And now that I was really looking at her, she was wearing more makeup than I had thought. A completely foreign concept before moving here, but everyone in Divlan with some sort of money seemed to wear it.

And thanks to the scholarship stipend, Avonly had money now.

And status.

Though you wouldn't think it from the way she avoided my eyes, how her hands kept moving from holding, then releasing, then back again. Where was that stuck-up girl who was disgusted to be seen standing next to me?

"I'm a terribly wicked person," she said, finally breaking the silence.

Yes, you are.

"No, you're not."

So much for my righteous indignation.

"Yes, I am." She looked at me and I felt my heart give a jump at the intensity behind her eyes. This was not a look she would have been able to give me before the exam. It reminded me too much of what I was feeling every day.

This was a mistake.

I leaned forward to leave.

"Wait!" She held up a hand and I sat back down again. "I need to get this out, then you can leave if you want to." She paused, staring at her hands, and I waited.

"That day on the road," she finally said, "I treated you terribly. And then by the fountain in that town, I thought I was better than you. I wanted to be better than you."

When I didn't respond she breathed out in exasperation. "I mean, could you blame me? For the first time in my life I was out of your shadow."

The room suddenly tilted.

"Out of my shadow?" I couldn't help but laugh, making her flinch. "Avonly, are you taste-testing strange herbs?"

"No!" she shouted back, then something caught in her throat. "Well, only once at that one party, but that's beside the point!" The tension was broken, thank The Great One, but she still looked uncomfortable.

Good.

"I've always lived in your shadow," she continued, her hands moving with her words. "You were the smartest, the fastest at memorizing, had the most natural skill—we all knew you had the greatest chance of getting into the Academy. And don't get me wrong, I was happy for you, but honestly, after years of you shouting out the answer during lessons before I could even think about raising my hand, it began to get more than just a little annoying."

I had no idea what she was talking about. I wanted to tell her so, but she kept going.

"Part of me felt justified that I made it and you didn't." In that moment she shot me a look that made me wonder if she didn't still think that just a little bit; but then she added, "and that makes me the worst friend there ever could be."

This was insane. I had gone insane and none of this was real. Waiting to be woken up, I turned my eyes to the ceiling and let out a long breath.

"I don't resent you for what happened," I said.

"Liar," Avonly said, leaning back in her chair. "I grew up with you, remember? I know you can't stand being looked down on, no matter how pathetically you would slink around the village. I've seen you give that death-glare of yours to everyone and I thought how much they all deserved it for the way they treated you. But then when you gave it to me...it has been haunting me. I've tried to block it out, but you just have this gift for making me feel guilty when I'm being awful—"

"All right!" I said. "I get it! You're forgiven! Just stop it already!"

Her blue eyes went wide, and we both burst out laughing.

"So you haven't been waiting around every corner to stab me?" She laughed.

"Well," I said. "Maybe not stab, but I was pretty mad. I've become quite lethal with my brush skills." I held up the brush I was still holding in a mock stab to prove my point. "But I guess you've done a pretty good job of punishing yourself."

"That's an understatement," She said, her face losing some of its ease. "Nothing about this place has been anything but a punishment."

"Really?" I said, leaning over and picking up the edge of her gown. "This doesn't look too bad."

"The clothes are nice," she said, smacking my hand away with a smug smile that was more Avonly than anything else leaking through. "But there are other things that haven't been."

She looked over her shoulder at the pile of books on her desk.

"How are classes going?"

"They could be going better," she said, still staring at that pile as if it would attack her.

"Avonly…" I said, leaning forward. "Tell me."

"Oh Kailin," she said, crumbling in front of me. "This place isn't anything like we thought it would be! The classes are more than hard, they are impossible! And I haven't been able to get the help I need from the other students because, because…" She paused, her eyes seeing me once again, but not in the way that had led to us laughing together. "The point is," she continued, blinking away the harsh look, "that nothing really matters now except that I've found you and we're going to be together again."

"Oh Avonly…." I had to stop her. Yes, I didn't hate her anymore, but she had to stop before she promised something that couldn't be. "We're in different rings now. Nothing has really changed since that day on the side of the road."

"No one has to know!" she said desperately, taking my hands. Even after only two months, her calluses were so much softer than mine. "Please give me a chance, there must be something I can do to get you to stay—"

"I'm glad you found me," I said, standing up. "I really am. And I miss you too, more than you could ever know, but we can't do this." She looked up at me with such utter loss, I had to get away before I caved—or started crying. I picked up my bucket and brush and moved to the door. My hand was on the handle when she grabbed my arm.

"Wait," she said.

When I turned around she was holding a notebook.

"Here," she said, handing it to me. "I want you to have it."

"Your notes..." I said in disbelief.

"Not my notes, *your* notes." She looked determined and wouldn't let me give them back.

"But you need them for your classes!"

"I'm going to fail out of here anyway. You at least enjoy learning this stuff."

Slowly, I began to leaf through the pages, my hands trembling from excitement. They were on the properties of two different plants I hadn't heard of before, and I could feel a hunger I had tried to ignore the last two months take control of me.

"I can't just take your notes..." I started. She tried to protest again, but stopped when I took her hand and smiled. "So I'll just have to study with you."

It was Avonly's turn to smile, and just as quickly as she had destroyed my heart she became my best friend again.

"Oh Kailin," she said, throwing her arms around me. "I've missed you so much!"

"I've missed you, too," I whispered back. I smiled as I felt her arms tighten around me, hugging me like we were children again. I held her tightly as well, trying to feel the Avonly I had known all my life, but instead all I could feel was the fine fabric she was now wrapped in.

CHAPTER
TWELVE

It was too bright. The blue fire had become nothing more than small, bright lights that danced around me in the forest. I giggled like a child with a new toy, even though I was almost blinded by their radiance. I reached out my hand to catch one, delighted and frustrated by the game.

Finally, one fell into my outstretched palm—and I gasped with pain. It felt like a hole being burned straight through my skin into my soul. I yanked my hand back, but it was too late; the blue lights were dancing again, a fast, possessive cyclone circling with me at its center. The one from my hand joined the rest, trailing a stream of bleeding blue light anchored to my palm. I turned in circles, trying to keep it in sight, when I saw something so obvious that I had no idea how I hadn't seen it before.

I had been standing on the edge of a cliff, a sheer drop to the crashing waves of an endless ocean. I could hear the roar, feel the vibrations of the waves breaking through my bare feet, smell scents I had never known in real life before.

The lights suddenly broke apart, and the one pulling my soul from me raced out toward the horizon. I shouted for it to come back, *to return the part of me it had stolen, but I was silenced by the appearance of another light racing toward me from the empty edge of the sea, identical in every way to my own captor, except this one was a deep red. My stomach clenched, and I screamed.*

It didn't matter. The two lights collided, releasing a burst of light so powerful I fell backwards, my whole body on fire with sensations that weren't mine. My heart stopped, my breath left me, and I could feel someone grasp my hand.

I banged my head on the shelf above my bed. Some shrub had installed it too low, but tonight I didn't mind. The pain gave me comfort that I was still alive.

I grabbed the hand the dream had seared, but there was no glowing light. As my fingers brushed over familiar calluses I took a breath, grateful for the feel of air in the back of my throat. The skin was still sore from the dream's memory, but there was no scar or hint that anything unnatural had happened.

Just the feeling that it had been held.

It was just a dream.

That was all. I lay back down and closed my eyes.

And saw another pair looking back at me.

I jumped out of bed and threw on my dress in the pitch blackness, slamming my toe against a chest and stifling a shout as I tried to find my boot. Feet covered, I stumbled to the door and creaked it open. The moon was glowing through the window in Lady Cathrina's sitting room, making my run across the open space to the door easier.

I stuck to the main halls, as it was well past midnight and my chances of running into anyone were almost nonexistent, and right now I needed the space. I needed to not feel trapped. My path was clear, as the lanterns were still barely burning.

I had no real destination in mind, just a restlessness, a need to walk, to get away. No, to escape, but from what?

I couldn't stop rubbing my hand.

It was a dream. It was a dream. That's all it was. A DREAM!

I collapsed to the ground in a hallway of classroom doors, pulling up my knees and leaning my head back.

If it wasn't a dream, then what was it? And more importantly, why was it happening to me?

My head snapped around at the sound of voices at the other end of the hallway. It was a teaching floor, no offices; no one should be here! But they were coming from the stairwell and in a moment two figures appeared, laughing as they stepped onto my floor.

They were obviously two students, from their dress and manner, laughing and bumping shoulders, one in a gown that pulled at her perfect figure, the faint light dancing on her pale skin. She was smiling at the other student as she leaned seductively against the wall by the nearest classroom door, the lantern behind her shoulder bringing her reddish-brown hair to life.

The second student leered in front of her, his arms full of books. The lantern light in front of his face made him easy to see. He was tall with dark hair, and was very handsome.

Too handsome.

With a long vest.

I let out a gasp, and Lord Aiden turned his head.

And saw me.

I couldn't move and was even afraid to breathe. He didn't move either, only stared back at me.

Then the girl reached out and touched his arm.

He started as he looked back at her, quickly saying something, their voices from where I stood just a series of mutters.

Look back at me.

Please.

In profile his face hardened, his jaw becoming tense. With

a deafening crash the books fell to the ground and his body was suddenly pressing the girl against the wall, enveloping her in his arms.

The girl shot out a hand to the side and found the door handle, and the two of them disappeared into the classroom.

I ran for the nearest servant hall, slamming the door behind me. I ran all the way to the top floor before I stopped, finding myself on the landing by my workroom. There, in the almost-dark, I tried to catch my breath, my trembling hand pressed against my chest.

That was dangerous. I knew it was. Lord Aiden could have come for me, as the other girls had warned, and taught me what it was they all feared so much. But instead he went for the student girl.

Because she's prettier than me.

No, that couldn't be it. I didn't want his attention.

Didn't I?

I ran back through the halls to my room and didn't leave it again until morning.

"Stop slouching," Lancy muttered, her face still bent over her own work. "It will kill your back."

I tried to sit up, but I was so tired the effort was beyond me. Besides, I doubted that slouching while emptying my basket of mending was the reason behind all the pains that were shooting through my back. I would think it was more because of the three flights of stairs I had scrubbed yesterday. Or that I wasn't getting any sleep anymore.

Either one.

The late morning sun was mockingly cheery in the way it entered the workroom window, giving light to the dust floating through the air and the stickiness of the lingering fall humidity. Autumn was meant to be cool, a hint and ripening for harvest and winter—not whatever passed for seasons here. If anything it was only heat and less heat—sticky heat and dry heat. At least I was told winter was the dry kind, so I had something to look forward to.

I looked up at Lancy sitting across the workroom table, confused again by her presence. For months she had treated me like one of her books, to be used and then closed, though she treated her books with more care than she gave me. But today she had come in, seen me working, placed her books on the end of the table, and sat down to help me without saying a word. Her stitching was small and neat, and though I had improved greatly since coming here, my work still seemed large and clumsy next to hers.

"Daugh!" I shoved my bleeding thumb into my mouth, glaring at the offending needle.

"Honestly, Kailin," Lancy said looking up at me, her face the perfect mask of righteous judgment. "You look like you're about to fall asleep mid-stitch."

"I'll be all right. I'm just having trouble sleeping."

"You should tell Lady Cathrina," she said matter-of-factly, returning to her stitching. "She'll make you a sleep tonic that will help."

"I thought we were meant to be invisible."

"Normally we are, but Lady Cathrina is different." Then muttering under her breath, "she always was."

I paused at her words, but dismissed them almost immediately.

Lancy finished the underdress she had been rehemming, and before I knew it she was halfway through another, her fingers never slowing down. The other girls were obvious in their own way, from how they acted to the way they talked like someone of the outer rings—but Lancy spoke the way Aunt Beredith insisted I speak, like someone educated. And as for her interest in books, and writing...The other girls knew how to read and write, but Lancy's education level seemed much higher than theirs. Or at least her interest.

She drew out more thread from her personal sewing box and threaded it through her needle in one fluid movement.

"Where did you learn to sew like that?" I asked.

Lancy hesitated for only a moment before continuing her rapid movement.

"My mother taught me." I waited for more, but she didn't offer anything else.

"Is she a seamstress?" I prodded. I could imagine a woman tall and thin like Lancy surrounded by a noble-woman's gowns and fine fabric, a perpetual frown like Lancy's on her face to counter the cheerful colors draped around her.

"No."

"Is she a lady's maid like us?"

Lancy stopped sewing and looked up at me. I had seen her look indifferent, bored, and even angry, but the look she was giving me now made me stop sewing. Her eyes were hard, then I thought I saw something else in them.

A bright, blue flash.

Bitterness. Grief. Annoyance.

I blinked, and they were just eyes again.

"She's dead," Lancy replied. Turning from my shocked expression, she got up and left the room, taking her books from the table.

"Lancy!" I shouted, but she was already through the door. "I'm sorry!" I dropped my stitching on the table and ran to the door, fully aware of how easily one could disappear into the servant halls if you weren't fast enough.

I started to pull open the door only to stop, closing it again so only an inch of space was left.

Lancy was on the small landing, and she wasn't alone.

A young man was blocking her path to the stairs.

He looked close to her age, with dusty blond hair to match hers. He wasn't beautiful like Lord Aiden, but had a strength about him that made it hard to look away.

He also didn't look menacing, though Lancy's stiff back made it clear she saw him as a threat.

"Tell me what happened, Lancy," he said, his arms moving up to her shoulders, but at the last second he dropped them again. "I haven't seen you this upset since—"

"Don't call me Lancy," she spat back.

"We've been over this, that's your name." He sounded hurt, and frustrated. "You don't make a scene when other people call you that."

"You're not other people!"

"Oh!" He smiled a little and leaned against the wall, looking up at her through hair falling on his forehead. "So you admit that I'm something special then?"

Lancy took a step back, then straightened to her full height.

"Get out of my way, Dustin."

The smile left his face and he straightened back up as well.

"So you can call me by my name but I can't call you by yours?"

"I've always been able to call you by your name," she said, lifting her chin a little higher. But as she met his eyes, it began to quiver slightly.

There was a pause, and the young man stepped back from her.

"Yeah, I guess you have." Abruptly he turned around and

stalked through the door opposite us. Instead of heading wherever she had been in such a hurry to go, Lancy just stood there as motionless as the walls.

It was ten breaths before she turned around and began to walk toward me.

I flew to the table, grabbed my sewing and made a terrible show of working, though I did manage to stab my finger again. Lancy came through the door and looked startled for a moment to see me there.

"Lancy," I said standing up. "I'm sorry about your mother; I didn't mean to pry."

"It's all right," she said, distracted. "I'm just so used to everyone knowing everything about me that it caught me off guard."

We stood awkwardly for a moment when the noon bell sounded through the walls.

"I should get down to help clean up the classrooms," I said moving around the table, grateful for the escape.

"Yes, of course," she said sitting back down. "And don't worry about your mending. I'll have it done in half the time it would take you anyway."

"More like a tenth of the time."

That got me a small smile, and I took my victory down the servant stairs.

A few of the servant girls who tended the classrooms were sick today, so for a promised favor from the hall's head maid, Markly had graciously volunteered me to help. I exited the servant stairs at the third level and kept my head down at the flood of first-years making their way chatting and laughing toward the stairs. I hid a smile that wouldn't be suppressed, knowing that tonight, once Lady Cathrina dismissed me, I would get to learn everything they had learned today.

I didn't regret all the reasons for why I was tired.

A crash made me turn my head, and I saw a girl bent over a pile of fallen books.

Avonly looked up with a forced face of exasperation, then acted surprised when she saw me. "You!" She said, sounding like a shrub in her attempts to sound lofty. "Come help me pick these up!"

I managed not to roll my eyes, but just barely, as I made my way over.

I leaned down next to her to pick up a book.

"I have to cancel tonight," she whispered. I almost dropped the book I was handing her, but managed to catch it.

"Why?" I whispered back.

"Can you believe it?" she said, her eyes lighting up with excitement. "Jesselle has invited me to come to her room tonight!"

"To study?"

"Oh no, Jesselle is a *Merchant* and her family owns, like, a fourth of the wool industry of Tamerin! She invites a group of girls to her room at night to gossip about clothes and boys and the court and things like that, and she invited *ME!*"

I quickly glanced around to make sure no one had overheard her squeals, but the hallway was empty now.

"But what about studying?"

"Oh, I'll catch up just fine tomorrow night. Making these types of connections is so much more important anyway."

I started to protest, but a door opened behind me and I quickly finished handing her her books.

Avonly's daydream smile melted off her face as her eyes looked over my shoulder, then she turned around and dashed down the hall to the stairs.

I shook my head, still dazed at her disregard for studying, and turned to go find Markly and the other girls.

And walked right into Healer Steverno.

He yelled as I hopped back.

"Forgive me," I said, looking up to apologize, only to remember a moment too late that servants were supposed to keep their eyes down.

I had just enough time to see the offended sneer when I felt the blow on the side of my head, sending me flying to the ground. My hands weren't fast enough to catch me, and the side of my check stung as it scraped on the stones. I could feel the sickening warmth of something wet on the side of my face as my head started to pound. I pulled myself up to my hands and knees, staring at his shoes.

"Eyes down." The Healer's voice was cool, in contrast to my rising temperature. I kept my eyes fixed on the flagstone in front of me.

His brisk steps echoed as he moved down the hallway, only to stop. Tensing, I waited.

"Also," he said, and I could imagine the sick smile in his voice, "my washroom bowl needs to be scrubbed. I want to see my face smiling back at me when you're done."

I could feel my hands ball into fists, but I forced myself to keep my head down, not trusting my eyes to hide what I was feeling if I looked up.

Then I remembered.

Maidservants weren't permitted in men Healers'chambers, including those of the instructors. It was grounds for dismissal. But if I didn't do it, I had no doubt it would be grounds for some other type of punishment.

I jumped to my feet, only to lean against a wall in my dizziness, and ran down the hall, opening doors as I went.

On the third door I found Markly, picking up scraps of paper from under the tables.

"There you are!" she said, putting her hands on her hips. "I was wondering—" she stopped and her eyes went large. My hand instinctively went to my forehead. Compared to other injuries I used to get back at Valehaven from a thrown rock, this was only a scratch. I guess it looked bad enough for Markly, though.

"What happened?!" she said, rushing around the tables. She stopped in front of me, taking out a rag and trying to wipe off my cheek, but I backed away. She may not know about infection, but I sure did.

"It's all right!" I said when Markly tried again. "It isn't as bad as it looks!"

"Oh really," she glared. "And how did you get this scrap that isn't as bad as it looks?"

"I made a mistake." I muttered.

"It wasn't with—" she started, the fear plain on her face, but then she shook her head, "No, if it was him you wouldn't be here. Tell me from the beginning. Was it one of the servants? Gabell?"

"No," I sighed. "I bumped into Healer Steverno—literally."

She whistled and nodded. "That would do it. Even the students avoid him."

"And there's something else," I said. "He asked me to clean his washroom bowl, but I don't know how. Aren't we not supposed to go into the men Healers' chambers?"

"Yes, and he knows that too! He's a terrible snob, but on the whole, harmless to servants." She looked at me as if expecting me to enlighten her as to why he would be picking on me.

There was no way I was going to tell her I lit him on fire.

"So if I can't clean it, what am I supposed to do?"

"Go talk to Dustin," she said stepping back. "He'll see that it is done."

"Dustin?" I asked, wondering if she meant the same young man I had seen with Lancy.

"Yes, he's in charge of the manservants for the men Healers. He'll get one of his lackeys to do it, and if he says no, remind him that he owes me a favor."

"But I," I started, not sure if I wanted to draw the attention of yet another servant who had more power than me. "I don't know where to find him!"

"Ha," Markly said smiling. "Ask Lancy to show you. It'll do her good to see him."

Now I was more confused than ever. It was obvious Lancy did not like Dustin at all, but Markly made it sound like she was doing Lancy a favor giving her an excuse to find him.

"I think that would be a bad idea—" But Markly was already back to picking up crumpled notes.

I turned for the door, finding the nearest servant stairs.

Lancy was exactly where I had left her, at the worktable with my basket of mending almost empty.

"Wow," I said walking over and tilting it toward me so I could see the bottom. "I was joking about you being ten times as fast as me."

"Aren't you supposed to be helping Markly?" she said, yanking the basket back toward her again.

"Um, yes. But she told me to get you to show me where the manservant workroom is."

Lancy stopped sewing.

"We aren't supposed to socialize with them," Lancy said looking up at me, eyes narrowing.

"I got an assignment from one of the Men Healers."

She stared at me for a moment, like I was a stain on an undershirt that wouldn't come out. "Fine," she finally said, standing up.

I wasn't at all surprised to see her cross the landing between our workroom and the one across the stair landing that Dustin had gone into only an hour earlier. She went right up to it and opened the door without knocking.

What I saw inside made my skin crawl.

The room was almost identical to ours, with a stove in a corner, shelves stuffed with things and a large worktable in the center. Where it differed was in the two boys holding a smaller boy over a tub of water, and they were in the process of dunking him in head first.

"Where is Dustin?" Lancy snapped, not fazed at all by what she was seeing.

The older boys dropped their hostage and looked sheepishly around. The younger boy, now free, ran to a pile of boxes and proceeded to hide behind them.

"Well, he's..." started the one on the right with black hair.

"Obviously he isn't here," Lancy cut in, the sharpness in her voice silencing anything else the two boys were going to say. I would be scared of Lancy, too, if I were them. The usually calm and reserved young woman now poured out a power that didn't match what I knew about her at all. Even Lady Cathrina didn't demand this kind of attention. Not that it was bad on Lancy. With the way she held herself straight and tall, she looked almost pretty.

"Kailin," she said without looking at me, "tell these boys which Healer needs to be tended to and what their assignment is. Since Dustin isn't here, we'll have to take our chances with these shrubs."

"They are pretty stunted," said a voice behind us. Lancy's entire frame stiffened, but I was the one to turn around to see the same young man from earlier standing in the hallway behind us. He was even nicer up close.

"If I may?" Dustin asked, nodding toward the room. I hadn't realized I had been staring, and I practically stumbled out of his way. He gave me a questioning look as he stepped through the door, but then all his attention was on the girl who wouldn't look at him.

"Now, Lancy," he said, a lopsided grin forming on his mouth, but Lancy just flinched as if her name stung. "You know that young women aren't allowed in our workroom."

Lancy fixed her eyes toward the wall, her hands clenched into fists.

"Healer Steverno needs his washroom bowl cleaned!" I blurted out. The two other manservants let out a collective groan.

"What did you do to tick him off?" whined the one who hadn't spoken yet. He had brown hair and an almost babyish face.

"Nothing," I lied. "He just stopped me in the halls and made his request."

"Really," Dustin said flatly, looking intently at my face. It was then I remembered the scrape on my cheek and the blood I hadn't bothered wiping off yet.

"Are you going to do it or not?" I hadn't liked the way he had looked at Lancy, but I liked the way he was looking at me even less. There was a pity in it that I couldn't stand.

"It'll be taken care of," he replied, still frowning at my face. The two other manservants looked smugly over at the younger boy, who was now sitting dejected on a box in the corner with his head down.

"Make sure one of those two does it," I said, pointing at the two torturers, their faces no longer amused.

"A great suggestion," Dustin said, his lips curling up into a smile. "And who is your new friend, Lancy?" I saw her wince again, but when she looked up and saw Dustin's eyes fixed on me, I could feel her entire body go rigid in a new way.

"This is Kailin, the new girl. Markly must have told you about her. And we need to get back to work."

"Of course," Dustin said, turning back toward her. "I know how important your work is to you."

The way he said it made me feel like he knew what sort of work Lancy slaved away on day after day. Her eyes bored a hole into him, throwing the full weight of that unnerving power she had shown earlier behind her glare, but he didn't so much as flinch. If anything he looked pleased.

Setting her jaw, Lancy turned and marched out of the room. I stood there, not sure what to do, then I turned to follow. As I shut the door behind me, I caught a glimpse of Dustin again.

And his blue eyes.

Wait, didn't he have brown—

Sorrow. Longing. Frustration.

I slammed the door.

THIRTEEN

My head still felt like it was underwater when I entered Lady Cathrina's chambers that evening with her nightly tea, and it wasn't just from the bump that was growing on the side of my head. I wanted to just get this done with and move on to scrubbing floors in solitude, but I had had my conversation with Lancy, and then the way she had acted toward the manservants, running through my head all day.

"Lady Cathrina," I started after setting her cup of tea on the small table by her chair. I wasn't sure how she would take my question, but if I had to choose between asking the other girls or asking her, it wasn't really much of a choice.

"Yes, Kailin?" she asked, turning to me. I don't know what my face must have looked like because she set down her book. "Is something wrong?"

"Oh no, nothing like that," I said, untangling my hands that had somehow gotten intertwined in front of me. "I just had a question about one of the girls. Her name is Lancy and she mentioned your name this afternoon, and, well—"

Her lips were thin, but not unfriendly.

"Did something happen between you two?"

"Not exactly...Lancy and I were mending this afternoon and I asked her about her mother. I'm worried that I might have offended her. I know I shouldn't pry, but she seems so different from the other girls."

Lady Cathrina's smile was completely gone now, but she didn't look angry. Now she just looked tired.

"She seems different from the other girls because she is different."

"Different how?"

She looked at me for a moment longer, then seemed to come to a decision.

"Have a seat, Kailin." She gestured to the opposite chair, the one I had sat in that first night. This time I didn't hesitate to sit in it.

"What I'm about to tell you isn't to become gossip, but because you asked, and because I believe you are a considerate girl, I'll tell you the details of how Lancy came to her current situation."

"Situation?"

"Lancy wasn't born a Tradesman. She was demoted."

Demoted. Even I knew how that happened. Only the Senate could take away someone's ring.

"What did she *do*?"

Lady Cathrina took a breath and looked over at me, her mouth forming into a hard line that looked unnatural on her.

"She didn't do anything. It was her father's doing. He was an important admiral"—then, adding as if it pained her, "and a Lesser Noble."

I waited for her to tell me it was a joke, that something as ridiculous as a Lesser Noble—the third innermost ring and only one ring below a Noble like her—dropping all the way to Tradesman couldn't actually happen.

"What happened?"

"There was an incident about three years ago. The flagship of the Tamerin navy had a misunderstanding with the Richark flagship in neutral waters, which resulted in the Richark ship sinking. This would have been a diplomatic disaster in and of itself, but then it was made known that Richark's second prince was aboard and drowned as well, creating an international catastrophe that has yet to be resolved." She reached over to the table without looking and brought the cup of tea to her lips, only to wrinkle her nose at the discovery that it had gone cold.

She set it down and looked at me again.

"Lancy's father was in command at the time and was the one who ordered the firing. I'm sure you've heard rumors about our strained relations with our neighbor on the other side of The Islands. Don't repeat this, but I can tell you right now they aren't just rumors. Some have even said war is inevitable, and all of the conflict can very easily be traced back to the order given by Lancy's father."

Even as remote as Valehaven was, we all knew about Tamerin's sworn enemy, the faraway kingdom of Richark. It was on an island like ours, but while we were covered in life and forests, theirs was a land where the sun was always warm and winter never touched. According to Aunt Beredith's map, it was west of the string of islands simply called The Islands that had always been declared neutral, but that didn't mean that the waters to the west, east, north, and south with the corresponding trade routes weren't up for, what Aunt Beredith called, debate. And by *debate* she meant an endless tension that always led every few decades to war.

"He was disgraced," Lady Cathrina spat out. "They took

from him his ring and status along with the status of his entire family reaching out as far as his second cousins, but instead of just a normal demotion out one ring to Merchant, they were reduced to Tradesmen. And the outer rings do not treat kindly those who fall from their positions of power."

"What do you mean?" I felt this was where the story became one I didn't want to hear.

Her mouth twisted.

"If you haven't noticed, the inner rings aren't exactly charitable to those outer than themselves, and the resentment—no, that isn't a strong enough word. The hate, the rage." She looked at me and saw my shocked face. "No, you haven't lived here long enough to sense it, but that fury always leads to tragedy."

"But the law—"

"There is no law in between the outer rings! Sticks, Kailin, how can you not know these basic things?"

I could feel myself go pale as a world that had never been real before was explained to me. I wished I could go home where the ring structure was nothing more than a theory that mattered to people who had nothing to do with my life.

"What happened?" I whispered.

"Lancy's family barely survived their first few months in the slums." Her voice lost its venom and she looked simply pained again. "Her father couldn't find work and was routinely beaten by the other Tradesmen and Peasants until he finally was left dead in a gutter. And her mother, who already had a fragile constitution, fell ill and died that first winter. I had known her growing up, and though the law forbade me from doing anything to directly help the family, I made sure Lancy found a position here, where I could have a little control over her protection."

She made a little self-satisfied huffing noise. "I made sure Dustin also found a place here."

"Dustin? What does he have to do with any of this?"

A small smile crept onto her face.

"The servant halls must have gone silent for you not to know this juicy piece of gossip. Dustin was a servant in Lancy's house before her demotion, and they, um, knew each other. On the times I visited, even though he tried to hide it, it didn't take a genius to see he would protect her."

She took a breath and leaned back in her chair.

"So now you know. I hope this will help you to treat Lancy with more charity than the rest of the world gave her."

"I will."

I had spent my entire life believing mine was the saddest tale there was to tell. But next to Lancy, I seemed to have lived a charmed life.

Then I thought of what Lancy said about how her mother had taught her sewing.

"If she was raised as a Lesser Noble, how did her mother teach her to sew?"

Lady Cathrina looked at me with amusement.

"You're right, her mother didn't teach her how to hem underskirts, but she did teach her how to embroider. She was actually one of the best in the city. Ironically, her tapestries are still hanging on the walls in the palace."

"But that doesn't explain why she is so obsessed with studying."

"She is?" Lady Cathrina looked honestly surprised. "That's wonderful!"

"But she's a Tradesman now. It isn't like she can get into one of the Academies."

"And is that the only reason someone should try and expand one's talents? She had always been a scholar and I made it clear to the librarian that she was able to have free access to the Academy's catalogue."

Then she gave me a searching look.

"It isn't like her demotion changed fundamentally who she is."

I looked away toward the fire.

There was no way she could know about my study sessions with Avonly, right?

She gave a long sigh and stood up.

"I think that's enough society gossip for one night." She gave me a real smile this time, but it didn't reach her eyes. "You have a lot to learn about how life in Divlan works. I hope along with anything else you've learned tonight you also take the warning that you need to educate yourself better in this regard."

Then she turned and made her way up the stairs.

I cleaned up the tea things, then made my way down the familiar halls toward Avonly's room, only to remember I wasn't going there tonight.

FOURTEEN

"I understand all this! We don't need to review it again!"

Avonly practically threw the page of notes at me, and I had to scamper to catch it before it fell to the ground.

"Good." I said looking over the list of traits and attributes she would be tested on in just a few days. "So tell me the difference between using a greyleave's bark vs. its leaves."

"Well," Avonly's face fell. "Sticks in a hole, I DID know it."

She laughed at my shocked face.

"What? Don't you know what that means? It means—"

"I know what it means!" I said turning red. "I just, how can you say something like that?!"

"Seriously, Kailin." She laughed again in that haughty way that was getting more and more on my nerves. "Don't be such a root. *Everyone* talks this way."

"Right." My teeth ground together as I looked back down at the notes. "Sticks and holes aside, don't get too worked up about getting that one wrong. The exam is still two days away. We have plenty of time to shove all this into you."

"Yes, I know," Avonly turned her head toward the fireplace, avoiding my gaze. She was wearing yet another new gown of soft pinks and greens, her hair pulled back on top of her head using six hair sticks. A blanket was thrown over her shoulders, and she looked comfy slouching against the headboard of her bed, even with her scowl. I pulled the worn fabric I had found in the corner of the workroom tighter around my shoulders, her wooden desk chair I had pulled up next to her bed not contributing very much to keep my backside warm.

I had never thought it would happen but the evenings *were* getting colder with the arrival of winter, and though it wasn't as cold here as it got in the Holy Forest, I still missed Aunt Beredith's warm kitchen.

"Let's review it again," I said, holding out the page of notes, but Avonly didn't move to take it. In fact she didn't move at all, except to chew on a fingernail. My eyebrows came together. She only did that when she was nervous.

"Don't worry, you'll get it," I said leaning forward to take her hand. "We'll just have to study more the next few days."

"That's the problem," Avonly said, pulling back her hand. "I won't be able to study the next two nights."

"What do you mean?"

She took out a hair stick and looked at its bright purple color, spinning the short string of beads.

"Jesselle's parents are hosting a Solstice party two nights from now." She twisted her hair and stabbed the stick back in. "The girls and I need to go shopping for it tomorrow night. So you see, I'm going to be busy."

All I could do was stare. I was sure I'd heard her wrong. The Winter Solstice wasn't even until next week!

"Avonly, you need to study. You don't have time to go shopping."

"That's easy for you to say!" She slid off the bed and

loomed over me. "I have a chance to be *in* with the most influential girls of my ring! And Jesselle is a *Merchant*! I'm not going to blow this chance!"

"But you're not here to make social connections!" I yelled back, standing as well. "You're here to learn how to heal people!"

"I'm here because I don't want to be a Peasant anymore!"

Both of us froze, the truth weighing between us like stones around our necks. We both always knew it, but having it said fractured something between us. Something inside me. I looked down and saw my hand still holding the paper that meant so much to me and so little to her.

"What about your rural duty?"

"If I do everything right," she said, her voice going flat, "I'll have enough friends to marry into a good family right after graduation and officially enter the Healer ring." I looked back up at her and the look on my face made her glare at me. "You get exempted from your rural duty if you're married into an established Healer family—believe me, I've researched *extensively.*"

I shook my head and Avonly turned from me, going over to her open wardrobe that now held her greatest treasures. She pulled one of the doors open a little wider, revealing a mirror attached to the inside. I could see both her and her reflection from where I stood, and I didn't like what I saw.

On the outside, in colors and fabric, eyes lined and hair sticks dangling, she was the perfect image of an inner-ring woman with all the confidence that distinction placed on her. But in the mirror the Avonly I saw was tired, her gown ties pulled too tight, her breath shallow, and her hand almost white as it gripped the door. But her eyes, oh her beautiful blue eyes that I had envied so many times, were wide with desperation. They reminded me of stories of hungry animals so wretched for food in the winter they would go mad at the scent of fresh meat. It was frightening, and so horribly heart-breaking.

Oh Avonly...

I wanted to reach out to her, comfort her....

I saw a flicker of blue light dart around her head.

My eyes opened wide, but just as quickly as it came it was gone.

I looked away to the embers, catching my breath as I fell back onto the chair.

"What are you going to do about the test?"

"I *can't* fail," she whispered, closing her eyes. "I can't go back."

My stomach sank further, but I could hear the truth in her words.

She really couldn't go back.

"I'm not hopeless," she continued, "I think I can pass the tests—I just need a little—" her eyes found mine in the mirror. "I just need some help."

"That's what I'm doing right now!"

"I know, but it's not enough. I need more than just help studying."

"What do you mean?"

Her face turned hard and she left that cursed mirror and walked back to the bed, sitting on the edge facing me.

"My test will be in the large classroom on the third floor," she said, talking fast. "The seating assignment is in alphabet-ical order, so my desk will be in the second row, third from the left. We get a break for lunch at noon and the room will be deserted except for some upperclassmen guarding the door. No students can go in or out."

"So how is that going to help you get you through the test?"

It was a stupid question. I already knew what she was asking.

"I said no *student*," she leaned forward and took my hand. "But as a *servant*, you can go wherever you want."

"I'm not going to cheat for you!" I said jumping up. "Not only is it a sin to claim another's work for yourself, but if we were caught—"

"I know that!" she said. "I'm smart enough not to ask that of you, you're much too honest." From the way she said "honest," you would have thought it was a bad thing. "I just want you to check my answers and then mark which questions I need to look at again."

I sat down and said nothing. It was cheating. It was wrong. But was it? It wasn't like I was giving her the answers or taking the test for her. I was just letting her know which ones she got wrong—like a second chance. Wasn't that what the Healer Academy was about? Giving the outer rings a second chance at respectability through the scholarships? Giving everyone a second chance at life through healing?

But Avonly wasn't looking for a second chance.

This was the Academy, where scholarship students got only one shot. I had my aunt's story to confirm that.

"All right."

"Oh! I knew you would!" Avonly shouted, jumping out of her chair and pulling me into a tight hug.

"But only this once," I said, pulling away.

"Oh yes, of course," she said through her grin. "Next test we'll have studied together from the beginning so it will be so much easier! I just need your help this one time."

She let me go and turned toward her wardrobe, pulling out gowns.

"So..." I said picking up the forgotten page of notes. "Shouldn't we get back to work?"

"You can if you want," Avonly replied while studying a bright-red gown with ties in the back scandalously dyed an orange color. "I need to figure out what I'm going to wear for the big shopping trip tomorrow!"

My face grew warm and the page in my hand wrinkled.

I left before I said anything I would later regret.

The hallways were crowded not only with first-year students, but also with anxiety. The first year was broken up into two large sections of study, one on herb properties and the next on anatomy. This test marked the end of the first section and the beginning of the second after the Winter Solstice. Some students were pacing, others leaning against the wall with their eyes closed, muttering facts about the three hundred or so herbs and plants they would be tested on. While I had at least heard of most of them throughout my years of helping my aunt, there was so much more to every flower and twig in the world that I doubted I could ever enjoy a walk through a meadow again. I hadn't seen Avonly since our study session two nights earlier, but I hoped she was holding it together better than some of the students I saw this morning.

I kept my eyes down as I went about my morning chores, trying hard not to look as nervous as I felt.

At five minutes to noon I made a stop in one of the storerooms to pick up some firewood. It was an unusually cold day, so I had my excuse for entering the classroom, but even with that, my hands just wouldn't stop shaking. I gripped the wood tighter to my chest and tried to remember why I had ever agreed to Avonly's crazy plan in the first place.

Steadying my breath, I made my way toward Avonly's classroom. As the clock struck midday, I scooted to the side of the hall across from the door. Classroom doors flew open and a herd of first-year students came out, creating a deafening roar as they discussed the first part of the exam.

Some looked confident as they told the others about how easy it was, while others looked as though they had received a death sentence. I had been confused why they were allowed to talk to each other during meal breaks while the exam was still going, when Avonly explained that even though they are being tested on the same material, no one actually has the same list of questions. Even if you had an hour for lunch and could pump those around you for answers, you would still pretty much be on your own.

Unless you had someone actually taking the exam with you.

Older students appeared in the stairwells, corralling the younger students down to the second floor with no detours back to their rooms to read notes. I caught a glimpse of Avonly leaving her classroom, chatting away with her new friends as they moved down the hall away from me.

I was glad. I doubted either one of us could have kept a straight face if we had seen each other.

In less than a minute the hallway was clear, and the older students took their posts at the doors along the hallway, two at each one.

Except Avonly's classroom. There was only one.

I let out a breath of thanks that something had gone in my favor. As I passed by the older students, it was obvious they weren't expecting anything. They were casually leaning against the wall talking to each other, some not even in front of their doors. No one looked at me. The student at Avonly's door was turned away from the door, busy chatting with a pretty girl guarding the next classroom over. I slipped into the room without him even turning his head.

The door shut behind me with an audible click that echoed in the empty room. The ordinary long tables facing the large chalkboard had been removed and replaced with individual desks, spaced apart so a Healer had enough room to walk between rows if they chose. Somehow it made the room seem even larger.

I rushed to the front and dumped my logs on the already full stack by the stove in the corner, then ran to the desk Avonly had said was hers.

On it was a neatly stacked pile of papers about an inch tall. The top page held Avonly's name. I gingerly lifted it and set it down face first next to the stack.

On the next page were ten questions and Avonly's answers.

This is it, I thought. I could still leave. I haven't done anything yet. I haven't helped her cheat yet...

Swallowing my fear, I read the first question.

Which part of the brown-wood tree would you use for pain?

That was easy. We had some brown-woods back in Valehaven.

"The bark around the twigs," I muttered. Avonly got it right so I moved on to the next one.

In which part of the country does the butter-lace grow?

Even easier. The butter-lace section was one of my favorites to read in my aunt's books.

"In the north mountains at the head of the Ural river," I said a little louder. She had gotten this one wrong. Taking up the pen she left on the desk, I put a tiny mark next to the question.

Each question seemed to be simpler than the one before, and soon I was caught up in the elation of knowing the answers. Time slipped by and I had made a note of eleven questions

Avonly had marked wrong. Better than I thought she would do, if I were being honest. She probably didn't even need—

"WHAT ARE YOU DOING?!"

I spun around, knocking over Avonly's stack of papers as I did so.

And froze, my hand reaching up to my throat as my heart pounded a death sentence in my chest.

Lord Aiden was at the door, perfect hair and eyes and long vest and everything. And he looked ready to kill.

"I was—I just—"

"Really?!" He yelled striding down the aisle toward me. "You're going to talk back to me *again*?!"

I tried to back away, to run, certain I was going to finally find out what my insolence would cost me, but all I did was trip over my own feet and fall.

Then he was standing over me, a descending angel bent on my damnation.

Then the corner of his mouth moved upward ever so slightly.

He was *laughing* at me?!

"I didn't do anything wrong!"

His eyes opened wider, and for a moment I thought he would strike me like Healer Steverno. At least this time I was already on the ground.

But when he reached out it wasn't for my face but for my arm, hauling me to my feet and pulling me behind him toward the door. I tried to pull back, but he didn't even act as if he noticed. For a Noble he certainly was strong!

"Lord Aiden!" The other boy who had been guarding the door turned to look at us. "What are you—" I met his eyes and he choked on whatever he was about to say.

"Eyes down," Lord Aiden hissed as we passed by other

students now turning to see the commotion. "You're making a scene."

"You're the one—"

"Just shut up until I get you to Healer Steverno's office."

My life was over.

Why had Avonly never mentioned the Healer I set on *fire* was her instructor?

Oh.

As Lord Aiden dragged me into the stairwell I knew the answer—because she knew I would never have agreed to her plan if she had told me.

Then we were there. The sixth floor where the Healers' offices were kept.

Where my life would end.

Please help me, I prayed. *I know I did something wrong, I shouldn't have helped Avonly cheat! Please, help me...*I frantically pulled on my arm, and Lord Aiden spun around, pulling me close as his grip tightened.

"Stop fighting!" he said. "If you didn't want the consequences you shouldn't have been acting inside your ring!"

"Please," I whispered. "Please, I'm sorry. Please don't do this."

And he froze.

He didn't move, didn't even breathe as his eyes locked with mine, and everything I had felt that first day when we had stared at each other on the stone floor came rushing back to me. My cheeks felt warm, and I could smell something earthy coming from him. It made me want to lean in closer. The hardness was still on the edge of his jaw, but his eyes lost their cruelty and was replaced with something else. Something I didn't understand and wanted to get away from. His grip became softer, but still refused to let me go.

Then he was pulling me even closer so I could hear him hiss.

"Who are you, and what are you doing to me?"

If I was scared before, I was now terrified.

Lord Aiden was insane.

"And where are you taking my servant?"

We both spun to the now-open door behind us. Just in the entrance to her office was a tall Healer with dark brown hair and her hands on her hips. I wanted to weep with joy as Lady Cathrina glared fire at Lord Aiden.

"Lady Cathrina!" he exclaimed, trying to bow and ending up pulling me down awkwardly with him. "I caught this servant taking the first-year exams and was bringing her to Healer Steverno for disciplining."

"The exams?" she said startled, looking at me. "Is this true, Kailin?"

I stared at her, then turned back to Lord Aiden. All the softness was gone and he was all high and mighty again, which I decided I preferred to him acting like a lunatic.

"Kailin?" Lady Cathrina asked again.

"I was in the classroom," I said, turning back to her. "But I wasn't stealing the exam!"

"I didn't say you stole it," Lord Aiden said.

My fear lessened slightly in the face of the puzzle. I glanced at him next to me, but he was still looking at Lady Cathrina.

"I think we should continue this discussion in my office," Lady Cathrina said, turning.

"But I need to take her to—"

"She is *my* servant," Lady Cathrina snapped. "And I will decide her fate."

It was then that I realized I might have fared better with Healer Steverno.

Lord Aiden tried to drag me into Lady Cathrina's office, but

I yanked on my arm and he surprisingly let go, following me in through the door.

Lady Cathrina's office was a large room only slightly smaller than her sitting room, with a beautiful large window to the right showing a view below of a street lined with potted trees. All along the walls were bookshelves, filled with volumes on every topic I could imagine, along with stuffed birds and delicate displays of dried flowers. In the center of the room, where she was heading, was a large, neat desk and three chairs, two in front and one behind. Like everything else about Lady Cathrina, it was elegantly tasteful without the clutter of a professor or the gaudiness of a Noble.

"All right," Lady Cathrina said, facing Lord Aiden with her arms crossed. "You're making a pretty extraordinary accusation, even for a Noble."

Lord Aiden's jaw tightened, but he didn't contradict her.

"Tell me exactly what you saw."

"I had volunteered to help with the first-year exams," he began, his voice formal, like a soldier giving a report. "I was running late from my class over at the hospital this morning, and when I got there Lucas was over at the next door talking to that third-year that talks too much and he's..." Lady Cathrina raised an eyebrow and Lord Aiden cleared his throat. "Anyway, when I yelled at him for slacking off, he said the only living creature that had been in this hall was some pathetic servant girl." He shot me a look. I felt my own jaw tighten in anger as I glared back at him. His eyebrows twitched together and he turned back to Lady Cathrina. "I thought it was strange and asked him where she went. He didn't know, so I opened the door and found *her*," he pointed at me, which I thought was overly unnecessary, "standing over one of the tests, reading through them out loud and answering the questions!"

He was fuming now, as if he couldn't believe what he had

just said either. Lady Cathrina didn't respond, didn't even move for a full minute. Then she said the last thing either of us expected.

"And how were they?"

"How were what?"

"Her answers." She released her arms and walked over to a bookshelf. "You said she was reading the questions out loud and then answering them. Was she answering them correctly?"

Lord Aiden didn't respond immediately. Instead he turned and stared at me, but I kept my eyes on Lady Cathrina.

"She was doing fine."

"I was doing much better than *fine*." I snapped, turning on him.

"And she keeps doing that! I know she's your servant—"

"Yes, she is my servant—not yours," she said taking a stack of paper out of a box that had been locked. "Now, you said she was doing 'fine' with her answers. This is a Healing institution, I'm sure even servants pick things up now and then."

"Not thirty in a row."

"Thirty? How long were you standing there watching her?"

He didn't respond but turned his head away from her as well as me.

I was in trouble, but I didn't care. I had confused him, and I liked it. A smile started on the edge of my own lips.

"I see. Kailin," she said, indicating one of the chairs in front of her desk, "please have a seat."

That brought his head around quick.

I did as she said, but my head was suddenly dizzy. "Please, I didn't mean to—I just—"

She had moved around her desk and sat down herself. "Lord Aiden, please have a seat in the other chair. I would like you to witness this."

He moved over to the chair with all the grace you would expect from a man of his ring, but his face showed a pouty teenager stuck somewhere he didn't want to be.

A little more of this and I would forget I was supposed to be terrified of him.

"Now," Lady Cathrina said. "I happen to have a copy of last year's first-year herbology exam. If you would be so kind as to answer the questions I'm about to ask you, I would appreciate it."

And it began. For the next hour and a half, Lady Cathrina asked me question after question on facts that had become a part of who I was.

And I felt myself come alive for the first time in months.

When she finally stopped I was lightheaded, but happy. Without having to ask, I knew I hadn't missed a single one.

I turned my head with a smug smile, but Lord Aiden wasn't looking at me. He was staring at his hands, which were white as he gripped them together.

"Interesting," Lady Cathrina said leaning back in her chair, contemplating me.

Suddenly Lord Aiden pushed back his chair. I turned around, but he was already out the door, slamming it on his way out.

"Very interesting." I turned back to Lady Cathrina, but her eyes were on the door.

"What's going to happen to me?" I asked.

"Right now? Nothing." She stood up and went to the opened box on the shelf, putting the stack of papers back in. "Lord Aiden won't turn you in, if that's what you're worried about. I doubt he'll even rat off to his friends. As for your test results, I'll have to think on this."

She locked the box, but instead of coming back to the desk she rested her head on the edge of the shelf above.

"I'm sorry," I said, breaking the silence. "I know I shouldn't have been there—"

"Yes," she snapped, turning back to me. "You *shouldn't* have been there! And thank The Great One I happened to be opening my door just then or you would be out on the streets right now after getting a good beating, if not worse!"

I shrank under her glare, a deep hole of shame opening up inside me.

She took a deep breath, then came back to her chair.

"What could you possibly have been thinking, Kailin?"

I hadn't been. Someone else had been doing the thinking for me.

"I know you are skilled enough to actually be a student, but I didn't think your ambition would have caused you to forget something as inconsequential as self-preservation."

"I hadn't forgotten."

Hadn't I? Hadn't I forgotten everything when she looked at me so helplessly?

"Your actions speak otherwise."

Avonly had risked nothing, and she would have gotten all the reward. And I risked everything, but would have gained nothing.

I wasn't a student here.

And never would be.

"I thought I had to."

"And why would you think that?"

I dipped my head down and stared at my clenched hands.

"Because I didn't think I could live with myself not knowing what I'd missed."

The silence that came after was worse than when she yelled at me.

"Kailin, please look at me." I raised my head. Her mouth was a hard line, but her eyes were bright with...pity?

The shame was gone in an instant. Now I wanted to yell, to punch something, break something—*anything*.

"I need you to understand," the edge in her voice quelled me. "I made a promise to your aunt to look after you, but I cannot be there to save you every time you get into trouble, so the only way to protect yourself is to *not get into trouble*. Do you understand?"

I nodded my head.

When she didn't respond I cleared my throat.

"Yes, Lady Cathrina. I will stay out of trouble; on The Great One's branches I swear it."

Her mouth formed a soft smile and some of the...

Oh, it hadn't been pity.

Some of the *fear* left her eyes.

"Good," she said. "I'll see you this evening."

"Yes, my lady." I stood and hurried out of the room, never feeling more grateful for my servant invisibility as I made my way to the servant stairs.

CHAPTER

FIFTEEN

*S*tay *out of trouble.*

I could do that. I had kept out of trouble for the most part since coming here, and it didn't seem very hard.

I met Avonly again that night and wished I had stayed away.

"What do you mean, you got caught!" Avonly yelled. "How could you be so sloppy! Do you have any idea what might have happened to me if you had gone to Healer Steverno?"

I apologized for my "sloppiness," then said I had chores and left.

After that the Academy was quiet with the post-exams break. Most students had gone home to celebrate the Winter Solstice with their families, but a few stayed behind. Avonly was one of them, but I didn't go visit her.

The morning of the Solstice I woke to the sound of bells tolling through the walls. I turned over in the darkness and pulled my knees to my chest, holding myself together as the longing washed over me. If I had been home I would have wakened to Aunt Beredith singing the familiar hymns to ward off the night and welcome the return of day. Then we would work side by side like every other day, but that night we would have a simple yet special dinner.

I knew that even though I was in a city brimming with people, I would be alone this year.

It was a particularly cold morning when I walked into the workroom looking for Markly to ask about my chores for the day. Holiday or not, I had learned long ago that work never stopped. Not if you wanted to eat, that is.

The room was empty except for Gabell, who wasn't in her usual spot on the bench under the window but huddled in a chair pulled near the stove.

I was just turning to leave when Gabell threw down the garment she was working on.

"These needles are useless!" She yelled. Then she looked up and saw me.

Great One, help me! After this long I should have known better than to be caught alone with her!

"Oh Kailin, dear," she said standing up, her face a mix of a smile and a sneer. "You're just the person I was hoping to see."

"I really don't have time—"

"I need you to go get me some more needles—these ones are dull beyond belief. And you'll have to go out to the market, as those shrubs in supply say that we already used up our quota for the month."

"Gabell!" I said, shocked beyond belief. "It's the *Solstice*! You're not supposed to go shopping today!"

The smile was gone.

"I. *Don't.* CARE!" She suddenly moved around me and slammed open the small cupboard right above my shoulder. She shoved a small bag into my hands, knocking me backwards. When I looked down I realized it was a coin purse.

The coin purse.

"Go to the market and buy more needles, or you'll be worshiping The Great One face to face!"

"But I can't! It's a sin!"

Then she slapped me.

My first instinct was to slap her back, to tackle her to the ground and smash the coin purse into her face until she had coin-shaped bruises, but her next words froze the boiling rage inside me.

"Markly has been too kind to you. You've forgotten that you're just a dirty, worthless Peasant. I could take that poker over by the stove and beat you bloody and no one would care. Now get moving and don't you dare come back without those needles!"

I turned and ran.

It wasn't until I reached the fifth floor that I collapsed against the stairwell wall, my hands shaking. With my back pressed against the solid stone, I looked down at the coin purse in my hand.

Go to the *market?* As in, *outside* the Academy? I had been here for almost half a year and had never been out into the city since the first day I arrived. I had seen the spread of the buildings from the windows and had grown to feel safe behind the Academy's walls, but along with that had been the acceptance that I would never leave them again.

Carefully I pulled a coin out of the bag and held it in my hand. I had never held money before; even back home our meager amount was handled solely by Aunt Beredith. I was strangely disappointed at how light the coin was. I had thought something so vital to existence would have had more heft to it.

But I couldn't use the money—not today. Today was the Winter Solstice, a holy day. Even if Gabell wanted to defile it, I couldn't do so. She could threaten all she wanted, but I couldn't go out into the city...

And I was hit with a longing that shook me to my bones.

I could leave the Academy. I had an excuse for the first time since I was locked away here. Even if I didn't actually buy any needles, a look outside wouldn't do any harm. I would even say an extra prayer of gratitude tonight.

I walked down the stairs and found the servant courtyard I had stood bewildered in all those months before. I saw Robert's back as he brushed a horse, and a few other servants moving to unload a supply wagon that had just arrived, but no one gave me a second glance as I walked to the gate. The Academy guard by the door gave me a questioning look, but when I raised the coin purse he nodded and let me out.

And I was assaulted by noise and cold. I clutched the coin purse to my chest and flattened myself against the Academy wall.

People were everywhere. The street choked with wagons and wheelbarrows, carriages, and people in lovely gowns, vests, and coats in every color of a meadow walking past without so much as a look in my direction. No, not walking, almost running along the street, everyone yelling and calling to each other.

Okay, I thought, you've seen the city. You can go back now.

But I couldn't. Clutching the purse to my chest, I stepped out into the street.

When nothing worse happened than a few people bumping into me, my confidence and stride grew. I looked up at the tall new buildings, gawked at a stone bridge that crossed from one building to another right over the street, smiled at the potted trees that were still beautiful even missing their leaves, wondered where everyone was going and where all the streets led, and wondered how far it was to the river, the bay, the ocean...

I let myself be pulled into the wake of the group of women in front of me down an avenue to my right. This street was different from the thoroughfare I had been on before. Along the sides weren't the entrances to great edifices, though these buildings were just as tall as any others. This street was lined with shops.

I knew I should feel disappointed by so many people out shopping on the second most holy day of the year, but I couldn't take my eyes off what I was seeing. One store sold painted pots from those small enough to be a thimble to those large enough for a full Family Tree, another sold bolts of sturdy cloth dyed in bright colors. One shop even sold cages of birds, singing above the noise.

It was all so magical, all so wonderful I thought I could go on like this forever.

And then I stopped.

More people bumped and cursed me, but I simply stood in front of the glass-covered storefront at the reflection of myself perfectly overlaying a lovely green gown on display. It had embroidered yellow and pink roses along the bodice with a matching sash, the sleeves reaching mid-arm. Another piece of green-sheen fabric draped around the shoulders to the front and then dropped to the side in an imitation of a vest, a style some of the inner-ring students favored. I thought it had always been a silly idea to mimic a boy's style, but seeing it here, as if on me...

"Hey you!" A woman stood in the door of the shop, "this is a respectable place, not something for a heap pile!"

I bowed my head and hurried on.

After a while the nicer shops traded off into smaller ones selling more practical items, and then even those smaller shops turned into pockets along the now narrow street, their wares hung around the edges of the opening and behind the peddlers, who were themselves behind half-doors, as if in no great hurry to associate themselves with their customers in the same way they were with their customers' money.

I held my purse even closer to my chest as the crowd pushed around me, eyes opened wide at the noise of everyone around me haggling at the top of their lungs. It was a holy day, but what was around me wasn't holy at all.

This wasn't the part of the city I had wanted to see when I left, and the spirit of my adventure drained out of me. I turned to make my way back when I saw it.

A shop selling sewing supplies.

The purse suddenly felt very heavy in my hands as I stared at it, the wave of people moving around me as if I were a stone in a river.

The shop was only a door-width wide, with the customary half-door in front, with a tall, thin man with a long, drooping mustache and short vest standing in front of it. He had a slab of wood balanced on top of the door holding what looked like junk to me, but he must have been popular from the crowd of customers surrounding him. Above him in a net over the doorway were an array of spools of thread and boxes of needles. What was beyond him was hidden behind a black curtain.

I'm already here.

I squeezed the bag tighter. I could feel the outline of coins within. And we do need needles. And it would help Markly. Helping others is something The Great One wants us to do. This would be like serving her, which is all right to do on the Solstice. What could be more a symbol of light than helping someone in need?

My stomach felt sick, but I stepped forward anyway.

I waited patiently for the brightly clothed Tradesman to finish with the woman he was assisting. When he was done I moved forward to make my request, but the Tradesman turned right past me to another customer. Frustrated, I waited again. When this happened again, I pushed my way to the front, holding up my coin purse.

"Excuse me!" I yelled.

"Yes, what is it?" the tall man replied, only partially paying attention to me. Then he saw the coin purse, and his eyes traveled down my brown dress. He leaned forward and gave me a greasy smile. "And how may I help a lovely lady like you?"

"Can I buy that pack of needles?" I blushed.

"Needles!?" his face brightening, "I have plenty of needles! But you don't want these ones, low quality that will snap in your fingers before you can finish a stitch! I keep them around to give to customers that I want to send on their way. But you!" He leaned forward, his eyes holding mine. "I would love for you to be a return customer." He quickly turned and pushed everything on the board into a hidden box, lifted and stored the board, and opened his half-door. With a smile he turned back to me as he pulled aside the curtain enough for me to walk through. "Follow me and I'll show you the high-quality needles I save for high-quality customers!"

I hesitated, but then remembered the showrooms I had passed. Maybe this shop's showroom was in the back? Ignoring the solid lump in my chest, I moved past him to the room beyond.

It was the same width as the door, went back about two yards, and was stuffed from wall to wall with more boxes of the same junk he had been hawking outside. That, along with a cot smashed in one corner, made it almost impossible to move at all, which would have bothered me under any other circumstances. Right now it all fell dull as a horrible realization hit me.

There were no shelves displaying needles.

The door slammed and I tried to turn, but the Tradesman's hands were already on me. I tried to scream, but his large hand wrapped around my face, his other hand ripping the coin purse out of my hands.

Then I was shoved through a back door I hadn't seen, landing in a pile of garbage. I turned around in time to see the door slam behind me.

I lay there for a minute, shaking in my fright as a terrifying parade of what could have happened to me raced through my mind. Then I realized what *had* happened to me.

I had lost Markly's money.

I sat up as something familiar began to boil inside me. I had lived my whole life being tortured, and every time I would shrink away. But I wasn't in Valehaven anymore, and it wasn't Dural or the other children. It was a stranger, and what he did to me had nothing to do with my mother.

I pounded on the door, but there was no answer.

My face felt hot as I ran down the alley. At the end was the break I was hoping for, and I was back on the street with the shops. I didn't stop until I was in front of the Tradesman who had robbed me and pushed my way to the front of the customers gathered around him.

"I demand that you return my money to me!"

He stared at me, as if he couldn't believe I would have come after him. I glared back, and he turned, purposely ignoring me, as did a man next to me who was handing him some coins. I shoved him out from in front of the Tradesman, making him drop his money.

"GIVE ME BACK MY MONEY!"

The Tradesman's eyes narrowed as the man he was striking a deal with walked away.

"Look you splinter," he said, grabbing my hair and pulling me toward him. I yelled as his dirty fingers pulled at my scalp. "This is how it's going to work. You have three seconds to run before I start yelling that you're a thief, which we both know will sound more believable to everyone than that a *Peasant* honestly came to have a full purse!"

"I need it back! It isn't my money—"

"Just as I thought! GUARDS! THIEF! THIS GIRL'S A THIEF!"

I stood dumbfounded for only a second as armed men who I would swear hadn't been there a moment ago started moving my way. Without thinking I lashed out with my free hand and left three, straight red lines across the Tradesman's worthless face. When he screamed and let go of my hair, I sprinted off without looking back.

Weaving in and out, I slid through the crowd that had only moments before seemed impossible for me to navigate. I had no idea where I was going, but I still found myself turning down this alley, and then that street, almost like I was—

I stopped dead.

It was the *pull*. I hadn't felt it since leaving home and had hoped never to again.

If it was back, after all this time, what did that mean?

Someone bumped into me so hard I almost fell, and that got me moving again. I had bigger problems right now than whether I was going crazy.

I didn't fight it as it led me deeper into the city.

One after another, I ran down alleys and streets until, exhausted, I stopped against a wall to catch my breath. I couldn't go any farther because I was now without guidance. The *pull* was gone. I looked around and saw to my relief that there were no men in uniforms in sight. It was a short-lived feeling, though, as a new horror sprouted in my chest.

I had no idea where I was.

The sun was behind the buildings now and long, dark shadows were growing along the stone fronts, giving everything a purple cast. Now that I had stopped running, the air had turned chill again and I could feel the bite of it, indicating more clearly than the shadows that nightfall wasn't far away. I wrapped my arms around myself as I started walking, and not just because my teeth were beginning to chatter. The street wasn't nearly as busy as the one by the Academy, but it took only a moment to see why. The buildings were covered in grime, some with plaster cracked with staircases zigzagging up the sides of buildings to doors. They were skinnier too, as though they had originally been no bigger than my aunt's cottage but then had been added to over the years. Instead of rebuilding, new buildings had been squeezed between the ones that were already there, and stories had been added to the existing ones, giving an uncomfortable fear that they would all tumble down at any moment.

The people weren't much better. They were in Peasant-brown like me, but their clothes were just as patchy and frayed as the buildings they were leaning against. The stalls were fewer and seemed to be run by men and women with a permanent scowl.

I walked faster.

Up ahead a door crashed open and a large group of men staggered out and began walking in my direction. They were dirty and large, with torn sleeves showing muscular arms, laughing loudly and swaying. Without even considering an alternative I turned down the next alley.

Only it wasn't empty. There was a woman dressed in a

brightly colored, very revealing gown in a doorway arguing with a short balding man.

"Come on, let me in, you know you love me!" the man slurred.

"Ha!" the woman barked. "Bring coin with you next time."

And she slammed the door in his face.

He yelled at the door using words I didn't even know the meaning of, then started walking down the alley.

Toward me.

I turned to run, but the group of men passed the alley entrance right then. I fell back a step and turned, but now the balding man was looking at me. He gave me a gaping grin as he looked me up and down. His two front teeth were missing.

"Hello little sapling! Looking for someone to start an orchard with?"

"N–no!" I staggered backwards, but he kept moving forward, the men behind me louder than before as I lay trapped between two horrible fates.

"Come on now," he said motioning with his hands. "Don't be like that!"

Please! I prayed. *Help!*

The *pull* yanked my heart so hard I gasped.

Then as if I were looking through a window, Lord Aiden's face appeared behind my eyes. He was standing in a brightly lit room surrounded by beautifully dressed people. He suddenly turned toward the door leading outside into the city, his eyes wide as he took two steps toward it, but stopped when a young woman in an expensive gown came up behind him, placing a hand on his arm. He looked down at her and smiled. He gave one last look toward the city before turning back to the crowd.

My eyes cleared and the man was there, grabbing my arm.

"There's a good sapling," he said pulling me close, his breath stinking of old fish.

I screamed, and a stick came down on the man's head.

He fell to the ground, and behind him was a pile of clothes hiding the oldest woman I had ever seen, a walking stick held high above her head.

"Inside, now!" she hissed, moving back toward an open doorway a few yards behind the man's unconscious body.

I hesitated. She was a stranger.

Then I saw it; a blue light danced from one side of her head, orbiting to the other, then disappearing within her messy bun.

I followed her through the door, but lights or not, I still flinched when she threw the bolt.

CHAPTER
SIXTEEN

Inside there was only a single, dimly lit room, but it was cozy in a warm, fire-lit way. It smelled of herbs and wood smoke, with only the faintest hint of the stench of the alley outside the door. At first I could see nothing but the piercing light coming from the few lanterns and a small fireplace in the center of one wall, but my eyes adjusted quickly.

I held in a gasp as a homesickness I hadn't experienced in months attempted to steal away my ability to breathe.

Everything around me might have been from my aunt's cottage, from the worn wooden table with a stack of vegetables on it to the clean, organized pots around the fireplace. She even had herbs hanging from hooks on the ceiling. But the thing that made my chest knot with a loneliness I thought had been rooted out of me was the simple, carved Blessing Tree on the wall by her door.

"You might as well sit down until that bark striper moves on." The old woman hobbled past me now using her walking stick for what it was meant for. Her voice was cracked with age, but it didn't seem unfriendly.

Maybe I was actually safe. For the moment.

My rescuer was about half my height, but she might have been taller in her youth, as she was bent over with age. Her wispy white hair was in a loose bun with trails flying all about a deeply lined face centered with clear brown eyes. Her clothes were little better than rags, but still gave the feeling of being well maintained.

"Thank you for rescuing me," I said, sitting on the stool next to the table. She grunted, then moved over to the fireplace, swinging a small pot on a hook over the meager flames, and began to stir.

"I really do appreciate you taking me in. I can go now if you want—"

"Dinner is almost done, so you might as well stay and have some."

"That's very kind of you," I said, "but I don't want to bother you and I have to get back before they close the gate."

She turned to me and smiled a little. "A servant girl then? That would explain how clean you are—all that scrubbing would keep any dirt from sticking under your nails. Good for you for finding a family that would take a Peasant."

I looked down at my calloused hands, noticing for the first time how clean they really were. It made me depressed. There had always been dirt under my nails from working in the garden.

"If you don't mind my asking," she said, pulling down a bundle of herbs from a hook on the ceiling. "What is a girl like you doing so far from any decent place, and on the Solstice no less?"

I winced at all the wrong choices that had led me here, starting with going out shopping on a high holy day.

"I got lost."

"Uh huh," the woman said, her eyes getting even smaller as

she narrowed in on me. I looked down at my hands, suddenly hit with the shame of my actions.

"I made a mistake," I said, my eyes stinging.

"Oh don't be too hard on yourself." She striped some leaves and put them in the pot. "If The Great One punished us every time we sinned, He would be so busy He wouldn't have time to do anything else! And since the trees keep growing and the sun keeps rising, He must be busy doing other things most of the time."

Her voice was warm, and I felt a tension in my shoulders lessen. I wasn't sure if I believed her, but it made me smile anyway.

"I was serious about getting back," I said, sitting back on the stool. "I don't want to get in trouble."

The woman was leaning over the pot and trying a sip. She smacked her lips and nodded.

"Cut those carrots first, then we'll have something to eat and I'll take you home."

I nodded, and picked up the knife on the table, pulling a carrot toward me. After I had worked my way through two of them I realized the woman had stopped moving. I looked up to find her staring at me.

"You're a Healer."

The knife slipped and almost took off my finger.

"The way you hold that knife," she said, nodding toward my hand. "You were taught by someone who uses plants for medicine, not food, at least not for hours at a time. Let me see your hands."

Without waiting for a response she grabbed my hands, pulling them so close to her face I could feel the tip of her nose on my palm. After what seemed like an eternity, she brought them down, her eyes large.

"You've been touched by The Great One."

I yanked my hands back like she had burned them. "Excuse me?"

"You have a special destiny," she replied, her eyes still seeing beyond me.

"Um, no," I said, sliding off the stool and taking a step back, but the room was small and there was nowhere to go. "You're wrong, I'm just a Peasant orphan."

Her eyes cleared and narrowed on me, her mouth in a hard line.

"A Peasant orphan who grew up in the shadow of The Great One's Holy Forest, if what I saw in your hands is right."

My mouth hung slack.

"How could you have known that?"

"They used to teach us Healers many things, before that thorn-choked Academy was built and the old ways were lost."

"You're a *Healer?*" I looked around the room again, then back at her fraying clothes. Her *brown* frayed clothes. "But you're, I mean, you don't—"

"Yes," she said, the corners of her mouth rising a little. "I'm a Healer, and I'm a Peasant. I was one of the last to be taught the old ways after Healing became a ring." I knew I was gaping, but I couldn't help it, couldn't wrap my mind around what she was saying. "Oh, stop looking at me like a dead fish! It isn't very attractive for a young lady to stare so!"

I closed my mouth.

"Much better," she said sitting down on a small chair next to the fireplace. "Now finish those carrots and I'll tell you what you obviously want to know."

Mechanically, I sat back on the stool, picked up the knife, and began chopping again.

"I thought all Healers were absorbed into the new ring when the king established it," I said to the carrots.

"Ha." The woman laughed without humor. "Only those who chose to give in to politics got that privilege."

I looked at her, then looked away again at her glare.

"I see you're more ignorant than I thought if you didn't even know that. I'm going to have to start a little earlier." She took a breath. "Surely you know how being a Healer used to be a calling from The Great One."

"I've heard something like that," I said, not sure about the whole *calling* part. "But then the king made it a ring to give the Peasants and Tradesmen a chance for a better life."

"A better life?" she snorted. "Talk to some of those scholarship students at that Academy and see how much better their life is."

I thought of Avonly in her comfortable room and new clothes, as much food as she wanted.

"But that doesn't matter," the woman said standing, taking the bite-sized carrots in her hands and dumping them into the pot. "What you need to know is the history, if I'm reading your hands correctly, where the Healers came from, because the only way to understand who you are is to understand your past. Tell me, what do you know of The Great One?"

"The Great One?"

"Yes. You know, big tree, lots of leaves."

Now it was my turn to glare.

"I was taught to pray, to always have a Blessing Tree in my home, and to follow the laws."

"So you were told to mutter before falling asleep, given tips on decorating and not to steal or plant any orchards before you're married."

My face turned red up to my hair.

"I didn't ask what you knew about His teachings, I asked what did you know about *Him*."

"I don't understand."

She squinted her eyes at me. "Are you sure?"

And as if she had summoned it, I remembered what I saw at the Holy Altar the morning of the exam.

"I'm sure."

"Right. If that is the case, then I think we should start at the *very* beginning."

"Five hundred years ago, when our people were young," she began. I wanted to roll my eyes; of course I knew *this* story, but while Father Gant's voice had the cadence of a storyteller, her voice was bland, as if she were in the Academy giving a lecture. "We sailed to these shores, seeking a new home. Where we came from, that is a mystery lost to time, so don't bother asking because I don't know, but the important thing to know is that when we arrived the land was cold and hard and we could not make it produce the food we needed to live. Afraid and on the brink of starvation, we fell on our knees and lifted our voices up to Heaven, to our forgotten maker, and that is when The Great One came to our aid."

I knew this part of the story, but had never heard our ancestors described like repentant apostates. It made me feel uncomfortable.

"You see," she continued, her eyes now turned on me as if I would be tested after she was done, "he was always our God, but our people had turned away from Him, so we were scattered on the sea. He waited until we were ready to accept Him again, and then He answered our prayers."

I wanted to tell her she had the story wrong, but something in her eye said she knew more than the Priests in the shrines.

"He led us and taught us how to live, advising our first leaders in the ways of balance. There were no rings then—all were equal and respected as part of the whole."

"But the rings give us stability—strong like a tree with life pooling to the outer edges." I whispered, remembering my lessons. "Our unity comes from being a part of something greater, being a part of the rings."

"Unity, my knot-covered foot!" She snorted. "Look around you, girl! Does this look like unity to you?"

I looked down at my hands. No, there was no unity. Even among the rings no one wanted anything to do with each other.

"I'm sorry," she sighed. "I shouldn't be so harsh on you. You're just a child and have been taught the way you were taught. But you need to know, all this division, all these *rings*, this wasn't how The Great One taught us. Those Senators and Priests have distorted and twisted His message, removing parts that don't fit with their view of themselves and adding new doctrine that would elevate their positions. They seek to be exalted in this life—and because of that the whole has suffered."

I looked back up as she shifted on her chair. I swore I could hear her bones creak.

"Oh, this chair was never comfortable to begin with. No, don't get up, I'm settled now. But I was going to tell you about the Healers. You see, our people were prospering and The Great One was teaching the principles that could lead to peace and life, when an illness broke out. It seemed that overnight half the population had been struck down to their beds, and there was a great cry let out for The Great One to heal them. But He didn't."

I thought of the village I had seen on my way to the Academy. Those people had cried out as well, but The Great One hadn't come then either.

"Instead," the old woman continued, "He called twelve of His closest companions, those He trusted more than all the rest, six men and six women. These He touched and dedicated them to the service of His people. They were to prepare and cultivate the people's lives, to make their relationships with one another wholesome and strong so they would find joy in this life and everlasting power in the life to come. To facilitate this, so none were taken until they were ready and to teach the sanctity of life and service, The Great One gifted the first Healers with the ability to heal."

Then her eyes took on a determination that frightened me.

"They were the ones to lead others to life—to bind them to the light. All they touched lived."

Light. Like the blue lights.

I gasped, almost falling off my chair as the *pull* erupted in my chest, resonating in my soul as if my entire body were a bell that had been waiting all my life to be rung. I closed my eyes, trying to make it go away, but as always, it stayed, growing.

"And you, my dear girl, have that gift as well."

I looked back at her, angry tears starting to well in my eyes.

"I have no gift," I spat back to her. "If I did I would be at the Academy learning, instead of just scrubbing floors!"

"I'm not talking about just setting bones and mixing herbs!" She got up from her chair and grabbed my hands again, this time shoving them toward my own face. "These are the hands of one who can bring the light back to a soul! This is the true healing! The type that really matters! The type that can heal our people from a worse illness than death!"

She's crazy, I thought. *She's just a crazy old woman whose mind is gone.*

Then I saw it. A blue light sparked up from the fire behind her. Then another, and another, dancing and moving around each other, leaving trails of glowing threads. In a moment there were over a hundred, their dance growing faster and more frantic, spiraling and weaving until they were no longer individuals but one of a whole.

I was not asleep. This was not some dream to plague me.

With horror I realized this was real.

My hand reached out on its own accord, and they came to me, wrapping around my arm like a glove.

Then one burrowed into my palm.

I gasped, not at the pain, but at the sensation.

Someone was holding my hand, and I was filled with such longing, such need, I couldn't breathe.

"You see them, don't you."

I nodded, not able to look away.

"What are they?" I asked.

"That I don't know, having never seen them myself. I have a little of the sight; all who were called by The Great One in the old ways do, but no Healer has seen the lights in hundreds of years. It's all just lore passed down now, but I could see it in your hands, and now I see them reflected in your eyes."

The lights spun faster, pulling tighter around my hand, and the feeling grew stronger, deeper.

"No!" I yelled, and pulled my hand to my chest, scraping furiously at the lights as if I could scratch them off.

I hadn't needed to. As soon as I spoke they scattered, then faded, and might have never been. And just as quickly that unholy connection was ripped from me, leaving me alone with emptiness.

But even that faded to the back of my mind as pain burst through my skull. I collapsed against the table, my hand on my head.

"Here." The old woman was at my elbow, handing me a cup. I drank and almost gagged, but the headache subsided. But nothing could take away the hollowness that followed. A hollowness that wasn't mine and that I wanted nothing to do with.

"You need to be careful," she said. "This power is not to be used lightly."

"But I don't even want it!" I shouted, shooting to my feet. "I just want to go to the Academy! To be a *real* Healer, not some messed-up folktale! Please!" I shoved my hands back into hers. "Take it away!"

"Oh dearie," she said gently. "I wouldn't, even if I could. You're needed—"

"What I *need* is to be getting back to the Academy!"

I felt bad for yelling, she had been so kind to me, but I wouldn't hear any more.

I couldn't.

I wasn't part of some mythical plan, I was just *Kailin*! Just boring, plain, useless Kailin.

The woman stared at me for too long, then nodded her head.

"If that's what you wish." She turned to the door, pulling down two shawls from a peg and handing me one. "Wrap yourself up good—it's cold out there."

I did as she asked, then followed her out into the night. She led me through the maze of streets to the gates of the Academy, the lanterns still burning bright, but the doors closed. I turned to thank her, but she was already gone.

I felt a pang of regret.

I didn't even know her name.

CHAPTER
SEVENTEEN

"Hello!" I yelled for the fifth time, "is anyone there?!" I banged again on the door to the servant gate, but there was still no answer. Someone was supposed to be on watch, but they were probably in the kitchens celebrating the Solstice. My stomach grumbled at the thought of the old Healer's stew I hadn't gotten to eat.

I pulled the shawl she had given me tighter around my shoulders.

It was very dark, and I huddled beneath the lantern next to the gate, feeling very alone and exposed. My breath was visible and my ears hurt from the chill. Two city guards materialized out of the dim blackness, making my heart race as one of them gave me a warning look before marching on.

I couldn't stay out here. But what could I do? I didn't think I could find the old Healer's home again even if I were suicidal enough to venture out into the city again.

Then a carriage rolled by, turning around the corner. I heard voices calling out, and a large gate being pulled open, then closing again.

And I had my answer.

I walked around the corner, just in time to see the main gate of the Academy shut.

I took a breath and walked up to the ornately carved wood.

"Hello?" I yelled.

"Keep moving, Peasant!" A sharp voice replied from the other side of the gate.

"I'm Lady Cathrina's servant and I've been locked out! Can you send someone to the servants' entrance to let me in?"

"Sure you are! Now scatter before I call for the city guards!"

I hit the gates in frustration and turned around, leaning against them. I was just about to accept the fact I was sleeping outside in the frigid air when I heard the jingle of harnesses. I ran to the shadows as a stately carriage appeared and a shout was given. My heart raced as the gates began to move.

I had been lectured repeatedly concerning the areas servants were allowed to be seen. I knew that entering the front gate was not an option.

On the other hand, I thought, remembering the stern eye of the patrolling city guard, *standing out on the street isn't an option either.*

Tightening the shawl even closer, I hurried in behind the carriage and quickly pulled myself up onto the shelf on the back that was used for luggage. I hugged myself as small as I could, hiding in the shadows of the larger carriage body, trying to keep my terrified breathing from being too loud. I remembered that first day and knew there was another gate to the side of this courtyard where the carriage and horses would be taken to the stables, so all I had to do was stay in the shadows as the passengers were dropped off and then slip out of my hiding spot once the carriage was back in the servants' area.

I held my breath as the Academy guards moved to close the gate behind us, but by some miracle they didn't see me. I was beginning to feel this might actually work when the carriage rounded the drive and stopped before the imposing front entrance, suddenly bathing me in light. I panicked as my face was illuminated and quickly leapt down from my perch to crouch under the back wheel where the shadows were deepest. I had no idea how I was going to get back up onto the shelf without a guard or, even worse, one of the passengers, seeing me, but at that moment I couldn't think of anything beyond surviving the next few seconds.

I heard a murmur of voices and then the servant who was driving the carriage stepped down. He was tall and kept his gaze straight as he pulled open the carriage door, though I was sure anyone with ears could hear the pounding of my heart.

Crouching deeper into the shadows behind the wheel, I watched as a tall man stepped down, followed by a younger man in a vest that reached past his coat to his knees. When the taller man turned into the lantern light, I suppressed a gasp. Though I hadn't seen him since my journey to the Academy, I would know that face anywhere. The servant shut the door, but the two men didn't turn toward the stairs. Instead Healer Arios stepped forward toward the carriage.

"Thank you, Lord Calvin, for a most entertaining evening," Healer Arios said, his voice light and pleasing. "The Winter Solstice was truly brightened by your hospitality. And thank you for the honor of accompanying me back to the Academy."

"It is nothing," a deep, vibrating voice said from within the carriage. "Parties bore me. A trait I apparently share with my son."

The young man turned toward the carriage, bringing his face into the light.

A small yelp escaped my lips.

Lord Aiden must have heard it because his eyes shifted

down to my hiding spot. They widened, but before he could say anything his father's voice commanded his attention.

"Remember what we spoke of," his father said, still from within the carriage. "You know well enough how important it is right now for you to make a good impression. Our family cannot afford a scandal with your coming of age so close."

"Yes, Father," Lord Aiden replied. The torchlight was casting soft shadows on his face, pulling distinction to his nose and forehead while keeping his eyes dark except for two points of light where they reflected perfectly. He looked like he could have been from another world, and, in his alien attraction, I forgot my place in the shadows.

His eyes met mine again, and my heart stopped. I knew he had no qualms in reporting me, but he only frowned slightly and turned back to the carriage.

"I will be sure to avoid any unwanted associations and practices that would reflect poorly on you and our family."

"I expect nothing less," the unseen man replied. "And Healer Arios—" The tall healer took a small step forward. "It was a most informative evening. I hope we have a chance to talk again soon."

"It would be my pleasure," Healer Arios replied with a slight bow. I had thought he was above playing the social games Avonly seemed to think so important, but I guess I was wrong.

With a shout the driver began to move the carriage.

It was only then I realized the catastrophic flaw in my plan.

The carriage was leaving! It was not going back to the stables!

I faltered in my step and fell to my knees, exposing myself to the lantern light illuminating the steps. Healer Arios had already turned to ascend the five front steps leading up to the door, but Lord Aiden was now at my side, yanking me to my feet.

"Hurry," he hissed, "get inside before the carriage turns around!"

For once I had no problem obeying an order. I ran up the stairs and flew past a now-startled Healer Arios. Once inside, I collapsed forward, my head down as I tried to catch my breath. Then my arm was grabbed again, jerking me around.

"What are you doing here?!" he demanded. "Do you have kindling for brains?! Servants are *not* to use this entrance!"

"Lord Aiden," Healer Arios said softly, putting a hand on my captor's shoulder. "Lower your voice. As a Healer it is more important to gather information through a soft inquiry rather than by ripping open the wound with an ax."

"But she's not a patient!" Lord Aiden snapped. "She's a defiant servant with a death wish!"

Healer Arios's hand tightened and let go. Lord Aiden's mouth hardened into a line.

"Fine," he said, practically throwing me from him. "Why were you hiding behind my father's carriage?"

"Because," I replied flatly, returning Lord Aiden's glare. "I needed to get into the Academy."

He snorted and turned back to Healer Arios, his look saying *See? This is what you get from talking to Peasants like people!* Healer Arios just crossed his arms.

Lord Aiden took a breath; then, as if it was the hardest thing in the world, he turned back to me.

"And *why* did you not use the servants' entrance?"

"Because it was locked and no one was answering my calls."

"So why didn't you just stay on the streets?"

"Now who's kindle-brained?"

"What were you doing outside the Academy in the first

place," Healer Arios asked. "I thought it was Academy policy to give servants the day off from outside errands for the Solstice."

That would have been nice to know.

"One of the other servants sent me to buy needles, even though I knew it was wrong to shop today, but a Tradesman robbed me and chased me into the city and I became lost and..." they were both looking at me, Lord Aiden's hard eyes now edged with interest. I remembered the thought of him when I was attacked by the bald man, how I had felt I could trust him. I narrowed my eyes, thinking instead of the rough way he had grabbed my arm a moment ago. "I have just now found my way back."

"There, Lord Aiden," Healer Arios said, "a perfectly reasonable explanation. Believe it or not, not all servants are up to something nefarious. Now," Healer Arios said, giving me a smile. "Can you describe where this unethical Tradesman was located?"

Confused at his request, I described the street of shops and how far I had traveled with a description of what the shop and the ones around it had looked like, finishing with what the Tradesman looked like, complete with the three scratches I had given him in my escape.

"You attacked a Tradesman?" Lord Aiden asked. He didn't seem so angry now, but I would hardly say his question was friendly.

"What would you have done if someone had been holding you by your hair?"

"That's enough." Healer Arios turned toward the door. "Lord Aiden, would you be so kind as to keep Kailin company until I return. I won't be long."

Lord Aiden choked, but before he could protest, Healer Arios was gone. His hands balled into fists, and I was reminded of how angry he was after I answered all those exam questions.

When he didn't turn around I wrapped my arms around myself, turning away from him as well.

That was when I suddenly realized where I was.

My breath caught, as the splendor of the Healer Academy's fabled front hall absorbed my heart and soul. I had never been here before, my place in the hierarchy of servants too low to be seen in such a place.

In front of me against the east wall was the largest image of a Blessing Tree I had ever seen. Life sized and carved into the stone, an immense tree was inlaid with gold, silver, and precious stones, the massive branches reaching out over the arches framing the front doors and opposite entrance stairs, covering the surrounding upper walls and ceiling. Saplings and flowers of every species grew up the walls from the floor made from the same exquisite materials. Standing in the middle of the room, I could almost feel that The Great One was striving to embrace me.

All these details in gold and stone work were impressive, but what held my eye were the images carved into the lower part by the trunk. Instead of just a nature scene with flowers and animals like those I was used to seeing in other large Blessing Tree images, here there were twelve life-sized men and women dressed in robes. Each had a branch delicately touching their forehead, heart and upraised hand.

I didn't need to read the inscription at the base of the image to know these were the first Healers the old woman had told me about, at the moment The Great One gave His blessing to heal as well as the charge to save His people. From their peaceful, virtuous faces my eyes seemed to drift to the motto of the Academy inscribed in the turn of the branches above the stairs.

Seekers of Life, Binders of Truth.

"You probably have never seen so much gold in your life, have you?"

I turned, surprised. Lord Aiden was looking at me, still annoyed but with a quizzical tilt of his head.

"No, I haven't," I replied. "But it isn't the gold that interests me." I turned to look at the room again and found myself drawn to a particularly beautiful replica of a butter-lace flower, so detailed it might have really been growing out of the precious metals encasing it.

"It's the attention to detail," I continued. "The original craftsmen must have really cared to bring such life and vitality to their work."

"I had never noticed before," Lord Aiden said, having moved across the room to look at the same flower. "It really does look like a butter-lace."

"Even with the faint stripe of red along the stem."

"And the fading from bright yellow to burnt orange in the petals."

He was next to me now, analyzing the same plant, so close that if I moved my shoulder it would have brushed against him.

He turned his head, and he actually had a smile on his face. His face that was suddenly so close to mine.

His eyes widened and he jumped back several feet. "But how would you even know what one looked like? They won't grow anywhere except in the North."

"I've read about them in Albertic's Herb Almanac." I turned back to the flower, my cheeks becoming warm for no reason I could think of.

"But that's a Healer's text."

I continued to stare at the flower, the edges of my vision turning hazy.

"Yes," I said, "it is."

The silence in the room became heavy with his unspoken questions and I was frightened to find I wanted to give the answers to him. Then I felt him move, slowly, carefully until he was behind me, close enough the edge of his vest brushed against my arm.

"And what would you need a Healer's text for?"

I let out a breath I had been holding; then just as cautiously I turned.

His black coat was open, showing the navy-blue shirt and knee-length vest underneath. His hands were at his sides, his fingers twitching, but they weren't in the hard balls they'd been in earlier. My eyes traveled up to his neck, the skin showing from his open collar that ran partway up his neck, the top two buttons undone.

Then I found his face. He was still the most handsome man I had ever seen, and this close I could see his hair wasn't black, but more of a deep, dark brown. And his eyes, his blue eyes, I became lost in them. I used to stare for hours into that same blue, the blue of a summer day when you could almost see the night behind the sky.

I don't know how long we stood like that, unmoving, barely breathing, until the door slammed open, making us jump apart.

"Oh good, you didn't kill each other," Healer Arios said. "I was worried for a while there. Here you are Kailin." He tossed a bag at me, making a very reassuring metallic sound as it hit my hands.

"The money?!" I stuttered. "But, I mean, *how?*"

"A good Healer never reveals his secrets!" He smiled a boyish grin, and I could easily imagine the rough, outer-ring boy he must have been when he earned his scholarship. "Actually, that is terribly inaccurate because good healing happens only when there is a free exchange of knowledge, but that's beside the point." Lord Aiden laughed, and when I turned to him he smiled back at me.

It was a nice smile.

"The important thing is that you can get most things from people if you know the right way to ask." Lord Aiden laughed again, and I couldn't help but join him.

At that moment the bell struck nine, and I realized I still might be able to tend to Lady Cathrina. She had told me she would be in her chambers tonight, despite the usual revelry the rest of her ring would be indulging in.

That Lord Aiden was supposed to be indulging in right now.

But wasn't.

"Thank you, Healer Arios, you have no idea what this means to me." I turned to Lord Aiden to thank him as well, but when I met his eyes, now bright from our moment of shared humor, the words stuck in my throat. I turned and ran up the stairs, hugging the coins to my chest.

EIGHTEEN

Lady Cathrina was more subdued than usual when I entered her chambers. Instead of working or reading, she was simply staring at her fire, her legs pulled up against her chest, her hair down.

She didn't even notice me until I leaned down to hand her her tea.

"Oh," she said, giving me a small smile. "When I told you I wouldn't be out tonight, I should have told you that you could take the evening off as well. It is the Solstice, after all."

"I don't mind," I said, setting the cup and saucer down on her side table when she didn't reach for it. "I don't think I would be welcomed down in the kitchen anyway."

She let out a sound that reminded me of a snort, then slid off her chair onto the ground.

"Here," she said, patting the ground next to her. "We'll have our own private celebration."

I smiled, still riding my high from whatever had happened downstairs and did as she asked, settling down in front of the fire next to her.

"Tell me," she said, her eyes staring into the flames again. "What did your aunt do for you to celebrate?"

"Oh, not that much," I said leaning back against the chair, "I mean, we didn't have that much to begin with, but she always found a way to make it special. Making a little honey cake or an evergreen crown for me to wear around the house. But my favorite part was the singing."

She turned to look at me, her smile back again.

"Singing?" she asked. "Your aunt *sang*?"

"Oh yes," I said, "When I was young, she used to sing from dawn until we went to bed, and she would keep singing until I was asleep." I looked into the fire, the dancing flames almost mocking me in their joy. "There aren't any songs here. You wouldn't even know today was anything special."

Lady Cathrina didn't respond, and I began to feel tired. It had been a long day.

But right when I started to think I should leave, a miracle happened.

My mistress began to sing.

Her voice was sweet, but definitely not refined, only making it more real in this unreal moment.

In the dark land,
Come hold my hand,
and we shall find His way.
The dawn is neigh,
The gloom shall fly,
And greet the breaking day.
Do not lose heart,
For though we part,
The void an endless wall.
Come, draw near,
His promise is clear,

His branches are over all.

My eyes stung, and using my sleeve I wiped at them. I took a breath and joined her voice.

Fear not your stride,
Where shadows abide,
The faithful heart is free.
With head held high,
Watch toward the sky,
Living light we again shall see.

An hour passed as we sang through every hymn I knew, and some that were new to me. When I finally left her, my heart felt as warm as the embers now low in her hearth.

I wandered down the stairs, hoping to find some dinner at last, when I met another servant carrying a tray up the stairs. I didn't know her name, but I recognized her as one of the servants for the young women's dormitories.

"Oh good," she said, shoving the tray of soup and bread into my hands. "take this up to room fifteen on the ninth floor!"

"But—" It was too late, she was already down the stairs. The lightness Lady Cathrina had put in my heart started to fade as I turned around and began trekking back up the way I had come.

Room fifteen was across the hall from Avonly's with the other scholarship students, and the girl who opened it curled up her lip when she saw me.

"I hope you didn't get your dirty hands on my rolls," she said, taking her tray, then slamming the door in my face.

"You're welcome, and happy Solstice!" I snapped at the door.

I turned to go, when Avonly's door cracked open.

"Kailin?" She asked, opening it wider. "I thought you weren't a servant on our floor."

"I'm not," I said, just as surprised. "I was just asked to bring up the tray. Aren't you supposed to be at a party or something?"

Her eyes turned hard, and I could feel a warning go off in my mind.

"Most people just celebrate with their families on the actual Solstice," she said, turning back into her room, leaving the door open. I took it as an invitation and followed her.

"That must be nice," I said, taking my usual spot on her desk chair. "To have a family to celebrate with."

"Yes," she said, flopping down on her bed. "I was glad for a night off; all this socializing is exhausting." She was dressed in one of her nicest gowns, her hair up and makeup perfect. I had the impression that her night off wasn't her choice.

"Well, at least we can celebrate together."

She snorted and looked down at her fingers, picking at some dead skin around a nail.

"What is it like for the servants?" she asked, not looking up. "Lots of loud laughter and drinking, I would imagine. It was always like that at the village celebrations, but I guess you wouldn't know that, would you."

Her words hurt. There was a reason Aunt Beredith and I would celebrate alone.

"I missed most of the celebration today," I said. "I had to go into the city and got lost for hours. I was even attacked. Twice."

"Attacked!" She said sitting up. "Are you all right? What were you doing out there alone?! Divlan is *huge!*"

"Yes, I'm fine," I smiled, taking her hands. She squeezed them back, and behind her makeup I could see real concern.

"Thank The Great One, I was rescued by an old woman with a very sturdy stick."

"It sounds like you should be thanking her instead of a tree." She pulled her hands back.

"I did thank her, and I helped her chop some vegetables, and then—"

I stopped, suddenly unable to go on.

"And then what?" Avonly asked, flopping back on her bed, her face turned away from me toward her fire. It was lower than it should be, but there wasn't any more wood. "Did she ask you to scrub her floors? Try to match you off to her dolt grandson?"

"No, nothing like that." My voice had become quiet. I looked at her, really looked. She seemed so different from the playmate who would steal off with me to the meadows to make crowns of wildflowers. But there, underneath, was my best friend.

I had to believe that, because right now, I needed a friend more than anything.

"Avonly," I said, bringing her eyes back to me. "She spoke of The Great One, and of me. And she said some things—"

"Oh I'm sure she did!" Avonly snapped, jumping off the bed. "When are you going to give up all that nonsense, Kailin?! You've been away from our backwards village just as long as I have, yet you still hold on to those stupid stories!"

"Avonly!" I stuttered, not believing her disbelief.

"Don't *Avonly* me like you're my mother!" She clenched her hands at her sides. "Maybe it is different down with the servants who still need some ridiculous story to give them a reason to get up and live their miserable lives every day, but for those of us who know better, we rely on reality to base our beliefs!"

"What are you talking about?" I shouted back, standing as well. "You're the one who used to lecture *me* on having faith!"

"Well I know better now. I know not to believe in something that is cruel enough to give you everything you wanted, only to—"

She looked to the side, breathing heavily through an anger I couldn't understand. After a moment she took a deep breath.

"Look, Kailin," she said, taking my hands. "I'm sorry I lost my temper, it is just so hard to see someone I care about so ignorant."

"Ignorant?!" I yanked my hands out of hers.

"Will you just listen to me!" She was furious again. "I know things now that you don't. If you had been accepted as a scholarship student instead of screwing up the exam then you would have dumped all that dung Father Gant shoved in us like the rot it is!"

I gaped at her words. Never had she been so cruel, and I stared at her through stinging eyes, desperate to find the answer.

Her blond curls had started to come out of their hair sticks and strands were falling around her painted face. I had grown used to seeing makeup on the faces of the other girls here at the Academy, but it never looked real on her, like a mask she used to hide what she really was underneath—a Peasant like me.

"I know it has been hard for you," I started, reining in my own anger. "But that doesn't mean you should stop believing."

"I'm not—look, Kailin. We have a chance here to actually learn about the real world, not some fantasy. We can make our own decisions about what matters—not simply follow the shrub-headed traditions of some rot-covered Peasants."

And something solid took over the place in my heart as the slur came out of her mouth.

"*Rot-covered Peasants* like your parents and everyone else we left behind?" I spat it back at her and felt a great deal of satisfaction when she flinched.

"Yes, actually," she said, folding her arms. "Looking back, I can't think of one word of sense my mother or father ever spoke to me."

I looked at her again, and suddenly she was a stranger to me.

Had I ever known her at all?

"You're forgetting something, Avonly." My voice had become hardly a whisper, my whole body trembling at the horrid feelings boiling in my blood. "I'm still one of those *rot-covered Peasants* who believes!"

I turned and threw open the door, no longer caring who saw me leave her room.

I was never coming back.

Avonly shouted at my back things I didn't want to hear, her voice becoming shrill when I didn't turn around. I slammed the door, letting its echo chase me down the Academy's corridors.

At that moment the bells in the city rang out, announcing midnight, and the darkest night of the year.

End of Part Two

PART THREE

CHAPTER
NINETEEN

The workroom door shut with a click, silencing the bickering voices behind it. It was the first day of classes since the Solstice, and Markly was using the unusually busy schedule of the Healers for us to scrub and polish their floors while they were out. I had grown used to expecting no help from the other girls. Working together, they would fly through the rooms, but since I was Lady Cathrina's *personal* servant, that seemed to mean they didn't need to help me.

Or just didn't care.

I was fine with that.

I didn't care either.

No one here seemed to care about anyone else, so why should I?

I pulled the bucket up by the handle, almost dragging it along the hall toward Lady Cathrina's chambers.

It is just so hard to see someone I care about so ignorant.

I took another step, the water threatening to slosh over the rim of the bucket.

If you had been accepted as a scholarship student instead of screwing up the exam.

Another step, my arms starting to ache from the weight.

Rot-covered Peasant.

The water spilled over the edge, and I bit a curse on my tongue as I bent over to wipe it up, but all I could do was stare, empty again as I had been over and over for the past week.

Avonly hadn't just been my best friend.

She had been my only friend.

Ever.

Now I really was alone.

I cleaned up the soapy water.

Yes, I was looking forward to the long hours ahead of me, when I wouldn't have to worry about another human soul. Setting down my mop and bucket, I put the key into the lock, only to have the door swing open. Lady Cathrina stared down at me, a look of surprise mirroring my own.

"My Lady!" I stuttered. "I didn't think you would be here or else I would have picked another—"

"It's all right," she said, backing into the room. "I was actually just going to send for you. We have something we would like to discuss with you."

It was then that I saw she wasn't alone. Sitting in the armchair I usually found her in was an older man with a brightly edged vest.

"Dean Rathord, this is the servant girl I was telling you about."

Dean Rathord? I had heard of him, the man who ran the Healer Academy, but I had never seen him before, let alone been brought to his attention.

His hands were peaked in front of him, resting on his generous girth.

"You didn't mention she was a Peasant."

"Peasant or Tradesman, it does not make a difference to me, only how skilled she would be as my assistant on the assignment. Please come in and shut the door, Kailin."

Assignment?

I stepped into the room, dragging my mop and bucket behind me, and used my foot to nudge the door closed.

"My Lady," Dean Rathord continued, "I really think you should consider—"

"The Senate has approved my request that I may bring an assistant of my choosing to the Peace Negotiations. They did not put any specifications on that assistant's ring, and neither will I."

"Yes, of course, but this other request of yours—"

"And in order for her to perform to the best of her abilities, I will need to train her."

Peace Negotiations? Train me for what? I looked back and forth between them, but neither one was paying any attention to me.

"But think of the Academy's image! We're under enough scrutiny as it is for still insisting on treating the outer rings for free—"

"Which is a great and virtuous tradition you should be commended for upholding, but that isn't the issue here. What is the issue is that in a few months I will be on The Islands in the center of a Richarkian fleet and would like an assistant I can count on, which I will only have if I have trained her properly."

RICHARK?!

"Very well," the portly man said, pulling himself to his feet. "I suppose sending a Peasant with you instead of a student less expendable, given the dangerous nature of your assignment, has some wisdom in it. Your request will be granted. Just please, *please,* make sure that she is not seen more than is needed."

My skin turned cold.

Danger?

"Of course." My mistress stepped back to give him room to reach the door.

He stopped as he passed me, looking down at my shocked face. Too late I remembered I was meant to look down, but instead of the slap I had come to expect, he only pulled his eyebrows together in concern.

The door opened and shut behind him.

"What was that about?" I asked, turning on my mistress.

"Just a bit of negotiations." Lady Cathrina was in front of her table by the window, sorting through a stack of papers as if she hadn't just upset my world.

Again.

"What did he mean by *assistant?*"

"What it usually means." She finished gathering her papers and turned to me, a smile on her face. "You officially have permission to assist me in my fourth-year class."

I was dreaming. I had slipped on the soapy water I spilled and had hit my head and—

"'Thank you' is what people usually say in these circumstances."

"But—I—*Islands?*" My mind was officially fried, but somehow I pulled that detail out of the mush my brain had become.

"The Peace Negotiations with Richark will be held this summer on The Islands in hopes of reaching a calm conclusion to the incident I spoke to you about earlier this year. I will be a member of the delegation to be sent and have chosen you to come with me as my assistant."

The look on my face must have shown how I felt about this,

because she stopped smiling. "I wouldn't worry about them too much; as I said, they aren't until the beginning of the summer and anything can happen between now and then. Maybe these tensions will run their course and we'll return to our normal levels of xenophobia before we need to step foot on a ship." She walked past me to the door, and I found my tongue.

"But how could you think I'm qualified for such an important position?! In case you forgot, I *failed* the entrance exam and am still just a Peasant! No one will take me seriously—"

"Kailin!" Lady Cathrina snapped, shutting my mouth better than if she had grabbed my jaw. "Do you really think that I am so unhinged that I would choose to bring an impractical assistant into a situation that could easily escalate into war?"

I wrapped my arms around my middle, sure that if I were to let go I would spiral apart.

She set her papers on the bookshelf by the door, then took my shoulders in her hands. Her eyes were a bright violet as she stared into mine. I held them fast, afraid I would drown in my own self-loathing if I let go.

"I know you've been forced to grow in barren soil for too long. Even if you can't believe in yourself, believe in me and the fact that I am rarely wrong—and I'm positive that this will not be an exception."

I felt something strange stir in my chest, different from the *pull* and yet it moved me in almost the same way. It was so much more than what I had felt when preparing for the exam or secretly studying with Avonly. Something even more powerful than the emptiness that had been burned into my heart.

I felt hope.

Lady Cathrina gave my shoulders a squeeze, turning toward the door while picking up her papers.

"Right now all you need to worry about today is following me, or else we'll be late, which would be very embarrassing, since I insist on punctuality from my students."

She opened the door, and I left my mop and bucket behind as I followed her into the hallway. We had taken only a few steps before she turned around.

"Kailin," she asked, "what are you doing?"

I felt panic as I stared at her skirt hem, trying to think of what I was doing wrong.

"I can hardly have you do the work I need you to if you don't look up."

I hesitated, I couldn't help it, but I did raise my eyes. She smiled, then turned and resumed her brisk pace. The Healers' floor was empty, but as we descended the stairs the thickening of students and Healers grew until we were weaving through their chatter like fish moving up a stream. I still tried not to meet the eyes of the students and Healers we passed, but I could feel their eyes on me as they stared after us.

I wanted to care, but I couldn't. It was as if I were seeing the Academy for the first time.

I saw that some students were pretty, and some were very ugly. They were not all angel-faced Nobles like Lord Aiden, but were as different from each other as the people in my village. I mean, of course they were quite a bit cleaner and better dressed, but if I really looked at them they didn't seem all that different from me.

How strange; I never would have guessed this if I had not looked up.

We continued through the halls, now new and strange in this sea of faces, until we reached an area I had not seen before.

Lady Cathrina stopped before a pair of double doors and smiled at me.

"You've never been in these rooms before, have you?"

I shook my head, and she smiled as though she had a secret she couldn't bear not to share.

"To the north of the Academy is the National Hospital, and these classrooms are a part of that institution. Instead of desks and chairs, you'll find something a little more practical." Her smile widened, and I couldn't help smiling back.

Then with one fluid movement, Lady Cathrina pushed both doors open and swept into the high-ceilinged room beyond.

The room was about thirty feet long with a long, jar-strewn table running down the middle. At the far end was another pair of closed doors, identical to the ones through which we had just entered, which must have led to the National Hospital. The walls were pristine white plaster leading up to large beams arching to the center of the room. High arched windows filled almost all the upper half of the walls. It was bright in the winter light, and for a moment I had to blink to adjust my eyes. When I could see again I realized with a start that the room was already filled.

Along both sides of the room were ten patients in identical beds with wheels, dressed in stark-white linen tunics and sitting up against tall pillows. Some looked on with interest, some simply looked ill, but all of them were silent and watchful. As we walked by the first few beds I looked at their faces and I could see I wasn't the only one questioning the wisdom of letting students practice on the living. I couldn't tell what ring they were in, as they all were washed and dressed in the same hospital-issued, easy-to-disinfect clothes. No dirt or vests here.

There were also students.

About twenty of them sitting around the center table, none paying any attention to those in the beds behind them. They had been chatting among themselves, but when Lady Cathrina barged in they all hurriedly snapped to attention like a regiment of soldiers.

Soldiers. Like those who would be fighting in a war against Richark unless my remarkable mistress could broker peace. And she had chosen *me* to accompany her? I found myself standing a little straighter. Lady Cathrina, like any true general, hardly acknowledged the efforts she expected and kept her pace with me trailing behind.

I was enjoying myself for the first few steps, then almost tripped. My heart raced as I met eyes with a student who was staring at me just as openly. But Lady Cathrina was still moving, so I focused on the wall at the other end of the room and got my feet under me. It was all I could do not to look at Lord Aiden as I passed, but there wasn't anything I could do about my cheeks.

At the end of the central table was a chair that Lady Cathrina sat down in. I took a spot standing off to her right, not having gotten any better instruction. None of the students had sat down again, and Lady Cathrina didn't look at them. Instead she was browsing through the stack of pages she had brought with her, slowly looking over each one before setting it down. I leaned over and saw that at the top of each one was a name and number in large print with neat handwritten notes beneath.

After a minute of this and still nothing happening, the initial tension in the room moved from Lady Cathrina to the other point of interest.

My skin began to crawl as it would back home whenever I had to go out into the village. The students weren't even trying to hide their stares, the whispers filling the room. Well, except for one student, who was leaning on the table rotating a jar around in circles as if it were the most interesting thing in the world.

I fixed my eyes forward, looking above all their heads, telling myself to breathe.

No one was going to throw a rock in here.

Another minute passed and Lady Cathrina continued to look through the stack. Another minute, and she still said nothing to the students. The students began to grow edgy, all their whispers toward her now. Still, Lady Cathrina read on.

Then, when I thought I would lose it as well, she set down the last sheet and looked up.

"Nothing too terribly serious, you can all calm down a bit." She stood up gracefully and went to a large cupboard by the door to the hospital, opening it to reveal an array of shelves with clothing. The larger pieces she ignored, but she did take a pair of thin gloves and put them on. Then she walked back to the table, took the first sheet she had read, and made her way over to the first bed.

In it was a boy who looked my age. She made a clear show of comparing the sheet in her hand with the sheet in a paper folder attached to the footboard, then reached for the stool that was against the wall.

"Hello." She smiled at him, sitting down so she was brought to his height. "My name is Healer Cathrina. Can you please tell me who you are?"

The boy had red-brown hair and a splattering of freckles across his nose. If he hadn't also been a shade of grayish-green, I might have thought he was cute. Keeping his eyes down, he coughed and answered in a hoarse voice, "you have my name, it's there on that sheet."

"Yes, but I need to make sure that you are who this sheet says you are. We don't want you mixed up with an old grandfather with the same name who just had his foot taken off, right?"

This earned her a smile from the boy, and probably a lot more than that because without hesitating he said, "Jareth. I work as a netting apprentice down by the pier."

"Well, Jareth," Lady Cathrina continued, her smile coloring her voice with safety and trust. "We're going to have you out of here in no time. I have the best students in the whole Academy to help look after you today."

Jared looked past her at the students behind her, and I could see the doubt in his face.

As Lady Cathrina did a quick exam of his throat, the hall filled again with whispers. I thought they were commenting on how amazing Lady Cathrina was at getting a complete stranger to trust her in thirty seconds, until someone said "crazy" a bit too loudly. I felt my face grow hot.

When she finished, Lady Cathrina reached out and patted the boy's hand, then stood up to face her class.

"Today you will be treating Elsberg throat. You have all encountered and treated it during your sessions at the hospital. As you know, it's not contagious and has a fairly straightforward treatment, if a bit finicky."

She collected the remaining eleven pages and handed them out to teams of two or three, making sure to assign a group to Jareth. I couldn't help but notice that Lord Aiden had moved to treat the patient at the far end of the room.

Then Lady Cathrina sat back down and the students moved toward the jars and bowls along the central table.

"They're herbs," I said under my breath. "For healing. Just like at the exam."

"Fond memories?" Lady Cathrina said without looking.
"Ha."

I had seen Elsberg throat back in my village and I knew

from experience it could be treated with a simple combination of three basic herbs with no preparation more complicated than mixing with water. But I also knew from experience that if not treated it could lead to weeks of painful sores on the inside of the throat and even loss of voice, which could become permanent if not treated in time.

Voices from the nearest group of students brought my attention back to the here and now.

"Not Elsberg throat," I heard the first student say to her partner. "I thought we were going to do something *interesting* in this class."

"I know what you mean. I remember studying this years ago. I was really hoping that Lady Cathrina's class would have more of a challenge to it. At least with the way everyone worships her you would think so, but then again, you know what people say about her."

"Well now I believe it! This is beneath us—a first-year could do this!"

"Exactly! And why is she making us make our own medicine instead of just letting us go over to the pharmacy at the hospital? I can't even remember the last time I made my own!"

"You're totally right! No *real* Healer would have to make their own medicine. But, you know..." The second student tilted his head toward Lady Cathrina. "We should humor her."

"Of course." They sat in silence for a moment before the first student asked, "So which herbs are we supposed to be using?"

The second student didn't know, so they went over to the next team to ask the students there if they knew. The middle-aged man they had left behind looked paler and I doubted it was from his throat.

As the minutes ticked by I couldn't believe what I saw. I could see the same air of conceit in the other students as in the first pair I had overheard, the same running around looking for someone who actually remembered anything about treating this illness, and the same disregard for the fact that their patients were human beings. My face grew hot again with that anger Aunt Beredith had constantly warned me about, and I had to bite on the side of my mouth to keep from saying anything.

I knew what to use. *I* paid attention on those healing trips back home. If this was the type of half-rated Healers the Academy produced, then I was better off following Aunt Beredith around the village back home.

The door at the far end of the room opened and shut, probably some student leaving to use the washroom, drawing my eyes that way. And that's when I saw that the room wasn't completely full of shrubs. Lord Aiden was quietly mixing his ingredients together and pouring them into a cup. Gently he helped the weakened woman in front of him slowly drink from it. When they were done, his partner went off to another group, but Lord Aiden stayed and talked to the woman. I couldn't hear what they said, but the woman smiled and patted his hand.

Then he turned his head, his eyes finding mine. My breath stopped, because he had that same smile he had given me a week earlier in the entrance hall.

Then it was gone, his mouth going flat, and he turned back to his patient.

I couldn't put together the two Lord Aidens I kept seeing.

A bright blue light suddenly flared out of the corner of my eye.

I snapped my head around toward it, but whatever it had been was gone. All I saw was the white winter light coming in through the windows above the bed of the boy named Jareth. He was smiling, looking more at ease now that he had gotten his medicine—while I was anything but so. I looked back and forth, but there wasn't anything else to see.

Finally the class was over, and I was amazed no one had toppled over dead. Student's stations were a mess, jars were placed back on the central table in a heap, and instead of paying attention to how their patients had taken their medicine, the students were congratulating themselves and making plans for lunch.

Without looking up from a pile of papers she had been examining the whole time, Lady Cathrina waved her hand and dismissed the class.

When the last one had exited through the far door, she finally set down the sheet she had been holding while letting out a long breath. She didn't move at first, her eyes trained on the door that had just closed.

"Come on, Kailin," she said, standing up. "Let's fix this mess."

CHAPTER

TWENTY

L ady Cathrina and I spent the next hour examining each patient individually, teaching me through example how healing should be done. She wasn't as brash as Aunt Beredith, but both, in their own way, managed to convince the patients that they cared about them getting better.

"Having them trust you is important, isn't it?" I asked after the last patient was wheeled back through the doors leading to the National Hospital.

Lady Cathrina didn't answer right away, but straightened the pile of patient reports from the students. The afternoon sun slanting through the large windows gave a warm glow to her hair.

"It is the most important thing."

She handed me the patient reports from the class while she picked up the pile she had been going through. But instead of going back to the Academy she walked to the doors leading to the National Hospital.

And that was when she led me to another world I had never dreamed I would ever see.

The National Hospital was as much a part of my childhood dreams as the Healer Academy, almost even more so because to work here, to become a member of the staff after graduation, was the hope and dream of every prospective Healer.

I would listen enraptured as Aunt Beredith would tell me of the quiet wards and the stress of emergency surgeries. With these stories now on my mind, I followed wide-eyed behind Lady Cathrina as she opened the doors.

I saw nothing magical behind them.

Actually, it was painfully dull.

Yes, we had to navigate through the bustle of Healers and older students talking about this disease or that broken bone, but there was nothing captivating in their voices. No one was running around in blood-covered aprons. We didn't pass by any wards full of agonizing cries.

It was nothing like I had expected.

Yet...it was better than any daydream I could ever have come up with.

The normality and reality of it all made me long to be part of it so strongly my chest hurt. I couldn't stop turning my head from side to side, struggling to take it all in.

We turned a corner and I finally saw a woman being rolled down the hallway going the other way. She seemed fine for the most part, though her leg was wrapped in a splint from her toes to her hip. As we passed she turned her head to look at me, and a flash of blue fire sparked behind her eyes.

I kept my eyes down for the rest of the walk.

Lady Cathrina took us down a flight of stairs and up to a large and imposing desk that seemed to be in the heart of the building. It was round, with several stations of Healers collecting and passing out folders. Behind it was a door with its own flow of traffic, each Healer carrying folders.

Lady Cathrina walked up to a rather busy-looking man with a balding head. He didn't look up as she approached. He didn't even acknowledge her until she had been standing there a minute.

I could feel my eyebrows come together. I thought everyone knew Lady Cathrina.

"Leave the files on the desk," he said without a glance, his metallic voice grainy against my ears.

"Thank you for your help." Lady Cathrina placed the papers in front of him and turned to walk away, her voice and manner unchanged.

I stared at him, then ran after her.

"Oh, get that pout off your face, Kailin," Lady Cathrina said without looking back at me. "That wasn't an insult to you or me or the ring structure; it is just that I'm here so often that it would seriously disrupt things if they jumped every time I walked into the room. They know it doesn't bother me that they don't grovel at my title, and to be honest, I prefer it this way."

"Sorry," I muttered. Nothing should surprise me anymore. My mistress lived in her own world when it came to social decorum. "Are we going to spend every afternoon cleaning up after students?"

"I should hope not. I'd rather that their performance improved after today."

We had turned a corner and ahead I could see the pair of double doors we had come through.

"Why should they?" I asked, failing to hide the disgust in my voice. "If *I* heard the stupid things they were saying to each other, I'm sure you did."

"Every class says the same things on their first day. And

every time after their abysmal display I fail them all. Shockingly, their performance drastically improves after that." A smug smile hinted at the corner of her mouth. "I have high hopes for the future."

"You fail them *all*?"

"Just on this first assignment. People say I'm hard on my students, but it is mostly because I don't accept half-hearted work when someone's health is involved."

"You sound like Aunt Beredith."

Lady Cathrina laughed. "Where do you think I learned how to be a good Healer?"

That gave me something to think about.

"So do all of your techniques come from my aunt?"

She looked over at me. "I wouldn't say *all* my techniques, but I did learn a lot from her. She was always a little more forceful than I thought necessary, but when it came to patients, I can't think of anyone who cared more. Could you imagine your aunt sitting quietly while a room full of self-righteous adolescents congratulated themselves after a performance like today?"

"No!" I barked out in a laugh. My aunt would have strung up every student in there by their toes.

"I picked some things up from her and she learned some things from me. I will admit that when I first got here, I was more interested in clothes than books and gossip than patients, but your aunt soon stamped that out of me."

I knew my aunt was very convincing in her own forceful way, and I was suddenly sick with the thought that maybe if I had been more like her then Avonly wouldn't have drifted away.

But I hadn't been. I hadn't cared, just like everyone else.

Everyone except the woman walking next to me.

"Why do you care so much about people?" I breathed, not even sure if she had heard me.

We had reached Lady Cathrina's office door and her face had a quiet, contemplative cast, her eyes looking back the way we had come as she bit her bottom lip. "I suppose," she started, her voice soft. "I care about people in trouble, because we all get into trouble sometimes."

With her words she seemed to diminish before my eyes. When she finally turned to look at me, her eyes had dimmed to a dull lavender.

"Thank you for your help this afternoon." She smiled, but it didn't give me the same sense of security it usually did.

I bobbed a curtsy, and she went inside her office. I stood staring at her door for a moment until warmth moved back under my skin. As I walked down the hall toward the closest servant door, dodging students with confused faces at my upturned head, I wondered at what she had meant. Not with her vague statement on altruism, but the honesty in her eyes.

Something had happened. Something that made her not care about her title or privileges.

Something that taught her what she was trying to teach me.

The class was understandably upset when they got their grades. We were in one of the smaller classrooms on the sixth floor with rows of tables and chairs placed in steps one higher than the one before, beneath tall, skinny windows along one wall facing the Academy Garden.

I had taken a spot at the back of the room by a window and tried hard not to let on how much I was enjoying the scene. After the students' protest had quieted down, Lady Cathrina launched into what can only be described as an Aunt Beredith lecture on humility. Her voice took on a forcefulness I had never heard from her before, and it shocked me as much as the students.

By the time Lady Cathrina finished, all the students were staring down at their tables. When she then began a lecture on good bedside manner, the room was deafened with the sound of scribbling pens.

Lady Cathrina didn't wait for me after she dismissed the class, and thinking of Markly's sharp gaze when I told her about my new assistant position, I stayed behind to clean up the classroom before starting my afternoon chores. I had just shut the door when I noticed someone waiting at the end of the hall. I was surprised, as most of the students had already hurried down for lunch, but what business was it of mine if a student was so stupid as to miss a meal?

Then he looked at me.

My eyes narrowed and I turned to walk the other way. I had only gone half the length of the hall when I realized I was being followed.

Lord Aiden was a few yards behind me, and his long stride was shortening the distance quickly.

Don't panic, I told myself. *He probably just has somewhere to go. It has nothing to do with you.* But when I had made an entire circuit of the sixth floor and he was still methodically getting closer I couldn't help the palpitations in my chest.

What did he want with me? If he was going to fulfill the threat I was warned of that first day, he could have done it when we were alone last week in the foyer. But he hadn't. All he had done was insult me.

And just like that, the feeling of being stalked prey turned into something more antagonistic.

I was done with this game of his. I turned at the next hall to sneak into a servant door, but realized too late that I had turned too soon.

And faced a dead end.

Scattered on this floor were about a dozen annoying mini-hallways, some leading to broom closets and servant doors, like those I had thought I had turned down, and others with Healer offices on either side and a large window at the end.

Guess which one of the two I was now facing.

I turned to backtrack—and nearly knocked Lord Aiden down.

"Rot!" I swore, jumping back.

"This time it was your fault," Lord Aiden said. He was wearing a blue vest today with gold embroidery, a white shirt underneath buttoned high to the base of his neck, but his hair was falling slightly to the left onto his forehead. I had a sudden urge to reach out and fix it—that is, until I saw his eyes.

They were hard as cobalt.

I looked down and stepped to move past him.

He stepped in front of me.

I tried the other side, but he moved in front of me again.

"I have some questions for you, servant girl."

"Kailin," I whispered through clenched teeth.

"What?"

"My name is Kailin," I said, raising my eyes. "And I have a *very* important appointment with a mop right now."

His jaw tightened, but he didn't strike me. Why didn't he strike me? None of the other Healers, students, or even servants had a problem hitting me when they thought I was being insolent. So why didn't he?

Never mind—it didn't matter. He was not my puzzle to solve but my problem to avoid.

"All right, *Kailin*," he said, "If you don't mind keeping the mop waiting, please explain to me what you are doing in my class."

"If you care so much, go ask Lady Cathrina." I tried again to step around him, only to have his arm shoot out in front of me, his palm on the wall, trapping me. He had moved so fast I hardly saw it happen. I met his eyes, paralyzed in shock. Something about my face must have amused him because his mouth twitch up for a moment.

"I'm asking you."

I should have been scared. I should have been terrified. Instead I was furious.

I let out a puff of air, accepting the fact that I wasn't going anywhere. I may have been crazy, but I wasn't unstable enough to try pushing past a Noble.

He must have seen my opinion in my set jaw because his own smile flattened.

"All right," I said, "I'm in your class because I'm trying to steal Lady Cathrina's technique for asking patients their names."

"If you were a spy," he said lowering his arm, "it would at least explain why you seem halfway literate."

"Literate?" I snapped. "What, do you think all Peasants are imbecilic cretins?"

"Yes, actually," he said, folding his arms. I could see the fabric pulling at the muscles beneath. "And the fact that you even know such *refined* words as 'imbecilic' and 'cretin' show that you are *not* a normal Peasant. Were you demoted? Is that why you act like you have some sort of right to an opinion?"

"*Right to an opinion?*"

"So is that a yes?"

"No!" I shouted. Then I remembered where we were and lowered my voice. "I was *not* demoted!" I hissed. "I have always been this *plebeian*!"

"Well pardon me for trying to figure you out!" he hissed back.

We stood glaring at each other for a moment, and I seriously considered pushing past him, punishment or not.

Until I realized what he had said.

"Why would you want to figure me out?"

He clearly wasn't expecting me to ask him that. His eyes lost their hardness and widened slightly, like he was afraid. But of what? No one was here except me. Then he looked to the side, his hand wiping down his face.

It was so normal a move I forgot for a moment to hate him.

"I don't know," he finally muttered. When he didn't say anything more, I tried to move around him, but once again he stepped in front of me.

"If you don't know, may I please be excused until you figure it out?"

"No, that isn't what I meant," he said looking back at me. There was a hint of panic in his voice that made me suddenly remember how crazy he had seemed the day he caught me cheating for Avonly. Then just as suddenly as it came it was gone again. "It is more like you're a puzzle, and it is a hobby of mine to figure out things that don't make sense." He let out a breath. "And *you* do not make sense."

I couldn't help but let a hint of smile leak onto my own lips. His confusion felt like a victory.

"You're not going to let me go until you're satisfied, are you?"

He shook his head.

Fine then.

I turned from him and walked toward the window.

"There isn't anywhere to go."

"I know," I said, pulling myself up onto the windowsill. I let my feet dangle as I turned back to him, enjoying the look on his face more than I thought I would. "Now that I'm comfortable, you may begin your interrogation."

"All right," he said stepping forward. "Let's start with your tonal quality."

"My what?"

"Your accent. How did you come to speak like someone inside your ring?"

I looked at him like he was crazy. Was he really asking about my voice?

"Everyone in my village speaks this way," I said. Then I paused; that first day I had noticed that the other servants spoke differently, but over time I had grown used to it, without even noticing that the inner rings *did* speak like me.

I looked down at my hands, picking at my dress. Markly had been surprised at the fabric, as if it was inside my ring. Were there other parts of me that diverged as well?

"That's—interesting," Lord Aiden said, drawing my attention back to him. He moved over to the wall next to me and leaned his shoulder against it, his eyebrows pulled together as he looked out the window.

And my heart did that pounding thing again.

It made his face look younger, more open. He was obviously older than me; he was taking Lady Cathrina's fourth-year class, so that would make him seventeen? Eighteen?

I chided myself. It didn't matter how old he was. After this I was going to do a better job avoiding him.

"It must have something to do with your village's location," he said looking back at me. "Was it remote? Did you have much trade?"

"We were in the heart of the Holy Forest, so no, we didn't get many visitors."

"The Holy Forest?" he asked, raising his eyebrows. "But linguistic analysis aside, there is still the matter of your knowledge of herbs. I hadn't realized Peasants were even capable of such expansive learning."

My cheeks flushed as my jaw tightened again.

"If we weren't, what would be the point of the scholarships?"

"Scholarships?"

"You know, where the Academy will pay the way for students from the outer rings to attend classes?"

Lord Aiden looked confused.

"Those scholarships are for *Tradesmen*; the exams aren't even offered to Peasants."

I stared at him.

But my aunt had gotten one. Avonly had gotten one, and the examiners came every year! There had to be other Peasants here too, I just hadn't seen them and Avonly hadn't mentioned them and—

"Next question," I whispered.

"All right," he said. "I suppose I can accept the fact that somewhere in this world there are Peasants who have the cognitive ability to learn and be taught. Now I want to know why you're in Lady Cathrina's class."

"And I said to go ask her yourself."

"But I want to hear it from you."

He leaned toward me ever so slightly, and I could feel myself lean the same amount away from him.

No. I wouldn't be intimidated by him.

I looked away from him.

"She needed an assistant," I said, gripping the stone edge of the window.

"Other Healers have had assistants before, but those have always been high-level Tradesmen servants from the Hospital *at least*. Why would she choose you?"

Why had she chosen me?

Because she needed someone expendable to take to the Islands.

"Because she decided she wanted me, which was good enough for me and it should be good enough for you."

"But *why* did she want you? It just doesn't make sense!"

"You really can't think of any reason someone would want a person like me as an assistant?" I said, my anger making me turn back to face him. It was one thing that I thought I wasn't worthy of the position, but for some reason I couldn't stand the fact that *he* thought I didn't deserve it either. I tried to glare, but how he was looking at me now....

He didn't look like a Noble interrogating someone rings outside him. Leaning against the wall like that, all the former tension and egotism gone...

He just looked like a boy talking to a girl.

I focused on the embroidered edging of his vest.

"For someone who is supposed to be a student of one of the most advanced places of learning in Tamerin, you sure are showing a lack of imagination."

"Oh, I have plenty of imagination."

And he smiled.

And I liked it.

I rolled my eyes.

And his smile grew wider.

"My first hypothesis," he said, "was that you were some sort of demoted relative of Lady Cathrina, but your explanation of your background rules that out. So my next theory is that you are some sort of social experiment."

"*Experiment?!*"

"What? Haven't you been around Lady Cathrina long

enough to know that she is, well, eccentric? I wouldn't put it past her to try to mix the rings just to see what would happen."

"I am not anyone's *experiment*."

"All right! Fine then. The only other possibility that I could come up with, after many long and tedious hours of using *my imagination*, is that you're the daughter of a Richarkian ambassador, who was actually a spy, and after your father was imprisoned they sent you to work here, hoping Lady Cathrina's sweet disposition would milk your father's secrets from you and that whole 'growing up in a small remote village no one had ever heard of' is just a cover story."

"I thought we ruled out my being a spy," I laughed. "Seriously, how much time did you spend coming up with *that* one?"

The smile reached his eyes. He leaned closer. "You didn't deny it."

"You're insane," I snorted, but when his smile got even broader and his eyes almost glowed, I knew I had to end this conversation. Quickly. "All right, I, Kailin, officially deny your ridiculous theories. All I am is a village girl who last summer became Lady Cathrina's servant. You can let me go now, because honestly there is nothing special about me."

You've been touched by The Great One.

No. I wasn't anything special.

I was just Kailin.

"Right," Lord Aiden said, standing up straight. The teasing smile was gone, his face serious as his eyes bored into mine.

"You're nothing special," he continued. "Except that you know more about herbs than most second-years, treat those inside your ring as equals, and that you make me—" He looked away.

Please look back.

His eyebrows came together.

He looked back at me.

Really looked at me.

My hands started to tremble.

"You're right," he said. "You're nothing special. Except that you're a Peasant who has somehow become Lady Cathrina's pet."

"*Pet!*" I snapped, jumping down from my perch.

"No!" He said stepping toward me, his voice panicked. "That isn't what I meant! I just was trying—"

"I think I need to go find that mop now!"

I took my opening and ran down the hall before he could block me again, turning into the servant door I had meant to escape through in the first place.

"Kailin!"

I slammed the door shut before he even turned the corner, knowing his pride wouldn't let him follow me.

Being a servant had its perks.

TWENTY-ONE

I sped through the maze of hallways and stairs, not caring in which direction I was heading. I hated the way Lord Aiden kept popping into my life, as if it was his mission to annoy me to death. Maybe *that* was the horrible punishment the other servant girls were worried I was doomed for. In that case, they were right to warn me. I honestly couldn't stand being around him, no matter how his hair always seemed to fall on his forehead or how his muscles pulled a little on his shirt or the color of his eyes or the way he smelled or talked or looked at me—

Why are you running away?

I passed a window, catching my reflection.

That's why.

The anger left me. My black hair was fizzling around my head as it escaped my braid. My skin had turned a strange pale beneath my caramel complexion from being inside too much. My violet eyes...I thought of Lord Aiden's eyes and knew mine would never be captivating.

There was nothing special about me, and him showing

interest in me was only a cruel joke the universe felt like playing on me.

A joke Lady Cathrina was in on by making me her assistant.

I was a servant, a Peasant who was ignored and hated by other Peasants, who didn't have a friend in the world and—

Avonly.

He had made me forget Avonly.

And I had smiled.

I couldn't remember the last time I'd smiled.

There is nothing special about you.

I turned and started running up the stairs again.

I stopped for only a moment where these stairs ended and only then to make the decision that I did *not* want to go to the workroom or really be anywhere where someone could tell me what to do no matter how I felt. So instead of turning right at the landing to the halls and stairs I would normally take, I turned left instead.

It wasn't a long rebellion, there really were just two directions you can go, but it gave me a precedent to make another. And another. Right instead of left, up instead of down, I didn't really care as long as it kept me from arriving somewhere until whatever Lord Aiden had done to me worked itself out of my system, until I had a certain amount of numbness back before I had to face them all again.

I had come a long way since that first day where each turn made me dizzy, and I was confident I knew all the servant halls by now.

So I stopped dead in my tracks when I realized I had no idea where I was.

It was the light that first hinted that I was in unfamiliar territory. The servant halls were never as well lit as the main corridors of the Academy, but these lanterns were out and looked as if they hadn't been used in years. I reached out my hand to straighten the one in front of me and had to catch it as it came free of the stone!

I set it down on the dust-covered floor.

The floor here was also no longer the soft, worn stone I was used to, but was made of a rougher, blacker rock I had never seen before. The walls were made of the same material, and the windows, when I came across them, were merely slits letting in a bare minimum of light. It was still winter, and I could feel the cold seeping down the passage.

Instinctively, I wrapped my hands around my arms.

Had I found some sort of attic? No one had ever mentioned an attic before, but then most servants weren't very interested in poking around beyond their workstations.

I walked forward to one of the windows and looked out, only to see a large, rectangular building several stories tall just below with a large, open green area in the middle connected to the one I was in by several raised sections. The Academy? Then that would mean I had somehow gotten into the National Hospital.

Somewhere I definitely was not supposed to be.

I turned to retrace my steps, but stopped.

This was something new.

Lord Aiden is something new.

I spun around and followed the hall farther. After a few yards the windows stopped, and I was faced with a wall of darkness. I reached out my hand, suddenly sure that I could touch it.

Just like another blackness I hadn't thought about in a long time.

I jerked my hand back, my blood pounding in my ears as my entire body began to tremble.

And I was suddenly back in front of an ancient slab of

stone, facing a wall of trees that was supposed to be harmless, but I knew were anything but that. My chest constricted as the *pull* tugged at the center, as if my heart were simultaneously being pulled and crushed at the same time.

As if it wanted me to keep going forward.

Which made me want to run away even more.

But then the *pull* had helped me on the solstice; maybe it wasn't completely evil...

I placed one foot in front of the other.

Minutes or years slid by as I felt my way along the wall, cringing as my hand brushed against spiderwebs and fearful of every mouse scampering in the shadows. The pressure was lessening, and I was beginning to wonder if it had been there at all, when I heard the faint murmur of voices. Stopping, I held my breath. Despite what Avonly thought of my religious convictions, I wasn't blindly superstitious and didn't believe in ghosts, but here, alone, in the dark, the muffled sounds made me feel more open-minded.

I was just about to turn and run when I heard one of the voices say something that sounded like "Richark."

Sure that ghosts had better things to do than keep up on current politics, I began moving down the passage again. Soon there was a faint brightening to the darkness and I came to a window looking down into a large room. It was still very dark, but I could make out the shape of long tables lined with benches. It must have been a dining room of some sort, with a great fireplace against the far wall, now dark and cold like the air that was seeping under my skin. The only thing I could see for certain was a single candle burning at the head of the center table with four hooded figures clustered around it.

"It's too risky," a man's voice said. It was low and deep, as if he were used to commanding everyone's attention whenever he spoke. "With a war about to start, everyone will be on high alert."

"This whole business involves risk," a nasally man's voice replied. "If you are scared you should have just stayed in your precious little boating town."

"How dare you question my conviction!" the deep voice retorted, slamming his fist on the table.

"Silence both of you." This was said by a new woman's voice. This voice was smoother and frighteningly composed, as if each word were a well-placed stab in the dark.

The other two quieted.

"This is the perfect time to set our plans into motion," she continued. "The war is a blessing from the one we follow, the perfect distraction and scapegoat. Yes, everyone will be more alert than before, but their eyes will all be fixed on Richark. While they are watching their supposed enemy, they won't be watching their backs, or anything that might slide between their ribs." There was a hidden pleasure in her words.

And I suddenly knew what it meant to be afraid.

She leaned in closer to the candle and I could make out her pale skin, her slightly pointed chin and colorless lips, but her hood concealed the rest of her face.

She looked like a corpse.

"But we must move forward with precision and accuracy," she continued. " We can begin to move our pieces into position, but I've received direction that it is far too early for any direct confrontation."

"So what would you have us do?" the nasally man asked.

"I would have you complete the targets on your list. We need to continue to vet those who could help or oppose us and our cause. Here are your new assignments." With a motion as accurate as her words she handed the other three figures envelopes. Each read what was inside, and then as one they placed the papers above the flame until they were charred to dust. "Do not fail in your missions—or you will be punished."

She turned and disappeared into the darkness, two of the figures joining her. The last one, who hadn't said a word, stayed a moment, as still as the empty room that entombed them. Then they leaned down and blew out the candle, leaving me alone in the darkness, shaking with fright.

I turned and ran the way I had come.

I found my way back to the servant halls faster than I had prayed possible, and ran to the workroom.

"Markly!" I shouted, throwing open the door. The other three girls were sitting and working on various tasks, their heads snapping up at my entrance. "I just—I saw—"

What had I seen?

"What is it?!" Markly said jumping up. "You're as white as a ghost, what happened?"

"I was running, because Lord Aiden—"

"Lord Aiden!" Markly yelled, taking a step back. "By The Great One—"

"What?! No, I mean, yes, he cornered me in a hall—"

"I don't want to hear any more!" She snapped, suddenly furious. "And you are *not* to speak of it again! I'm sorry Kailin, but it's your own fault for bringing yourself to his attention, but if you tell *anyone*, you could get us all dismissed! What a Noble does, even if it is as horrible as what he did to you, cannot be complained of. *EVER!*"

"But all he did—"

"STOP!" She shrieked.

I was petrified. I had never seen her so angry or so scared.

"You are relieved from your chores today," she said, tears brimming at the corner of her eyes. "Now, go to your room and pull yourself together." She came closer and put her hands on my shoulders. "I'm sorry Kailin, I really am. But we're just outer-ring servants. No matter what happens, we, *you*, need to let it go."

I looked at the other girls, but neither of them was looking at me.

I looked back at Markly, but she wouldn't meet my eyes. My vision blurred at the edges as my jaw tightened, enough that I thought it would crack.

I turned and ran, but not to my room.

Instead I ran to the classroom that only hours earlier I had sat in and forgotten for a time who I was and what that meant. I collapsed into a chair bathed in Divlan's miserable excuse for winter sunlight.

And cried like I hadn't since that first night when I was brought to this awful world.

CHAPTER
TWENTY-TWO

Time moved forward.

No matter what happened or what my opinion on the matter was, every day the sun would come up, and I would get up as well.

I thought of trying to tell Lady Cathrina of what I had seen in the Hospital attic, but after that first class Lady Cathrina hadn't spent more than two minutes alone with me. She would see me and instruct me before and after class, but she was out every night now at meetings until after I had gone to bed. Other than my chores around her chambers, I might not have had a mistress at all.

Except for the reminder in the gift she had left me.

One evening I had come back to my room to find a Blessing Tree above my bed. It was small, no bigger than my palm, but its metal branches were polished to a silver shine. I was in awe, my fingers tracing the delicate little leaves attached to the swirling branches. Lady Cathrina never mentioned it, and neither did I, and at the time I was grateful for the small symbol of hope.

I wasn't grateful anymore.

I didn't remove it, I wasn't that faithless; but looking at it only reminded me of everything that was wrong. Of Avonly hating me, of the old Healer's words, and of the pair of dark eyes that followed me in my dreams every night.

Because every night I dreamed the same dream, not of blinding lights, but that I was in a forest, always looking for something I desperately needed but couldn't find. Always feeling those dark eyes watching me.

I would throw myself into my work as quickly as I could the next morning.

The only thing in my life that gave me any semblance of peace was Lady Cathrina's classes, but even those were starting to lose their magic.

"UG!" I groaned, opening the workroom door. I had just come from another one of Lady Cathrina's classes and wanted to punch something.

"What happened now, Kailin?" Lancy asked, her eyes not leaving her notebook. She was working again on, well, whatever it was she was always reading and writing about, with a large basket of laundry to be ironed and folded next to her. I didn't need to ask to know it was going to be my amusement for the afternoon.

It had been two weeks since I had barged in here, and through a healthy dose of ignoring the issue, the tension I had always felt with the other girls returned to some sort of normal. I wouldn't say Lancy and I were friends, but at least she acknowledged my existence when she was in the mood.

If anything she would listen—or at least ignore me—so I could vent a little.

"It's just these students!" I said, flopping down in the seat across from her. "They've been given this amazing opportunity and they act like they just don't care!"

"How frustrating for you," she said without looking up. I snapped my mouth shut. Here she was struggling to get some semblance of an education, while I was whining about the miracle that I got to attend an actual class.

I was just as bad as the students I was complaining about.

But I couldn't help it. Even though I should have been elated at being able to attend a class at all, I found that it was actually causing me to lose my mind. Lady Cathrina was an amazing Healer and everything she said sounded like gold to my impoverished ears, but today was the students' second patient-practice day, and though it had gone much better than the first, there was still a bitter, flippant edge to everyone's healing that set my teeth on edge.

Well, almost everyone.

I was startled when Lord Aiden had chosen the patient closest to me. He never even so much as looked in my direction, but I swear I saw his lips turn up into his stupid cocky smile every time my eyes turned his way.

Not that I was looking at him.

I hated him. Even if he was a really talented Healer. A really talented, tall, handsome, smart, perfect blue-eyed Healer.

UG!

I was saved from whatever kindle-brained daydreams would pop uninvited in my head when Markly opened the door.

"Oh good, you're here, Lancy." Markly turned and opened the forbidden cupboard by the door and took out the coin purse.

"Where else would I be?" Lancy's tone was flat, but the bitterness got across easily enough.

"Errands, cleaning, you know, doing your job," Markly said. She came over to the table, and with one finger flipped Lancy's notebook closed.

I thought Lancy would bite her.

"Get that look off your face," Markly said, turning. "I need your help running to the Market."

"Isn't that why we have supply rooms?" Lancy hissed.

"That's the theory, but they decided that I needed to actually start spending my monthly supply allowance—so we're going shopping."

Markly turned toward the door, and with sharp movements Lancy followed, only to stop and look back at me.

"Kailin should come, too."

"What?" Markly and I said in unison.

"She should learn where the Market is, just in case she feels the need to wander outside the walls again."

The story of my failed errand had spread quickly among the servants, not because of any worry as to where I had gone, but because Gabell had used my going to get her more needles as an excuse for why she didn't finish her chores.

Markly stared at me as if she hadn't even noticed I had been sitting there the whole time, then nodded. "Good point. All right, come on, Kailin."

I had to run to keep up with them as they flew down the stairs, and as we walked out into the courtyard I was proud of the fact that I wasn't winded. I turned to head toward the servant's gate, but Markly was making her way to the stables.

"I should have known," Lancy muttered.

"Known what?"

"That Robert would be coming along as well."

I didn't think it was a problem. I liked Robert. He was always nice to me the few times I'd run into him, but when I saw him and Markly walk out of the stables holding hands and gushing an adorableness that turned my stomach, I understood why Lancy wasn't thrilled.

But then someone else followed them out. A step behind

them walked another, dusty blond young man. Lancy gave a yelp, and the young man looked up and froze in his step.

"I hope you don't mind that Robert and Dustin are coming with us," Markly said, her eyes holding a new twinkle I had never seen in them before. "I ran into Dustin on the stairs and he's having the same problems with the supply room, so I invited him to come with us."

Now I understood why Markly had hesitated on letting me come, and suddenly I really didn't want to be there either. Lancy was pointedly looking at the stable's roof and Dustin was pointedly looking at her.

"All right," Robert said, his deep voice setting everything in motion. "Let's get going before someone notices I'm gone."

We made it out onto the street, and this time, surrounded by older servants who knew what they were doing, I moved easily with the flow of traffic. I noted with a twinge of bitterness that we were moving in the opposite direction from the one I had guessed all those weeks ago. Markly and Robert had taken the lead, still holding hands and laughing every now and then.

It was so cute I couldn't help but glare.

I got the fun job of being between Dustin and Lancy, both of whom were as silent as a memory grove. I couldn't decide which couple was making me feel sicker.

"So," I said, turning to Dustin. He looked down at me, as if noticing me for the first time. I tried to think of something to say, but my mind was suddenly blank.

His face softened.

"Yes?"

"When does it start getting warm here?" I blurted, throwing out the first thing that came to my mind. I had forgotten a shawl again, and the chill air was already making goosebumps on my arms.

A gentle smile crossed Dustin's face.

"It won't be anything spectacular, but in a couple more weeks you should start to feel a difference."

We walked in silence again, but I could feel Dustin relax a little.

"Are you liking working at the Academy?" Dustin asked.

"Yes, well, no—I mean—"

"Kailin is from the less civilized parts of Tamerin," Lancy snapped. "She doesn't like the lack of dirt here."

"There's plenty of dirt," I muttered. "I just hate having to clean it up every day."

Dustin laughed. "It must have been a hard adjustment," he continued, his voice brightening, "but I promise that with the warmer weather the trees along the avenues will start getting their leaves again. I'll take you out to see them if you'd like. It's nice to know *some people* still appreciate the small things."

I wanted to tell him that would be great, but he wasn't looking at me anymore. Lancy's cheeks had turned pink, though it could have been from the cold. She met his eyes, and I noted that she didn't have a look of absolute loathing on her face.

Dustin was brooding at her.

"I need to talk to Markly," Lancy suddenly said, rushing forward to join the couple in front of us.

He didn't protest, but I could feel Dustin let out a sigh of either victory or defeat, I couldn't tell which.

"You should be nicer to her," I heard myself say before I could stop.

"What?" Dustin said. The look on his face made me wish I had bit off my tongue instead.

"Lancy." I took a breath, wondering where I had lost my sense of self-preservation. "Stop pushing so hard. It is like you're picking at a scab with your random comments like that."

"I just want her to stop wishing she was still—," he looked away from me, his eyes fixed on Lancy a few yards ahead of us.

"Then show her what she has to be happy about being a Tradesman."

"You're joking, right?"

"I mean," I said, my cheeks flushing. "Show her how her life can still be happy *now*."

"I don't think she wants to be happy," he muttered, but I could see the gears starting to turn in his head.

"So figure out what it is that she actually wants, not the fancy stuff that made her seem happy back then, but the things that really make Lancy feel good about herself. Even as a part of the outer rings, we're still people and can still be happy. Show her that her life isn't completely hopeless."

He might have said something more, but we had caught up to the others.

"Oh no," Markly said.

I didn't understand until I saw the group of soldiers in front of us, almost hidden in the shadows of an alley. They were standing in front of a cart with men tied up inside.

"Are they prisoners?" I asked.

"*Recruits*," Lancy hissed. "We need to get out of here before they see Dustin and Robert."

It was then I noticed there were other soldiers milling around the crowd. A man without a vest and a heavy load on his back was following behind another man in the short vest of a Tradesman. They were too busy focusing on getting through the throng of people to notice the soldiers.

Until they grabbed both the Peasant *and* the Tradesman.

They both tried to break free, the Tradesman yelling about how he wasn't eligible because he wasn't a Peasant, but the soldiers didn't even seem to notice as they hauled the two men toward the cart.

Panic hit the crowd as everyone with a vest shorter than the waist scattered.

"Come on!" Robert yelled, grabbing my hand, running after the others who were already sprinting down an alley. When we were three streets away they finally slowed down.

"What was that?!" I asked.

"Recruiters for the army," Markly answered. "With the war coming, they need to increase their numbers—so they look for *volunteers* from the outer rings to sign up."

"Those didn't look like volunteers to me! Why doesn't someone stop them?"

They all looked at me like I had spoken in another language.

"Who would care?" Dustin said, his voice bitter. "Even among our own ring, no one even notices when injustices happen unless it happens to you."

"People aren't really so heartless, are they?"

I looked around, but none of them would meet my eyes.

"You seem to care," I said to them all.

"We're not really like everyone else," Dustin continued. "But we are smart enough not to stick our necks out where it can get chopped off."

I looked at the people on the street around me. Most of them had run like us, but I didn't see any concern on their faces. In fact, they hardly looked frightened anymore, as if the event hadn't even happened.

As if someone's life hadn't just been ruined.

Only the four people I had thought were heartless before showed any sort of anger at all.

"What Dustin said isn't fully accurate," Robert said in a low voice to me. "There are others out there, others like us who are angry—"

"Don't listen to him, Kailin," Dustin growled. "He'll just fill your head with the lies of his new 'friends.'"

"They will bring justice to the outer rings!"

"They just want to bash in some heads!"

"Stop it both of you!" Markly snapped, looking around fearfully. "If someone heard you two talking—"

"Let's just get to the Market, then get home," Lancy muttered.

The topic was apparently closed, but Dustin and Robert kept throwing glares at each other.

Then we turned a corner.

I wanted to turn and run, because we were now standing in front of the most frightening place I had ever seen.

The Market was enormous.

A towering, six story mass of stone, bodies and *noise* that rang in my head until I thought it would fall off. It was an open structure, with no walls, held up by thick pillars. In front of us on the ground floor were pens and cages, wagons and carts of animals. So many animals I thought I would gag from the smell they were creating. I said a silent prayer of gratitude when Markly led us up a set of stairs.

This level was worse.

My mind ground to a stop, unable to believe that so many people could fit in so small a space. I had thought the side street I had found on my misadventure had been overwhelmingly crowded, but I couldn't even see how someone could force their way into the mass of bodies in front of us.

There were stalls that looked something in between temporary and permanent, made of wood but looking as if they had been there for decades by the amount of wear and clutter decorating each one. Some were no larger than a slab of wood, others had small showrooms you could enter. And there were hundreds of them just on this floor. My breath was shallow as I fought the urge to cover my ears against the din of a thousand haggling voices.

"You all right, Kailin?" Dustin asked, leaning close to make himself heard. "You look pale."

"Are all the floors like this?"

"No, just the lower levels. The upper levels are nicer for the Healers and Merchants—you know—farthest away from the smell of the animals and people like us."

Despite arguing with Robert, he had the same anger and bitterness in his voice.

"All right!" Markly said, clapping her hands together with a big smile on her face. "Kailin, you come with Robert and me, and Lancy, you can help Dustin get his things. We'll meet back here in an hour!"

"Thanks, but I don't need any help." Dustin moved into the crowd, disappearing almost instantly. I smiled as I saw Lancy watch after him.

"Ooookay," Robert said, turning toward the first row of stalls. "Let's get started!" They jumped in, and it was all I could do to force my feet to follow.

Before I knew it Markly was hurrying from stall to stall as if this was what she was born to do. She haggled and bartered better than even Aunt Beredith, and soon we were all loaded with boxes filled with everything we would need for the next month.

We were somewhere in the center of the Market now, the roof too close like a cage of its own with no exit in sight. I had to trust that Markly knew how to get out, when someone started shouting. The fact that it could be heard above everything else was a miracle, but whoever was yelling had a different ring to his voice that made everyone stop what they were doing.

He sounded desperate—no, more than desperate.

Like he was dying.

We turned with the rest of the people around us to see a short, skinny Tradesman shouting and waving his arms at a man who was dressed volumes finer than any of those around him, with a red striped vest down past his waist and shoes so bright they shone in the dim Market light.

He also had a group of armed men behind him.

"That's a Merchant!" Robert growled next to me. "What's he doing down on this level?"

"You can't be serious," the Tradesman yelled again, his voice high in alarm. "I would lose everything! You can't just claim my goods!"

"I'm not claiming them, my good man," the Merchant replied, his voice so slimy I felt the need to take a bath. "I'm offering a fair price and you are agreeing to it."

"You're offering less than a tenth of what everything is worth! I would become poorer than a Peasant! I won't accept it!"

"Very well," the Merchant said stepping back, an unholy grin on his face. "If you insist on giving me all your goods for free then I will be happy to take them."

With a flick of his finger the men behind him surged forward. They looked nothing like the city patrol I had seen outside the Academy's gates. These men looked rough and filthy, each wearing a tunic with an unfamiliar insignia on the front. Two of them grabbed the poor man, holding him back while the other brutes began looting and destroying his stand.

It looked so sad, so hopeless I wanted to look away, but like everyone else I just stood there and watched. Well, not everyone. A large man with an even larger mustache from two stalls down walked calmly up to the Merchant.

"Sorry sir," he grunted, "but I'm afraid that you're going to have to pay for those goods."

"Go back to your pen," the Merchant said, not even looking at him. "Or would you like to make a donation to my House as well?"

"I can't," he said, stepping even closer. "You see, what you're doing is stealing. And there are punishments for thieves in this market."

"Really," the Merchant said, finally turning to him. He should have cowered; this man was easily a head taller and looked as if he could break a post in two over his knee, but instead the finely dressed man sneered and crossed his arms. "You, a Tradesman, are going to *punish* me, a Merchant of the Trading House Calmron?"

"Put the man's goods back, or pick which finger you want broken first." The people around me moved as one, away from the Merchant and the man, wooden doors slamming for those stalls that had them. I took a step back, but Markly grabbed my arm to keep me from getting pulled away in the rush.

"Captain," the Merchant said, sounding bored. "Please remove this *thing*—it's bothering me." The Tradesman didn't back down, didn't even move. Until one of the guards placed a hand on his shoulder.

Then the Trademan's fist flew at the guard's face.

Chaos broke out, screams shattering my ears as a new wave of bodies pushed forward toward the fight, adding their own fists to the mayhem. Someone rammed into me and I dropped my box, screaming as I stumbled forward. Then someone's arm was around my waist, and Robert was pressing me against a closed stall door, flattening me next to Markly and Lancy.

"You all right?" He asked, looking from me to the other two girls.

"Yes," I sputtered, my heart pounding somewhere between my throat and my forehead.

"Good!" He smiled at us, showing all his teeth as something horrible lit up his eyes.

"Robert! No!" Markly lunged to grab him, but he let out a jubilant howl and jumped into the fight.

I turned toward her, expecting her to yell at him to come back, but instead all she did was sigh in annoyance, as if he had just stopped to look at a stall she hadn't planned on visiting and was going to make them late.

"Not again..." Lancy muttered.

Then another shout was raised, yelling that the City Guard was on its way.

"Come on," Markly said. "We'll wait for him at the edge of the Market. We need to get out of here before those pruners get here." She grabbed my arm and pulled me into the tumult of bodies, some moving away from the fight, others fleeing the approaching guards.

"What's happening!?" I shouted as we crushed our way down the stairs to stop in front of an alley across from the Market.

"It's another riot!" Markly yelled back, holding on to my left arm as Lancy gripped the other. "I'm sure that wasn't what that man was planning when he stepped in, but it sure is one now! Ugh, this happens almost every time we go out, but I guess it's good for Robert—helps to get out his frustration so maybe he'll stop complaining for two minutes."

"Frustration?" I asked, my voice shrill. We weren't moving fast enough and Lancy pulled me and Markly back between two stalls as a guard and what looked like a Peasant, from his frayed brown clothes, ran past us.

"Come on, Kailin," Markly said. "You're a *Peasant*! You of all people should hate being stuck at the bottom, where the inner rings can do whatever they want and you can't do anything about it."

"Not enough to join a street fight!"

"Even after what Lord Aiden did to you?" Her face was cold. It was the first and only time she had brought up what she had thought happened to me. She said to never talk about it to anyone, but maybe being here, outside the Academy with people from the outer rings fighting, made her bold.

I didn't feel bold, I felt like shrinking at her words. At the truth in them of what she believed Lord Aiden could do and get away with.

What any Noble could get away with.

Or Lesser Noble, or Merchant or Healer.

What was I to them but a nameless brown dress?

By The Great One, what was this world I was now in? I thought it was just a slap here and there, an order to clean and a fear of getting dismissed. I didn't know, hadn't even guessed....

Tears stung my eyes as I wished for something I'd never thought I would.

I wished I could go home.

Markly must have seen it because she wrapped her arms around me, pulling me to her.

"That's why Robert's fighting," she whispered. "We can't talk about it, never seek justice, but out here, where there are so many other Tradesmen and Peasants...It won't make a difference in the end, but sometimes it is good to be angry."

I nodded my head—and banished Lord Aiden's smile from my mind.

He was just a faceless monster, like those running past me

to arrest the men and women who were fighting for me, even if they didn't know my name.

The fight had spread until it seemed like no matter which way we turned there were men and women attacking each other, some with fists, a few with swords and knives, others with pots, boards and anything else they could use as a weapon. The Merchant's personal guards had been joined by Divlan's, and between the two of them they were leaving a wake of broken heads and bones. But the outer rings refused to back down, their numbers giving them an advantage. The look on their faces was one of defiance and pleasure as they beat the guards into pulp. Like they were enjoying it.

And it dawned on me that Markly was wrong. They weren't unselfishly fighting for injustice, they were simply letting out their hate. I felt sick, the light darkening, and I could almost see the poison pumping through their veins as dark as what the inner rings felt for us. There were no heroes in this fight, only thugs looking to spill blood.

Heal our people from a worse illness than death.

The old Healer's words rang in my head, and I understood.

This wasn't a sickness of the body, though there were plenty of broken ones surrounding me now. This was a sickness that ran deeper.

Much deeper.

I gasped as I doubled over out of Markly's arms, my chest tightening like someone had reached into my chest to pull out my heart.

No! Not now!

And the world exploded in blue light.

There were thousands of them, all around me, swirling from one person to the next, the lines they drew behind them snapping one after the other.

It was chaos reborn, reflecting perfectly the flaming

passion of those fighting for no other reason than their need to fight. I screamed and fell to the ground, but just as quickly as they'd come, the lights were gone.

I couldn't breathe even though my chest was heaving, my vision splotchy and racing from darkness to a brightness that was even worse. I thought my rib cage would break, my heart beating so hard, and I was boiling in my own sweat. Someone grabbed my arm, and I screamed again, batting away their hands.

"Kailin!" Someone yelled. "Get ahold of yourself! We need to get out of here!"

"But the lights!"

"Lights?"

"I DON'T WANT THEM!"

The faces of the two girls above me looked at each other, and I wished these strangers would just leave me alone so I could properly cower.

"Kailin," the blond one said, squatting in front of me. "Kailin, just breathe. Did you hit your head?"

"But, the lights..."

"The lanterns aren't even lit."

Then I knew them.

Markly. Lancy.

How did I forget? *Why* did I forget?

And the horrible, destroying realization—they hadn't seen the lights.

It was only me.

I really was losing my mind.

A familiar yell shook me out of my stupor, as all of us turned to see Robert tackle a city guard only yards away from us. He seemed to be making progress rearranging the man's face when more men in city uniforms grabbed him from behind, holding him while the first punched him in the gut.

Markly screamed and tried to run to him, but Lancy held her back.

Then suddenly Dustin was there, and he was holding a very large stick. He knocked out the first guard, but one of the other two punched him hard in the face. He rocked back, but it was enough to give Robert an opening to kick at the distracted guard who was still holding him, sending him to the ground. Then he was on the last one, pushing him into a cart full of chickens. For a moment our corner of the universe was still.

"ROBERT!" Markly screamed, and both he and Dustin came hobbling over to where we were hiding. I scrambled to my feet as they got closer.

"I think we need to get the ladies back to the Academy," Dustin said, his face purple and bleeding. His shirt was torn on one sleeve and he had a bad limp, but as he stood next to Lancy he tried to hold himself tall.

If he was trying to impress her it didn't work.

"YOU SHRUB!" Lancy screamed, then she snatched his hand and turned to run. The rest of us followed.

We didn't stop until we made it to the stables inside the Academy gates, hiding in one of the stalls.

Then a new chaos broke out.

"You stupid, irresponsible, bark-stripping shrub!" Lancy yelled, as if she would begin beating Dustin herself.

"I'm sorry, Lancy, if I offended you," Dustin said, his own face furious, "but that guy was getting robbed—"

"I don't care about your social justice! I care about you putting yourself in danger! You could have been killed!" The words were out before she could take them back. Dustin's face instantly went slack, his eyes wide as he consumed her whole. Lancy didn't look away this time.

And she was still holding his hand.

She quickly dropped it and stepped back, hugging herself.

"I mean, I just," she floundered, and I could see tears start to come. Dustin looked like he had been hit in the head again, his mouth hanging open in a way that was both stupid and cute at the same time.

They stood there in silence, until Dustin choked out, "Um, my leg kinds of hurts, a lot. Can you help me to my room?"

Lancy didn't answer, but with careful movements she slid under Dustin's arm and the two of them began the slow walk toward the servants' door.

"Well," Markly breathed, her voice light and airy, as she started babying Robert as if he had simply tripped while doing his work. "I couldn't have planned that any better myself!"

"They'll be together by the end of the week with you working on them," Robert said, suddenly grabbing Markly and pulling her into his lap. She laughed and kissed him, not seeming to care that he was still bleeding.

I ran from the stall, feeling sick again, only to remember I couldn't go toward the door yet. Lancy and Dustin were still there, her constant stream of chastisement easily heard from this far away, and his arm holding her tight.

TWENTY-THREE

I don't know how to accurately express how difficult my life became.

I was used to having to work from morning until long after dinner. I was used to the other girls throwing their chores on me. But now Lancy was a nightmare, her emotionless reptile-like demeanor replaced with the frantic spontaneity of a cornered rodent.

One minute she was pacing and wringing her hands, the next she was yelling, and then quiet and agitated again.

Markly was loving it, and she let Lancy get away with *everything*.

Including not doing any work. Which meant I now had to do all her chores on top of mine.

Boys were the stupidest things to have ever been invented, if they could make someone as levelheaded as Lancy turn into a useless, annoying drain on my life.

But all this could have been manageable if I had been getting any sleep at night. The return of my nightmares made sure that didn't happen. Neither Lancy nor Markly had asked about what had happened to me in the Market, and I had done my best to forget it for my own sanity's sake. I might have succeeded, but whenever I closed my eyes at night the lights would be there, worse than ever before, the forest now infested with them as I ran, never knowing if I was trying to escape or follow them.

And always the sense that I wasn't alone.

To say I hadn't been sleeping well would have been an understatement.

Days after the Market incident, I had just finished Lancy's mending when it was finally time to leave for Lady Cathrina's class, my only moment of peace anymore. As if I had been under water, I burst from the servants' entrance to the hallways, taking in a deep breath of air.

I was reviewing the details of her last lecture in my mind as I marched down the stairs between the seventh and sixth floors, when my concentration was shattered by the hollow chiming of the Academy clock, followed by the familiar bang of classroom doors flying open. I had been hoping to get to the sixth floor before anyone saw me out of the servant halls, but suddenly I was surrounded by bodies moving up and down the stairs.

And that is when I heard her laugh.

It was still far off, but my eyes instinctively looked up, trying to find her face in the crowd.

Avonly was with some of her new friends, all done up pretty in their colorful gowns, holding their books and moving toward me up the stairs. They were laughing about something when Avonly looked my way. Our eyes met, and I could feel the hurt and anger begin to build up inside me. I wanted her to know that I still hadn't forgiven her, but what I saw in her eyes made me stop walking. They were the same color as the stream by our village when it froze over in the winter, unmoving yet oh so dangerous.

I put my head down as we passed. Then there was a foot, and stone scraping at my face, tearing the sleeve of my dress and bruising my arms and legs as I fell to the sixth-floor landing. I looked back up the stairs in rage, even though I already knew who had tripped me. But Avonly wasn't looking at me. She was blowing her nose on a handkerchief, then dropped it, letting it float to the step above me.

"Take care of that, Peasant girl."

Avonly and her new, sophisticated friends continued up the stairs, their laughter fading away. I couldn't move as the surge of students continued to flow around me as if I weren't even there.

The last student had left, but I didn't move from my seat. My left knee stung, my right forearm had a purple bruise the size of my palm, and I knew I had several scratches along my cheek, but it was the pain in my chest that kept me from standing up.

Lady Cathrina had raised an eyebrow at my appearance, but she was gone before the first student was out the door.

I didn't care. I couldn't. It hurt too much.

The light, white and cold, was coming in the classroom at a sharp angle through the long, thin windows, but did nothing to heat the side of my face. I couldn't believe the warming of the seasons Dustin spoke of would ever come. I turned my head, letting the light fall fully on my face, and looked out into the gardens below. It was still too cold for most students to spend much time outside, but there were a few faithfully tending to the plants the Academy and Hospital would use for healing. My heart ached to go out and join them, to feel freshly turned soil between my fingers. Maybe then I would feel like myself again.

There were flower and herb beds and groupings of trees all accented by low walls and benches. There was even a greenhouse at the far end for growing plants needing the extra warmth.

"Hagsfoot is a large root that has a very small, deadlooking stem found in the desert plateaus of south Tamerin."

The words came back like a whisper on a breeze, wrapping around me like the blanket my aunt had given me as a child, which always kept me warm.

"The dry weather makes most of the plant grow downward so as to avoid having its moisture evaporate," I recited, the words tasting sweet on my tongue. "When digging it up, use gloves, as the outer layer can cause—"

"A painful rash, which is no joke. I thought my skin would melt off when I grabbed one by mistake last year."

"Lord Aiden!" I shrieked, jumping out of my chair so quickly it fell over backwards.

He was standing by the door diagonal from me. His hand was still on the doorknob, as if he had just shut it, his other hand holding a notebook.

"I'm used to people being excited when I enter a room," he said letting go of the doorknob and rubbing his ear, "but I don't think anyone has ever screamed before."

"What are you doing here?!" I didn't want to see him. Not now, with everything that was happening. All I wanted was my life to feel *normal* for just a few minutes.

And the way he was looking at me was anything but normal.

"I'm sorry to have startled you," he said moving across the front of the room to the side lined by the windows. "I just want to talk, and you're really hard to track down. The last two times you had already left by the time I made it back here."

Not normal at all.

"I need to go." I moved down the row at the back of the room away from him.

"What?" He said mirroring my movement along the front row. "That's all you have for me? No witty retort that could end you up in a cell?"

I reached the end of the row and I turned to make a break for it, but Lord Aiden was there at the end of the aisle, blocking me.

Just like his ring.

Just like the hopes and dreams the inner rings blocked from those outside them. I thought of the Peasants and Tradesmen being "volunteered" for the war, of the man in the Market getting robbed legally, of the poverty I saw in the slums I got lost in; and I remembered Markly's accusation of what she thought this boy had done to me and how scared she was.

But I wasn't afraid.

All I wanted to do was push him out a window.

All I could see was his nice clothes and his long vest.

"Fine," I said, my hands balling into fists at my side. "I don't have the time or patience for any of your *kindle-brain* antics today. Your behavior is more in line with a deranged stalker than a sound-minded human and makes me wonder if you were dropped on your head as a child or if stupidity just runs in your family."

His mouth set into a hard line at the mention of his family, and I wondered if I had gone too far; then I remembered that I wasn't supposed to see him as human.

What did I care if I offended him? Wasn't that what he'd just asked me to do?

"Is that really the best you can do?" His eyes were hard, but his mouth curled up at the corner.

"Believe it or not, I don't actually want to end up dismissed." I moved down the aisle toward him, planning on pushing my way through if needed. "Now that you've gotten your fix for your weird addiction, I'm going to go."

"Wait," he said. "Please. Don't go."

Please?

And just like that he was human again. A boy again.

Lord Aiden stepped closer, closing me in with the table on one side and the wall on the other. I had an escape path behind me, but I couldn't bring my feet to step backwards.

"Why are you doing this to me?" I asked.

"I told you. I want to talk to you."

"No, I'm not just talking about today." I finally found the strength to step back. "Why are you always following me?"

"I'll tell you if you tell me why you are always staring at me during class."

"I do not!" I sputtered, then turned down the first row and pushed in a chair, as if that's what I had been meaning to do all along. I didn't have time for this, and if he wasn't going to let me leave, then I had a classroom to tidy up! Then I realized something. "And how would you even know I was, unless you were looking back!"

"I'm a Noble, I can look at whatever I want." He sauntered after me, as if he was just out for a stroll instead of being weird and creepy. "Besides, you are more interesting to look at than the walls or Lady Cathrina's 'don't be an ass' lectures."

I let out a laugh, then covered my mouth quickly with my hand, my sleeve falling down to my elbow from being torn on my way down the stairs. A look of triumph still spread over his face at making me laugh. Then it faded, his eyebrows coming together as his hand reached out and grabbed my wrist. My heart shook in a thousand ways, both horrifying and embarrassing, but he wasn't looking at my face. He was pulling back my torn sleeve and studying the purplish bruise and scrapes.

"How did you get this?" he asked, studying my arm.

His grip was so different than when he had dragged me through the halls. It was still firm, but held a gentle give, like if I pulled away he would let me go.

So I did—and he did.

"I fell," I said, pulling my arm to my chest.

"Right." Something sharp sparked in his eyes.

I turned, pushing in the next chair.

"I'm a servant. You get lots of bruises when you're cleaning."

"And the scrapes on your face? Did a mop do that to you too?"

"Why do you care?" I snapped, spinning around to face him. "Why would you, a high and mighty *Noble*, care about a Peasant like me?"

"I don't!"

"Then why are you following me?!"

"I DON'T KNOW!" He looked at the back wall and wiped his face, just as he had done the last time he cornered me. "All I know," he said, turning back to me, "is that I want to talk to you. Can't you just humor me and not run away again? Constantly being on the lookout for you is starting to impact my social life."

I wanted to look away, I wanted to run—but he held me in place without even touching me.

His eyes were so blue...No, it wasn't just the color. They had so much need in them, but that couldn't be right. The only thing he was looking at was me.

He's a Noble...and he is so close I could pretend to trip and he would catch me and—

No! Stop it, Kailin! He's a Noble...and I'm just a Peasant.

I'm just Kailin.

Rot, my head hurt.

He took a step forward. Then another, slowly as if he were afraid I would try and bolt again. Then Lord Aiden was in front of me, looking down at me as I looked up at him.

"Please stop," I moaned, my eyes stinging. "I'm having a really bad day. I'm very tired and you're only giving me a headache."

"Would you like something from the pharmacy?" he asked. "I have access as a fourth-year. Tellow-leaf oil is great for headaches, which you probably already know since you apparently have the first-year texts memorized, or you could try—"

"STOP!" I yelled, making him jump. "Just go back to your perfect, pompous life and leave us rot-covered Peasants alone!"

A week of no sleep and too much work had ruined my self-control. I was so tired, both inside and out, that I just collapsed into the nearest chair and hid my face in my arms as unwelcome sobs poured out of me. I didn't want Lord Aiden caring about my headaches.

I wanted Avonly to care.

I wanted to be a student and make Aunt Beredith proud.

I wanted a life without blue lights and old Healers and dark eyes that followed me in my dreams.

A life that made me want to wake up in the morning.

The chair next to mine scraped back.

I had thought he would leave, but I could feel him warming the air next to me.

When my shoulders finally stopped shaking and I could breathe normally again, I turned my head, peeking out. Lord Aiden was looking at me, his eyebrows almost touching in his concern.

Then he looked down and pulled something out of his pocket.

He held out a handkerchief.

I stared at it, not sure what to do.

"You blow your nose with it."

"Is that allowed?"

"Is anyone watching?"

I took it, and tried to carefully clean my face in a dignified manner, but there really is no good way to go about getting snot out of your nose.

"I'll wash it and return it to you tomorrow," I said folding it into squares.

"Don't be ridiculous. There are servants for that—well—other servants." He grabbed it and shoved it into his pocket.

"Thank you," I said. "I still don't want you here, though." The corner of his mouth moved up again.

"I got that impression, but I'm annoying and arrogant and am going to do what I want." He looked down at the notebook in front of him, his fingers playing with the top corner. I had forgotten that he had been holding it. "I don't know why I keep running into you, following you. You're right, I shouldn't care. I've never noticed servants before, not in any meaningful way. They're just sort of there, like furniture." I snorted and it made the corner of his mouth go up again. "The only sane reason I can think of is that you're a novelty in my otherwise dull life."

I knew I should be insulted. Even if I didn't want him to care, no one wants to be sought after for being a *novelty*.

But then he smiled, and my heart started to pound.

Maybe being a novelty wasn't such a bad thing.

"I thought we went over this," I said, folding my arms again and looking at them. "I'm not special or interesting. I'm just Kailin."

"Kailin," he said, rolling over the word easily like he had said it a thousand times. "I've never known a Peasant's name before. It's pretty."

I slammed my head into my arms and groaned.

"What!?" he said. "What did I say now to make you mad at me?! I'm *trying* to be nice!"

"I know!" I said my voice muffled in my arms. "That's the problem! No one is nice to me—no one has *ever* been nice to me, except the one person in the entire world whose opinion I care about who thought it would be fun to trip me just to show off to her new friends!"

He didn't say anything, and when I peeked back out, he was leaning his forehead on his hand, his eyes closed.

"I knew you didn't just fall," he said, opening his eyes at me.

They were so blue, and I finally figured out why I kept being drawn to them. They were the same color as the sky in the summer, so much like home and safety and long afternoons when I could let myself dream.

Let myself hope.

And it came back to me, that same feeling I had in that horrible alleyway all those weeks ago. That I could trust him.

"Her name is Avonly." I couldn't believe what I was saying, but somehow the words came out anyway. "She is—was—my best friend. My only friend. We had studied for the entrance exam together our entire lives, played together as children when no one else would come near me. Then she got her scholarship, and everything—changed."

"Scholarship?"

"The examiners come to our village every year, and all the Peasant fifteen-year-olds take the exam."

He opened his mouth, then shut it.

"I've never heard of anything like that."

"Maybe you're not as knowledgeable as you think you are."

We stared at each other, until he took a breath and looked at the notebook in front of him again, playing with the corner.

"So this friend of yours, she thought she was too good for you?" He looked back at me all serious. "I might have some practice in that category."

I snorted a laugh and he smiled.

It made me want to smile too, but I didn't.

"That was the original reason for her ditching me, but then we found each other later and she apologized, and I believed her. She was having trouble with her classes, and I began helping her after my chores were done. It was nice, just like we'd always imagined, minus the whole guilting me into cheating for her."

"Ah." He said, his jaw set. "That makes more sense."

When he didn't say anything more I continued. "But then we had a disagreement over...something important, and I couldn't stand who she had become anymore. I hadn't seen her before today..." I looked away from him at the windows and their weak light. "I guess it is my fault I'm alone again."

I could hear him playing again with the cover of the notebook. The methodical softness of his finger running on the underside, then the sharp snap of the pages pushing themselves back down past the edge of his finger.

"You aren't the only one alone here."

He said it so softly I barely heard him. In fact, I wasn't even sure he had meant for me to.

"What do you mean? You have lots of friends. I see them

fawning all over you, and your—" I took a gulp of air. "And you have your girlfriend—"

"My *what?*" His eyes were wide as if I had just bit him.

"That girl," I said, my cheeks turning pink at the memory. "The one you were kissing and you went into that classroom—"

Just like this one.

"Oh," he said, looking down at his notebook, again. "She's not my girlfriend. And all those *friends* of mine are just friends with my title. They only care about me as long as they think I'll grant them and their families favors someday. Even the other Nobles see me as only a potential alliance, not someone to talk to about the weather."

"The weather is boring. No one wants to talk about that. You shouldn't hold people accountable for trying to avoid boredom."

He chuckled and looked back at me. "So you see, it is refreshing to have someone treat me like a person, for a change. I was serious when I said I wanted to talk to you. It makes me feel real, if that makes any sense."

It did. More than he could ever have guessed.

"I suppose talking to you is nice as well," I said, finally allowing myself a small smile. "It's nice to feel like I exist, beyond just someone to shove all your chores on because you're too busy swooning over a boy."

"You're joking, right?"

"No! There is *so* much drama in my workroom right now I almost wish I were assigned kitchen duty!"

He laughed with me, and I felt like I could float away.

"You're kind of an enigma, you know," he said, his eyes bright. "You're a servant, but for all intents and purposes you are taking Lady Cathrina's class. You have no formal education, but are more knowledgeable than a second-year. And now you've decided to leave your evil best friend who is two rings inside you, and are hurt about it."

"You're missing one other obviously unordinary occurrence in my life," I said leaning on my hand, my elbow on the table.

"And what is that?" he said mimicking me.

"For some reason, a Noble has taken an interest in me."

He froze, then looked down at the table. He had mirrored me perfectly, complete with his other hand on the table, so close to mine.

"I guess you're right about that," he said, pulling his hand down onto his lap. "Like I said, I like puzzles, and you are by far the most puzzling thing that has ever happened in my life."

"Is that a compliment or an insult?"

"I'll let you know."

The Academy clock vibrated through the walls.

"Rot!" I yelled jumping to my feet and running to the front of the room. "Markly's going to kill me! I need to go."

"Wait!" He said following me. "There was another reason I was looking for you."

I stopped and turned to him, frustrated all over again that he was making my life harder. He looked down at the notebook in his hands, his eyebrows pulled together again. Apprehension spun in my chest, and I wished he would smile again.

"I wanted to know," he said, pushing it out toward me, "if you would like to borrow this."

I reached for it, confused. As I wrapped my fingers around the edge closest to me I saw drawn on the cover a doodled femur bone.

My eyes shot up. He was looking down at me again with a seriousness that made a shiver run up my spine.

"Your class notes?" I breathed.

"I know you know everything about herbology, but I didn't

know how good your anatomy was. I still have my notes from the first year if you're interested."

"I would like that very much," I whispered. He hadn't let go of his side of the notebook yet, even though my hand was already on them, and without meaning to, our fingers touched. Neither one of us breathed, and the moment seemed to last forever.

Then I pulled a little harder, and he let them go.

"Thank you, Lord Aiden," I said, taking a step back.

"Aiden," he said, his eyes suddenly wild. "I want you to call me Aiden."

He could have knocked me out of the window and I wouldn't have been more shocked.

"But, I couldn't—"

"Yes you can!" he said, stepping forward again until his chest was almost touching mine. "Yes," he breathed, "you can."

And something pulled inside me. Not the normal *pull* that made me want to cry from the intrusion in my chest, but something soft yet steady. Something that made me feel like the ground under me was solid and wouldn't let me fall.

"Thank you, *Aiden*," I said, and he smiled like the sun breaking through a cloudy day. I could almost feel the warmth of it on my skin. "You know," I said stepping out of his shadow. "I'm not *actually* a student, so I might have some questions about these notes of yours."

"I could help you with that," he said eagerly. "That is, if you want my help."

I had reached the door, and I couldn't have stopped the smile on my face even if I had wanted to. Which I didn't.

"I would like that very much."

"I can do lunch tomorrow. Unless you have more mop appointments."

"I think I could reschedule." I reached for the handle, but

he got to it first, opening it just wide enough for me to slip through. "Until then, my lady," he said with a bow, his eyes never leaving mine.

"Until then. Aiden."

I left with the memory of his smile as I slipped into the hallway, his notes tight against my chest.

TWENTY-FOUR

The clock sounded up through the walls and resonated with the anxiety I was feeling, igniting the familiar bang as classroom doors opened up and down the halls with freed students.

I had read several pages of the notes he had given me the day before and it was *wonderful*. I had absorbed the knowledge in them like it was food and I had never eaten before. The fact that I would get a distracting flutter in my stomach whenever I thought about how much I liked his handwriting had little to do with the fact that I had pored over every word and sketch until the oil in my lantern burned out. And the excitement I was feeling now was solely based on my need to have him explain some sections. It had nothing to do with the fact that I got to see Aiden again so soon.

Aiden.

Just Aiden.

My stomach did a little flip.

I slowly made my way down the hall with a bucket in my hands, Aiden's notes safely tucked into the bottom. I was only a few yards away from the classroom where Lady Cathrina taught, but it felt like miles with the massive number of students milling around me. When the last of the students came out through the door and passed me, I hurried the remaining distance and slipped into the empty classroom.

Well, what was supposed to be an empty classroom.

"Kailin!" said a warm, commanding voice. I froze by the door, shocked into immobility by the appearance of Healer Arios in front of me. "What a surprise! I've been meaning to ask Lady Cathrina how you were doing since becoming her assistant, but now that you're here you can tell me yourself."

He was standing at the front of the room, erasing what must have been his lecture from the chalkboard. When he saw the panic I was doing a terrible job of hiding, he froze as well.

"Is everything all right? Did something happen? I didn't think Lady Cathrina had her class today—"

"I'm fine!" I said a little too loudly, then taking a deep breath continued. "I mean, yes, I'm loving being Lady Cathrina's assistant. And she doesn't have class today; I just forgot something I'd left here yesterday and came to look for it."

"Oh good," Healer Arios smiled, finishing up the last of the board. "For a second there I could have sworn that something terrible had happened from the look on your face. You know that you can relax when you're around me. I'm not like the other Healers."

He was being so nice, and everything from his open and friendly manner to the kind, supportive look in his eye spoke the truth of what he'd just said. I could feel myself smile back.

"That's better," he said. "You have a nice smile, and should wear it more often."

"Thank you."

"Don't be silly. I'm a Healer, facts are important to me, and your smile is a fact."

"No," I said. "Thank you for treating me like a real person."

He had turned to the small table at the front of the room where his teaching notes were stacked in a neat pile, picking them up while looking at me, his face now grave.

"To me, Kailin, everyone's a real person."

Then the door opened and Aiden slipped through it. When he saw me he grinned, and completely missed the panicked warning in my eyes.

"Oh good, you're here already. I was worried I would have to…" Then he froze, the same hysteria suddenly reflecting in his own eyes.

"Hello, Lord Aiden," Healer Arios said, his face serious, as he looked from me to Aiden and back again.

"Healer Arios! Hello! I mean, good morning—afternoon, I mean." I thought for a moment that he would choke, his face was so red.

"It's afternoon now, I believe," Healer Arios said cooly.

"Yes!" Aiden said, trying desperately to regain some composure. He quickly shot a look at me, but I was just as close to unraveling as he was. "Oh look! A servant! I mean, of course it's a servant, there are servants everywhere, no reason there shouldn't be a servant here too. And I was just here looking for something, something that I left here yesterday, in class, because that's why I'm here."

Healer Arios glanced at me again, and his eyes held a humor and suspicion that made me both embarrassed and nervous at the same time.

"Well then, Lord Aiden," he said, moving toward the door. Aiden jumped out of his way as if dodging a runaway carriage. "And Kailin," he added, nodding at me, "I'll leave you both to look for whatever it is you both left here yesterday." I could swear he was trying not to laugh, but then his eyes found Aiden's and a hardness came into them that made me feel sorry for the young man. "And I hope that you're careful with whatever it is once you find it."

Aiden's red face paled instantly. As Healer Arios left the classroom he caught my eye again and winked. Everything clicked into place, and I suddenly knew with certainty that his warning to Aiden had nothing to do with meeting a servant secretly—it had to do with meeting *me* secretly.

I could feel a smile come across my face at the thought. I turned and sat down on the table in the front row, setting my bucket down next to me, elated that I could pretend that this was where I was meant to be.

"Stop smiling. He knows about us now." Aiden was still standing where Healer Arios had immobilized him.

"Oh, he knows, but we don't need to worry."

"Weren't you paying attention?" Aiden snapped, a wild panic in his eyes as his hands pulled at his hair. "He may not have said anything flat out, but he clearly knows what's going on!"

I had never seen Aiden so upset, and I quickly got up and rushed over to him, only to remember at the last minute not to actually pull his hands away from his abused hair.

"Aiden, it's going to be ok," I said, trying my hardest to project a calm I was beginning to lose myself. His mouth was set in a hard line as an unseen tension took over his frame. I saw behind his eyes his brain running faster than a humming-bird's wings.

Then it stopped.

"I can't do this," he whispered, and spun around toward the door.

"No!" I shouted, but he was already there opening it. In one movement I threw my shoulder against the wood, slamming it shut.

"Get away from the door," Aiden said, his jaw tight. He was

looking down at his hand still wrapped around the handle. It was beginning to turn white from the fierceness of his grip. There was so little space between us, but Aiden's face was anything but the one from my daydreams. He looked scared, more scared than I had ever seen anyone before—and I could see the proud, heartless Noble crawl across his face.

"He isn't going to tell anyone," I pleaded, my entire frame trembling.

I suddenly had a flash of memory of a hand coming across my face, my entire body spinning, then crying out at the impact of Healer Stevero's strike, and the disgusted, heartless look he had given me.

The same one now on Aiden's face.

"You don't know that," he said, finally looking down at me. I closed my eyes against the pain I knew would suddenly scream across my face, but it didn't come. Instead there was a gasp and the sound of him stumbling back, crashing into the first-row table. When I opened my eyes he was staring at me as if I was the one who had struck him, his chest rising and falling like waves in a pond during a storm.

I wasn't doing much better.

The light suddenly changed, a cloud moving from the sun or some other heavenly intervention, and the rays through the window became warm on his tan face, his dark hair falling off to one side of his forehead, the fabric of his shirt straining as his strong arms grasped the edge of the table as if he would fall without it there. He looked so handsome I thought my heart would break.

And here I was, still pressed against the door with my messy black hair in a loose braid down my back, wearing the only brown dress I owned. I had always thought it the least flattering thing in the world and just one of a thousand things that made me undesirable, but Aiden was looking at me like I was anything but that. It wasn't a fleeting glance or a penetrating glare, but a scrutiny that stripped away all the walls I had, as if I were more than just a person passing through his life, but someone he desperately needed. I felt exposed, as if I weren't wearing anything at all.

"Please don't look at me like that," I whispered, turning my face away from his toward the windows. I had to fight the urge to pull my dress tighter around my neck.

"What?" Aiden croaked.

"You're looking at me like—" I stopped, not sure what I was going to say. "Never mind. And calm down, you don't need to worry about Healer Arios."

"Why not?!" The hysteria was back in his voice. "Didn't you see that look he gave me?"

"Aiden," I said, and the sound of his name only made his eyes more manic. One hand came up to cover his eyes as his head bent forward, his breathing heavy in hyperventilation. "Will you calm down and listen to me?!" I rushed over to stand in front of him, but he still hid behind his hand. "That look he gave you wasn't a warning that he was going to tell anyone. It was to warn you against..." A sudden warmth filled me, and I couldn't tell if it was from the thought of someone actually protecting me or from what his warning implied.

"If it wasn't from a threat to reveal me, then from what?"

His other hand came up and joined the first, completely covering his face now.

Reveal?

I hesitated, weighing the risks, then disregarding them as I slowly took both his hands in mine, gently pulling them away from his face. He opened his eyes, and stared at me like I was some sort of salvation from whatever nightmare he believed his world to be. His hands were warm, calloused, and as they instinctively returned my grip I could feel how strong they were as well.

"Healer Arios likes me," I whispered, holding his hands a little tighter. "His warning was about protecting me, not threatening you, because to him I'm just a girl, and you're just a boy."

Recognition flashed behind his eyes, and the fear that had consumed them shifted to a new understanding—one that made me feel just as panicked as before.

"Oh," was all he said. He let go of my hands and I dropped his as well, turning my eyes toward the wall as his turned toward the windows.

We stayed that way for I don't know how long, until I took a deep breath in and turned to face him.

"I got through a good chunk of the notes you gave me yesterday," I said. "But there were some places that I didn't follow what you were saying."

I calmly walked around the table and sat down next to where I had placed my bucket. Aiden's eyes followed me, the corner of his mouth moving up slightly as I pulled out his notes from my bucket.

"Which parts?" His voice was still flat, but there was an underlying warmth to it that was promising.

At least he wasn't trying to run away.

"Here, with the rib cage," I said, turning to the right page. He scooted back to where he was fully on top of the table and turned his body to see the page I was pointing to.

"Yeah, that was a confusing lecture, if I remember right." He suddenly swiveled around, smoothly sliding into the seat next to mine. It was so quick and fluid that all I could do was stare. "Go back a page and I'll take you through what Healer Clara was trying to say."

I woke myself up from staring and turned the page back.

The light shifted from one window to the next, indicating the passing of the hour. During that time I became lost in his explanations and my questions, the strange ecstasy I always seemed to feel when I immersed myself in something I loved. I almost didn't even feel the way being so close to him affected the rhythm inside my chest.

Almost.

"Do you need me to go over any of that again?" he asked.

"No, I think I got it."

Rot, I should have played dumb. Then he would have had to explain it again and we would have had to stay here longer and—

"You sure," he prodded, "it's a lot to remember."

I sighed, letting go of the daydream.

"I have a good memory."

"Oh yeah," he smiled. "I had forgotten how brilliant you are."

"I'm not brilliant," I muttered looking down at the notebook in my hands.

"You're right," he breathed, and I could feel myself hurt even though I had just told him as much a second before. "It is too early to tell anything like that—all we know for certain is that you're crazy."

"What?!" I snapped, looking back at him, but instead of an accusation there was only humor. "Well, if I'm crazy, then so are you!"

"I won't argue with that," he said, stretching his arms over his head. "I hope you know that I gave up a very productive nap to help you out. If that isn't insanity I don't know what is." He yawned and I laughed.

It felt good.

I hadn't laughed very much lately.

"Thank you for your sacrifice, oh great and powerful lord!"

I stood up and exaggerated a curtsy. "My gratitude knows no bounds!"

He gave me a look that wasn't quite a glare, but it held the same accusation.

I laughed again, then turned back to the table, putting the precious notebook back into the bucket. "I really am grateful," I said, almost a whisper. "You don't have to do this—and if you think it is too dangerous—"

"Don't worry about it," he said, standing as well. He didn't say anything, only watched me until I had it well hidden.

"I'm sorry," he said. "For earlier. I don't know what came over me. You must have been scared to death. You *looked* scared to death..."

"Not as scared as you looked." I turned my head to look at him and swallowed a gasp. His face was only inches from mine, his eyes both kind and confused and beautiful.

And oh so serious.

"I won't hurt you," Aiden said, earnestness pouring into every word, as if he weren't just stating a fact but also making an oath. "No matter what happens, I want you to know that I will *never* hurt you."

"I know," I whispered before I could stop the words. But it was true. I did know, and I was suddenly gripped with fear at how much I trusted this young man who was still a stranger. My reply must have been what he wanted, because his mouth tweaked up into that half smile I had started longing for.

"Good," Aiden said, straightening up, and as if a bag had been removed from over my head I could breathe again. "Because I think I need more time to analyze you and I would hate it if I had to track you down again."

"Oh really?"

"I don't give up my puzzles that easily."

I laughed as I walked around the end of the table, my back

to the window so the light fell around me. His eyes brightened, and I could feel myself stand up a little straighter.

"So all of this, the notes and the tutoring, isn't from some sense of ring guilt or social philanthropy?"

"Of course not," he said, laughing as well. "I'm a rich, spoiled Noble—everything I do is about me."

"Good," I said smiling. "So that means I get to use you for my own purposes as well, right?"

His smile took on a new edge, and I suddenly wished I were dead.

"To teach me anatomy! That's what I meant—I mean—no!" I could feel my face flame in embarrassment while Aiden laughed. I ran over to the door, suddenly desperate to get away. In one motion he vaulted the table and was leaning against the door, his smile stretching from one side of his face to the other.

"You're funny," he said as I gave him my best glare.

"And potentially hostile if you don't let me through!"

"When can you meet again?" His voice was still light with humor, but now had a hint of something so close to longing that the hardness melted from my face.

"If I keep disappearing every day the other servants will notice."

"So—every other day?"

"I am still swamped with chores, remember? And don't you have to study?"

"Bah, don't worry about me. I could still get top grades in all my classes even if I spent all my time with you."

"How about after next class?" I ventured. It was only two days away, and I thought I could last not seeing him again until then. "The other servants already expect me to be gone, and that would give me a little bit of time to finish all the notes you've lent me so far."

My answer must have satisfied him, because he backed away. I reached out for the door handle at the same time he did, and we both froze as our hands overlapped. It was only a hand, but I didn't think I could have felt more encompassed if he had drawn me into his arms. He pulled his hand away first and quickly stuck it into his pocket. His face had gone pale as he turned from me to look out the windows over my head.

"I'll see you then?" I asked, but all he did was nod his head, still looking away.

I turned the handle and left, carrying a heaviness in my chest that hadn't been there before. I knew that what we had just done, and what we were planning on doing, was dangerous. For me I would be turned out onto the streets—but Aiden had acted like his very life was on the line. And I wondered, as I remembered the way he had looked at me when I pulled his hands away from his face, like I was now all he could see, if my life wasn't as well.

I had just opened the door to the servant stairs when I barreled into Dustin. I panicked and almost dropped my precious bucket, but caught it just in time.

"Kailin!" He fumbled what he was holding and caught it before it fell as well.

"What is it?" I asked. "Did something happen?" Dustin wasn't one for emotional instability. If he was worked up about something then—

"No!" He said a little too loudly. "I mean, no, nothing has happened. I was just wondering, that is—are you going up to the workroom?"

"Yes—"

"Because I was going to go there to drop something off, but if you're already going there…"

He looked down. He was holding a package about five inches long and four inches wide and only about an inch thick. I didn't need to open it to know it was a book.

"Is it for Lancy?" I asked, as his eyes shot up.

"Can you give it to her?" He asked, his deep voice uncharacteristically shy.

I nodded my head, and he handed it to me.

"Tell her if she wants to talk I'll be in my workroom this evening." With that he turned and headed back down the way he had come, his feet moving too fast.

Annoyed that I'd gotten sucked into Lancy's drama, I dropped Aiden's notes off at my room, hidden under my mattress, and went to find the overly emotional reptile girl.

Lancy and Gabell were both in the workroom when I got there. Lancy was at the table with her books open, but she was staring in front of her as if they weren't even there. Gabell, on the other hand, was asleep on the bench. I shot her a glare, but she continued snoring.

"Here you go," I said, dropping the package in front of Lancy, turning to leave.

"What is this?" she asked, picking it up.

I considered just ignoring her, but Dustin had always been nice to me. I owed him.

"A certain young man stopped me on the stairs and asked me to give it to you."

She dropped it like it had burned her.

"Take it back to him!"

"Lancy…"

"Do it!" She slammed her hands on the table and stood up, turning to march out the door.

"Well, if she doesn't want it, I'll take whatever it is." Gabell was apparently more awake than I thought as she grabbed the package and tore off the paper. "Ugh, it's a book!"

Only Gabell wouldn't have recognized its shape.

"It's for Lancy, what did you expect?"

"Something edible. Whoever heard of a boy giving a girl a storybook?"

"What did you say?" Lancy asked. She was halfway through the door, but had stopped.

"*Madam Clearance's Collection of Northern Stories*," Gabell sneered. "How boring."

Gabell unceremoniously dropped it on the table. Lancy bounced from foot to foot, like she couldn't decide which way to run, the door open wide behind her, the book almost mocking her from the table. The book won, and in two steps she was back in front of the table. I watched her as she carefully lifted the cover, her hands brushing the edge of the binding with delicate fingers.

"That was nice of him to get it for you," I said, leaning over to see the artistic scrolls on the title page.

"It's our book," she whispered.

"What?"

She closed her eyes and took a breath. "When I was a girl, a stray dog had gotten into our garden and was chasing me. I tripped and was positive that I was going to die, but Dustin appeared and kicked it in the stomach. It ran off, and he helped me to my feet. I hadn't been as *conditioned* as most children my age, and since Dustin wasn't one of my personal servants, I didn't see him as anything other than a skinny boy who had just saved my life."

She sat down and held the book close to her chest. "We used to spend so much time together, playing and talking. He taught me how to climb trees, and I taught him how to read..."

She pulled the book back and looked down at it, her eyes shimmering. "I used this book, well, one just like this—"

She flipped to the back cover, and dropped it on the table, covering a gasp with her hand. I leaned over and there, on the last page, was Lancy's name scrawled in a childish hand.

"How?" she whispered, then louder, picking it back up. "How did he get this?! It was left in our mansion's library to be auctioned off with the rest of our possessions! He would have had to go back and...and..."

"Steal it?"

We both jumped and turned to find Dustin standing in the open door.

"Dustin!" Lancy said. "You could be arrested for this! Beaten! Made a cripple!" She was in his face, yelling her accusations, but the book was still held tight against her chest.

"They should have let you keep it," he said, his eyes hard and pleading. "And they're not going to arrest me for something that they don't even miss. When I snuck back in there the library hadn't even been opened since you left."

She looked down at the book again, one hand brushing along the cover. Dustin's face softened as he watched her.

"Do you remember any of the stories?" she asked, barely loud enough for me to hear.

"All of them."

Lancy seemed to wilt, but Dustin quickly added, "But I'd love to hear you read them to me again."

He stepped to the side as Lancy hesitated, then she walked past him into the hallway. Before he shut the door, he shot me a grateful look.

"Well, that was overly sappy," Gabell said, collapsing back onto the bench, one leg hanging off.

"Yes," I said with a smile. "It was, wasn't it?"

CHAPTER
TWENTY-FIVE

The door shut with a click. I walked a few yards down the hall, then stopped. I knew I should have kept going as we had agreed, as I had done now a dozen times, but I couldn't. The hallway was empty, and I felt as though I was the only person in the world.

Well, almost the only.

I heard the door open again, and every single one of my hairs stood on end as I felt him see me. I finally turned my head, and I couldn't help smiling as I saw Aiden for one last moment, watching me with a smile as well.

Our secret meetings over the last three weeks had fallen into a very efficient routine of me asking questions and him answering them with little else, as exemplified by how today we spent the whole time covering the minute details of the foot bones. Though I was amazed at how competent Aiden proved to be as an instructor and was brimming with pride at how quickly I was flying through the first-year curriculum, I always left our session unsatisfied.

I was beginning to suspect why.

I counted my heartbeats as Aiden's smile faded into something serious, taking mine away as well. Then I became afraid by how his eyes reflected perfectly the intensity that was suddenly inside me.

He took a step toward me.

"Kailin!" Lady Cathrina's voice rang down the hallway as she came out of her office only a few doors away, her arms full of folders and jars. I jumped as I turned toward her, then quickly turned back to Aiden, but he was already walking in the other direction. Disappointment wasn't even the beginning of what suddenly consumed me.

"I'm so glad I ran into you," Lady Cathrina said, marching up to me. "Could you help me? I need to take these over to the Hospital—that is, if there isn't anywhere else you need to be."

"No," I replied, hiding the bitterness I felt at her appearance. "And I'm *your* servant, I always have time to do whatever you need me to do." I tried to smile, and knew I did a terrible job, but she was so distracted by not dropping anything from her load to have noticed.

"Yes, but in this case you're my *assistant*," she smiled, handing me one of the jars. "And we're lucky you have that bucket with you, these are more than a little cumbersome!"

I hesitated for only half a second, then with a steady hand placed jar after jar carefully on top of Aiden's precious notes, praying to The Great One that their lids were tight.

Lady Cathrina's efficient stride took us in the same direction Aiden had taken only moments before, and my heart caught as I remembered Aiden mentioning that his next class was over at the Hospital.

I paused at the classroom that was used for patient practice, expecting Lady Cathrina to open it and cut through to the Hospital, but instead she kept walking toward the stairwell.

"Aren't we going to the Hospital?" I asked as she stepped off the steps onto the fifth-floor landing.

"We are," she replied without slowing. "But since we're not using one of the classrooms, it is polite to use one of the more standard entrances to the Hospital from the Academy."

"Through the library?" I asked. Then she opened the heavy, ornately carved door, and everything inside me stopped and stared.

Every wall was crammed with more volumes than I had ever dreamed. I could see through open doors that there were rooms the same as this one extending what felt like indefinitely. I had never been on this floor before, never having a need, warned countless times that common servants would be punished for approaching an area so valuable. Lady Cathrina had an extensive collection in her chambers, or at least I had thought it to be extensive, but now I felt like it was nothing but a drop in the ocean of knowledge which had always lived only a few floors below me and I had never known.

I could feel my eyes begin to hurt from how wide they were, and my fingers to itch as I took in the titles along the bound covers.

Lady Cathrina was in the next room before she noticed my absence.

"Kailin?" she asked, returning and seeing my shocked face. "What happened? Are you all right?"

"There's so many of them," I whispered.

Understanding dawned on Lady Cathrina's face, and she smiled kindly. "Yes," she said, "and when we're done dropping these off, I could use your help finding some volumes I need for my research."

My heart skipped in a new way very different from how Aiden's smile messed with it, and elated, I hurried after her.

The entrance to the Hospital was just a few rooms down in

the middle of the floor on the north wall, with nothing indicating its specialness other than an enclosed bridge from this building to the other with an image of The Blessing Tree carved above it.

We were almost to the imposing desk when Lady Cathrina turned to me.

"How about we cut our time in half? I actually need to discuss some of these files with the clerk, so how about you go down to the second floor and find Healer Arios to drop off those jars. He should be in the open clinic today, and I'm sure he wouldn't mind you watching while you wait for me. I'll come find you when I'm done."

She smiled as she took in my now-excited face, knowing how much I loved watching a real Healer in action. I had been to the open clinic once before with Lady Cathrina a few weeks earlier and knew the way, so I nodded and turned toward the stairs, still holding the precious bucket as if my life depended on keeping it steady.

I arrived on the second floor and stood there at the base of the stairs for a moment, not sure which way to go.

"Oh good!" said a gray-haired Healer I had never seen before. "There was a lot of blood over in exam room five that needs to be cleaned up immediately."

I stared at her for a second, and then realized that without Lady Cathrina next to me I must have looked like any other servant.

"I'm sorry, I'm actually here to find Healer Arios."

The Healer's face puckered in confusion, then transformed into an expression I had seen once before. Right before Healer Steverno had backhanded me. "Where did you learn to talk that way to your betters?! And get those eyes on the ground!"

She raised her hand and every muscle in my body stiffened

as I prepared for the shock of impact, but before she could, a hand rested on her shoulder.

"I think I can take care of this, Anna." Healer Arios gave his hand a squeeze and the Healer narrowed her eyes at me as she lowered her hand. I shot my eyes to the ground as she stormed past.

I breathed like I had never felt air in my lungs before, blinking away the tears that were forming.

"You can look up again, Kailin. She's gone." I raised my head and took in Healer Arios's kind smile, and then noticed the ten students standing behind him. They were all dressed in Healer aprons, and they all wore confused faces at Healer Arios's intervention. I did see a few students I recognized from Lady Cathrina's class not looking as surprised at seeing me, but they still held a lack of interest in my plight.

That is, all except for one face that held a mixture of shock and outrage.

Aiden's eyes found mine, pleading to know if I was all right. I gave a small nod, and he looked relieved, only to then glare beyond me to where we could hear the horrible old Healer ratting out some other unfortunate soul.

"That's better," Healer Arios said. "Now, can you tell me what you're doing here without Lady Cathrina?"

"She's up at the filing desk," I said, still shaken. "She sent me down here to find you, and to give you these." I held out the bucket full of jars; then realizing I didn't want to give him everything in the bucket, I pulled it back.

Healer Arios frowned. "She sent you down here *by yourself?*"

I nodded as he muttered, "By The Great One, Cathrina, I swear..." while looking at the stairs.

"She did tell me to stay with you until she came for me."

"Good. Go grab an apron from that closet over there, leave

the bucket on a shelf where no one will bother it, and join the class."

Join the class?

My stomach thrilled at the words.

I almost ran over to the supply closet he'd pointed to and stepped inside. Frantically, I emptied the bucket and shoved Aiden's notebook down the front of my dress, then grabbed an apron. It was similar to the one Aunt Beredith used, but hers wasn't of such quality. I pulled it over my shoulders, savoring the feel of the thick fabric reaching high on my neck, so familiar yet so new. I tightened the strings around my wrists, then almost laughed with a sense of freedom when I looked down.

It completely covered my brown dress.

I was reaching around back for the ties when I felt someone else grab them first.

"What are you doing here?" Aiden whispered down my neck.

"I'm doing what I'm told. Don't worry, it's a servant thing, you wouldn't understand."

He pulled the strings too tight.

"Aiden!"

"Sorry," he muttered, loosening them again. "I really hate it when you say things like that."

Then he was gone. When I came out I saw him with the other students. They were laughing and pointing back at me. He gave them a flippant smile as he shrugged.

He's playing a part, I told myself. I knew it was true, yet why did I still feel nauseated?

"All right, everyone follow me!" Healer Arios had gathered his small group together and they were approaching the first examination room. I decided to stay as far away from Aiden as I could, which wasn't hard as he was right in front while I was pushed to the back. The examination room was small, and with ten other students I was left in the doorway looking in.

Healer Arios was over by a bed on which was a middle-aged man whose skin looked yellow with matching eyes. His skin was also sagging as though he had recently lost a lot of weight. Healer Arios did a quick examination of his vitals, then he turned to his students.

"All right, now what should be done?" He was met with silence.

But I knew.

The open clinic was where people who were having ailments would come in from off the street. You could see everything from food poisoning to traumatic amputations, so it was a good place to teach students about quick thinking.

It also was the most like what I had seen every day following Aunt Beredith from cottage to cottage all my life.

And I had seen more than one villager who had the same characteristics, and I knew what questions should be asked next.

I kept quiet though. I wasn't a student and knew I would be pushing my luck by answering a question meant for them, but I could feel my face grow redder as the seconds turned into a full minute.

Finally, someone spoke up.

"You should look for swelling in the extremities, showing water retention." Aiden had stepped forward and was now next to the man on the bed. "Hello, my name is Healer Aiden. I'm just going do a quick exam."

He looked at the man's arms and legs and found that they were swelling, then lifted his shirt, revealing a spider webbing of vines around the belly button. Then he had the man sit up.

"I'm going to push on your hands," Aiden said, "try and hold them still."

The man looked confused, but held up his hands. Aiden pushed on them, then pulled back. We all watched as they nearly bounced forward and back in a tremor.

"I would order a biopsy of the liver taken."

"Very good, Aiden. Thank you for answering—again."

Suddenly there was a shout and the entire clinic erupted into chaos as a dozen bloodied men and women were brought down the hallway from the Hospital entrance. Some wore the insignia of city guards, others with a brand I did not know, but most of them were dressed in Peasant browns or Tradesmen drab.

"What happened?" Healer Arios shouted as he grabbed a Healer assistant running toward the entrance.

"Another riot!" His eyes had a panicked excitement that frightened me. "Get those students either helping or out of the way! And we're going to need to double up rooms, or even triple! There's more coming from where these came from!"

"Students!" Healer Arios said, turning back to us. "Those of you who have taken my second-level course on surgery may stay and assist; those of you who haven't please return to the Academy. The ones staying pair up and report to Healer Marko for assignments."

"But do we really need to help them?" one of the students, a tall blond boy, asked, as he made a face at a Peasant who was quickly carried past us on a stretcher. "The guards I can understand, but why should we waste time and resources healing the outer rings?"

My stomach turned, my eyes narrowing. I should have been afraid or sick at his blatant hate for those like me, but instead I wanted to put him on a stretcher as well.

But before I could do anything illegal, Healer Arios glared at the young man.

"Your calling is to heal, not to pass judgment." He spoke so forcefully I thought the now-pale young man would pass out. "If you feel that you cannot fulfill your calling, then you can leave the Hospital and the Academy and find a new profession that aligns better with your view on social morality."

He then turned and entered the fray, leaving us in shock and confusion. I could see half the students make a beeline for the stairs and the Academy, while the other four, including the blond boy, quickly paired up and moved toward the clinic entrance.

I was frozen in indecision. Lady Cathrina had told me to stay with Healer Arios, but he had disappeared. I was about to return to the Academy when a hand grabbed mine and pulled me forward.

"I haven't taken Healer Arios's class!" I yelled at Aiden over the noise.

"Just do what I tell you and you'll be fine. Besides, they need every Healer they can get."

He just called me a Healer.

Aiden didn't need to pull so hard—I would have followed him to the ends of the world.

I didn't say anything more as we made our way forward toward the admittance desk directly across from the large doors leading onto the street and into the city. A large man in an apron like ours was standing behind it with two assistants on either side of him, a chalkboard map and paper lists on the flat surface in front of him. As more and more men and women were brought in, some limping and others on stretchers, he would efficiently wave his hand as to where they were to go, which was then noted by the assistants on the lists and map.

Aiden didn't hesitate as he walked up to the man. "Two of Healer Arios's students—we've taken second-level surgery, third-level medicine, and third-level trauma treatment."

He sounded so confident, so efficient, that I thought Healer

Arios had possessed him for a moment, but it was all Aiden. He was calm and steady, even though the smell of blood and the cries of pain were reaching a crescendo as the rooms around us filled with the injured. I turned to look at him, and the light coming in through the flung-open door highlighted his hair, face, and eyes with a power that had nothing to do with the rays of the sun. This was what Aiden was meant to do—and he knew it.

"We're sending second-level trauma patients to the third floor," Healer Marko said, glancing down at the map. "Take room twenty-six."

Aiden was already dragging me toward the stairs when we heard a faint "And don't forget to fill out full reports!"

"Aiden!" I yelled once we had reached the third-floor landing, pulling my hand out of his. He turned to face me, anxious to keep moving. "Do you really know what you're doing? I mean, you're great with bone structures and bedside manner, but this is people's lives!"

I didn't know which emotion was the strongest on his face, amusement, exasperation, or offense.

"Yes, Kailin," he hissed, leaning closer, a determination in his eyes that held a challenge. "I know *exactly* what I'm doing. If either of us is biting off more than we can chew, it would be you."

And something inside me solidified, pushing away my insecurities. I returned his glare with my own challenge, then marched past him toward the crowded hallway. He was next to me within two steps, and side by side we entered examination room twenty-six.

What I saw there churned my stomach. The floors patched with blood from the two men inside, one on the bed and the other still on a stretcher. Assistants were hurriedly putting pressure on the wounds and doing what they could.

Aiden turned to face me for only a moment as he pulled out a mask and gloves from a box by the door. I did the same. He didn't look afraid at all as his face disappeared behind the fabric. His eyes told me to trust him.

I put on my own mask.

"Ok," he said turning to the assistants, his voice miraculously calm. "I'm Healer Aiden, and this is Healer Kailin, tell us what we're looking at."

With that we stepped into the room and didn't leave it again for five hours.

I lost count of how many patients were brought to us, and the hours melted into each other as Aiden and I worked side by side to assess and treat each one. They never sent us the serious ones, only ones with deep gashes or broken bones, but we cleaned, stitched, and administered medicine. Once they were declared stable the assistants would bring one of those beds with wheels and take them away, servants quickly mopping and disinfecting the room and us, then the next patient would arrive.

The first time the assistant pulled off my apron and saw my brown dress she paused, staring at it as if she didn't know what to do. Aiden shot her a glare, and with a pale face she pulled it the rest of the way off and finished disinfecting me.

She didn't hesitate again.

The whole time Aiden never lost his rhythm. No matter what we saw or how long ago the light outside dimmed and the lanterns were lit, he kept moving forward treating each patient as though they were his first, and I fell into step next to him as if I had always been there. I couldn't understand how we were able to read each other so smoothly having never worked together before.

Finally, the last of the riot victims were treated and settled in their own rooms on the other floors of the Hospital, and we were told we could go back to the Academy.

Slowly I walked out of the examination room that had become my world. Pulling off my face mask I leaned against the wall. I saw the Healer who had almost struck me earlier walk down the hall with two assistants, but she didn't even look my way this time. Numbly I looked down at my hands. My gloves and the front of my apron were still soiled. There was something inside me that felt like I should be repulsed, but I was so tired the thought wouldn't process.

Then there was movement in front of me, drawing my face up.

I met Aiden's eyes, now glossed with fatigue.

"They expect you to clean yourself up if you're not seeing another patient," I heard him say from a thousand miles away. "I'll show you where the washroom is." I nodded and followed him to a small room with a trough-like basin with two faucets, tubs of soap with ladles, stacks of towels, and several sealed hampers. Aiden peeled off his gloves and threw them into one of the hampers and his mask into another. I did the same, then followed him to the basin.

He pushed his foot down on a pedal that was under it, and water came out of the faucet, flowing over his hands.

He stood there for a time, watching the water take away what violence and then compassion had put there.

"I can't believe we just did that," I said, my voice tired as I stepped next to him.

"It's what we're being trained for, isn't it?" Aiden's voice was flat, his fingers moving back and forth through the flow of water, his eyes blankly taking it in.

"It's what *you're* being trained for." I turned on the other faucet like I had seen him do and cringed as the cold water hit my skin. Aiden reached for some of the soap, taking off the lid and ladling the clumpy powder into his hands. I did the same, mimicking the steps, as he used different ones in a specific order to make his hands pure again. They smelled of strong herbs and stung my skin as I used them to rub off whatever remained and disinfect my hands and arms; then I rubbed moisture back into them from the last jar of ointment.

Aiden had already gotten his apron off and was putting it into the assigned hamper along the wall when I finished. I leaned against the sink, looking at him. His hands and arms up past his elbows were pink from washing, and I could see the muscles and tendons flexing with his movements.

He smiled tiredly at me and I noticed that a smudge of something was still on his cheek.

"Here," I said stepping forward, licking my thumb. His eyes grew wide, then softened as I touched his cheek. It was soft, and I found that I couldn't pull my hand away. "There was something there," I tried to explain, but suddenly I couldn't think past his blue eyes looking down at me.

"Let me help you with your ties," Aiden said suddenly. Before I could answer he was behind me, and I could feel him standing close as he undid the knots, so much like the ones he had so carefully made a lifetime ago.

I thought I wouldn't be able to breathe, like moments earlier when I had been lost in his eyes, but the drop in adrenaline and the exhaustion of hours of strenuous work had taken away my ability to be careful. I could feel myself sink into the feeling of being near him, as if having him so close was the most natural thing in the world.

I was just reaching the peak of relaxation when I felt, more than heard, him sigh. My eyes flew open as his forehead rested on the back of my head.

"Kailin," he whispered. "I'm so tired."

His weariness flowed into me. I could suddenly see the two of us curled up on a bed somewhere, him holding me as we both slept off the insanity of the day. I knew it was a dangerous thought for a thousand different reasons, but in my fog I couldn't see anything wrong with it at all.

He pulled on my apron ties and I let it fall.

Then I felt Aiden's hands on my waist, and his head moving down to my neck. My heart stopped working, my breathing suddenly shallow.

"So tired," he whispered.

I closed my eyes as he turned his head toward my neck, only to have my euphoria shattered by loud voices shouting from right outside the door.

I spun around as if my heart had been hit by lightning, time slowing as I could see each millisecond of what could be our last moment together. Aiden's face was beyond panicked as the realization of what could happen if we were caught together was reflected in his dilated eyes. Then I saw the supply closet in the corner of the room. Before I could think twice I was pushing him into it with me after. I had just closed the door when two angry voices entered.

"You're wrong! It was *poison!*" Lady Cathrina's voice fumed. "And someone left their apron on the floor! Incompetence is just running rampant today!" I heard the hamper open and shut with a vengeance it didn't deserve.

I looked up in the dark toward where I knew Aiden's face should be, and felt his breath brush down on me. Somehow we weren't touching, but that didn't stop my imagination exploding at the thought of how close to being in Aiden's arms

I really was. A flash of a daydream streaked across my mind, of me falling forward, the two of us exploring what could happen here in the dark, but then a second voice snapped both our heads back to the scene only feet away.

"Oh really?!" Healer Arios shouted back, as I heard one of the sinks turn on and the jars of soap fall over on the counter. "And here I thought I was Tamerin's leading expert on poisons, which is a title that clearly should belong to you! So go ahead, if you're so smart and well read, put me in my place and tell me what type of poison it was!"

"I don't know!" Lady Cathrina spat, as the other sink was turned on and I could hear the angry splashing of water. "But that doesn't mean that it was liver failure like you're trying to pull off!"

"The liver failed, which, I believe, is what is called liver failure! Or maybe I should go back to a first-year class and retake that lecture!"

"Yes, the liver failed—but not in the way it is *supposed* to fail!" Both sinks were turned off at the same time and replaced by the sharp opening and closing of the towel hampers. "And what about the timeline?" she snapped. "That doesn't raise your suspicions at all? That a high-ranking Lesser Noble, one known to be exploiting the outer rings into recruitment for the war, suddenly has liver failure right in the middle of a riot only a few streets over from his house?"

"Oh, so now you are subscribing to conspiracy theories!"

"I don't know what sort of poison it was, but that doesn't make it something that it clearly isn't!"

"Whatever you say, your *grace*!" I could almost feel Lady Cathrina burning him through the closet door.

"It just doesn't make sense..." Lady Cathrina sounded tired now, but there was a bitterness that was unmistakable. "I just have this feeling that something isn't right, like someone used the riot to cover up—"

"Just let it go, Cathrina," Healer Arios pleaded. I could feel Aiden's head snap around toward the closed door at the drop of her title. "Please, just this once, don't go chasing after a problem that isn't there."

"I can't; you should know that about me." There was only the sound of their breathing for ten long, excruciating seconds until I heard Lady Cathrina say, "here, let me help you with that."

There was the sound of moving fabric, and the hamper lid being lifted and closed, but this time it wasn't with the same violence as before.

"Your turn," Healer Arios said, a new somberness to his voice that made me shiver.

I could hear the rustle of what must have been Lady Cathrina's apron, as Healer Arios slowly untied her strings. Then there was silence.

And more silence.

Why weren't they saying anything?!

"Arios, please," I heard Lady Cathrina finally whisper, followed by a sharp sound of fabric moving and the hamper lid being opened and shut.

"Why?"

Nothing again, then the washroom door opened and shut. After a minute it opened and shut again.

Slowly, I eased open the door, and seeing that the room was again empty, I stepped out into the light, Aiden following. Looking back at the closet I couldn't possibly imagine how we hadn't been smashed up against each other in so little space.

When I turned around Aiden looked like he was about to laugh.

"So," he said, the half smile I loved so much crawling onto

his face despite how worn out he was. "Lady Cathrina and Healer Arios…"

"Don't even say it," I snapped. "We don't actually know anything."

"You sure?" he asked, a new light brightening his eyes. "Because that was *a lot* of not talking we just overheard."

"Stop it!" I said and smacked his arm.

His eyes opened wider than I had ever seen them before.

"Did you really just hit me?" He said, feigning astonishment and outrage. "I believe that goes under the category of 'attack on a Noble person'; I could have you arrested for that!"

"I'd like to see you try. But seriously, don't say anything about the two of them. Lady Cathrina has been so good to me and—"

"You worry too much," he said, all joking gone, but he still had a lightness about him that kept away the dead look from earlier. "Of course I'm not going to tell anyone—you should know me better than that by now."

Did I?

"But I don't. Other than that you are a talented Healer and have outer-ring thrill issues…" His eyebrows came together as he waited for me to continue. "I've seen you with your friends —how am I supposed to know which Aiden is real?"

He looked away, and then back at me with an intensity that was inflamed only by the lack of restraint the trials of the day had drained from him. In a heartbeat I could imagine him pulling me into his arms and giving me my first kiss, and I gulped down a breath of air as if it had already happened.

But he didn't pull me toward him. His eyes seemed torn for half a second, but the battle was quickly won as his hand came up to brush a strand of hair from my face. "I'm always the real me when I'm around you. You have to just assume that everything else is an act to survive."

"Survive?"

A heartbeat passed, and then another, and his hand lingered by my ear, still holding the strand of hair. Finally he closed his eyes, and I felt myself released from the hold they had on me.

"We should go," I whispered.

"Where?" he asked. His eyes flew open and he looked embarrassed, as if the word had come out before he could have thought better of it. "I mean, yes, we don't want someone else to come barging in here and get shoved into that closet again." He tried to smile, but his eyes suddenly flared and I wondered if it really would have been that bad.

This time he went first and I counted the necessary thirty seconds before opening the door.

And froze.

He was there, only a few paces down the hall, with his head turned back watching me.

I smiled at him, but he didn't smile back. I tilted my head to the side, searching his face for a hint. Then a Healer turned the corner entering the hallway and he turned, walking back to the Academy as if I didn't exist.

CHAPTER
TWENTY-SIX

The trees were strange here, with large branches of leaves near the top, on the edge of a spread of water bigger than I ever thought possible. Blue sparkled into the distance, with white-crested waves moving with a force and rhythm that was both beautiful and terrifying. I was sitting on the ground and there was sand under my toes. I enjoyed the feel as the grains brushed against my skin. I leaned back on my hands, watching the waves move back and forth in their endless dance beneath a sky of brilliant blue and orange in the setting sun.

I had never seen anything so beautiful.

Then he was there.

He hadn't walked over and sat down in any way that would have made sense. One minute I was alone, and the next I wasn't.

I kept my eyes on the horizon, petrified at the sound of his breathing, the slight rustling of movement that made him something real. I had always hoped, prayed, that he was nothing more than just a haunting of my imagination, but I couldn't deny it anymore, not with him right there next to me.

The intruder in my mind. The one I had felt in my dreams all year was finally here.

We sat side by side for a long time, neither one of us moving. I began to wonder if he was even aware of me.

Then he reached over and took my hand.

Terror.

I gasped, my vision overlaid with a soul that wasn't mine, my heart split open with a knife as everything that made him who he was and everything that made me who I am came pouring through the breach.

Hopes, wishes...

Pain.

He had so much pain.

But then so did I.

Impressions of a whole life lived, of a whole identity forged one heartbeat at a time, fixed and woven into the strands of my own. I still couldn't see his face, anything about who he was or where he came from, but now I knew him, this stranger, better than I ever knew myself.

And the pain grew into pure ecstasy.

Joy. Wonder. Fear.

Was it my fear or his?

Then I realized I couldn't think that way anymore. Because from now on it was our *joy,* our *wonder.*

Our fear.

His hand tightened around mine until I thought the bones would break, and I squeezed back as if my life would be snuffed out without him there holding it. His hand began to shake as a new burning grew in our chests.

Who are you?

Longing.

I turned my head to finally see the face of the boy that was always lurking just on the other side of my dreams.

But instead of a face, I was met with a pair of dark eyes illumi-nated by a glowing red fire within.

I CRIED OUT, my entire body writhing from being pulled away from him.

Where was I?! Why wasn't I with him?!

I dashed my limbs, tangling them in the fabric that had been covering me.

Where was the beach, and why was it so dark? Where was I?

WHERE DID HE GO?!

I needed to know. I needed...

I needed to sleep.

Because I was a servant. At the Healer Academy. And I would need to wake up soon to begin my chores.

How could I have forgotten any of that?

Dreams will do that to you.

And it was only a dream.

So why was I sobbing?

I clenched my hand to my chest, cradling the fingers he had almost broken, the answer echoing back through my hollow cries.

It was because he wasn't there anymore.

And I had never felt so alone.

"Hurry up, Kailin!" Gabell snapped from the doorway of the Healer's chamber we were cleaning. I had a bucket full of ash and was just getting the last of it from the back of the fire-place while Gabell stood at the door glaring.

"Done!" I shouted, and carefully carried the bucket to the hallway, giving Gabell my own glare as I passed. "Maybe if you helped it would go faster."

"I'm management," she said loftily; then closing the door she took out her key and locked it. I might as well have done this job by myself, for all Gabell helped, but she held the keys to this hall of Healer's chambers, so I had to endure the chore with her.

We made our way to the servant stairs and started the long climb down to the storeroom on the first floor where the ash was kept. We were just passing the third floor when the stairs suddenly became clogged with crisp white sheets and a familiar young boy frantically picking them up.

"What'd you do now, kindle brain?!" Gabell snapped. I recognized him as the manservant for the men Healers who was constantly being harassed by the other boys.

The boy cringed and tried to move faster.

I set down the bucket and asked as calmly as I could, "Did one of the other boys trip you on your way up?"

His hands paused, but he didn't lift his eyes. Finally he nodded.

My mouth flattened into a hard line.

"Here," I said reaching out, "I can help—"

"NO!" The boy yanked away the sheet I was about to touch.

I stared at him wide eyed as he looked back at me, his chest rising and falling as if he was about to die.

"Your hands..." he finally whispered.

I looked down and saw they were still black from the ash. I drew them back, careful not to let any flakes fall.

"Then what can we do?" I asked, my heart aching for him.

"Nothing," Gabell snapped. "*We* have a job to do." But instead of marching on the sheets and ruining their pristine whiteness she turned around and stomped back up the stairs. I could only wonder at her unexpected mercy for a moment before the boy drew my attention back to him.

"It's all right," he said, and a shy smile worked its way at the edge of his mouth. "It won't take me too long to clean this up."

I gave the boy as encouraging a smile as I could muster before running after Gabell.I didn't have far to go because she was waiting for me at the door to the open halls.

"We'll take the main stairs down to the second floor and then cut back into the servant halls." Her voice was still hard, but I could hear the apprehension in it.

"You sure you want to go out there? The halls will still have students in them."

"Just don't get me in trouble," she grumbled.

We were on the third floor and the hallway didn't have as many students in it as I expected, but the stairwell quickly made up for it. I was suddenly reminded that it was dinner-time for the students, as the mass of them made their way to the second floor and the meal that awaited them. I was worried someone would yell at us for being out in the open so blatantly, but I shouldn't have bothered.

No one noticed us at all.

When we got to the second floor we followed the flow of students passing study and social rooms on our way to the nearest servants' door.

I slowed down as we passed the first one, risking a quick peek into the world that could have been mine.

The room was large with two grand fireplaces at either end, the darkened windows lined with fine wall hangings. Some of the students curled up in chairs, their faces hidden behind books or napping, while others were gathered in groups around tables or on couches. The sound of laughter filled the air like as if they hadn't a care in the world.

"What are you doing?' Gabell hissed at me, but instead of yanking me forward she turned to look as well. I glanced at her, and she was almost unrecognizable. The sneer I thought was a permanent part of her face was gone, the edges of her eyes and mouth now softened with something I had never seen in her before but was so obvious I should have noticed it the very first day I met her.

Longing.

I turned back to the open door, forcing myself to forget the two blue sparks that had danced on her shoulder.

We stood there side by side for longer than we should have, two outsiders looking in on a world we made possible but would never be a part of.

Finally Gabell shook her head and started walking down the hall again. I followed, determined to ignore the other study rooms and save myself the pain.

Then I heard his laugh.

The one I loved so much.

I froze in my step, then slowly moved backwards until I could look through the door of the room I had just passed.

And he was there.

It was just like the other room, with students sprawled everywhere, talking and laughing and studying, except sitting at one of the tables was a boy in a long vest.

He was focused on the group of students that were gathered around him, most of them female, when all of a sudden they rocked back in laughter at something he had said.

He looked triumphant, as if nothing could have pleased him more than catering to this horde of imbeciles.

Then one of the girls placed a hand on his shoulder and leaned in to whisper something in his ear.

And he smiled.

I thought I would be sick.

"The biggest catch of them all," Gabell said, suddenly next to me.

"What?"

"Lord Aiden," she said nodding toward him. "That's who you were staring at, right?"

"No, I was just—"

"Oh, don't worry," she said, her voice strangely kind. "After the first time a Noble, Lord Larsion, took me I couldn't help but look for him as well. It turned out pretty good for me once he realized that I was more fun willing than not, but I wouldn't recommend looking to see if Lord Aiden would be interested in a playmate."

My stomach made a movement that I had to swallow down.

"I mean, it would be *amazing* to be his mistress," she continued looking back at him wistfully. "Could you just imagine the lifestyle?! I would probably have servants of my own! But with his family...it just isn't worth the risks."

Risks?

"What do you mean?"

"You don't know?" she asked, looking back at me with honest surprise. When I stared back at her, she just shook her head.

"Look," she said, "I'll be honest, I don't like you. You're lazy and stupid and I wouldn't be bothered at all if you were thrown out on the streets, but you don't deserve, *nobody* deserves what the men in his family do."

She looked at me meaningfully, but I couldn't imagine what she was talking about that would be worse than what she thought Aiden had already done to me.

"Sticks in a hole, you have kindle for a brain, don't you?!" I narrowed my eyes, but she didn't seem to notice. "Lord Aiden's father, he—he takes outer-ring girls, especially *Peasant* girls, and he doesn't just have a round of fun with them like a normal man. No, he does things to them…things that make them not the same afterwards…" There was genuine fear in her eyes as she turned back to Aiden.

"I still don't know what you mean," I said, following her gaze.

"As much as I hate you, I honestly hope you never do."

The boy next to Aiden had just told a joke and Aiden laughed, pounding the boy on the back.

"But Lord Aiden isn't his father," I said, my own heart beating quicker.

"Not *yet,*" Gabell said with a snort. "No one has admitted to him doing anything that his father has done, and honestly you're the first servant he's ever taken, he doesn't even visit brothels, but with how he burns through inner-ring girls, even those as inside as Lesser Nobles, everyone knows it is only a matter of time."

"*Other girls?*" I was outraged, I couldn't help it, and confused about why I felt that way. We were only friends, he could do what he wanted with other girls, what I had *seen* him do with other girls.

So why was I so angry?

"How do you not know *anything?*" Gabell asked. "Everyone knows that Lord Aiden is the biggest planter in Divlan! They say that the only girl *not* chasing him is Princess Mayorla, and that's only because she's marrying a foreigner. Sticks in a hole, he doesn't even have to try! Girls of every ring are practically dragging him into their rooms trying to win him over! Because a marriage with him, into his family—it would be the accomplishment of a lifetime." She turned back to the group, her eyes empty and sad again. "And no one would ever look down on you again."

We stood side by side for only a few moments more, both our hearts broken but for different reasons.

Finally Gabell turned, and I followed her the final yards to the servant door.

She's wrong, I thought. Gabell is always wrong. What does she know anyway—she doesn't even know him.

I tried to think it with conviction, but then I saw in my mind the girl's hand on Aiden's shoulder. Could he be the heartbreaker Gabell said he was, destined to become someone who did unthinkable things to Peasant girls?

Peasant girls like me?

Then I was back in that small washroom two days ago, his dark blue eyes pleading into mine.

I'm always the real me when I'm around you. You have to just assume that everything else is an act to survive.

I wanted to believe him—but, now in the light of the poorly lit servant lanterns, the fear wouldn't leave me.

TWENTY-SEVEN

Lady Cathrina gave her class a pop quiz—again.

Seriously, how could these students still be surprised when the days she didn't end class with a quiz were the exception? The room had emptied and I tried to swallow my fear. At the end of our last study session, right before we worked together in the hospital, Aiden and I had agreed to meet after this class. I should have been excited, with butterflies crashing against my inner organs until I thought they would carry me away, but after what Gabell had told me I was seriously considering whether it was wise to continue meeting with him.

The skin on my neck where his lips had almost touched began to sting.

I rubbed the spot, savoring and banishing the memory.

Even if Gabell was wrong about everything she had told me, I couldn't escape the reality that there was so much I didn't know about him.

I shook my head, deciding that I would skip today's

meeting to take some time to figure out a decision. I didn't need to commit to anything today; one missed session wouldn't destroy our friendship.

My plan made, I was free to focus on picking up the quizzes.

That is, until I got to Aiden's seat.

Once I lifted the sheet, a small piece of paper hidden underneath slipped off the table and floated to the ground. Reaching down, I quickly recognized the handwriting.

North-east stairwell, tenth floor,
when you're done tonight.

My chest was doing that pounding thing again, and mechanically, I finished collecting the quizzes to take to Lady Cathrina's office.

The day stretched on forever. Each hour was an eternity, and I couldn't decide if it was a comfort or a torture as my mind frantically bounced back and forth between meeting him and not.

Then it was nine o'clock, and I was serving Lady Cathrina her tea. She was reading a book in her chair, distracted as I waited. I shifted from foot to foot, trying not to fidget. Finally she looked up, dismissing me for the evening.

I curtsied, and forced myself to calmly walk out the door.

Once out I raced the deserted length of the south side of the Academy. I couldn't help it. In spite of all my brave, sensible talk, I was just as jittery as Lancy had been the last few weeks.

I didn't want to think about what that comparison could mean.

Common sense finally gained control of me only as I was

about to turn the corner of the East hall. Once I rounded it, I would be able to see the north-east stairwell at the other end.

And anyone there would be able to see me.

Why did he want to meet with me outside our classroom? And why so late at night? Something inside me said we wouldn't be discussing healing tonight.

He takes outer-ring girls, especially Peasant girls.

Gabell's warning pounded in my chest with each beat of my heart.

Everyone knows it is only a matter of time.

I stepped around the corner.

He was at the far end, wearing a cloak and leaning against the wall reading a book. He hadn't looked up, hadn't seen me. I could still turn around, walk away.

Then his hand came up and scratched the side of his nose.

And just like that my fear dissolved.

Besides, who ever heard of someone bringing a book when planning to seduce someone?

As I began to walk down the hall, Aiden's head snapped up at the sound of my footsteps. For a second he looked surprised, but just as quickly the corner of his mouth turned up. I stopped before stepping onto the landing.

"You must be the slowest tea server on the planet," he said, closing the book.

"Serving tea is easy—it's the waiting to be dismissed that takes forever."

"Are you really so good at making tea that people forget you're there?"

"Maybe I am. Why, would you like to order some?"

"Tempting, but I have no desire to forget you." My cheeks reddened and he smiled triumphantly. Which just made me glare. "Besides," he laughed, closing the gap between us, "tonight I get to be the one serving you."

I took a step back, losing control of the temperature of my face as a hundred possible implications of that statement flashed across my mind.

"Oh come on," he said rolling his eyes as he took my hand, fresh calluses on his palm rubbing against the calluses on mine. "I'm not going to murder you. There's something I want to show you."

Then he started pulling me toward the stairs.

Gabell's cautions and even Markly's warning of being thrown out on the streets if I was found in the room of a male student suddenly became the least of my worries compared to the crash of emotions that suddenly hit me. For a split second I could imagine a world where Aiden's room was exactly where I wanted to go.

But I knew I shouldn't. The Great One said so.

And everyone had always thought I would end up like my mother. I couldn't prove them right, no matter what I felt when he smiled at me.

I yanked my hand back. He turned, a question already forming on his lips, when he saw my face. His eyebrows pulled together, but instead of reaching for my hand again he turned to face a broom closet at the top of the stairs. It was skinny, not much wider than two feet, with an unassuming door and handle. It could have been any number of storage closets scattered around the Academy, though it was strange that it was at the top of the stairs instead of along the halls.

I was about to ask him what he was doing when he knelt in front of its keyhole.

Broom closets didn't have keyholes.

More curious now than scared, I stepped next to him as he pulled out two pieces of metal and started moving them around inside the lock.

"What are you doing?"

"I'm opening a door."

"I can see that. *Why* are you opening it?"

"To get to the other side."

I glared at him, but he just smiled smugly and kept working.

"Where did you learn to do that?" I asked squatting down to watch him work.

"Well," his smile faded an inch, his eyes fixed on his work, "you probably think, as everyone else does, that growing up as a Noble means a free ticket to a perfect life, but as a kid you actually spend a good amount of time locked in your room. I wouldn't be surprised if most of the other Noble kids know how to pick locks or climb out windows."

I waited for him to tell me he was joking, but he didn't. I stared at him, trying to make sense of the Noble I saw yesterday in the study room and this boy who knew how to pick locks. I hadn't made any progress when the door clicked open.

Aiden jumped to his feet and yanked me through the opening, shutting the door and all light behind us. He let out a sigh of relief, then a nervous chuckle as his thumb rubbed the top of my hand.

"That's always the most stressful part," he whispered in my ear, making me jump. He was much closer than I thought.

"Obviously," I said, trying to sound calm. "So, um, why did you want to show me a broom closet?"

"Well..." His voice turned low and smooth, setting off every alarm inside my head. He pulled on my hand, but I couldn't have moved if I wanted to.

"I'm only joking," he chuckled, "Come on, there's a staircase just a few feet forward."

He tried to pull on my hand again, but I didn't budge. His hold loosened, and I could feel him shift from one foot to the other, then back again. I thought of what Gabell had said, and wondered when was the last time Aiden had had a girl in a dark room who wasn't throwing herself at him. And if he thought I would be just like them, he was so wrong and should—

His hand tightened. "Please trust me."

There it was again, that *please* that had made me pause before.

That had turned him into something real.

I let out a sigh, and squeezed his hand back.

I could almost see his smile in the dark.

"Besides," he said, "I make it a point never to seduce a girl without first having her permission, which, I believe, you have not yet given me."

"You're a shrub," I breathed and he laughed, leading me forward. And just as he'd said, in a few feet there was a staircase.

We had gone only a few steps up it when I tripped, letting out a yelp before his arms wrapped under me, steadying me back on my feet.

"I thought you said you weren't going to kill me!" I snapped. "Why didn't you bring a lantern?"

"If you fell and snapped your neck that would *hardly* be my fault. Besides, there's no way I could explain a lantern if someone walked by while I was waiting for you."

"Couldn't you have just said it wasn't their business, because you're a Noble and everything?"

He laughed, but instead of light and fun, it was edged with something I didn't recognize. He began climbing again. "You have no idea how the world really works," he muttered under his breath.

My eyes narrowed at where I thought his head should be. I was the Peasant and he was the pampered boy who had never worked a day in his life. I wanted to pull away and march back the way we came, but the fear of breaking my neck kept me from doing so.

We kept going up for a long time, or maybe it just seemed long from the slow pace he marked for us after my slip. Neither one of us spoke, with the only sound coming from our feet scuffing against stone, until Aiden stopped. Then something metallic scraped against something in stone and light hit my eyes. Aiden stepped aside.

And the world changed for me again.

Beyond the door was a small landing, no larger than a harvester wagon, and below us were hundreds of thousands of burning lights. Divlan, the ugly maw of poverty, sin, and stone desolation, was now alive with a beautiful orange and yellow glow rivaling its mirror in the sky. I dropped Aiden's hand and moved to the low stone wall at the edge. The roof angled down from it for about ten yards before dropping, revealing us to be a dizzying height above the city streets below, but I couldn't give them more than a passing glance before my eyes were drawn upward again, trapped by the endless radiance.

"It's really something, isn't it?" Aiden said, stepping next to me.

"I've never seen anything like it."

"I thought not."

Then something changed. Maybe it was the weight of the air, or the temperature of my skin, or something that had everything to do with him and nothing to do with me at all. The lights blurred together as I stared unseeing, the air becoming thick and unbreathable.

The space between us was so small, and this was no washroom where someone could walk in at any moment.

I didn't turn my head, but I could still feel Aiden decide

something. I saw movement where his arm and hand were. I waited, not breathing, not hoping...

And he turned away.

A disappointment that I didn't understand hit me. I found I could breathe again, but the lights didn't seem quite so bright as they had a minute earlier. I turned to see where Aiden had gone and found him sitting on a bench beside the door. It was carved into the wall, a tiny alcove just below the roof. Aiden's back was against the roof on the far side from the door, his feet pulled up as he stared off beyond me. He looked sad until he saw I was looking at him, then his smile was back.

"I thought about what you said in the Hospital, about how you didn't know anything about me, and I realized that I really don't know anything about you either. So," he added as his smile spread a little more, "now that I've lured you up here, I can interrogate you without worrying about being interrupted by highly sexually charged Healers—"

"Ugh! Did you have to describe them like that?"

"How would *you* have described them?" He laughed at me. "I seriously thought that they were going to start—"

"Stop it! She's my *mistress!*"

"Fine. I'll cater to your delicate sensibilities. But that doesn't change the fact that I have you *exactly* where I want you."

"On my way back down the stairs?"

"Somewhere where we don't have to pretend to be something we're not."

Something we're not.

I was suddenly furious.

"Maybe that's easy for you, but I can't just pretend I'm not wearing this brown dress!"

"Well, there is an easy solution to that problem."

I turned toward the door.

"No! Wait! I'll behave! I promise. Please don't go."

And there was that *please* again.

"No more inappropriate jokes, about me or anyone else."

"Word of honor."

I glared at him, but I did sit down next to his feet on the bench.

"So now that we've established that I'm here against my will," I said, "what is it you wanted to know about me?"

"Everything."

It came out of his mouth so quickly, and his look was suddenly so intense, I knew he was telling me the truth.

"That's an awful lot to want."

"I'm used to getting an awful lot of what I want. Spoiled Noble, remember?"

"It is still a lot. I wouldn't even know where to begin."

"How about we start with something simple. What was it like growing up in Valehaven?"

"How did you know—"

"Please," he said, like he was offended. "During my last interrogation you said it was a village in the heart of The Holy Forest. It didn't take that much research to figure out where you can from, as there is only *one* village anywhere near The Holy Forest." Then he snorted out his nose. "If you could even call it a village."

"Hey! We might not have had much, but we had everything necessary."

"What? A cow? And maybe some chickens?"

"If you want to know about me, then you need to be nicer."

"Ok fine. What did your village have?"

I sat up straighter and made my most serious face.

"We had *multiple* cows and *many* chickens, along with a baker, a blacksmith, a Healer—"

"A *Healer?*"

"Who did you think taught me?"

"I—I don't know. But your village is so remote, how did it even get on the rolls to be considered for a Healer assignment?"

"We didn't have one assigned to us…my aunt was our Healer."

"But I don't understand." He looked so confused it was almost cute. "If your aunt was a Healer, then what was she doing in a remote Peasant village?"

"The answer is pretty obvious. She's a Peasant. She received a scholarship, but then—but then she had to drop out halfway through her fourth year."

"But why would she do that?! It's a miracle, beyond a miracle, that she got in as a Peasant in the first place, so who in their right mind would throw away a ring advancement?"

I felt my blood pump in my ears.

"She didn't have a choice. She *had* to come home."

"What could have been more important than a ring advancement?"

Me.

"Her sister got pregnant. She was sick, and no one was going to help her."

"That sounds heartless. Not just to her sister, but also to make her come home."

"They didn't have a choice! If they helped her, then it would show that they approved of what she did."

"I'm pretty sure what she 'did' was how most people get made."

"You don't understand!" I took a breath, unable to stand the feeling of abandonment that always stabbed me each time I thought of the father who didn't even know I was alive. "She didn't have a husband."

"So?"

So?!

"So I know that here you can shove your stick in any hole, but for followers of The Great One's laws, giving yourself to passing tramps is considered *a sin!*"

That disgusted look was back. "You sound as though you agree with them."

"I don't! I mean, I do think having sex with someone before marriage is wrong, but my aunt always said our neighbors were more interested in worshiping themselves than The Great One."

And like the sun rising, I saw him place the pieces of the puzzle together.

"Your aunt."

I looked away from him, unable to stand knowing how he must be looking at me.

Instead I looked out at the lights. Those beautiful, unending lights. I brushed away at my eye.

"Kailin?"

If I kept going, if I said what I knew would come next, everything would change. He would know. He would be disgusted and look at me the same way everyone had always looked at me.

And I would never see him again.

Could I stand, could I *bear,* to never see him look at me like I mattered again?

But could I stand to hold this secret close to my heart, to always wonder if I was only one moment, one sentence away from finding out that everything I thought I had with him could shatter if he ever found out?

"The whore was my mother." I dropped my head in shame. "I'm a bastard. My aunt gave up her future because of me."

"It's not your fault." He sounded so angry I looked up at him in shock. When I saw his face I realized that he wasn't angry. He was furious. "And your aunt is a *bitch* for making you feel like it was."

"She never did! She never even so much as hinted that she regretted her decision!" My cheeks were wet now and I didn't care. "She took care of me, raised me, protected me, and I'll never, *never*, be able to repay that!"

His look of anger didn't disappear; if anything, it grew stronger.

"What do you mean, she protected you? Protected you from *what?*" His jaw clenched. "Or was it *who?*"

"Everyone!" I said standing up. "Are you happy I told you now? I was born from a sin, remember? I am *cursed!* I bring bad luck just by breathing!"

"That is the most kindle-brained thing I've ever heard!" he said, standing as well.

"I'm sorry that my life feels kindle-brained to you!"

"You're right! Your life is bark stripping and you don't deserve it!"

I stared at him. I had been afraid that he would be disgusted, and he was, just not in the way he was supposed to be.

"How could you know what I deserve?"

He closed his eyes and pinched the place between them, taking a deep breath.

"Anyone sane who has ever known you would know that you deserve more, more..."

I couldn't look away.

"More what?" I whispered.

He took another breath before lowering his hand and looking at me.

"Everything."

I had to turn away from him, to make him talk about something, *anything* else. It took a full minute to calm down my breathing.

"Is that everything you wanted to know?"

"It's enough—for now."

I could still feel the undertone of anger in his voice, but it was calmer as well.

He took my hand, and I let him lead me to the bench again. I didn't hesitate this time when he handed me his handkerchief.

"So," I said, folding it, "is it my turn to ask you questions?"

He chuckled. "Go ahead. I'm an open book."

"All right then. Why are you here?"

"To interrogate you."

"No, I mean here at the Academy. You aren't in the Healer ring."

"All inner-ring youth are expected to receive an Academy education."

"So why not one of the other Academies? Why *here*?"

He looked at me, horribly uncomfortable. This wasn't where he was planning this conversation to go, but if he was going to force my life from me then I was free to do the same to him.

He started to say something, then stopped. He took a breath.

"You're right, I was supposed to go to the Law Academy. It was where my father went and was where I was expected to go, but then the spring before I was going to start, my mother got sick. She —she didn't get better. But every day I would watch the Healers, and by the end I knew that this was where I wanted to come."

He looked down at our hands. "I've never told anyone this before."

I rubbed my thumb over the top of his.

"Thank you for telling me."

He smiled a little.

"I have to admit I did enjoy the look on my father's face when I told him I was planning on switching Academies." He let out a bitter laugh. "I don't know why he bothered—we both knew that I could have studied poetry for all it would have determined my future."

"But you're a great Healer! You don't have to stop just because you graduate next year."

"That's sweet of you, but in case you missed this rather fine point, I am a *Noble* and can't just do whatever I want. I have to 'uphold the family's honor and get ready to take my place as Chair of the Senate. So you see? My future was determined before I was even born, no matter what I want." He didn't even try and hide the bitterness now. "After graduation the only way I'm getting back into a hospital is on a sick bed."

I was furious that he would give up so easily on who he obviously was, when something he said pushed all other thoughts out of my head.

"What do you mean by *Chair of the Senate*?"

He looked at me like I had just grown another head, but when he saw my face he just doubled up laughing.

"Sticks in a hole, you really didn't know!?"

"I don't see what's so funny."

"It's just the one girl—and she didn't even know!"

I felt my face turn red. With a huff I stood up to leave when Aiden, still choking on his infuriating laugh, threw himself lengthwise on the bench to grab at my skirt.

"Don't go!" He laughed, gently pulling on it, "I just think it's *amusing* that you of all people didn't know that I'm destined to—"

I turned on him and ripped my skirt out of his hand.

"Be the second most powerful man in Tamerin!"

"Calm down, it isn't that big of a deal. Ok, it's a *very* big deal, but—"

"And you have no choice at all? But you're such an amazing Healer!"

He stopped laughing and looked at me in that way I had hated so many times. Like I was a—how did he put it? Like a puzzle he couldn't figure out.

"That's really what you're hung up on?"

I knew what he meant, but if I let myself focus on what he had just told me, what I had just pieced together...

He was practically a prince, and I was—no, I didn't want to think about that right now. Not with the lights out there making everything seem possible.

"But you love healing."

"And how would you know that?"

"Because I've seen you heal! And it's like that's what you were *made* to do."

I sat back down next to him.

"What about Lady Cathrina?" I continued. "She's a Noble *and* a Healer. You could do both, too, couldn't you?"

"Lady Cathrina lives in her own little world," he said while leaning forward onto his knees. "She also has a few things I don't. For one thing, she is the last of her family—there isn't anyone to complain or even care what she does. She also isn't heir to the most powerful Senate seat in Tamerin. The only way for me to get out of it is to do something so terrible that I lose my title and it goes to my sister."

I remembered he had mentioned during one of our sessions that he had a sister.

"Wait, even *Nobles* can be demoted?"

"You're acting like a foreigner!" Then an evil smile spread across his face. "Unless, of course, I guessed right the first time and you really *are* a spy..."

"I'm not a spy!"

"You're right. A spy would know a whole lot more about our country."

"Just stop it and answer the question. How could you lose your title?"

"I see I have to go back to the basics with you. How much do you know about the system of selecting Nobles?"

"Isn't it just like all the other rings? You're born into it?"

"Yes and no. The law says only a hundred direct-line Noble immediate families are allowed to exist at any one time. A Noble keeps their title until they die, but only *one* of their children is allowed to inherit the title. With this in mind, by law the title goes to the oldest child, unless their parents can present to the Senate a reasonable argument before their child's twentieth birthday as to why that person would be unfit to inherit. After that the only way one could lose their title is to have it stripped from them by the King."

"Wait, so you're *not* a Noble yet?"

He rubbed the back of his neck.

"I was hoping you wouldn't notice that. No, after my birthday next month I still have a whole year of good behavior before I'm at last free. But don't worry, I'm pretty sure I'm going to make it. I'd have to do something pretty kindle brained for my father to even take the time to notice me, let alone go to the Senate to have my title inheritance removed."

"And what if it was?"

It was a wicked thing to ask, but I couldn't help thinking of Dustin and Lancy.

It wasn't lost on him either, because he gave me a suspicious look.

"As long as I wasn't drastically reduced, I could always marry back into the Nobility—that's the other way you could gain a title, but the girls of the court are *so* dull I'm always pretty sure I'm about to throw myself out a window whenever I'm stuck at one of those awful parties they throw at the palace."

"You're hopeless," I said, not even trying to hide my eye roll. When I did I caught the view of the lights again.

They were so lovely, and up here, away from all my problems, all my realities...

I rested my head on his shoulder. He stiffened, then his arm came around me, and slowly his hand began to slide up the side of my arm.

I froze. My mind was flooded with Gabell's words.

"Aiden." Something in my voice must have warned him because his hand stopped moving.

"I have another question for you. One that I don't think you'll want to answer."

I pulled away from his shoulder and he let me go.

I opened my mouth once, then twice, then chickened out at the last minute.

"That night in the hallway, I know you saw me. You were with a girl, and everyone says that you have a lot of—girl-friends."

"Oh is that all? I thought you were going to ask for some terrible confession."

I let out a sigh of relief.

I knew Gabell was lying.

"Having a fun night with a girl would hardly be called having a relationship."

I stared at him, my mouth hanging open, my brain freezing mid-thought and then tripping over itself as I realized what he was actually saying.

"Why are you looking at me like that?" He asked. "Sure, I've probably had more fun than most people, it kind of goes with being a Noble, which is probably what you've heard from the other servants, but it isn't like they really meant anything and I always use protection, it's just that classes are stressful—but I haven't all year! Not since, I mean, doesn't that count for something? Why are you still looking at me like that?!"

"Because it's wrong! The Great One's laws—"

"Oh please, you don't actually believe the laws mean anything, do you? And are you really telling me that you have never been with someone?"

"No!" I shrieked, jumping to my feet, startling him. "So it's true? You have sex with every girl that throws herself at you?"

"Well," he said, rubbing the back of his neck again, not looking at me. "Not *every* girl."

I felt sick.

"What? Am I too *sinful* for you now? No, don't answer. It is written all over your face."

There was disgust on his face now, and I was shocked how much it looked like how the villagers back home used to look at me, only for the exact opposite reason. And it made me wonder if I looked just like them as well.

"I'm sorry. You're right, I'm being judgmental. It's just... this specific law is important to me. I don't want to be like my mother."

The disgust disappeared.

"I'm sorry, too. I didn't think of that."

I sat down again.

"But you're not your mother," he continued, "you have to know that. And I can't believe that everyone in your village believed that you were, what did you say, *cursed?* I just can't believe that there weren't any boys that wouldn't want to take a beautiful girl like you, I don't know, behind a haystack or wherever it is that Peasants go."

Beautiful?

"I've never even thought of it."

No, that wasn't true. There had been one time when I was thirteen and Dural had suddenly grown up and I started having thoughts that it would be nice to be kissed by him and maybe one day, once we were married, of course...

Too many rocks had made it clear that my daydreams were pointless—so I stopped having them.

No boy from home would ever touch a cursed girl.

But Aiden wasn't from home.

And I *had* started having daydreams again.

What if Aiden had turned to take me downstairs instead of up here?

My cheeks reddened as I looked at his handsome face, the memory of what it was like to be held in his arms, the smell of him...

"I find that hard to believe."

"I've never even been kissed."

He gave me an incredulous look.

"Now I know you're lying."

"I'm not."

His gaze fell down to my mouth, and my heartbeat became frantic.

He raised his hand, hesitated, then gently placed it on my check. "Never?"

I wanted to die. I wanted him to kiss me. I wanted him to kiss me and then die from ecstasy, from how I knew it would make me feel.

He moved his face closer to mine.

"Never?"

I could feel his breath on my lips.

Things that make them not the same.

I gasped for breath as I pulled away.

He sat up as well, turning away from me to look out at the lights.

I faced toward them as well, gripping the edge of the bench, trying to keep from having to ask what I knew I needed to ask.

"Aiden, I'm sorry, but that wasn't the question I wanted to ask earlier."

He was silent, everything about him that was open and giving a moment ago now closed.

"What do you want to know?"

I tried to form the words, but they wouldn't come. Then he turned to me, forcing me to look at him. The coldness I saw made it clear he knew exactly what I was about to say.

"Some of the other servants...after that first day when you ran into me..."

"You mean when you ran into me."

Please stop talking.

His mouth shut.

"Afterwards when the other girls found out, they all became afraid."

His face became unreadable.

"They all said to stay away from you. That if you caught me, got me alone, that you would—"

I couldn't say it. Not when he had never hurt me.

"What did they say that I would do?"

"It doesn't matter."

"Clearly it does, or you wouldn't be leaning away from me."

I sat up straight.

The corner of his mouth lifted, but there was no humor there. And the words poured out of me.

"They say that your father takes outer-ring girls, and that it isn't just that he, he..." I closed my eyes. "That they are never the same afterwards."

It's only a matter of time.

"And that you were going to be just like him."

He shot to his feet and strode to the edge of the landing, his fists clenched at his side. His voice was so soft I almost didn't hear him. "Why are you here?"

"Aiden—"

"WHY ARE YOU HERE!?!" He spun on me, and his eyes were the same manic I had seen before. "If you think I'm going to rape you, then why did you spend hours alone with me? If you think I'm going to do what my father does, and believe me I *know* what he does, then why, WHY would you come up here with me?"

"But you didn't hurt me…"

"You think all because I didn't hurt you *before* that that would somehow protect you?!"

"I don't care what they say!"

"You should!"

I've never seen him so upset, his eyes wild with what I was shocked to see as fear.

"Aiden," I said standing, reaching out to him, only to have him stumble away from me, as if I were the one that would hurt *him*. The shock I was feeling must have been on my face, because he suddenly turned away from me, his hands covering his face as his head tilted toward the sky.

"Aiden, why did you bring me here tonight?"

"I don't know."

"If it wasn't to hurt me, then why?"

"I already said I don't know! Whenever I start to think I've figured it out, that I know why I can't just leave you alone, it all comes unraveling apart again!"

His shoulders were moving like he couldn't breathe. And I knew then why *I* was there.

A light flashed on his shoulder. It circled his head, flick-ered around his shoulder, then came toward me, trailing a thread of light. It reached me, rested on my chest, then faded.

Shame.

I walked around until I was in front of him. Gently I reached up and pulled his hands away from his face.

"I know you, Aiden," I said, squeezing his hands so he knew I meant it. "I trust you because when you're with me I know that you aren't just trying to survive."

His gaze held mine like he was lost in a dark forest and I was a light through the trees.

"That's not true. I've never felt more like I'm about to die than when I'm with you."

I couldn't help but smile at something so absurd.

"If I'm so dangerous then why are you still here?"

He gave a half smile in return, and his hands tightened around mine.

"Because you've trapped me."

"Now you're being ridiculous." I turned to walk back toward the bench, and he followed, not letting go of my hand. "You know where the door is. You can leave any time you want."

"Maybe," he said, flopping back down. "But maybe I want to be trapped for a bit longer."

The flirty smile was back and I rolled my eyes.

But I didn't let go of his hand.

"So!" He said, gratefully dissipating the tension. "Does my story surprise you?"

"Definitely not. You have 'poor suffering rich boy' written all over your face."

"Hey!"

"Oh what a hard life!" I jumped to my feet and threw the back of my hand against my forehead. "To be bored at a party at the palace, being stuffed with wine and fine food by a hundred servants! My pity knows no bounds!"

He laughed, and I was reminded again of how much I loved the sound of it.

"Are the girls at court like this?" I stood up on my tiptoes as if I were wearing a pair of those awful shoes I had seen them wear, one hand holding the edge of my skirt while the other one was pretending to hold a fan. "'Oh my, Lord Aiden! You must have grown a full inch since I saw you last! I'll have to get even higher heels. Let me tell you all about my shoes!'"

He was doubled over now, rolling to one side of the bench, and for a second I thought he would roll right off.

"You're a dead copy of Lady Alexia! She said almost the exact same thing to me two months ago! Only she then went off about needing to be high enough to see my blue eyes or something."

Blue eyes?

Of course I wouldn't be the only one to notice. Every girl in Tamerin, if given a chance, would fall in love with his beautiful eyes. Girls that were born to inner rings—girls that he would actually be able to be with.

What had I been thinking?

It was the lights. They made me hope again.

When was I ever going to learn?

I turned away from him toward those very same deceptive lights, wrapping my arms around myself.

"Kailin?" He wasn't laughing now. "What happened? Did I say something wrong?"

"No."

"You're lying."

"I'm just cold."

I could hear him stand up and felt him move behind me. He was so close the night air was blocked.

I hugged myself tighter.

"Would you like my cloak?"

"But then you'd be cold."

A moment passed, then another.

"Do you have any other ideas?"

Slowly, I reached my arms behind me. He took my hands, the edges of his cloak in them, pulling me close while wrapping us both inside its warmth.

"Better?" he whispered into my hair.

"Yes. Much better."

TWENTY-EIGHT

It was eleven the next night, when I returned to the workroom after cleaning up another sticky mess on the stairs. I hadn't seen Aiden since the roof, and I felt a hole searing in my chest every time I thought of the way he had held me. He had been the perfect gentleman and walked me back to the stairwell after I was sufficiently warmed, but in the craziness of the moment we had completely forgotten to arrange our next meeting.

I was counting down the hours to Lady Cathrina's class the next morning.

I was surprised to see Lancy still awake when I opened the workroom door, but I shouldn't have been. Sometimes she would stay up late studying if the mood struck her.

"Hello, Lancy," I said, closing the door behind me.

"Kailin," she muttered, not looking up.

"What's tonight's topic?" I tried to sound nonchalant, but I had always wondered what it was she was constantly reading and taking notes on.

"The history of the ring system," she replied. I almost

dropped the mop, but caught it in time to stare at her. Oblivious to my reaction, she picked up her pen and wrote something down in her notebook.

"The history of rings?" I moved over and sat across from her at the table. "*That's* what you've spent all this time studying?"

"There's a lot to study."

The history of the ring system?! If I thought that she was odd before, this just made me sure she must have lost a few branches when she was demoted.

Yet...

"So what have you found out?"

She looked up at me, her eyes gauging how serious I was. I guess I succeeded because she turned her precious notebook around toward me and flipped to a page near the front. On it was a long line covering both pages with years marked off at even intervals marked with notes every now and then.

A timeline.

"This," she said pointing to one end that showed a picture of a boat with some notes underneath. "Is when our ancestors first arrived five hundred years ago and when The Great One supposedly found us. At that time our first social order was established—one that was based on what sort of work you did for society rather than who your parents were. A system that you can easily move up or down in, even from year to year. A system where no one was, by definition, less than anyone else."

I knew my mouth was probably hanging open. I had already known everything she just told me from the old healer in the city, but Lancy had said she had found this out in a *book*?

"What book told you all that?"

"No *one* book said anything that specific, and all the newer books from the last hundred years don't say anything about it at all. I had to piece it together from books they keep in the back of the library from before then. The librarian didn't even know what they were when I found them."

"So where did the rings come from?"

"The first mention of rings occurs at the same time as the first mention of Nobility, happening around here." She pointed at her timeline from about four hundred years ago, "But back then it was mostly wealthy people with land who passed on their wealth to the next generation. The idea of rings came from a tree—obviously, everything in our society comes from trees—where the growth of a tree happens in the most inner rings and then it expands and goes outward as new rings form in the center. The idea was that these landowners were the ones that were the center of all prosperity, the source of society's *growth*, hence the inner ring."

"That makes sense...in a perverted kind of way."

"Exactly, but even back then it was more of an idea than a true definition of legitimacy. Even though Nobles had more power than most, it wasn't exclusive. You could still work hard, buy land, and join their ring, with well over fifty documented cases I could find in the next hundred years of people doing so, though to be honest there were twice that many people losing that title after blowing their inheritance."

"Blowing their inheritance?! Like, not have any money left? How does a Noble not have any money left?" The only way I could think of a Noble becoming poor was if Tamerin didn't have any money left to give.

"Because they couldn't just take what they wanted. They had to *buy* what they needed, same as everyone else."

Same as everyone else.

"Then here," she said pointing to about a hundred years later, "is when the first mention of the laws of ring inheritance were drafted, where a Noble was able to inherit the title as a form of honor even if they were landless, letting them have a few more privileges. This is also when Tamerin got its first King, who was at first just a really rich Noble that the other powerful Nobles of the time liked. But they didn't just hand all the power over. Those same 'friends' started the first Senate as a way to check the King's power, but they kept it at one hundred seats to keep that power concentrated. There were still other Nobles who weren't in the Senate, but after another hundred years they either merged their families with the Nobles who were in power or just conveniently disappeared from the records."

"Which is where the rule of only a hundred Noble families comes from," I said.

"Exactly! And here," she continued without pausing, now pointing to the spot about a fifty years later, "is the first mention of the term *Peasant*, which back then just meant someone who wasn't a Noble—it had nothing to do with poverty until about 97 years later when the terms Merchant and Lower Noble appeared, the first being just a Peasant who was rich like a Noble but didn't have any Noble blood, the second being someone who was from a Noble family but wasn't on the Senate. Land started being divided up here as well, on the first level with the Merchant families, then the whole of Tamerin divided up by the Nobles. This is also where the term *Tradesman* became important, which back then simply meant 'not farmer.' Those three lower rings had constant mobility, where a Peasant could take up a trade and a Tradesman could get rich like a Merchant; and likewise, a Merchant could lose it all and become dirt poor, until hundred and fifty years ago when it began to get harder to move out of the bottom two rings. Then nearly one hundred years ago, they wrote it into law that you could never leave your ring; where you were born was where you stayed."

She paused then, and a shadow crossed her face.

"Unless the Senate decides to move you, that is."

"So," I said, "you're telling me that the rings, as we know them, have only been around for a hundred years?"

"I believe I just gave you a *very* in-depth summary leading to that conclusion."

"But it just—it just feels like it has always been this way—at least that is what they teach."

"Exactly," Lancy said, a new hardness coming into her eyes. I wondered what other conclusions she had drawn from her studies.

"Wait, you're forgetting Healers!" I leaned over to look at her notebook and she pointed at the hundred-year mark again.

"They were created at the same time as the solidification of the rings. Apparently the original Healers were causing a lot of trouble. People were becoming Healers from all the different rings, and were acting as a rogue group outside of the prescribed social order, not only healing anyone who came to them but also, and this was the important part, *teaching* whatever they wanted, usually the same history I just told you about what society used to be like. As you can guess, the Senate didn't like that, so the government did what it always does when it wants to stamp something out—it makes it official. This was also when they separated the role of Healers and Priests."

"What do you mean separated?"

"Because for hundreds of years Healers weren't just the ones who were in charge of, well, healing everyone. They were also the ones who taught and led the worship of The Great One."

I couldn't breathe.

"Once Healer was established as a ring and people began studying at the Healer Academy or at the Priest Seminary, the leadership of the Healers was broken down, and what was taught at both became standardized and controlled. The few random naysayers who refused to comply were made Peasants and never heard from again. And that is how we've gotten to the perfect, happy Tamerin of today."

I stared at her timeline. I felt lightheaded. Here it all was, the history of how Tamerin had fallen into the state it was in now, put together by a demoted girl in a room little better than a broom closet.

"It seemed like the other rings just sort of happened over time, but that the Healers were specifically targeted," I said.

"Look at that, she's paying attention! You're right, they *had* to get rid of the Healers, because they had something the Senate would never have."

She leaned closer.

"They taught the people to have faith, not just for this life but for the next. They had answers to those questions we all ask ourselves if we're ever given enough of a break to ask. And no one, not even the King, can give you a belief about your eternal soul."

She leaned back again.

"And then there was the issue of the prophecies—none of them really liked that at all."

I suddenly felt very cold.

"Prophecies?"

She looked at me like she could see I cared, and disproved.

"That Tamerin would be destroyed unless they returned to the old ways. But that is all just a bunch of religious mysticism. From what my research has concluded, the real problem with the dissolving of the traditional Healers is the lack of stability it created. Having them come from all the rings and then serving all the rings held society together. Without them the rings have become more and more inwardly focused, which will cause a collapse unless something is done. You don't need an old prophet in a hovel somewhere to tell you that."

She looked back down at her notes, her mouth turning down in a little frown.

And I felt it—the *pull*. It was tight in my chest and my hand went up to where I could imagine it coming out of me.

A light flew out of my chest and trailed a thread to her, and then both faded.

Determination.

"Lancy, why are you studying all this?"

Her jaw grew tight as she stared at the page in front of her.

"Because it has come to my attention in the last few years that the way things are is wrong. This isn't how life is supposed to be and I wanted to figure out what went wrong so that maybe, someday, someone—"

"Kailin!"

Markly had burst through the door. Seeing me she grabbed my arm and pulled me off the bench, dragging me toward the door.

"Markly! What's happened!" I said, yanking my arm back.

"It's Robert! I need your help!" She turned on me and her face was covered in tears.

I glanced over at Lancy, who was now standing up at the table, her face just as shocked as mine must have been.

"Markly," I started again, "I'm not any good with relation-ship advice—"

"He was in another riot! You said once that your aunt did a little village healing, right? She must have taught you something!"

I could feel my face pale as the magnitude of what she was asking sank in.

"You should take him to the hospital." My voice was flat, but my hands were shaking.

"I can't! If it was found out he was involved he would be dismissed! Please, Kailin." Her eyes were pleading as she pulled on my hand toward the door again. "I don't know who else I can trust."

I paused for only a moment, but I knew what my answer would be. It was the only one I could ever give. I turned toward Lancy. "You're coming too."

"What?" she shrieked. "I don't know anything about healing!"

"But you know how to stitch much better than me, and knowing Robert, we're probably going to need a lot of thread."

Together we ran out of the door. The two of them turned to start descending the servant stairs, but I turned toward the main halls.

"Where are you going?!" Markly yelled after me.

"If I'm going to do this I need more than just my hands!" I was through the door at a run, the other two girls following me through the deserted halls as we took the turn to the north-east stairwell and ran down the stairs two at a time until we reached the sixth floor.

Without hesitating I yanked the practice room door open and went straight to the supply closet in the corner. I opened it and breathed in the scents of all the herbs that had surrounded me since I was born. I didn't have access to the pharmacy, so I was going to have to make everything from scratch.

Just like in Lady Cathrina's class.

Just like at home with Aunt Beredith.

Markly's eyes opened wide as I began putting jars and bandages into her arms.

"Kailin," she whispered, "do you know what you're doing?"

I snapped my head around, suddenly back on the third floor of the Hospital the week before, when a dark-haired young man had asked me the same question.

"Yes." I grabbed two good mixing bowls and a pair of aprons, gloves, and masks.

On the next shelf down were the sterilized surgical packets. I looked at Lancy, her arms now holding half of the things I had given to Markly.

I grabbed the one on top and slammed the closet door shut.

"Where is he?" I yelled behind me as we cut into the servant's stairs.

"He's down in his room—there was so much blood! He might even be dead now! I shouldn't have let him go, I told him that he was kindle-brained for going, but Robert seems to *thrive* on that."

"Word must have leaked," she continued as we rounded a bend around the second floor, "because there was a whole platoon of guards waiting for them! It was a massacre! Dustin barely made it out carrying Robert."

Lancy tripped but managed to catch herself. "Dustin was there?!"

"He said he only went to keep an eye on Robert, and I thank The Great One that he did! He's in Robert's room with him now trying to keep him from bleeding out!"

I quickened my pace.

We turned down and around the confusing corridors hidden inside the walls of the Academy until we reached the first floor where they opened out into the wider halls of the servants' rooms. I let Markly lead the way, but I could have found the room without her from the trail of blood that was still slick on the ground.

When Markly reached his door and opened it, I froze.

Robert was grimacing in pain on his bed, and he was covered in blood—whether his own or someone else's I didn't know. Dustin looked almost as bad, only I knew that it was all

Robert's blood on his clothes as he appeared to be unharmed. I took a breath, then handed Lancy my pile and quickly moved to the other side of the bed, pulling on one of the sets of protective gear I had brought.

"What are his main injuries?" I asked, mimicking the way Aiden had behaved that day in the Hospital.

"One of the guards got him with a knife! He probably has a few broken ribs as well, but—" Dustin pulled back the towel he had been using to stop the bleeding and Markly let out a cry. It was easily about three inches long along his abdomen and looked terrible, but from a quick examination I could see that it was shallow and hadn't pierced any organs.

Now it was my turn to give a prayer of thanks that Robert's injury was one I could actually treat and that I had had plenty of practice from that day with the riots.

"You," I said turning to Dustin, "keep putting pressure on that wound, let's try and save as much of his blood as possible. Markly," I said, turning toward her, "go get some boiling water and clean towels." She was gone before I was finished saying the words, but I knew she would get what I asked for. "And you," I said, turning to Lancy, "go find a mop and soap and clean up that blood out in the halls before someone sees it!"

Lancy normally hated mopping, but she didn't hesitate as she ran from the room as well. Now with some space in the small single bedroom I turned and lit the remaining lanterns, then laid out my supplies on the small side table he had in the corner. Organization wasn't just a matter of professionalism; knowing what was where was a matter of life and death.

Then I began to mix the dry ingredients as Aunt Beredith had taught me, forming the familiar salve that would numb the pain, disinfect the wound, and help the blood congeal.

Markly was back with a small pot of boiled water within a few minutes.

"I can go get more, but I thought you might need some now," she said, out of breath.

"This is perfect," I said, mimicking the way Lady Cathrina always spoke to her patients, inspiring confidence and calm in every syllable. I measured out the water I needed into the other ingredients and stirred it until it was a soft, pasty consistency.

I poured the rest of the water into the second bowl and mixed in some greenflakes.

"This will sterilize the water. Now Markly," I said as calmly as I could. "Dustin is going to pull the towel away, and I need you to use one of the clean towels and the water I just sterilized to quickly clean. Don't worry about making him bleed again, I'll be taking care of that in a moment.

Markly was as pale as a sheet in the lantern light of the room, but she nodded her head and dipped one of the towels she had brought into the water.

I looked at her and then over at Dustin. His eyes were scared, but they also held a steadiness in them that I had begun to associate with him. He nodded his head to my unasked question.

"Now."

He pulled away the towel and Markly began cleaning the wound with the same efficiency she did every other chore in her life. Only the look in her eyes betrayed how emotionally taxed she was becoming.

When it was clean enough I pulled her back and quickly began using the spoon to apply the salve.

"AH!" Robert yelled, but it dimmed into a moan as the wound began to numb. The injured muscles underneath tightened at the touch of the medicine, but soon relaxed. When I had finished the last of it, Lancy opened the door.

"Done!" she said; then taking in the scene, she froze again.

"Good," I said, stepping back and handing her the second

set of protective clothes. "Because now it's your turn." Her face paled to the point of turning slightly green. "Go clean your hands in the water in that bowl, then gear up. I'll get the surgical packet ready for you."

"Kailin!"

"You are the best seamstress I've ever met, much better than I will ever be." She still looked scared. I threaded the hook-like needle with the thick surgical thread and held it out to her. "You are strong and brave and powerful—and you *can* do this."

A determination came into her eyes, and the Lancy I had always known, the one determined not to just let the world impact her but to push back as well, was standing in front of me.

She grabbed the other apron and mask I had brought with me, washed her hands in the remaining water, put on the gloves, and took the needle. I stepped back as she went to work over the now-moaning Robert, and with movements that couldn't have been taught better in the Academy she sewed up the wound. She had never sewn skin before, but she adapted her stitch with a skill that showed her talent and intelligence in a flawless combination. When she stepped back, I was amazed at how beautiful it actually looked.

I applied more of the salve to disinfect the stitching and stop the bleeding of the needle marks, and then using the bandages began wrapping him up.

Everyone was quiet while I worked, and I hardly noticed when Dustin left the room.

"Am I dying?" Robert moaned.

"Not if you do what I tell you to." I smiled, knowing that if he could talk then the pain couldn't be as bad anymore. "No moving for at least two days. Change the bandage once a day, applying more of the disinfectant from this jar. And if there is any sign of infection or fever you need to come and get me right away."

Robert started to mutter a protest, but Markly cut him off.

"Of course, whatever you say, Kailin." She was looking at me as if she had never seen me before. "Where did you learn to heal like a real Healer?"

"My aunt..." I started. The adrenaline was leaving my system, and as I had felt in the Hospital a week earlier, my body was beginning to shut down on its own. "We used to deal with farmers cutting themselves on equipment all the time—which is actually a lot like getting gutted with a knife in a riot apparently."

Markly smiled slightly, and I knew then that no matter what, she was never going to treat me as just an underservant again.

I returned her smile, then turned to tell Lancy what an amazing job she had done, but she was watching the door.

"Go to him!" Markly snapped.

"I can't—"

"Yes, you can! I don't care what your past is, he loves you and you love him! And when you get a gift from life like that, you don't just stand around!" She wrenched open the door. "Go! NOW!"

Lancy paused for only a moment, then ran past her.

"Finally," Markly sighed, shutting it again. "For all her studying she's one of the most kindle–brained people I know." She leaned in to kiss Robert and I quickly jumped up, suddenly feeling how horribly small the room was.

"I'll be right outside," I muttered, and closed the door behind me.

The hall was dim from the low lights of the lanterns set for the night. I leaned against the wall by the door and breathed. Then a movement down the hall caught my eye. I turned my head and could make out two figures standing in the shadows. Lancy was standing in front of Dustin, her with her arms around her middle, him as tall and straight as any unfeeling mountain. I couldn't hear their words, but then she reached out and took his hand. When she brought his hand up to her face, he yanked her to him. They merged into one shadow.

"I'll clean up the room." Markly was suddenly behind me, watching the long-awaited scene as well. "I know how. You've done so much, go get some sleep."

I nodded, and slowly began to make my way toward the stairs.

TWENTY-NINE

I didn't go to sleep.

First I snuck into the hospital to use one of the washrooms, throwing the borrowed aprons, masks, and gloves into the hampers. I used the special soaps on my hands as well, but mostly I just let the water flow over my hands and stared unseeing as I moved them back and forth in the stream.

Once I was clean, I began making my way back to my room, but I never made it. I found myself wandering, until I came to the alcove on the sixth floor where I had once been trapped. I climbed up onto the sill, then turned to bring my legs up and lean against the wall. I looked down at the garden below, and then at the sky above. I watched the moon rise and fall and the lightening of the sky as the sun began to warm the world.

I thought I should think through everything I had just done in one short night—how I had taken charge of the people who had always controlled me, how I drew upon my knowledge to actually heal someone by myself...but for some reason my mind just couldn't stay on those thoughts for long.

Instead, I couldn't stop seeing Lancy and Dustin in that

darkened hallway, when all their doubts and fears had been pushed aside for something greater.

I couldn't stop thinking about everyone who had ever meant anything to me.

I could see Avonly and myself hiding by the small creek back home giggling when we were six years old—and how far we'd come and how much had changed. I'd always have in my heart the little girl who ignored her parents and befriended me when no one else would.

I thought of Aunt Beredith—tall and imposing with her no-nonsense attitude toward life. Then with complete clarity I saw what I had never realized before.

My childhood had been a happy one.

I had believed until this moment that my past was just a string of sad incidents because of how cruel my neighbors were and because of what I didn't have—but now I knew that what I *did* have was infinitely more than most people, Peasant or Noble.

I grew up knowing I was loved.

Closing my eyes, I could see my aunt throughout the years, watching over me, teaching me, reprimanding me—but never dismissing me. Finally, I thought of the last time I saw her as the wagon pulled away.

Of how she watched me as if she didn't know how to stop.

I leaned my head back and stared out the window toward the morning-lit gardens.

I was loved. I might never see my aunt again, but I could live every day knowing what that meant.

And that's when I saw him.

He was the only one out there this early, carrying a box of young plants toward a grove of evergreen trees in one of the corners. It was still cool from the season and the early hour, but he was wearing only a shirt and a vest hanging open at his sides, as if he were above such things as climate. He paused and looked up as a bird flew from one side of the garden to the other. His hair fell down over his forehead, his lips curled in a smile, his eyes following its path.

He turned back to the trees and disappeared around the edge of them.

I flew down the stairs two at a time and went out the forbidden door into the open air. Without checking first to see if I would be caught, I strode across the lawn and stepped through the thick branches.

And there he was, kneeling on a pad in front of an open garden shed near the wall, planting the plants he had brought with him. He turned when he heard me move through the trees.

"Kailin?" He said standing up. "What are you—"

I threw my arms around his stupid neck and kissed him.

Aiden only hesitated a second before his arms snapped around me, making me gasp.

Then he dropped me, making me stumble backwards.

"WHAT THE HELL!?" he shouted. I had seen him look like he was about to come unhinged before, but now he looked almost feral.

"Aiden?"

This wasn't how it was supposed to be.

"I," he stuttered, his eyes going wild, his hands now pulling at his hair. "I, I can't, I am, you are, can't—"

He closed his eyes. I waited for him to open them and laugh, smile at me in that way that made me feel all funny in my stomach.

Then he actually did open his eyes.

They were cold. His hands let go of his hair and fell as solid fists at his side.

I paled, taking a step back.

He took a step forward.

"You are a servant," he said.

This wasn't Aiden. This was *Lord* Aiden who had dragged me through the halls to Healer Steverno's office.

And in his hard eyes I could see all the things I was supposed to fear from him that he had worked so hard to make me forget, and I could see my future so clearly.

A future where his hand strikes me just as Healer Steverno's did. A future where I ran for the door and went back to my servant halls and chores. A future where I would never see his face again and prayed that he not notice me if I passed his mud-encrusted shoes because if he did, then—

No!

I *couldn't* believe he was gone.

I tightened my jaw, planted my feet and looked back at him with all the fire I had, challenging the eighteen years of social conditioning that told him I didn't have a name.

His eyes flickered, but his hands were still clenched.

He took another step.

"You are a Peasant..." His voice wasn't as strong as it was before.

He took one more step, and he was there in front of me, me looking up and him looking down.

"You are..."

I'm Kailin! The girl you tutor, who helped you heal, who makes you laugh and tell secrets and hold in front of a thousand lights!

He collapsed sideways against the wall. Catching himself, he turned so his back was against it, his head in his hands.

"Aiden?" I asked, reaching out my hand, then pulling it back. "What's wrong?"

"Everything," he muttered from behind his hands.

When he didn't move, I leaned against the wall next to him.

"You looked like you were going to punish me," I whispered.

"Punish you?" Aiden snapped, looking at me. "Why in the world would I punish you!?"

"Because I attacked you."

"Yes..." his eyebrows were pulled together. "I guess, given the strict definition, you did."

"Aiden," I said, raising my hand to touch his face. He closed his eyes at my touch. "You scared me."

"I scared myself."

Then his eyes snapped open, and I could see his mind moving at speeds I would never be fast enough to understand.

I dropped my hand, and the enormousness of what I had just done crashed on top of me.

I had kissed him.

I really had done it.

And he looked like he had *hated* it.

"I need to get back to work," I said, turning away.

I gasped as I was yanked back and through the door of the gardening shed.

And then Aiden was kissing me.

If my kiss had been an attack, then his was an all-out siege. My stomach shot into my throat and my heart crashed to my feet and my arms wrapped around his neck like a lifeline above a cliff.

He gasped at my grip, and pulled me closer into his chest.

I was the first one to pull back, and when I did I could see the light from the cracks in the wood of the door reflected in his eyes. They were full of fear and shock and joy all rolled into one incomprehensible emotion.

"Kailin!" he gasped.

"What?"

"You are Kailin." He brought his mouth next to my ear, and

even though it was warm in his arms I still shivered. "You are a servant and you are a Peasant and you are Kailin—and you are amazing. And *that's* why I could never, *ever* leave you alone."

I could feel myself melt at his words and my fingers found his hair and pulled his face toward mine again.

This time his kiss was soft, and I could feel how gentle Aiden would always be with me.

It was a kiss that hinted of the possibility of danger in every shadow of this world, yet for the first time in my life I felt truly safe.

Because it wasn't just a boy kissing me—it was *Aiden*.

The one I knew—the one I trusted.

The one I had fallen in love with.

We pulled apart again and I laid my head on his shoulder.

"Aiden, why did you act like that?"

His lips brushed my hair.

"Because I didn't know yet who I was. I do now though. And that person wants to be with you."

I pulled back and looked up at him, my unasked question pleading from my eyes.

"I don't know how," he breathed, his forehead gently falling onto mine.

"Couldn't we, I mean—it was working before, wasn't it?"

"I don't think stolen moments would be enough for me."

"But then what can we do?"

"I—I don't know." He pulled me against his chest again, his arms firm in their hold of me.

"Aiden..."

"Please don't go yet," he whispered, kissing my hair. "Just a few more minutes. I want to remember everything."

I sank back into his arms and they became sweet and kind, his hand tracing my face, his lips kissing my cheek, my neck, the top of my head; and I could feel him breathe in the scent of me.

I nestled my face into his shoulder and felt him take a breath as I turned my head up to his neck, pressing my lips against his skin there. I breathed in his clean and earthy smell, and I suddenly knew it was because he spent so much time out in the garden. I smiled and pressed a little harder until I could feel his rapid pulse just barely under his skin. If I was never held again I would still be happy, because this memory of being encased in his arms was perfection.

After what seemed like only seconds or maybe days, his hand found the side of my face and turned me up to look at him. His eyes were sad, but he still smiled as he took in my face. I smiled as I pulled him down and he pulled me up.

This kiss was different, lacking any of the desperation and fear the other ones had. This one was just me and Aiden, sharing our secret friendship building into this secret moment.

I smiled against his lips and I could feel him do the same. I giggled and he pulled away.

"What?" he asked, a laugh in his voice.

"I'm happy."

"Happy?"

"Yes," I said as his eyebrows pulled together again in that way that drove me insane. I reached my hand up and touched the spot between them, and laughed again. "How does it feel to have your puzzle solved?"

"What makes you think I've solved you yet?" he said, taking my hand from his forehead and drawing my wrist to his mouth. I shivered again as he kissed it and placed it on his chest as if it was his most prized possession, his other arm around my back pulling me somehow closer to him still. Then he dropped his forehead onto mine, not like a lover seducing his soulmate, but like Aiden would if he were holding me in a dark storage shed and I was his best friend.

I smiled again, closing my eyes.

After a minute I could feel him take a deep breath.

Then blow it right into my face.

"Blaa! Aiden!"

"We should probably go before someone comes looking for a shovel."

"Yes," I sighed, reluctance pouring into the syllable.

He gave me one last quick kiss, his lips tasting sweet; then let me go and reached for the door.

"Wait!" My hand grasped the top of his before he could turn the handle. "We haven't figured it out yet! How are we going to make this work? When—" I took a deep breath, begging for reality not to swallow us whole yet. "When do I get to see you again?"

He wouldn't look at me, but I could see his jaw tighten.

"Aiden..." I whispered.

"Meet me at the stairwell after Lady Cathrina's class this afternoon," he said turning toward me. "We'll go to our roof and figure this out." I smiled when he said "our roof," but it froze on my lips when he didn't smile back.

I let go of his hand and he stepped out into the light, quickly making his way through the trees.

He didn't look back.

The light was pouring into the shed now, but without him there it seemed as dark as midnight.

My fingers went up to my lips, and I closed my eyes, not believing that it had really happened.

But it had.

It was real.

It was the most real thing that had ever happened to me.

THIRTY

It was patient day, which was both good and bad.

Good because everyone was so busy with their own assignments that no one would be looking at my face. Everything inside me kept jumping from shock to excitement to overwhelming joy and finally to terror. I'm sure that all of it would be obvious to anyone looking my way.

Good thing I was standing *behind* Lady Cathrina.

On the other hand, patient day was *very* bad because I had nothing to do *but* try not to look at Aiden—which was impossible, since he kept looking at me. He had kept his head down when I entered in Lady Cathrina's wake, but throughout the hour he kept looking my way. It was all either of us could do to look away and pretend to be thinking about anything other than what I knew was on both our minds.

Ten more minutes.

My head felt light at the thought, and instinctively my eyes gravitated again to his face halfway down the room. He was leaning forward, trying to hear what the old woman he was treating was saying. I allowed a smile, imagining her telling him every detail about her fifty grandchildren.

Then, just as he had three minutes earlier, he turned his head and I could feel my heart crash against my ribcage at the smile on his lips.

His lips.

I looked away first and focused instead on the back of Lady Cathrina's head, knowing how pink my face was.

Nine more minutes.

Lady Cathrina was leaning back in her chair with her arms crossed. Instead of going through patient reports or watching to make sure no one killed anyone, she was staring at the far wall. I tried to see what she was looking at when her voice made me jump.

"Kailin." I moved quickly next to her chair. "I have a meeting after this class. Can you please go around and collect the patient reports now? We can go over them before I have to leave and fix anything the students missed."

The Great One loved me! I would be able to leave right when class ended!

"My meeting should last only an hour or so. Afterwards I want you to come to my office."

I tried to move as quickly as I could, but students kept jumping in front of me, switching stations as their chatter about plans for after class created an annoying background noise. I was about to yell at a girl who had nearly knocked me over, but I bit my tongue in time.

I was supposed to be invisible.

Even if I wasn't to the boy at my next station.

Taking a deep breath, I hugged the patient reports closer to my chest and focused on the folder at the end of the old woman's bed. He wasn't looking this way; he wouldn't know, which was best, because...I reached out my hand.

"And who is this young lady?"

Aiden's head snapped around and with complete disregard for self-preservation he smiled at me.

"She's Healer Cathrina's assistant."

"You must be very accomplished to have such an important position." Then she gave Aiden a smile. "on top of being very pretty, of course."

"She most definitely is."

I quickly turned away, ducking my head to hide my smile.

"Now," I heard him say behind me, "what was the name of your youngest granddaughter again?"

Five more minutes.

I was stepping on air as I reached the end of the room, and I wouldn't have thought anything of the argument happening at the last station if they hadn't been arguing about whether or not to kill someone.

"You can't mix minkroot and wipsal together!"

Not entirely true, I thought, suddenly very interested; *you could if you wanted to melt someone's tongue.*

A tall brunette was dumping the contents of a drinking goblet into a spare bowl while her red-faced partner bristled next to her.

"You're the one that doesn't know anything!" He was a pudgy boy with too large of a nose and pockmarks, which wouldn't have condemned him if it hadn't been for the shallow eyes completing the picture. I recognized him as a boy who hardly ever showed up for class, but he was here today for some reason.

"Don't you know who I am!?" he hissed.

The girl froze, and I thought I could see her gulp down a breath she hadn't taken.

"I don't care who you are," she muttered bravely. "I'm not going to fail because of you."

The girl stalked away toward the front of the room where Lady Cathrina sat, leaving the boy fuming behind her. Once she was past the group next to theirs he grabbed the goblet she had left on their small worktable. Then he did the worst thing he could have done.

He started to pour the poison from the bowl back into it.

I looked at their patient, waiting for him to yell out that he was about to be murdered.

But what I saw there scared me more than what the boy was doing.

He was a man with a worn brown face, with white hair and beard. He might have been any grandfather I passed in the streets.

But his eyes were anything but normal.

Or sane.

They were devoid of anything remotely resembling a will to live.

His face was strangely peaceful with an apathy that both fascinated and repulsed me. I had seen death before, but there had always been at least some fight, some hope that even through the pain they might heal...

He didn't even blink as he watched the boy shake the last drop from the bowl into the goblet.

I couldn't move, each of my muscles rigid with indecision. I shouldn't, couldn't, draw attention to myself, but how could I let—

My eyes fixed on the goblet in the boy's hands.

I couldn't see anything else.

I gasped, dropping the patient reports on the ground as my hand grabbed the base of my throat.

The *pull!*

It was suffocating me!

I desperately tried to scream but nothing would come out.

Oh no...please, no!

The blue lights.

I'm just Kailin!

They were everywhere.

Leave me alone!

Every person was burning with them. Threads of fire running from one to another. Through the ceiling, the floor, the walls. To a bag, the jars, the patients.

Two threads were running into my own chest.

The old man!

I turned back to him, tuning out everyone else, and saw—I didn't believe what I saw.

Lying just under his skin was a universe of stars burning, so much like those I had seen the night of the fire. They moved as one, connected in a way I didn't understand as they pushed and pulled on one another, holding everything that made the man in front of me human and alive.

It was wonderful.

It was horrible.

I begged to wake up, but this wasn't a dream.

Then with a flare, the lights inside him drew out their own threads of fire, like cords made from the rays of a blue sun, but where most of the threads of fire from the students and other patients were thick like cords, his were all as thin as hair.

And there were only four of them.

One toward the light from the window. One toward the soft hospital blanket draped across his lap. One out through the floor connected to something somewhere else.

And one reaching toward the jars of medical herbs on the central table, branching out to touch five of them.

The ones that when combined correctly would make the medicine that his assigned students were supposed to have made for him.

Then even those threads began to dim. I turned and saw the boy walking toward the man with the goblet. The liquid inside wasn't just black to my new sight, it was devoid of anything.

It was a perfect darkness.

"Now just drink this, old man, and we'll show her not to question those better than her."

I blinked.

A pudgy monster was underneath me with the goblet spilled on the ground next to the bed.

The lights were gone.

And my brain exploded.

I screamed, sitting up and holding my head.

"HOW DARE YOU!" The monster under me screamed. I screamed back and tried to scramble off of him, but his claws —hands—fist—came at me first. I screamed again as my head snapped to the side and hit the floor.

What were the lights?! What did the threads of fire mean? Why—

I sucked in air, a backwards yell, as my body skidded a few inches along the floor, my ribs becoming flashes of white pain. More of the horrid voice yelled, calling me things, each contact with his foot making me curl into myself.

I wanted to be angry.

All I was was scared.

Not of the monster. Not of the pain.

I was afraid of what I now knew of all the sources of light in the room. They were galaxies sending off flames of joy, hope.

Reasons.

"LARSION!"

I looked up at the new voice and saw an angel.

He was tall with dark hair falling on his forehead and

endlessly blue eyes that were so full of fury I knew I was going to die when he reached me.

But it wasn't me he attacked.

He pushed the monster off me and helped me sit up.

"Are you all right?"

I kept my eyes down, afraid of him.

"Kailin, can you hear me?"

Kailin?

I looked up into Aiden's face.

How could I have forgotten him? His face meant everything to me now.

I reached out to him as I started to sob, but instead of pulling me close he yanked me to my feet and shoved me behind him. Other pains were breaking through the surface, and I held my now-bruised body with both hands, my eyes jumping from one face staring at me to another.

But there were no lights.

I was safe.

"What Aiden?" I stopped looking around and focused on the boy in Aiden's face. I recognized his voice as the one I had thought belonged to a monster, but in reality it was just the gross boy from earlier. "Didn't you see her attack me!"

"Shut up Larsion! You were going to puncture a lung the way you were kicking her!"

"Oh, now you're going to be all high and mighty! When everyone knows that if it'd been you she had attacked she wouldn't even be breathing any—"

"I SAID SHUT UP!"

"I don't have to do what you tell me!" He had to be crazy to stand up to Aiden's anger. "And I have as much right as you to claim whatever outer-ring whore I want, and she"—he pointed at me and I cowered behind Aiden— "is going to become an example of what happens when you attack a Noble!"

Noble?

I felt the room grow fuzzy as Lord Larsion grabbed for me, but it snapped back into clarity when Aiden grabbed Lord Larsion's passing wrist and bent it backward. He screamed as he was brought to his knees.

I looked at his face from around Aiden's shoulder, unable to understand how *THIS* pathetic human was a Noble. Anyone could see just from looking at Aiden that he was a Noble, and it would have been a crime against humanity if Lady Cathrina weren't one, but this shrub?

Then with chilling certainty I knew that it wouldn't matter what I thought of him.

He was a Noble.

I had assaulted him.

I was dead.

"You're making a big mistake, Aiden!" Lord Larsion yelled. "Wait until I tell my father about this!"

"Oh really? If that is the game you want to play, then I'll be sure to get *my father* involved as well."

The room went silent.

Lord Larsion's face had turned the color and consistency of raw dough.

"That won't be necessary, Lord Aiden," Lady Cathrina said, pushing her way through the gawking students. Everything must have happened faster than I had realized if it had taken until now for her to reach us.

"Everyone leave." There was no request in her tone.

There was a rush of students grabbing their books, and in less than a minute the room was empty.

"Lord Aiden, please don't break Lord Larsion's wrist."

Aiden twisted Lord Larsion's hand more before letting go,

making him yelp one last time. Lord Larsion cradled his wrist as he got to his feet.

Lady Cathrina didn't even pretend to look concerned.

"Now Kailin," Lady Cathrina said, turning to me. Aiden shifted slightly so he was between us.

As if he were protecting me from her.

As if he saw her as a threat as well.

Lady Cathrina's eyes widened only slightly, but it was enough.

She knew.

I touched Adien's arm. Still rigid, he moved out of the way, now just keeping himself between me and Lord Larsion.

"Can you explain your actions?" Lady Cathrina's face had returned to its mask of professional interest, but her eyes fixed on my forehead where I could feel something warm dripping.

"He—" I tried to take a breath, but my ribs only made me wish I hadn't. "Lord Larsion was about to give his patient minkroot and wipsal—at the same time." Aiden said a word I didn't even know the meaning of while Lady Cathrina didn't move at all—which somehow was so much worse.

"She's lying!"

"I'm NOT! If I hadn't stopped you he would be dead!"

Because I *knew* that if that man had drunk what was in that goblet he would have died. Lord Larsion would have put the void inside him and all the lights were going to fall in and the threads would be snapped and...

Was that what I saw?

I felt dizzy and weak. I thought I would fall, but then Aiden's arm was there.

"Kailin!"

"I'm all right." I got my feet under me, but Aiden didn't let go. Lady Cathrina frowned while Lord Larsion smiled.

I pushed Aiden's arm away from me.

Lady Cathrina walked over to the old man's bed and crouched down over the floor where the goblet had spilled. Then, using two fingers she touched the liquid and brought it up to her nose. She stayed like that for a long time, not moving, her shoulder hardly rising and falling with her breath. Then she stood up, and not looking at us, she reached for a cloth on the tray with the station's supplies.

"Lord Larsion," she began, wiping her fingers on it. "I would like to speak with you and your partner in my office immediately."

Lord Larsion looked like he was going to explode, but he turned around and moved toward the door.

He stopped next to Aiden and whispered loud enough for me to hear.

"She's not worth it. You of all people should know the skinny ones aren't as much fun."

Aiden practically growled, but Lord Larsion just laughed and walked out the door.

When we turned back Lady Cathrina was fuming.

"Go back to your room, Lord Aiden, and stay there!"

"But Kailin's hurt!"

"NOW!"

We both staggered back. Aiden looked like he was going to yell back, but I put my hand on his arm.

"It's all right," I said. "Just do as she asks."

My heart broke at the look he gave me, it was so desperate and worried, but I gave him as much of a smile as I could and pushed him toward the door.

He walked backwards, his eyes not leaving mine until he bumped into the wood.

Then he turned and was gone.

I gasped and sank to my knees. I hurt *so badly*.

Gentle hands reached under my shoulders and lifted me up, then one went around me and helped me to a bench.

Just then the doors at the Hospital end opened and Healer assistants rushed in and began wheeling the patients back to the Hospital.

"The patient reports," I said pointing at the scattered papers on the floor.

Lady Cathrina nodded and went to pick them up. She straightened them and handed them to an assistant, then went to the very supply closet I had ransacked the night before.

She pulled out the things she needed, then knelt in front of me and began to clean my face.

"How long has Lord Aiden had an interest in you?" she asked, her full attention on her task.

"He doesn't. He was just being nice."

She pushed down on the cut and I yelped.

"Sorry," she said, keeping her voice calm.

Silence stretched between us as she took out some ointment, and using a clean cloth she dabbed it on my forehead.

"He started following me around when your class started."

She froze mid-touch, said a word I never thought I would hear her say, then looked sharply at me.

"Has he made you sleep with him?"

"No!" I yelled. "He would never do that to me!"

"Kailin, you don't know Nobles."

"But I know him!"

She looked at me as if I were crazy, and I wondered if I was.

"All right, let me put this to you another way. Whether or not Lord Aiden is *currently* hurting you, he will eventually. But more importantly, by drawing attention to you he has put you at the mercy of *every other young man inside your ring*, which is *everyone*. If you had to pick whether Lord Larsion or Lord Aiden was the most dangerous for you, the answer is Lord Aiden."

"No!" I said again, tears starting to come to my eyes. "He'll keep me safe!"

"And who will keep him safe?"

What was she saying? Aiden was a Noble, no one could hurt him.

Except...

Except they could demote him.

"Come lie down," she said standing up, her voice gentle again. "Let's see how many broken ribs you have."

I lay down on the bench and she started pressing on my chest and sides, making note of places when I winced.

"It's isn't as bad as I thought," she said, helping me back up. "Just some extensive bruising. It'll be awful for a week, but I can give you something for the pain."

"I knew I never should have let Lord Larsion take my class," she continued, sitting on the bench next to me. "I'm sorry that you were brought to his attention, but we aren't helpless. There are things we can do to keep you safe. First, you have to stay away from Lord Aiden. I'll talk to him myself once I sort out this mess and tell him something along the lines of 'don't try to plow my servant or else.'"

"But he wasn't—"

"*Then* you will be restricted to behind walls. I should have seen this coming, but I thought—but it doesn't matter what I thought. You're no longer to be my assistant."

No more classes. No more healing.

No more Aiden.

"But what about the Islands?"

She hesitated.

"I'm sorry, but I'm going to have to train someone else. But the important thing, at least for the next little while, is we need to get you away from here."

"I'm being dismissed? But that man would have died!"

"I'm not dismissing you, Kailin, I'm hiding you for your own safety until things calm down around here."

I pulled my braid over my shoulder, my fingers grabbing the end.

"But where can I go?"

Lady Cathrina didn't look at me. Then slowly, she pulled a letter from her pouch.

"The Great One knows all things. He was already making arrangements."

"What sort of arrangement?"

She tapped the letter in her hands a few times. It was poor paper, water stained and ripped a little at the edge. It must have been very cheap, something only a Peasant would buy.

Then she looked back at me, and this time there were tears in her eyes.

"I was going to tell you this after my meeting this afternoon, but I've made travel arrangements for you. You're going back to your village. Something has happened to your aunt."

End of Part Three

PART FOUR

CHAPTER

THIRTY-ONE

Night had fallen but I couldn't feel the chill. Full-out spring in all its glory was a few weeks away, and standing outside my aunt's house I could see the frost beginning to form on the cracked mud from the early spring rains. But even if it had been a warm summer night I wouldn't have felt it. I was too numb to feel anything, even a cold that was raising goosebumps on my arms.

Aunt Beredith was resting now, and Healer Jonk was in the kitchen preparing for the next dose Aunt Beredith needed at midnight. He was highly recommended by Lady Cathrina, another student from their school days having set up a practice in one of the merchant-owned villages we had passed through on our way here. Though he had done an acceptable job stabilizing my aunt in the day we'd been here, I still didn't trust him.

I didn't trust much of anything anymore.

I wandered back inside, putting on my mask as I closed the door quietly so I wouldn't wake her. Our small common room had become Aunt Beredith's sick chamber, as it was warmer out there by the fire along with more light to see by.

They said she had protested any help, which I could easily believe, and had sent for me only when it became clear she had caught the Winter Fever.

I closed my eyes to try and fight back the tears my sudden anger called up. That letter most likely had cost her her entire savings.

But she had sent it, and Lady Cathrina had sent me home to help her get better.

Because that's why I'm here, I told myself.

I definitely wasn't here to say good-bye.

"You'll catch your death without a cloak, you shrub."

I opened my eyes and turned toward the small bed that had once been mine. It once was a sitting nook in our front room but became my own private alcove when I had outgrown my crib. Aunt Beredith was awake, her eyes catching the firelight. She was bundled up so only her head poked out, and her hair was matted down around her face, making her look like something that had died out in the woods.

Despite how terrible her appearance, it was what her speaking meant that filled me with dread. She had been drifting in and out of consciousness since we got here yesterday, but this was the first time she had spoken.

Anyone else would have felt relieved, but I knew better. Right before Winter Fever either kills you or breaks, there are a few hours where the symptoms almost disappear. My heart stopped at the implication of what tonight might hold.

"You're one to talk," I replied, placing my hands on my hips. "You really want to treat Winter Fever without a face mask?"

"It was dirty and I was in a hurry," she snapped, but her

eyes still lit up. "Did Lady Cathrina teach you to talk with such disrespect to your elders?"

"I missed you, too, Aunt."

Her mouth moved, and though it wasn't a smile, it was something.

"Come over here and tell me about what you've been up to."

I moved a stool over and told her about the last seven months. About the ride to Divlan and how big it was. About the Academy and the size of the kitchen and garden. How beautiful the halls and classrooms were, and how stupid all the students were. She laughed as I told her about the time the head of the kitchen thought the stable boys had stolen the chickens, and I was glad I had come home.

I didn't tell her about Avonly or Aiden, or that I thought it was a good idea to tackle a Noble. I wanted her to feel better, to believe I was happy—not that I was risking my life on a boy I could never have or that I might very well have a death sentence waiting for me when I returned.

We sat in silence after that, each glad we had returned to some semblance of what had been, when Aunt Beredith broke into a fit of coughing so violent that Jonk came in from the kitchen.

"Keep her conscious for a few more minutes, I'm almost ready with her next dose," he said.

Like I could make Aunt Beredith do anything, but I still pulled on one of the sets of gloves Lady Cathrina had sent back with me as I moved to help her sit up.

"Kailin," she whispered between coughs.

"I'm right here." I tried to move the covers tighter around her but she waved me off.

"Kailin," she started again, "you know enough about Winter Fever to know that after tonight, it can go one of two ways, and that there's nothing other than luck and the blessing of The Great One to determine if this final dose will work."

"Don't talk that way," I muttered, feeling myself grow numb.

"Listen to me! We have only a few minutes before that shrub comes back and then I'm put to sleep. I have something I need to tell you. Something about your mother."

That caught me off guard. My mother had been dead for over sixteen years and my aunt had already told me everything I wanted to know about her.

"What do you mean?" I asked, my voice flat.

"My sister," she paused as another fit of coughing came. "I had to leave the Academy because of my sister."

"Yes, I know that." I was beginning to worry that the fever was making her delusional.

"But you don't know that I didn't come home alone." I could feel my eyes widen. This was new. "There was another girl who was also pregnant, a friend of mine from the Academy, who needed a safe place to have her baby. I cared for the two of them, until the night they gave birth."

"They both went into labor on the same night?" My aunt had never told me about the night I was born, and I had never asked, assuming it hurt too much to talk about her sister dying. From the pain in her eyes I could see I had been right.

"You should rest."

"Shut up, girl, and listen!" The pain was still there, but there was also a desperation that frightened me. "Yes, they went into labor the same night, and believe me, having to deal with one delivering mother is hard enough, but two..." Her eyes closed and I could see a younger version of my aunt, alone with two equally frightened teenage girls, trying to help them both and...She opened her eyes again and I thought my heart would break. "One girl and one baby died."

She was quiet for a moment, reliving a pain and guilt I was inadequate to understand, and I wondered if she blamed herself for what happened. I had seen my aunt deliver every person younger than me in our village, and she was perfect. She had lost only two babies in all that time but had never lost a mother.

But that wasn't true, was it. Is that why she was telling me this story when she should have been resting? That she wasn't perfect?

"So my mother died and the other girl lost her baby? It's all right, Aunt. It sounds like a situation that would have tried even the most skilled Healer."

"No." Aunt Beredith said, her eyes hardening, pushing out the pain that had been there only a moment before. I felt small under her gaze, as if I were a child again, and wished I could disappear. Whatever she was about to say, I suddenly knew I didn't want to hear it.

"My sister and her baby died. The other girl and her baby lived."

I stared at her without seeing. If I was breathing, I couldn't tell.

I had been right.

I hadn't wanted to know.

Now it was my aunt who looked small, something I never thought possible, but she did.

And I was glad.

"Why?" I asked, my teeth clenched.

"Why? Aren't you more curious about the who?" Aunt Beredith's voice was weaker now and I remembered faintly that she was fatally ill.

"Why are you telling me this?"

"Because you needed to know..."

"No. I didn't."

"Yes, you *do*."

"Fine," I spat. "How about why didn't you tell me *years* ago? Why did you *lie* to me?"

There was a crash from the kitchen as Jonk knocked over some bowls, something he seemed to do a lot.

Aunt Beredith sighed, her eyes leaving mine to look at the ceiling, and for one frightening moment, I thought she would pass out.

"Because," she said, still looking up, "I had to protect her."

"Protect her?!" I yelled, standing up in my outrage. "This random girl who is actually my mother? Save her from a life of ridicule so I could be tortured my whole life?!"

"I knew I could protect you from a life of too much shame and poverty," she said, her breathing becoming labored. "But I had to keep her safe from the ruin that having a child so young could do before she inherited her title."

I froze at the word.

"Her title?" I whispered.

"For a girl as smart as you, I'm surprised you haven't figured it out yet. I was sure that *she* would; you do have her eyes, after all." My aunt turned her gaze toward me, and a new determination tinged with sadness was burning in them. She knew exactly how much she was destroying my world, my very existence, but she was going to do it anyway.

"Your mother is Lady Cathrina."

I sat there in silence.

"She doesn't know." It was meant to be a question, but I already knew the answer.

"No," my aunt replied. "After she gave birth she passed out. When she woke up, I told her that the dead child was hers. She stayed only a few days after that to get her strength; then one morning I woke up and she was gone." Her voice was little more than a whisper now, the conversation sapping her strength, but I wasn't done with her yet.

"You still haven't answered my question."

"Why did I lie to her or why did I lie to you?"

"Both!" I yelled, but quickly checked myself. The last thing I needed was that stranger barging in and putting my aunt to sleep. At least until I got my answers; then he could do whatever he wanted with her for all I cared.

My aunt looked away from me and sighed, and for the first time in my life I thought she looked old.

"Because she would have lost everything having a child. Are you familiar with how Nobles pass on their titles?"

I suddenly remembered a conversation I had had with another young Noble who was afraid of what would happen to him if he were disgraced, and I reluctantly let understanding solidify.

"Yes," I started, banishing Aiden from my mind. "It goes to the oldest child, unless they do something disgraceful before they turn twenty and inherit the title. The level of their degradation is determined by how upset their family is with them and what the Royal Senate decides."

My aunt smiled a little. "So you have been learning something while washing floors. Your mother was next in line to inherit the family title. Her family consisted of only her parents and a cousin that was more than eager for your mother to mess up her life. I had met him once at a party your mother dragged me to, and he made it no secret that he would have loved to ruin her, which is exactly what would have happened if anyone had found out about you. Your mother was just eighteen when she became pregnant with you—it would have been the end of her."

"It was her own fault for getting herself pregnant."

She slapped me.

"You will never, *ever*, speak like that again."

She took a breath and continued. "As I was leaving to return home Cathrina came to my room and told me she was pregnant. She was scared, with no idea what to do. I tried to get her to tell me who the father was, hoping to pressure him into helping her, but she wouldn't say, completely panicked at anyone ever finding out. I thought of a plan and told her to say that she needed a holiday. Nobles did that sort of thing all the time, sometimes being gone for a year or more if they felt like it. I gave her a place to meet me in one of the towns on the way home. We met up, she disguised as a Peasant, and I snuck her into our cottage when we got here. My sister was surprised, but she kept our secret. I took care of her along with my sister until their time came, and then I told you the rest..." She was quiet for a moment, the pain back in her eyes.

"The next time I saw her was when she was standing up there with the Examiners. She knew exactly where she was— and I knew she was coming to see you, the one who lived."

I saw the night of the exam all over again, highlighted with this new information. The two friends who hadn't seen each other in sixteen years, the shyness of my mother was now guilt for never thanking her friend who had done everything for her. And then the way Aunt Beredith had thrown herself against the door, the steel in her eyes when she said, "you owe me."

If only my mother really understood how much she owed my aunt.

Aunt Beredith was silent again, and I wondered what images she was seeing in the fire. The months of secrecy, of helping a friend and a sister, of delivering two babies at the same time only to have her sister and niece die. And then to let her friend go, free of all responsibilities, saving her from a future of ruin and degradation.

"All right," I started, my voice betraying how overwhelmed I truly was. "But why didn't you tell me?"

"Because I had to wait until she had her title," she said, her voice straining with frustration.

"But why didn't you tell me once you knew she had her title?!"

"Because," my aunt said, her voice growing weak and tired again. "Because I knew that if I told you, you would go and find her. And then I would never see you again."

"What are you talking about? We *both* could have gone to live in Divlan together! She would never have turned us away, not once she knew the truth. She doesn't care about ring status. You could have been friends again!"

"Kailin, do you know the rest of the laws governing how ring status, even for Nobility, is passed down?"

My blood had stopped moving in my veins. Of course I knew.

"A man can have as many affairs with as many chambermaids as he wants, because it is written into the law that someone's ring isn't determined by the father. It is determined by the *mother*."

My aunt closed her eyes, as if she couldn't bear to see what her words were doing to me. "If I had told you and you had left me, you would never have returned to me again, not as my niece, not as my equal. According to law, you are next in line to inherit Lady Cathrina's title and her seat on the Royal Senate." She opened her eyes, and I saw my frozen disbelief reflected in her steel-gray ones. "You're not a Peasant, Kailin. You're a Noble."

THIRTY-TWO

The wind was cold, blowing my hair into my face so I couldn't see. I didn't need to. I knew where I was going. Or really where I wasn't going.

I wasn't going back.

I could still see my aunt—well, the woman who I had thought was my aunt's face in the firelight. It was as hard as ever, but the fever was making it grow softer by the minute, like melting wax. While she was metamorphosing into something simple and moldable, I was becoming stone.

A Noble?

I stopped walking, put my hands over my face, and screamed.

My entire life I had envisioned my mother, or at least the woman who I thought she was.

My aunt had told me she was a slim girl, with dusty blond hair and a quick laugh—pretty but with nothing really going on between the ears. She liked fun and life, but was the most irresponsible person you would ever meet. I wanted to hate her like everyone else did, but my aunt never hated her, so all I ever did was long for her and wonder what it would have been like to have a mother. When I would lie in bed late at night and wish for my mother to hold me, the face I had imagined for her was the one I would picture.

But it was all a lie. Instead, my mother was the most brilliant woman I had ever known.

I *hated* it.

I hated that she had been alive and could have raised me. I hated that I had been alone when I didn't need to be. And I hated that she had been so close, sleeping no more than yards above my head every night and never knew to love me.

She was everything I could have ever hoped for, my fantasy mother made reality. This should have been the happiest day of my life.

But no, her *title* made it so I could never be happy again.

I threw myself against what I thought was someone's field wall and vomited. When there was nothing but acid coming up my throat, I braced myself against the low wall, letting the cold night breeze dry my face, my hair blowing back as I breathed in the fresh forest scent.

Forest?

I looked down at what I was leaning on and jerked my hands back as if it had burned them.

I had just thrown up on back side of The Great One's altar.

The moon was full, but when I raised my eyes to the worn carving of the Blessing Tree, a cloud moved in front of it.

That's when I didn't see them.

There, deep in the wall of trees that no one passed through, I felt, more than saw, movement. The breeze stilled and all the sounds of the night silenced as one, as if the whole world were trying to hide from whatever was in there.

I felt another movement, and then another. My heart was beating faster and faster into my throat, my whole body frozen with the fear of my childhood nightmares. My eyes finally confirmed what my heart was telling me when I saw a tree bend under an enormous weight, and then another tree bend as well. In seconds the entire wall in front of me was filled with their shadows.

Then I heard them.

A chattering noise that made my already racing heart explode.

I didn't know how I knew, but the certainty was there that they had come for me.

And I was about to die.

For the first time in my life, I prayed for The Great One. Not just in a distant way, hoping He would have some slight influence for good in my life, but honestly calling on Him for help.

The *pull* answered, small and nudging.

And I reached out to it.

Instantly the blue lights appeared and the world erupted in light.

My knees buckled and I fell on the altar, using it for support as I watched the lights reveal too many long hairy legs attached to bodies as large as horses. The heads were small, but covered in eyes on every side, with large mouths filled with moving fangs.

They were the perfect monsters.

No one had ever come out of the northern part of the Holy Forest alive. Now I couldn't understand why any of us were still alive.

The fear only made me hold on to the lights more tightly.

The creatures hissed in their strange chattering language. The lights around me flared and the creatures bounded back into the forest.

The danger now gone, I tried to let go of the *pull*, but it was too late. The lights swirled around me as they always did in my dreams, and I began to shoot out threads of fire like those I'd seen in the old man, but mine were as thick as ropes and were being pulled from me in every direction. Then all at once they twisted themselves into one single cord that shot directly over the altar, under the arbor, and straight into the darkness.

The darkness that had been calling to me my whole life. The source of the *pull*.

The trees pulled back, and the same tunnel of darkness that haunted my waking memory opened up before me.

"No!"

I stumbled back and fell, my head making contact with something hard.

And all went black.

CHAPTER

THIRTY-THREE

When I opened my eyes, I knew that I was not in my body.

I must be dead.

It made sense; everything around me was bathed in a soft glowing light. I had been taught that those who were good would go to heaven, a garden surrounding The Great One. Loved ones would be there, and we would never know want or loneliness again.

But looking around I knew I had actually been sent to some sort of special hell. I was still in my village. I had a brief moment of panic until I saw Aunt Beredith stepping out of her cottage. There was no way she was going to hell.

She must have died, and I was consumed with guilt that my last moments with her had been filled with anger.

Her angel state was lovely. She still looked like she could flatten any man in our village she no longer had gray hair or a face that was lined with the stress she carried every day.

In fact, she looked younger. Much younger.

She was calling my name, and I saw a child who couldn't be older than three hiding behind the house. With a start I realized it was me. I must have thought it was a game because I was giggling to myself.

That's when I realized this wasn't the afterlife. This was a dream, but not one I could have made up on my own.

I was remembering.

My aunt moved to come around to the back and I was up and running.

Then this dream became a nightmare. In front of my little figure the trees moved aside, revealing the dark path that had been calling me my whole life.

I screamed at myself to stop, but no sound came out.

Still giggling, I ran into the forest.

My vision followed into the tunnel of tree branches and bushes to a small figure crying while sitting on the ground in a large clearing. I had become lost and wanted to go home, but I was so young that there was no hope for me. I crawled onto my stomach and lay on the ground, hoping for who knew what, when a blue light burst from a bush. Then there was another, and another, and before I could believe what I was seeing, thousands of small blue lights were floating about my younger self.

I saw myself sit up and laugh, trying to catch one of the lights in my tiny hands. The lights seemed to be moving in a pattern, drawing the younger me toward a massive dark shape I hadn't noticed before. I thought at first it was a trap, but my heart felt warm and happy.

Giant tree roots appeared around me and the child-me yawned. I curled up between two roots and fell asleep in that perfect, peaceful way that only children can sleep. The lights continued to dance until they surrounded my sleeping little frame. The roots moved, pulling closer and twisting until they formed a bed, holding me gently as I slept.

The next image I saw was of me waking up only a foot or so into the forest, right behind Aunt Beredith's cottage. The child-me rubbed her eyes and yawned, and then, as if nothing at all extraordinary had happened, I ran to Aunt Beredith's kitchen door.

The child-me was almost to it when another child appeared, running across my path. I thought they would collide, but the boy passed right through the younger me as if she were made of mist. He looked to be nearly the same age as my vision self, with a head of messy black hair wearing clothes in a style I didn't recognize. I turned my head to follow him, and with the movement I was no longer in my village, but was on a dry, craggy mountain. There was a cliff dropping off onto a great plain on which a sprawling city lay with twinkling lights, and beyond that the sea reflected by the moon.

The boy was crying and not looking where he was going. I yelled out for him to watch out for the cliff, but once again I had no voice.

He fell off the edge.

I wanted to close my eyes before his body broke on the rocks below, but I couldn't tear my eyes away.

At the last moment, the air below the falling boy swirled into darkness and solidified.

When the boy hit it, he disappeared.

The scene darkened, and I wondered if the vision had ended.

Then I saw a light.

It was only a faint pinpoint, but I felt drawn to it as strongly as I had felt the call to the forest's edge. I walked at first, but the *pull* in my chest grew into an urgency that sent my feet flying beneath me.

When I reached the light I found it wasn't as bright or as big as I thought it would be. Just a small, glowing orb of red fire dancing above the outstretched hand of the little boy.

He wasn't crying anymore. In fact he was laughing.

Then he turned, smiled at me and then looked back at his light.

"Pretty," he said.

I knelt down, and the little boy's eyes followed me. His skin was darker than mine with dark brown eyes that appeared almost black. I didn't recognize him at all, but that didn't stop me from smiling when he reached out his hands with the red fire dancing in his palms.

"Hold?" He asked, still smiling.

I did not want to hold it. I was afraid enough of my own blue lights, let alone his red one. But somehow my hand came up anyway. At the last moment, instead of reaching for the light I placed a hand on the little boy's cheek.

He lowered his hands holding the flame and looked up at me, his mouth dropping open as his eyes turned huge.

I couldn't blame him. I was amazed myself.

Wonder.

Just like the boy in my dreams.

"Pretty," he said again, but this time he wasn't looking at the light.

I smiled, then called on my own lights and it appeared in my other hand.

"Home?" he said.

I nodded, then placed my hand with the light over his own, cupping both of them. The darkness around us lightened into the bottom of the cliff I had seen before.

He smiled at me one last time, then ran away toward a line of moving lights and voices calling out a name I couldn't make out.

I could only watch his retreating shadow for a moment before the *pull* at my chest flared again and I turned to see the outline of a young man standing in the darkness. I could not see his face, but I knew he was watching me. In two steps the boy who shared my dreams had crossed the distance between us and pulled me into his chest, encasing me in his arms.

Awe.

We stayed that way until the darkness thickened around us and I was wrenched from his hold.

I could feel the wet grass pricking the skin on my face when I opened my eyes. Everything was bathed in a soft, gray glow as the very first signs of dawn entered the sky.

I pushed myself into a sitting position, suddenly very, very cold. I had been out all night, lying on a ground covered with a thin layer of dew.

Stiffly I got to my feet and rested against the altar, gazing warily toward the wall of trees. There was no sign of the tunnel I had seen before blacking out, or the terrifying monsters. All was as an early morning should be, with birds singing and leaves gently rustling in the branches.

I stood there for a long moment, knowing that it was all a lie.

There was something much bigger happening here in this forest than I ever could have imagined.

I looked into the darkness and remembered what I had looked like being held by those large roots.

You have been touched by The Great One.

I sucked in a breath as my eyes pricked with tears.

It was all true. All of it, and I couldn't deny it any longer. I felt so alone, then I remembered that Aunt Beredith had always been a strong believer. She would be able to help me figure all this out.

A scream broke the morning stillness.

My aunt.

My *dying* aunt, who could already be dead!

I turned and ran back to the cottage.

I flew in through the door, half afraid to see her cottage filled with members of the village mourning the loss of one of their own. What I saw instead made me burst out laughing.

Healer Jonk was hiding behind the doorframe to the kitchen while pots and boxes were being thrown at him. He let out another scream as one managed to find his head. The kitchen door opened and slammed shut.

The living room was a mess and there, standing in the center of the room, another herb pot raised above her head, was a mad woman.

My aunt looked as though she had walked up to death's door, knocked, said something rude, and then came home again. Her face was pale and drawn, but her eyes were alive and bloodshot.

Laughing again, I ran into her arms.

"Kailin..." she whispered, dropping the pot with a crash. "I thought...after what I said and the way you ran out..."

"So you thought to destroy the house?" I buried my face in her shoulder. "Where would I have gone?"

"I think we both know that answer."

"I don't care whose daughter I am." I looked up at her. "I'm your niece and I will always come home."

My aunt's eyes were shining. I had never seen her cry and I doubted she was going to let me see now. She looked away and put her weight on me.

"Help me back to bed."

I let her use me as a support as we covered the short distance, maneuvering around the broken furniture. Once she was comfortable I took her hand and started rubbing it. It was something she used to do with my hand when I was little, but she hadn't done in years.

"Feeling nostalgic?"

I smiled as I continued the familiar motion.

"In a way. I was actually wondering..."

If you ever had any hints that I was some sort of divine servant?

"Did I ever run away when I was little?"

"All the time. I used to be beautiful before the stress of finding you every day made me ugly."

"But was there one time I was gone all night?"

Her eyes narrowed, but she nodded her head. "Yes. When you were three you disappeared for a night, and then the next morning came dancing into the cottage as if I hadn't had the entire village scoring the countryside for you."

So I had been right that it hadn't been a dream but a memory.

My aunt missed nothing, and she turned her hand over to take mine. "What is it, Kailin? What aren't you telling me?"

"Everything."

She didn't say anything for a moment, then in her no-nonsense way said, "well, you'd better start at the beginning."

And that's when I told her. About my dreams of blue fire, and the things the old Healer had said. About my waking nightmare at the market during the riot and again when I saved the old man.

Finally, I told her about the vision I'd had the night before, but only the part about me. I didn't know why but I didn't want her to know about the young man.

At some point she started rubbing my hand.

"Do you think I'm crazy?" I whispered.

"No." Her face was grave but her eyes had a softness to them that I had never seen before. "We studied mental illness at the Academy, and you don't show any symptoms of someone whose mind is failing them. In fact," she leaned back. "This explains a lot."

"A lot of what?"

"A lot of why you've never acted like a normal child. Most children would have stayed away from the forest, sensing the danger we feel whenever we get too close. But not you. Oh no, from the moment you could crawl you were always trying to make your way to the trees."

I stared at her, my mouth hanging slack. I hadn't realized it, but up to this moment, a part of me had hoped that I really had been suffering from some sort of mental failing that could be explained away by a Healer.

"And the way you took to healing!" my aunt continued, rolling her eyes. "I could understand your interest, *everyone* had an interest in learning for the scholarship, but you—you breathed it in like air. I had never seen someone with so much natural talent, like somehow you had already learned it all and was just going through the motions of being taught all over again."

"But did you, I mean, could you tell that I was—special?" I felt myself cringe as the word left my lips.

Blessed? Touched?

My aunt stared at me for a long time, her mouth in a hard, straight line. Finally, when she spoke, it was in an eerily quiet voice.

"Yes. You were always special. I thought it was because of something you had inherited from your mother, but I can remember times now when I would come to your bed at night and swear there was a glow, blue, like those lights in your vision. I brushed it off as a trick of the firelight, but now I can see it. And more than that, I always had a feeling that you were meant for something more. That's why I pushed your mother so hard to take you—because I knew you weren't meant to stay here."

We sat together a long time after that. Jonk had regained his courage and had come back to the cottage, coming in at times to give my aunt broth and medicine. Remarkably, my aunt didn't complain.

An hour passed, and my aunt sighed.

"What is it?" I asked, after having sat in silence for so long.

"It's just that I'm going to miss you."

"You don't have to worry about that yet. It's going to be weeks before you're strong enough for me to go back."

"No, we need to get you back to Divlan as soon as we can. Those wagoners your mother paid to bring you here should still be around and should be leaving today or tomorrow."

"Don't talk nonsense. You called me here to help you recover and that is exactly what I'm going to do."

"No I didn't, as you very well know. You were here for my deathbed confession, which is now done. I have no other use for you."

"But I don't *want* to go."

"Grow up, Kailin!" my aunt snapped. "You have a job to do, and it isn't to live and die obscured in this hole! You have a destiny to fulfill. I don't understand it, but The Great One doesn't choose random nobodies to be His advocates. He has arranged for you to get to Divlan, so that is where you need to be."

"But I don't know what I'm supposed to be doing!" I was panicking. Aunt Beredith was supposed to be helping me figure out my destiny, not throw me out! "You've been to Divlan; you know just as well as I do how hopeless it is. If anything, it's gotten worse since you were there. How can one person like me make any sort of difference?"

"By using the gifts that were given you." My aunt no longer looked old. Though still weak from her illness, her eyes shone with a new life I had never seen before.

"You need to heal Tamerin."

CHAPTER

THIRTY-FOUR

I let out a breath as the wagon stopped next to the servant gate of the Academy. It had taken a little over two weeks to return, which had given me plenty of time to mull over everything that had happened while I was home.

Every night I had dreamt of lights and the blue fire until they almost felt like old friends. And every night *he* was there, never showing his face, but I could feel his hand in mine, his soul asking who I was as much as I was trying to find the answers about him.

They never came, but every day I found I was looking forward to falling asleep more and more.

I thanked my driver and jumped down, returning his wave as he moved off into the traffic. No one acknowledged me when I entered the courtyard, but that wasn't surprising. I may have been a servant, but I worked on the upper floors while these servants worked below.

I stopped on the threshold before going inside and turned to take in the sights and sounds. The stables were off to my left, with their five or so carriages and twenty horses ranging

386

from those that would pull carts to the thoroughbreds owned by Healers and students. I saw a pile of mousy brown hair standing by one stall window and smiled as I recognized Markly flirting with Robert, which meant that he had survived his wound and hadn't been dismissed.

I was happy for them.

Off to the right were stacks of crates of every shape and size in front of the large loading door. Throughout it all, servants were running about, fulfilling their duties or at least appearing to. Loud and busy, with the smell of manure, dust, and light from the setting sun.

I wanted to remember it all because this would be the last time I came through this entrance.

I turned and began the climb to the tenth floor and my mother's chambers.

I wanted to get this over with while I still had the nerve. Even with everything Aunt Beredith and I had discussed about what my abilities with the lights meant, I knew I couldn't face any of it until I settled this first.

I had spent the past two weeks rehearsing in my mind what I would say. My initial hateful emotions had calmed down in the rational light of day, and a new burning curiosity and frightening awe filled my waking hours.

My mother is alive.

Lady Cathrina is my mother.

The thought made me lightheaded. I imagined the scene of me telling her, the way she would light up and open her arms and tell me that she always knew. That she couldn't have wished for a better daughter.

I smiled as I rounded another bend in the stairs. My small bag was over my shoulder, and I could almost feel the weight of the letter Aunt Beredith had written at the bottom of it.

The letter was meant to be proof that I wasn't lying, but I

hoped she would recognize me as her daughter as soon as I told her, because there was another scene in my mind that played just as often as the first one.

This one ended with me out on the streets or worse.

I paused on the stairs and held on to the wall, suddenly feeling sick.

Yes, this scenario was just as likely to happen as the happy ending. The part of me that still saw myself as the pathetic nothing of a girl held on to this possibility, hoping in a sick way that it would happen and confirm all my self-loathing.

No. I'm not that girl anymore.

What happened at the altar had made that clear.

I couldn't afford to be insecure.

I started to climb again, suddenly desperate to get this over with, one way or the other.

But when I got to her chambers she wasn't there. I turned around immediately and headed for her office, not caring that I was using the main halls. It was dinnertime, so they were almost empty anyway.

I was almost there when I was grabbed from behind and thrown into the nearest classroom.

I screamed but quickly had my mouth covered. I bit down on the hand and was rewarded with a yell, but instead of being released I was jerked around to face my favorite pair of blue eyes.

"Aiden!" I shrieked, throwing my arms around him. He hugged me back and smelled of soap and earth, and I never wanted him to let me go.

Which was when he dropped me.

"WHERE HAVE YOU BEEN?"

I took a step back, shocked not only by his shout but also by his appearance. He had stubble on his chin and upper lip and his hair was a mess. His red vest was unbuttoned over a wrinkled white shirt. His eyes were bloodshot with deep circles under them. And somehow, even with all these things that would mar anyone else, he *still* managed to look unearthly beautiful.

I shouldn't have hugged him. I should have run as soon as I saw it was him.

I hadn't planned on seeing Aiden again at all, and it had nothing to do with what my mother had told me.

I hadn't *wanted* to see him again.

I knew he probably had waited for me that day in the stairwell, but we had only shared one kiss and then I had left right afterwards.

Aiden's history showed how short his memory was for relationships, and those had been with inner-ring girls.

I couldn't think of any reason he still would have felt anything for me.

But instead he was putting his arms around me again and was leaning down...

"Wait." I breathed a moment before his lips touched mine.

My hands were on his chest and I could feel how frantically his heart was beating. He was looking at me, but I was watching my fingers and how they were rising and falling with his breath.

"Kailin?"

When I had thought I would never hear him say my name again I had tried to banish from my mind how he always said it. Deep and then light, emphasizing the "k" at the beginning, like it was a force of nature he wanted to hold instead of just the jumble of sounds my aunt had given me.

"I was so worried!" He said, crushing me against him again. "And Lady Cathrina wouldn't tell me anything. And when you weren't in class and I never saw you in the halls—" His voice was controlled but still with an edge of hysteria I didn't like. "I didn't even know how to ask for help without making things worse."

I didn't answer because I was crying so hard.

He pulled back and held me at arm's length.

"Did they give you to *HIM?!*"

"No!" I shouted, stepping out of his reach. "Lady Cathrina kept me safe." He seemed to relax a little, at least enough to reach into his vest and pull out a crumpled handkerchief.

My sleeve would have been cleaner, but I took it anyway.

This was not the Aiden I had left behind, the cool, collected, cosmopolitan boy. This Aiden was about to lose it.

"What was I supposed to think?" he said, "you've been gone for *weeks*. Were you sent to work in Lady Cathrina's mansion? To her family's land? Were you—"

"You and your theories!" I turned to walk to the front row of tables in what I could now see was *our* classroom.

"Well you're not being very forthcoming with information."

I turned, only to stumble back into the table when he was right behind me. I pulled myself on top of the table to give me more space, but he just put his hands on either side of me and leaned forward.

Then just as quickly he stood up again.

"You've been avoiding me, haven't you?"

"What?!"

"It's the only theory that makes sense!" He was shaking his head as his hands grabbed his already disheveled hair. "I scared you off. I just couldn't see it, because I'm a shrub and of course the idea of a girl not wanting me would never have occurred to me, because hey, everyone wants me!" His hands were now over his face. "Everyone except the one girl I actually want..."

I was across the room in two steps and pulled his hands away only a fraction of a second before I pressed my lips to his.

So much for never seeing him again.

I closed my eyes and placed his stiff hands around my waist, then slid my arms up around his neck. He didn't respond at first, but when my fingers found his hair he melted into my arms and pulled me tight against his chest.

I could withstand his charm, his good looks, and his captivating intensity.

But I was powerless against his utter and complete stupidity.

"You," he said, when I finally pulled back, "are confusing me." The hysterical look disappeared and my Aiden, the quirky young man with just the right edge of arrogance, was back.

"I'm sorry," I said, resting my head against his neck. "I had to get you to shut up."

"You succeeded," he chuckled. "So all I have to do is annoy you and you'll kiss me? I should have tried that a long time ago."

"You're ridiculous," I said, shaking my head and pulling away. "I wasn't avoiding you. Lady Cathrina sent me home for a little while to keep me safe, but now I'm back."

I sat down on the tabletop again and this time Aiden did as well, still holding my hand.

"Will you please tell me what happened?"

Which part?

My aunt almost dying? Giant monsters almost eating me? My prophetic destiny?

"Where should I start?"

"How about the last time I saw you. You remember, right? You were bleeding like something out of my nightmares and Larsion was threatening—"

Oh good. Something easy.

"First, I wasn't as badly hurt as I looked. Lord Larsion's kicks turned out to be pathetically weak." I laughed, but Aiden wasn't smiling anymore. "And I'm sure you see much more blood than that from most of your patients over at the hospital."

"It was from my nightmares because it was *your* blood."

"Oh." His free hand came up and slowly traced the faded line on my forehead. Then he leaned forward and gently kissed it.

I shivered.

"All right. I was a bloody pulp on the ground, you had just gallantly rescued me, nearly broken Lord Larsion's wrist, and then was thrown out by Lady Cathrina."

"There we go. Now what happened after that?"

"Lady Cathrina cleaned me up, then she told me…"

That I could never see you again.

"That she was going to gut me if I ever slept with you?"

My cheeks flared.

"Sticks, I've missed this," he said, stroking the side of my face, only making it hotter.

"She would be furious if she knew we were together right now."

"Then I guess we'll just have to make sure she doesn't find out," he said smiling. "Leaving a note for you to find after class worked pretty well last time. We can schedule different times and different places each time we meet. You know…" his smile turned stupid. "Like we were *spies*."

I thought I would start crying again.

"I'm no longer Lady Cathrina's assistant. I'm being restricted behind walls."

The smile left as I'd known it would, but in its place he looked…relieved?

"That's probably the smartest thing to do. Even with

Larsion getting kicked out of the Academy I don't like the idea of you being so vulnerable to inner-ring boys where I can't be there to keep you safe. You're much too pretty not to be noticed."

"Did you hear me?!" I yelled, standing. "I lost it all! I'll never be allowed in a classroom again! And I won't be able to go with Lady Cathrina to the Islands!"

"What?!"

Too late I remembered I had never actually told him why I had become my mother's assistant in the first place.

"It's the only reason the Dean allowed a Peasant to become her assistant. So she would be able to train me for when I went with her to the peace negotiations. "

"You're luckier than I thought," he said, taking my hands again.

"I lost it all and you call me lucky?"

He pulled me to him, pressing his face into my hair. "Yes, I do. When I couldn't find you I thought the worst. And now to hear that you've avoided going on that suicide mission? It almost makes me believe in The Great One."

"But I *want* to go to the Island to help Lady Cathrina," I said, pulling back.

"Kailin, no one is expected to come back."

"That's ridiculous. They wouldn't send her if they thought she was in danger. She's a Noble."

"I heard my father talking to some of the other members of the Senate. It's being paraded as a grand gesture toward peace, but the reality is we're going to be at war by the end of the summer if not sooner. Anyone going will be taken to Richark or killed outright."

"But Lady Cathrina!"

"They've tried to talk her out of it, but she insists on going."

NO!

I just got a mother and I wasn't going to let her die!

"I need to go."

"You're not going to change her mind. I know you two don't have a normal Noble-and-servant relationship, but there's no reason she would listen to you when she hasn't listened to anyone else."

But I did have a reason. One I'm sure she would listen to. And if she still didn't...

"Then I will just have to go with her and help her reach peace like we had planned."

I turned to walk toward the door, but Aiden was instantly in my way.

"No, Kailin. I won't let you go."

"You won't *let* me? I'm *her* servant, not yours!"

"You know what I mean! But, but—" He turned in a circle, pulling at his hair. "Why? WHY does she matter so much to you? Why would you risk your life just to be with her?!"

"Because she's my mother!"

He stared at me, and then slowly let go of his hair.

"What did you say?"

Oh no.

I ducked under his arm and reached for the door, but he shoved his shoulder against it.

"*What did you say?*"

"You heard me! She's my mother, and if she doesn't listen to me then there is no way I'm not going with her!"

He stared at me.

Then he smiled.

"She's your *mother?* Why am I just finding out about this now?"

"Because *I* just found out about it. My aunt told me when I was home. They had been friends at the Academy, and my aunt helped my mother have her baby in hiding when she was eighteen. She then switched me with her sister's dead baby and told my mother I had died, saving her from being disinherited. But now my aunt wants me to tell her the truth and ask her to officially acknowledge me."

"And you can prove this?" he asked eagerly.

"I have a letter from my aunt, if you can call the word of a Peasant as proof, but I know my mother will believe her."

"This is AMAZING!" He laughed, lifting me and swinging me around.

"Aiden!"

"Don't you see," he said, setting me back down. "This solves *everything!*"

"Not if I don't get her to back out of being part of the delegation!"

"Forget the Islands, this solves everything *for us!*"

"Us?"

"Kailin, she's your *mother!* That makes you"—he looked down and laughed. Then he looked up, spearing me with his eyes. "Like me."

My eyes started to sting again. I pulled away and turned back toward the door.

"Where are you going? You don't even look happy!"

"I'm not!" I said, spinning on him. "I'm furious! I've had my entire world shattered and turned upside down!"

"But your life is going to be so much better now!"

The sun was all but set, and the light coming in through the windows was a deep red that gave a malicious elegance to the shadows across his face. I was reminded of that night so many months ago when I had seen him dimly lit by the lanterns in front of the Academy entrance. I had thought he looked alien and untouchable in his shadowed perfection that night.

Untouchable because he was a Noble and I wasn't.

Which wasn't true anymore, was it?

Now we were in the same ring.

But all those days riding in silence in the back of a wagon had clarified one piece of important insight.

No matter who my mother was, I would never be his equal.

Why couldn't he understand that even if my mother officially acknowledged me—meaning I would share her ring and be her heir—I was still an illegitimate child who was raised a Peasant? I doubted I would be accepted by my peers.

And him?

Would he still want me when I became the fool of the court?

Where he saw an end to our problems, I could see the start of worse ones.

Where he saw a happy ending, all I could see were his eyes now black in the shadows of the setting sun.

He was still unreachable.

"I thought I wanted an interesting life where I did great things in great places, but now I know that all I want is a simple life, where I am a Healer who helps people. I feel just as robbed of the life I want now as I did on the day I failed the exam."

He came to me and I fell into his arms.

"I'm scared, Aiden."

"Don't be. I'll be with you every step of the way."

He tilted my chin up and looked at me for a long moment.

"I don't know how I didn't see it sooner," he said. "Your eyes are the only proof anyone would ever need. You have hers, and not just the color. You have their fierceness, even when you aren't angry." He placed his hand on my cheek and I leaned into his touch. "Even when you're scared."

I buried my face into his chest.

"Do you want to know the *real* reason I couldn't leave you alone?" he said. "When I knocked you over that first day of classes, I thought you were just some crazy servant and I was going to brush you off, but I couldn't get your angry, defiant, beautiful eyes out of my head. I told myself it was just the shock of having someone yell at me, but then when I caught you again in that classroom blabbing off every answer like it was the easiest thing in the world, I felt drawn to you. That realization and not knowing where it came from *infuriated* me."

"Then on the Solstice when I saw you underneath that carriage, I was sure that it couldn't be true. How did this girl keep finding me? Couldn't she leave me alone in my perfect world? Then seeing you in the foyer, staring at that flower made of jewels, I couldn't help but think that you were the real treasure, and that *terrified* me."

"After that I thought about you all the time. For the first time in my life I started watching servants to see if you were there. It was driving me crazy, wishing I knew how to find you and not even knowing why I needed to! And then when you just danced into my class behind Lady Cathrina I knew I had to do something, *anything*, to talk to you again."

I remembered that afternoon when he caught me in the hallway, how he had seemed so angry and yet so determined.

"Were you mad at yourself because you had fallen for a Peasant?"

"Would you forgive me if I said that I was? I am a son of a Noble. My entire existence has been based on the ring system, and I had believed my whole life that this was the way the world was supposed to be. But then I met you and somehow, just by existing, you forced me to see that it is all wrong." He stopped to brush my check with the back of his hand. "You finding out about your nobility is simply the universe finally letting you know what a remarkable woman you really are. And if the *universe* couldn't leave you alone, then what chance did I ever have?"

I didn't care about the tears this time, and with a smile I threw my arms around his neck. He lifted me from the ground again and spun me around, making me fly along with my heart.

I needed him. He was more than just my best friend, he was an anchor in my now chaotic life. I should have been scared, and a part of me still screamed that nothing good ever happened in my life, so why hope?

It was easy to ignore that voice while Aiden was holding me.

"You're a Noble," he said when we stopped, as if he were still dumbfounded by the idea.

"I'm glad that you're having a hard time accepting it," I laughed. "It makes me feel a little more normal with how I reacted."

"And how was that?"

"I ran out of my aunt's house in the middle of the night while she was dying, wandered around in the dark, and then threw up on the back side of The Great One's altar."

I had never heard him laugh so hard.

"But seriously, Aiden, your shock and initial denial is going to look like a paper cut next to the traumatic amputation of what we're going to face when I'm acknowledged, and I'm not sure that us being together is going to help or hurt. I'm still an illegitimate child and you're still the heir to the Chair of the Senate."

"Details. At least it is possible for us to be together publicly, and illegitimate or not, you're still the heir..." His eyebrows came together. "Who's your father?"

"I don't know. My aunt said my mother refused to say."

He didn't look satisfied.

"Excited for another puzzle?" I asked, putting my finger between his eyebrows.

He smiled sheepishly. "I do love my puzzles. Especially this one."

I let out a happy gasp as he kissed me.

When I could breathe again he pulled me against his chest, and I let myself be enveloped. I could hear him breathe me in and I wondered what I smelled like to him.

"You're a Noble," he whispered again, kissing the top of my head. "Lady Kailin."

I froze.

"What's wrong?" He asked looking down at me.

"What did you just call me?" The room began to spin.

"Lady Kailin? That's your title now."

I pulled out of his arms, but before I could take another step my legs gave out. Aiden caught me and set me down on the nearest chair.

Lady Kailin.

If I could be called that, then all of this really could be true as well.

I heard Aiden's voice coming from far away. He was kneeling in front of me and looked so concerned. How did the great Lord Aiden worrying about me become the second most unbelievable thing in my life?

"I promise never to call you Lady again!"

"That's a stupid thing to promise, as you'll be using my title all the time when talking to other people about me."

"Sticks, Kailin, I thought you were going to pass out!"

"After the last month I've had, I wouldn't mind if I did."

"Well," he said, smiling again now that it looked like I would stay conscious. "I could think of a few places that have a bed that I wouldn't mind lending you, but only because I'm very—what did you call me earlier? Gallant?"

"Aiden!" I smacked his arm.

"I'm just trying to be helpful! That's what good boyfriends do, don't they?"

"So you're my boyfriend?" I said grinning.

"Unless you have someone else in mind."

"So that would make me your girlfriend?"

"I hear that's how it works."

"So Divlan's biggest planter is now officially snared? Between that and announcing my nobility, which one do you think people will have the hardest time believing?"

"Ha ha."

I laughed as he helped me to my feet, because even if I wanted to spend all night in this classroom with my *boyfriend*, I had somewhere I needed to go.

"Thank you for your kind offer, my gallant hero, but I really should go find my mother."

He practically glowed with happiness.

I wanted to smack him again.

"It could still go all wrong, you know. She could reject me. And if I get dismissed"—my heart seized up—"how would you even know?"

"Don't worry," he said, "everything is going to be fine." Then he paused as my words seemed to sink in, smothering his smile. "But because I can't stand to have you leave and not know when I will see you again, how about we plan to meet here during lunch tomorrow?"

He held my hand as we walked to the door, retrieving my bag with the precious letter inside.

"That is, of course, unless I see you sooner."

"If everything goes right, then I will be able to see you tonight if I want to."

He gave me a wicked smile.

"I'm sorry Kailin, but after this I'm planning on going to bed. So unless you're planning on visiting me *there...*"

"Aiden!"

He pulled me to him one last time and gave me the kiss I had been waiting for all night. One that said he was euphoric to see me, that he had been going crazy without me, and that hinted, just enough at the end, that being with me was going to drive him crazy as well.

We were both out of breath when he finally let me go. His eyes had a new light in them, a mixture of hope and excitement, from the kiss or from my new title I couldn't tell.

But what I was sure of was that they screamed of the one thing that had been missing in our relationship before.

They screamed of possibilities.

"Good night, Lady Kailin," he said, opening the door for me.

I ran all the way to my mother's chambers.

CHAPTER
THIRTY-FIVE

When I entered my mother's chambers I was surprised to find them still empty. I stood in the center of the room and tried to figure out what to do. She could have been out of the Academy for dinner. She didn't make a habit of it, but I had helped her prepare for an evening out every now and then.

But most likely she was over at the Hospital.

Just because everything in my life was converging on this moment didn't mean that it was for her.

Not sure what to do with myself, I entertained the thought of finding Aiden in an empty classroom again, when I heard shouting coming from under the stairs.

I picked up my bag then inched over to the half-hidden door leading to the storage room where I slept.

It was open.

I was about to go in when I heard the voices again. No one was ever in there except me. Even my mother only told me what to get and where to find it, but she wouldn't actually go in there herself. With me gone, if she needed something it should have been one of the other girls in there, but it wasn't their voices I heard.

It was my mother's voice.

"There isn't anything else to discuss! I've already made my decision!"

"Why won't you ever listen to me?! If you go they will eat you alive!"

I caught my breath when I realized Healer Arios was down there with her.

"Then I'll be sure to give them indigestion!"

I had never heard my mother so angry. No, not angry. Hysterical.

"Listen, I'm not saying that you can't handle yourself. May the Great One help the man who thinks he can cross you."

"Are you praying for yourself?"

"It's just that out there you'll be completely in their power!"

"And you think the fifty warships going with me won't provide enough protection?"

"No! The fact that they moved up the meeting isn't a sign that things are getting safer; it only means that things are moving so fast and hot that this charade can't wait any longer without looking like the complete farce it is. And I don't like you being in the *middle of a war zone* when that happens!"

"Then I'd better do my job right and make sure a war *doesn't* start!"

I risked another inch and looked inside. My mother was bent over a trunk, her back toward me, folding and packing clothes with a vengeance. Every wardrobe was flung open and the mess was obscene. Healer Arios was behind her, his body stiff with his hands opening and closing into fists.

"Cathrina..." My hand flew to my mouth to hide my gasp. Not from him dropping her title, but from the intensity in his voice. "Please, I'm begging you. Let them send someone, *anyone* else."

My mother stopped packing, the pleading in his voice catching her off guard as much as it had me. She stood motionless for so long I thought for a moment she would actually give in.

"No," she whispered, "Tamerin needs me."

"I need you."

Healer Arios spun her around and kissed her with a passion I had never even imagined existed. My mother responded in kind, and I thought the walls would begin to crumble around them from being too near.

Then she jerked away, sobbing.

"I can't!"

I turned and dove into one of the armchairs facing away from the stairs just before Healer Arios bolted through the room, slamming the door behind him as he left.

And I had thought *Aiden* was intense.

They were both always so composed, so aloof from everything and everyone. And here they had been in love with each other this whole time.

But if she loved him, why did she push him away?

Aiden was going to be insufferable when I told him.

I didn't get up until I couldn't hear her crying anymore. Then I went to her chambers door, opened it, and shut it loudly.

"Lady Cathrina! I'm back!"

"Kailin?" my mother said, coming out of my room. "What are you doing here?"

My mind went blank when I saw her, unable to process that this woman was my usually put-together mistress.

Her gown was sliding off one shoulder, and her hair was sticking up in a snarl at the back of her head. Her face was blotchy and her wet, red eyes looked manic, but even as I watched they were slipping from their striking violet to a dull lavender.

This my mother.

Somehow, sixteen years ago this incredible woman had given me life, and then years later took me with her to give me a chance at life again.

"Kailin?" she asked again when I just stood there staring. "Why are you back so soon? Is your aunt..."

There was suddenly such pain in her eyes that it snapped me out of my stupor.

"She's fine!" I blurted, forcing myself to look away from her shoulder. "The fever broke the day after I arrived and she is recovering."

"That's a relief," she said smiling. Then she followed where my eyes had slipped again.

She quickly pulled the sleeve back into place and tightened the ties behind her back. "But why are you here? You had permission to stay with her until she was fully recovered."

I'm back because I found out you were my mother and because I'm supposed to save everyone and I don't know how.

"My aunt sent me back."

"I guess I shouldn't be surprised," she replied. "Refusing help to recover now that she knows she's not dying sounds like something she would do. I'm actually really glad you're here."

Tell her! a voice screamed in my head. I tried to move my lips, to force them to say the words.

"Come with me to the storage room," my mother said, turning back to the door under the stairs, "I need your help packing."

My feet moved without my having to tell them to, running after her. "Packing?" I asked as innocently as I could. "Are you going on a trip?"

"They've moved up the peace negotiations. Our ship leaves at dawn."

I stopped at the door, stunned. "Ours? I thought I had been dismissed as your assistant."

My mother turned on me.

"I don't care what those shrubs say! I will make my own decisions and *you* are coming with me. Now help me pack, I have no idea where anything is in here."

Aunt Beredith had said she believed The Great One had arranged for me to go to Divlan.

My stomach sank as I realized that He had also arranged for me to go to the Islands.

So that is where I needed to go.

"Well it *was* organized before you tore it apart."

She gave me a smile that made me blink back tears.

My confrontation would have to wait.

My heart beat against my chest in fear and anticipation.

My mother had kept me packing until well past midnight and I had only a few hours left before we were to leave.

I needed to sleep.

I needed to see him more.

The stairwell was deserted, the only light coming from the dimmed lanterns on the walls. Trying to breathe and failing, I stepped off the stairs onto the eighth floor.

It was one of the very first things Markly had told me: that if I was ever caught here I would be dismissed.

Female servants and students were forbidden on the boys' dormitory floor. Where we differed was that while the students would receive a severe reprimand and a report home to their parents, servant girls would be thrown out.

And until I actually told my mother who I was, I was still very much in the servant category.

Yet here I was, creeping close to the walls, scared out of my mind but determined to find Aiden's room.

The last time I disappeared, I came back to a lunatic. I didn't even want to imagine how he would react to my disappearing without a trace again. The only thing I could think of that could be worse was for him to then find out *where* I had gone.

I needed to explain things, calm him down from the way I knew he was going to react, say good-bye, and then sail off into a war zone.

Easy.

Of course if I was caught first and thrown out, or if one of the boys came out of their rooms and saw me...a servant girl... in my *brown* dress....

There it was. Each floor had a roster pinned up the first day with room assignments. I gave a silent prayer of thanks to The Great One that the boys in charge of cleaning this floor were as sloppy as they were with the rest of their chores. I ran my finger down the list of room assignments.

Found it. It was only one hallway away on the South wall. Motivated by the thought of being safe in his room, I picked up my pace.

His room.

My face turned warm.

Finally, I stood outside his door. It was a corner room that would have had two windows facing the city. A room reserved for a Noble.

I raised my hand to knock when I heard voices inside. I held my breath to hear better, but I wasn't mistaken.

There were two voices in the room—and one was a girl's.

And she was giggling.

Mechanically, I lowered my hand.

I was a fool. A rot-covered Peasant fool.

I turned around and ran, wishing now that war *did* break out while I was there.

I turned a corner and crashed into a boy coming out of the washroom.

A very much shirtless boy.

The lanterns were behind him, hiding his face, while they were in front of me clearly showing my very female features.

He grabbed me and put his hand over my mouth, cutting off the scream that had started.

"Don't you dare bite me again."

"Aiden? But—"

"Come on."

Grabbing my elbow, he steered me halfway down the hall and through a door.

Inside it was completely dark except for a few red embers in the fireplace and the light coming in from a floor-length window facing inward to the Academy. Aiden went there first and snapped the curtains closed. He then threw two more logs on the fire and went around raising the light on the six lanterns spaced on the walls around his room.

Because *this* room was very obviously his.

Two floor-to-ceiling bookcases where every space was taken. A large desk covered in notebooks and Healer texts, facing what must have been a nice view of the Academy gardens out the window. Two plush armchairs near the fire-place, one looking nearly threadbare from use, the other looking like it had never been sat in.

A weapons rack with every known blade in the universe.

Wait.

"When I said you could come and visit me I was joking."

I turned again to Aiden.

And snapped my eyes shut.

He was still *very* much shirtless.

"Kailin? What's wrong? Are you hurt?"

"Bark rot NO! Put on a shirt!

"You have to be joking."

But I heard him move away, then an opening and closing of what must have been a wardrobe.

"You can reveal your virgin eyes now that my nudity has been banished."

I opened my eyes and he was standing in front of me with his arms crossed.

With his bed behind him.

His very large bed.

Oh, why had I thought this was a good idea?

"If you wanted to come here for real I would have met you in the stairwell. If it had been another guy coming out of the washroom they could have seen you and grabbed you and—"

He closed his eyes as he brought up his hand to squeeze the ridge of his nose.

"It wouldn't have been a problem if your room had actually been the one assigned to you."

His eyes snapped open as he grabbed my shoulders.

"Tell me you didn't knock!"

"No! I stopped before I could because I heard—"

He looked at me expectantly but I just *couldn't.*

"Heard what?"

My face burned.

Understanding hit him like a rock.

"Is that why you were running so recklessly?"

I bit my lower lip and looked away.

"Kailin," he said, pulling me close. "How could you have believed that was me?"

"Because it said so on the roster."

"Roster? I changed rooms with that Merchant boy *years* ago for a view of the gardens. I had no idea that the official records hadn't changed."

His arms tightened around me. "The thought of you knocking on that door and then having him opening it and seeing you—" He pressed his face into my hair. "But he didn't, and that's what matters."

He held me like that until the tension left me and I relaxed into his hold. He smelled different, more soap than earth, but still so much like the man I loved.

Then that man chuckled.

"Wandering around the boys' dormitory. And here I thought you didn't want to spend the night with me."

I shot out of his arms.

"I still don't!"

"Then why were you hunting me down in *my room* in the *middle of the night?*" He smiled with a tease.

"I came because..." My eyes started to sting. It was so unfair. We had spent less than a day total from our first kiss to when I left him hours earlier. And now I was going to have to leave him again.

So unfair.

"Because I wanted to see you again."

His face softened.

"And ended up seeing too much, apparently."

"Aiden!"

He laughed as he pulled me down with him into the heavily used armchair.

I didn't protest.

"I'm guessing that the fact that you're here means that your conversation with your mother went well?"

I traced the inside of his hand with one of my fingers, going along one finger, then back, then up the next.

"As you can see, I'm not thrown out."

He let out a long breath.

"When is she going to go to the Senate?"

"She didn't say."

Which was one hundred percent true.

"That's annoying. We'll go talk to her tomorrow."

"You're not afraid of getting gutted?"

"For you I would risk it." I closed my eyes as he turned my head just enough to kiss my forehead. "I promised you that I would be by your side through all of this. I don't care how terrifying your mother turns out to be, I'm going to be there for you."

For a long, wonderful moment I let myself simply be held by him. Eyes shut, my hand in his, my head on his shoulder, the rise and fall of his chest as his breathing became more rhythmic, his body relaxing, his arms loosening...

"Aiden?"

I sat up and looked at him.

His head was tilted back into the crease in the chair, his eyes shut and his mouth slightly open.

Gently I touched the dark circle under one of his eyes.

So this is what my gallant hero looked like when he was asleep.

I smiled, but it quickly turned sad.

This was probably for the best. He had seen me and knew that my mother hadn't thrown me out. I didn't really *need* to explain things to him. My fears were just exaggerated. He would be fine.

I kissed him on his newly shaven cheek and slid out of his lap.

I was almost to the door when I was spun around and kissed.

And kissed.

And then my back was against the door and my hands were around his neck dragging him closer, and—

I'm leaving for the Islands in three hours.

His mouth went down to my neck and my hands curled tight in his hair.

I had to get out of there.

"Aiden, wait."

He dropped me and leaned forward with his hands on the door on either side of me, his forehead on mine as we both gasped for breath. I left my hands on his chest—I couldn't seem to be able to pull them away.

"I'm sorry. I was just going to kiss you goodnight, I didn't mean for it to go that far."

"I haven't talked to my mother yet."

He stopped breathing.

"That's all right," he said, meeting my eyes. "You can talk to her tomorrow."

"No Aiden. I'm not going to tell her tomorrow either."

His mouth flattened into a line.

"But that isn't what we decided," he said stepping back from me.

It was so cold without him there.

"I know, but things have...changed."

"How much could have changed in six hours?!" He spun in a circle, his hands in his hair, then stopping to face me, he dropped them. "You can't *not* tell her! This is our only chance!"

"I know!"

"And I *refuse* to have you be my mistress!"

"*Excuse me?!*"

"That's our only other option if we don't want to sneak around for the rest of our lives and I wouldn't do that to you."

"That's great, but I *wouldn't do that to myself*! And if our options really were being either a Noble or your mistress, then what did you think you were doing all those times in the classroom and the roof and…"

"What *I* was doing?! You're the one who kissed *me*!"

"Which was clearly a mistake!"

I had my hand on the handle ready to yank the door open when his appeared on top of it.

It was firmly there, but gentle enough that I knew if I decided to go he wouldn't stop me.

"I'm sorry. I shouldn't have said that."

I let go of the handle.

"I know what I was thinking all those times we were together," I said, turning to look up at him. "I knew it didn't matter what I did or didn't do because you were always a dream too wonderful to ever really happen. I never had to worry about tomorrow because I knew there would never be a today. But *you* never had that excuse."

He looked down at my hand in his.

"You're right. I don't have any excuse. I knew how real and yet impossible we were from the beginning, but I kept seeing you in that classroom anyway. I told myself that I was risking only my heart because I had to bait you with class notes to even see me, while I was having trouble focusing in every class from thoughts of you. I tried to lie to myself that I was just helping you, but I knew in reality I was doing everything in my power to make you fall for me."

He rested his forehead on mine again. When did it become so natural to have him so close?

"You becoming a Noble is going to save me from this

endless black hole where I can't live without you anymore but I also couldn't find a way to be with you that both keeps you safe and also keeps your dignity."

"Aiden," I put my hand on his check and tilted his face up to look at me. I was shocked to find his eyes flooded. They were a faded blue and were so empty, so desperate. He didn't move at all as one tear escaped and trailed down his check.

"Oh, Aiden."

His chin trembled and he turned away, pulling his hands to his face. I wrapped my arms around him and rested my head on his back as his whole body shook silently.

"I'm sorry, Aiden," I said, turning my head so my face was buried into his back, "I do want to be with you, you know I do, but I just can't tell her right now."

"But why?" He moaned into his hands. "What could possibly be more important than us being together?"

This was it. This was when he lost it.

"I can't tell her right now because I'm leaving with her to the Islands in a few hours."

He turned to stone.

"You said you weren't her assistant anymore."

"She decided she didn't care what anyone said. She wanted me, so I'm going with her."

"No, you aren't."

His voice was dangerous.

"That isn't for you to decide. I'm still a servant, remember?"

He spun around and yanked the door open.

"Aiden! No!"

He was already halfway to the stairs when I caught up with him.

"Aiden!" I grabbed his arm. He didn't shake me off, but he

didn't stop either, pulling me along until I couldn't hold on anymore.

"Please stop and let me explain!"

We had just reached the stairs when he suddenly stopped and turned, making me crash into him.

It felt like running into a wall.

"I'm listening."

I felt my pulse accelerate.

Oh this was so much worse than I ever could have dreamt! What could I possibly say to keep him from going to my mother right now and demanding that I be left behind?

Because I *couldn't* be left behind.

Because I was needed on the Islands.

Because someone more important than my loving boyfriend—more important than anyone—had orchestrated who knows how many lives to get me there.

"I have to go, and it has nothing to do with my mother."

He had no compassion in his eyes now.

"It has to do with something else, something bigger than you or me."

"Our pathetic excuse for a country isn't worth your life either," he said, his eyes narrowed.

I felt myself pale.

"It's bigger than Tamerin, it's—"

I couldn't tell him. I was too much of a coward.

He guessed anyway.

He was always good at puzzles.

"Don't tell me you think it has something to do with *The Great One*?"

I looked down, wincing at the venom in his voice.

His fists by his side were white.

"Kailin. Please look at me."

I looked up at him.

"I need you to listen to me very carefully. I know you have your beliefs and I'm fine with them if they make you happy, but I draw the line at putting your life in danger."

"It isn't just a belief! It is real and I can prove it!"

"That's cute, but that's not how fairy tales work."

He turned to go up the stairs.

And I reached for the lights.

My world exploded.

That night at the altar had given me some idea of what to expect, but nothing could have prepared me for seeing millions of streaks of fire burning out from my Aiden. I had always thought that he was angelic in his handsomeness, but seeing him like this made me nearly fall on my knees. Though all began in his chest, they each differed in direction. While almost all of them were really just variants on differing thicknesses of threads, there were several leading toward the hospital as thick as cords.

And then there was the one burning toward me.

It was like a rope mooring a ship to a pier, and woven into it was a cord of pure gold.

Instinctively, I reached out and touched it.

Aiden spun around, staring at me in horror.

"What did you just do?"

"I'm not just a believer. I've been given a calling."

Then he was in front of me, grabbing my shoulders.

"WHAT DID YOU JUST DO?!"

"I've been touched by The Great One, and because of that I have certain abilities."

I looked down at the fire between us again. Hesitantly I touched it with one finger and willed it to burn brighter.

Aiden gasped.

I pulled my hand back and stared at it as if I had never seen it before.

The lights left.

And a terrifyingly angry man was in front of me.

I wanted to run. I wanted to cower back.

But then he started talking.

"No, you're wrong," he said, stumbling back, his eyes wide.

His eyes the color of a summer sky.

Aiden.

His name was Aiden! And I loved him enough for my heart to be cracking with each word he said.

"It was something in your *voice* just now that pulled me back toward you!" he yelled. "And it was your *novelty* that day I caught you cheating, and simple *boredom* that made me desperate to be with you at that party on the solstice, and—"

"Aiden," I begged. "Please believe me. Please believe *in* me."

"Can't you hear yourself, Kailin? Can't you hear how crazy you sound right now?!"

"I don't want to but I *have* to go! He wants me there for some reason."

"*HE?!* Oh sticks in a hole, you think The Great One *talks to you?*"

"No, I mean yes, I mean it doesn't matter! What matters is that I'm leaving for the Islands whether I want to go or not." I was sobbing, but he made no move to hold me. "Whether you want me to or not."

His eyes were wide as they looked at me. His hands crawled up to his hair, only to be yanked down and slammed into the wall behind him.

Then he laughed.

"I knew it would all go wrong, I just didn't think it would be because of *this*."

"Aiden—"

"What?!" he said, turning on me. "Because unless you're

about to tell me that you were just playing some sick joke on me, there really isn't anything left for us to talk about, is there? You said you're going, whether I want you to or not. So I guess you should just go."

"AIDEN!"

"Maybe if you come back alive I'll believe any of this rot."

He stalked past me back down the hall toward his room.

I ran up the stairs two at a time.

He didn't come after me.

CHAPTER

THIRTY-SIX

She was an unstoppable force, the harbinger of peace, the conqueror of minds and wills.

My mother only had determination in her bright violet eyes as she stood on the bow of our ship and watched the Islands grow closer.

For as long as I lived I would never forget how she looked, with the wind whipping the hem of her deep-red gown and gold cross sash and pouch, hair in a low braided bun held in place with four silver hair sticks, loose strands flying unheeded across her face.

At her side, I was less inspiring and even more unrecognizable in my light-green gown. It had a pale pink sash in the same style as hers, with a matching pouch. I was still getting used to how the pouch should be placed on my hip. I adjusted it...again.

"That is the last time you will do that, Kailin," my mother said, never taking her eyes off the ever-growing line of green. "Remember, you have worn that pouch on your hip since you were a child. It would look odd to have you constantly fiddling with it."

"Yes, my lady," I said, knowing that it wouldn't be the fiddling that gave it away that I was acting two rings inside where I belonged.

It was only a week ago that I had returned to my mother's chambers after my convulsing sobs died down. I was only just shutting the door when she called down to me to join her in her private rooms.

When I reached her bedroom, I could see laid out on her bed the green gown she had picked as the one she would wear that day.

And a shorter gown in blue.

"ALL RIGHT," my mother said, stepping out of her washroom. "Shed that rag and get in the bath."

"What?"

"You heard me. You will be useless as my assistant if everyone thinks you are just my servant. So for the foreseeable future you are now in the Healer ring."

"But I can't!" She was already pulling at the ties on the back of my dress. "The punishment for forging your ring is death!"

"Then it is a good thing you're only doing it because some psycho Noble told you to."

She pulled the dress over my head.

"But everyone will know that I'm not a Healer!"

"I doubt it," she said, dragging me to the washroom. It was warm inside with the tub filled with hot water. "You already have the correct ring accent, a more- than-basic education, and the most important criterion of all."

She all but shoved me into the scented water.

"I'm going to tell everyone that that is the ring you came from and no one will question me."

SHE WAS RIGHT.

As soon as I stepped out of her chambers wearing color for the first time in my life, with hair washed and pulled up behind my head with two beaded hair sticks, I was a different person.

Even Aiden wouldn't have been able to recognize me.

No one questioned us when we left the Academy. No one acted suspicious on our ship or treated me differently when she wasn't there.

She had remade me just by saying I was someone else, but it came with a skin that didn't quite fit.

I still knew what I was.

"You're looking a little pale again." My mother was looking at me now. "Do you want some more medicine?"

"Ugh, no thank you. I'm almost tempted just to be seasick rather than having to take that sludge ever again."

My mother's mouth rose in a small smile before she turned forward again.

Besides, the vile stuff wouldn't take away the biggest cause of my stomach rolling.

That was now close enough that we could see a gold line of beach.

There were hundreds of small islands in the ocean between Tamerin and Richark, but only a cluster of five nearly exactly halfway between the two nations that made up what was known as The Islands. For some reason neither nation could claim them as part of their territory, so they were an ideal place for meetings such as these. The largest was the traditional meeting place, as it was the only one with a bay for ships to anchor.

Tropical in nature, as the daily increase in heat and humidity reminded me, they were uninhabited except by pirates, politicians, and other unsavory visitors.

So our imminent arrival at our destination was a likely candidate for causing my queasy stomach.

But then again, it was just as likely caused by the warships dotting the sea behind us.

Or the warships flying the Richark standard on the sea in front of us.

"Do you think they will attack us?" I asked. The warships that had accompanied or preceded us would be left ten miles back from the Islands as per agreement with Richark with their own warships following suit, but instead of feeling grateful for this clear sign of goodwill, I couldn't stop feeling overly exposed.

"Not at this point. It would not be nearly as strategically rewarding to burn down our ship as opposed to taking us hostage. If we're to be attacked it will be once we're on land."

Aiden's fears slapped me in the face.

"*Hostage?*"

"Don't worry," she said, giving me a smile that was completely inappropriate, "I'll make sure they take you as well. Nobles have always been extended the courtesy of retaining a handmaiden or someone like that."

"Oh, well, if that's the case then I guess everything is just fine, isn't it?!"

I looked forward again, glowering at the now-moving dots on the shore.

"I'm sorry, Kailin," she said, wrapping an arm around me. "I'm nervous too. But we can't show that we're afraid, not in front of the Richarkians and *definitely* not in front of our own people."

I nodded and she lowered her arm.

It wasn't just my clothes that had changed in our week at sea.

Sailors started shouting at each other as we came close enough to make out the two docks. I leaned over the railing to get a better look at our encampment as our ship slowed and then nearly stopped, the monstrous anchor crashing into the water.

Our ship, as well as the other one carrying the rest of the Tamerin delegation, would be permitted to anchor in the bay, along with two Richarkian ships. We, along with our soldier escort and supply train, would then be rowed to the dock proudly waving the Tamerin flag. I could see from here that our encampment had already been erected ahead of our arrival, along with a platoon of soldiers between us and the neutral meeting area already set up in the center of the beach.

On the other side of the bay and beach I could make out colorfully clad men and women moving about even more colorful tents in what must have been their encampment.

And just like ours, a platoon of soldiers stood between them and the neutral ground.

A final shout was given, and my mother turned toward the boats that would be lowered with us inside them. I hurried after her through the soldiers waiting to board the boats as well, still horribly unnerved in the way they moved out of my path without my having to say a word. What was even worse was the way the officers acknowledged me with "Miss Kailin" as if I were someone they were obligated to respect.

I would never get used to it.

The captain of our ship had just helped my mother into our

boat, when he held out his hand to me. I stopped and stared at it, until I met my mother's eyes behind him.

"Miss Kailin?"

Oh yes. Of course. This was a thing.

I took his hand and he helped me into our boat.

As soon as I sat down next to my mother she gave my hand a squeeze, then let go.

I needed to think faster once we got on land.

The swinging of the boat was terrifying, but not as unpleasant as when we began pulling through the waves, when I was instantly hit with another round of nausea. I put my head down between my hands.

"Are you all right?" My mother asked, rubbing my back.

"I should have taken the sludge."

"Deep breaths. We're almost there."

I gave a faint nod and focused on my breathing.

Then I felt the *pull*.

My head snapped up, startling my mother, but I barely noticed because my eyes were fixed on the Richarkian dock on the other side of the bay. On it was a squad of soldiers watching as our boat was pulling toward our own dock. Nothing really surprising there, so I doubted my lights would be wasting their time drawing my attention to something I already knew to watch out for.

Then I noticed it wasn't just soldiers on their dock.

A young man was wearing a long green shirt in the Richark style, his black shoulder-length hair tied to the side with a scarf waving in the ocean breeze. He stood with his legs slightly apart and his hands behind his back, and though we were too far away to see his face, I knew he was the one the *pull* was warning me about. I tentatively reached out to my lights, but at that moment he turned and stalked back through the crowd of soldiers. I continued to stare after him until our boat bumped against the dock on our side.

The soldiers that were with us secured the boat with help from other soldiers that had been waiting on the dock. Then they got out and turned around to help my mother and me onto the rickety planks of wood. I could see that it had been repaired in several places with fresher-looking wood, but I didn't trust that it would hold the weight of all these people.

I had no problem scurrying after my mother onto the sand where a group of people were waiting for us.

"My lady," the man in front said, giving her a bow. He looked to be in his late forties, but he wore his stiff uniform with the pride and energy of a man half his age, newly commissioned and ready to prove himself. I knew in an instant that this must be Admiral Cress, a member of our delegation as well.

His hair was blond and slicked back, with only a few streaks of gray, and atop his lip rested a mustache that seemed to itch for conflict. He was to be the voice of our armed forces, which didn't make any sense. According to my mother, before this mission he had only marginal advisory power with the Commanders back home, though you never would have guessed by the way he ordered around the men we had brought with us.

There were two other less imposing people behind him, a man and a woman, who I figured were Gerald and Linken, the other two members of our delegation.

"Admiral," my mother said, "I trust that your journey went well."

"Of course it did," Admiral Cress said impatiently. "My only complaint was having to sit here and watch those doornails just sitting there and not be able to do anything about it."

"Well, now that I'm here we can begin, as you said, to do

something about it in the form of words instead of swords." She said it so coolly that I thought for a moment I would stop sweating. She moved to walk past him and he joined her on her other side.

"Whatever you say, my lady," he huffed.

I thought she would go toward our camp, but instead she turned toward the center of the beach where a group of Richarkians were waiting for us at the invisible line between our two territories.

"My lady!" Admiral Cress said, realizing what she intended as well.

"Come along, Kailin," she said walking away toward the middle of the beach as if she hadn't heard him, forcing him to follow.

Then she breathed only loud enough for me to hear, "we have work to do."

As we got closer to the neutral area I was able to get a better look at our sworn enemies.

There were four of them, the same number as ours, with three women and one man, with other people I could only guess were servants gathered around them.

The men all wore long somber-colored shirts opened down to their clavicles. Each of them had long hair either left down or held back with a thin strip of fabric tied across their foreheads. The decorative knots that held them in place sat to one side of their head with the tails dangling freely. They were also all clean shaven except for the older man in front who sported a long drooping mustache. He also had on a vest that went only to his waist, with long, thin, trailing cords leading from its edges to cuffs at his wrists, like some sort of binding chained to criminals.

The women, on the other hand, wore gowns of the brightest fabric I had ever seen. Though the necklines were higher than our own, they didn't have any sleeves, exposing their entire shoulders. Their hair was done so that thin braids or straight strands dipped down on their foreheads in loops while the rest of it was pulled back high and covered with trailing translucent scarves that went almost to the hem of their gowns.

They were striking. That is, until we got close enough to see their faces.

Then I felt even more uneasy under their openly disdainful expressions.

I kept myself a step behind my mother, as I used to do with the doorframe back home a lifetime ago.

Their leader, the older man, obviously didn't share their opinion as he broke into a grin as we approached.

"Lady Cathrina!" he bellowed. I was shocked to find that I understood him perfectly though he had a different accent than us, before remembering that my mother had explained to me that though they lived so far away we somehow shared a language. When I asked how that was possible she just shrugged and said it was another mystery that only The Great One knew the answer to.

"I hadn't been informed that you would be part of this blessed meeting or I would have dressed up a little bit more!"

"Believe me, I am just as surprised and pleased to see you, Your Honor." She placed both of her hands on her heart and inclined her head forward.

"Oh, come now!" he said, waving his hand. "I thought we had moved past such gestures during your sabbatical."

"Yes, I remember you pestering me endlessly about that!" She laughed. "But may I remind you that the depth of my bow wasn't nearly deep enough for the office you hold, but rather was just the right amount for a loved uncle."

The women across from us stiffened at her words, but the

man she had called *Your Honor* only threw back his head and gave a jolly-sounding laugh.

"Oh my dear child, it is good to see you again!"

Again?

Clearly my mother had some explaining to do.

"And this must be your beautiful daughter!" he said looking straight at me. "She looks the image of you when you were that young, all the way down to her striking eyes."

I panicked as I looked up at my mother. She looked shocked at his words, but took a full moment of staring at me until she came to herself and rested her hand on my shoulder.

As if I truly belonged to her.

"I'm afraid not, though I would have been *honored* to have had such a daughter." There were murmurs from the Richarkian delegation, but Your Honor only smiled wider. "This is Kailin of Divlan and she has come from The Healer Academy as my assistant and is no relation of mine."

Her words moved me in more ways than one. Her praise raised me up, but the way she dismissed the possibility of being related to me pulled me down so hard that I felt myself break on impact.

But I had many eyes on me, so I dipped into an awkward curtsy. Then remembering how my mother had greeted him I put my hands on my heart and did an even more awkward bob of my head before scurrying back to my spot slightly behind her.

Your Honor smiled kindly at me, and in that smile he said I missed the mark on the gesture but he still appreciated the effort.

"Well, I consider it a privilege to meet any of your students, for wasn't it said by your Great One that a Healer's prodigy is knit closer than blood? If she is learning from your hand, I can only expect great things from her."

I beamed at the man, instantly thinking he was the nicest man in the world no matter which country he was from. I had never in my entire life heard such praise, and now here it was coming from a complete stranger simply because I was associated with my mother. What would my life be like once I was officially her daughter?

"I'm also accompanied by a youngerling myself, though not as lovely as yours," he continued. "My nephew is here as well."

"Your nephew?" My mother asked surprised. "Are you saying that Prince Trishton is here?"

If I had thought the men and women standing behind Your Honor were stiff before, they became still as stone.

Prince?

They brought a Richarkian prince to a peace negotiation to stop a war that had begun with the death of another Richarkian prince?!

My stomach dropped at the implications if things went badly.

"The very same! He turned sixteen last winter solstice and is plenty old enough to accompany me on state missions such as this." Then he looked over at me. "And while we blabber on about the dull things of state and treaties, I hope Miss Kailin and he get to know each other. You know what they say, that it will be the generation of tomorrow that will redeem the sins of today."

My mother stiffened at his suggestion, but what she was feeling was nothing compared to the all-out panic I felt at the idea of being left alone with a boy who probably would have rather stuck me with a stake rather than have our own cultural exchange.

"I hope they get along as well," my mother said, coming to

my rescue. "But as I said earlier, Kailin is here to assist me and will be by my side during our negotiations."

"Then I hope that her pretty face inspires him to participate as well."

The woman behind him to his right in a blue gown clenched her fist so tightly it began to shake.

"But we've been neglecting the other members of our delegations! Let me introduce you to my companions."

The rest of our time was given to him introducing the three women who had accompanied him while my mother introduced Admiral Cress and the two bureaucratic officials from the foreign relations department.

Two expendable civil servants and one quickly promoted admiral to command the warships that would most likely be active within the week.

No. My mother was here, and she and the leader of the Richarkian delegation seemed to be getting along great, so there was hope that they would not be used at all.

"I hope this spirit of friendship follows us to the negotiation table," my mother said when the introductions were finished. "Now, if you will excuse us, as you know we've only just arrived and my assistant and I need to rest."

"Of course, of course, forgive me! You must be sweltering! I forget at times how frigid of a world you come from. We look forward to seeing you again this evening."

Evening?

Ug. My mother had a lot of explaining to do.

THIRTY-SEVEN

As soon as we were in the tent that my mother and I would share I turned on her, but she was ready to pounce.

"No, first get out of that sweat-drenched gown and into this."

She had already opened one of our trunks that servants had aligned on the side of our tent between our two cots. In her hand was an undyed linen underdress in a style I had never seen before. It was very simple with no adornment or even any sleeves, mimicking the style of the Richarkian women's gowns, except with a neckline even lower than our own normal gowns. It also had no shape to it, billowing out tent-like, and looked like it would barely cover my knees.

"This is what we will wear when we are in here. You will find it much more comfortable in this heat and humidity. Now turn around so I can take care of your ties, then once you are in it I'll teach you how to do your hair so it will be off your neck."

When I was thus de-robed and much more comfortable, I

assisted my mother. Then she insisted I lie down and rest. I wanted to protest, but when she did the same I gave in.

But I didn't fall asleep as she said I should.

"All right," she said, her hands behind her head while she stared at the ceiling. "Ask your questions."

"How do you know Your Honor?"

"The year after I graduated I used my new and very useful title to get as far away from Tamerin as possible. I wanted to go somewhere where no one would bother me or try to trap me in a marriage for a while and ended up deciding on Richark. I met him while I was staying as a guest of the royal family."

"But I thought they were our enemies!" I said rising on my elbow to look at her. "How could you go there and think that you would be safe?"

"I didn't know, but we were at peace at the time and, if I can be frank with you, I honestly didn't care what anyone else thought."

She didn't care what anyone else thought. Like how she worked at the National Hospital or taught at the Academy or sailed off into a war zone.

"So who is he?"

She got up on her elbow and turned to me as well.

"His name is Alabakle Reed Smitheral Keel, but his official title is The Honor of the Keeper of the Keys to the Door Between the Light and the Dark, which is a mouthful, so he is referred to as Your Honor."

When I started she gave me a half smile.

"He's Richark's High Priest."

"They sent just a priest to the peace negotiations?! But the other delegates treated him as if he were a Noble!"

"You have to understand that in Richark their religion is everything to them, even more than in Tamerin. We have Blessing Trees in our homes; they have an entire *door* that they never use. Our children are taught the laws and that's it. Their children, no matter how rich or poor, attend state-sponsored school until they are twelve years old, where they learn the intricacies of their faith. So with all this regard and reverence you can imagine that the High Priest is next in power only to the King."

I listened not only with curiosity but also with my calling in mind. Was this what The Great One wanted of me here? To learn how they keep their faith alive so I could know how to spark that same devotion in Tamerian?

Maybe that prince would be useful after all.

"How long were you there?"

"Two years," she said, lying back down. "And honestly, I was sad to leave."

Then an image came to my mind of her front room.

"The picture above your mantle. It's of their capital, isn't it?"

"Yes it is," she said smiling. "I wanted to bring back something to help me remember a time I was free."

I thought of how Aiden had always ridiculed her, calling her "eccentric" and saying that she "lived in her own little world." I always thought it was from the disdain of his ring toward anything different, but maybe it was also said with some envy that he couldn't do as she did and just run away for a while.

"That sounds wonderful," I said, lying back down. Then, thinking back to that painting of the beautiful city, I was suddenly filled with my own need to wander.

To forget for a while the memory of a pair of blue eyes and strong arms that caused me pain every night while I fell asleep.

"I wish I could see it someday."

"If we do our job right, maybe someday you will."

Her words were so matter of fact that my heart broke.

How could she forget that the only way I would ever see these other cities is if she went and I followed in my brown dress?

I would never see them, not like she did.

But maybe, once I was acknowledged...

Maybe we could go there together someday.

"Get some rest. Tonight will be warm and you'll need your strength."

I sighed and rolled away from her so she wouldn't see the tears that fell every night as I was haunted by someone's kisses and his words.

Maybe if you come back alive.

I drifted off remembering how he looked when he walked away.

THIRTY-EIGHT

The evening was much cooler than it had been that afternoon, but it was still so hot that even though it was dark outside, I wore only my gown to the banquet. No cloaks here, just elbow-length sleeves that still felt too long and a skirt I wished I could hike up to let some air onto my sweaty legs.

My mother was in an evening gown of midnight blue to match the color of the sky, her beauty as bright as the moon we were walking under as we exited our tent into the lantern light.

"My lady," Admiral Cress said in a stiff uniform, meeting us at the edge of the encampment. "Best to stay close tonight, you never know what sort of games these savages might have in store!"

"I'm sure it will be just fine, Admiral Cress," she said, her voice flat. "And they are hardly savages, they are just as technologically advanced as we are."

"That being so, I wouldn't be too sure about our safety, my lady," Gerald said, stepping out of his tent to join us. He was in a more traditional suit of a light yellow shirt and green vest but while the front was the correct length for a Merchant, the back went down to his thighs—a style that Aiden had strong opinions on if I remembered right. His brown hair was cut short like a soldier's, but as he was from the Foreign Affairs Department, I bet the most dangerous weapon he knew how to use was a letter opener.

"I've made a point of studying these sorts of meetings in the past," he continued. "These diplomatic banquets have been known to be poisoned before."

"Do you really think so?" said Linken, as she emerged from her tent, dressed in a bright-lavender gown that set off her dark hair nicely. She was also a Merchant from the Foreign Affairs Department, with big brown eyes and a naivety about her that was startling to see in someone older than seven.

Gerald sighed and extended his arm for her, which she quickly grabbed.

"The only time an official diplomatic banquet was poisoned," my mother said, shooting Gerald a look I knew she saved for those students who were particularly annoying. "Was a hundred and fifty years ago. And I believe it was *our* side that did the poisoning at the closing banquet."

"If you say so, my lady." Gerald's face was impassive, but there was a spark in his eye that I had seen before, only from the outer rings looking in.

My mother gave him one last warning look, then turned toward the edge of camp, leading us all along while holding Admiral Cress' arm. I had to hurry to keep up with her, which was no small feat as I was still getting used to walking on sand.

I hated the way my slippers would sink into it as we walked, slowing me down, but not as much as I hated that it reminded me of something I couldn't remember. I had spent plenty of time running around barefoot in the dirt outside as a child, but this was different. It moved too much and felt too rough against my skin.

"The barbarians," Linken hissed to Gerald as we became close enough to see how the Richarkians had set up for the banquet. "It is uncivilized to make a woman sit on the ground!"

I didn't see what she was talking about at first. They had erected a platform, which was great as I could eat without worrying about tipping over if I shifted my weight the wrong way.

Then I saw that the tables were too low, almost to the ground; and scattered around were large pillows as long as my bed.

My mother did not hesitate to lower herself across from Your Honor, who was already seated. I quickly followed suit and sank into the seat next to her and found the pleasant man smiling at me. Admiral Cress took the seat on her other side with Gerald next to him, while Linken reluctantly took the seat next to me.

"Barbarians," she muttered again.

The other ambassadors from Richark were taking their places as well, filling all but the seat across from me.

"My Lady!" Your Honor was saying with his perky accent, "you look ravishing tonight! And your student's own beautiful smile will be a blessed relief to all these old, tired faces."

"The treasure of youth should be praised, especially in these circumstances," my mother said, smiling back as servants appeared and filled her goblet. I thought of poison, but she didn't hesitate at all to take a sip. "I believe it is said in your own scripture that all youth wish to be adults, and all adults wish to be youth, but those who live in the moment should be commended."

I felt uneasy at how easily she expounded heathen beliefs,

but then she *had* lived there for two years, so it made sense that she picked up a few things, even if Linken went stiff next to me.

All the dignitaries were now seated and more servants appeared with platters of food. According to custom, Richark would host the welcoming banquet while Tamerin would host the closing, as their country was closer to the setting sun and ours to the rising, signifying the end of conflict at the beginning of negotiations and the rising of peace as we departed. This was one of the many lessons my mother had given me on our long voyage here, along with how to sit and eat in a dignified way.

Though I felt like I was doing a passable job sitting up straight, I quickly discovered that her lectures were grossly lacking in preparing me for the strange food placed before me. I could feel my stomach turn at the foreign smells and felt like I was back on the ship. There were cooked vegetables and meats I did not recognize and breads as flat as paper. My mother was having no problem navigating the exotic platters, eating it all without utensils but with the thin bread instead, but I simply stared at my plate wishing something familiar would appear.

That's when I saw the latecomer walking through the darkness from the Richark encampment. He was younger than everyone else here, maybe my age. As he stepped up onto the platform and entered the lantern light, I could see that he was dressed in the same long shirt as the other men from Richark, but his was green and shorter and ended at his knees, showing tight black pants around his calves. On his head he wore a matching green scarf around his head tied on the side in a style that would have looked ridiculous on any boy at home, but on him it looked, well, attractive. His hair was as dark as the shadows he had just come from, with skin a few shades darker than mine.

The thing that caught my attention, though, was the slight frown on his face. It wasn't from pain or discomfort or worry—it just seemed to be a part of him. I quickly went back to examining my plate when I realized he was moving toward us. I chose one of the less threatening-looking breads and began to break pieces of it into my mouth.

"Ah! My own vision of youth!" Your Honor exclaimed as the young man came to our table. "Come! Sit, and eat! Lady Cathrina, you remember my nephew Trishton?"

"Of course, hello, Your Highness," my mother said with a smile and a slight nod of her head. "But when I saw you last you were no more than a skinny little thing running around trying to steal apples from the kitchen."

Prince Trishton loosened his frown for a moment. "I've grown up. It is the way of things." His voice wasn't as deep as Aiden's, but was still solid enough to make those who listened take notice. Admiral Cress and Gerald were giving him appraising looks while the other Richark ambassadors seemed to be pointedly ignoring him.

"Of course it is," his uncle said, cleaning his fingers on a napkin. "We were just talking about that and how you young people are always trying to grow up. But I hope that you and Lady Cathrina's assistant remind us all that we're here to work toward a future that you both can look forward to together."

It was then that he turned his eyes on me. I looked up at him as well, and found that I couldn't move. He seemed to freeze as well, and the chatter around us seemed to fade.

His eyes were the darkest brown I had ever seen, almost black, and I felt like I had seen them before. The frown softened on his lips slightly, and I wondered what he felt looking at me.

"This is Kailin of Divlan," his uncle continued, completely oblivious to whatever momentous occurrence had just happened. "Isn't she just the loveliest young woman you have ever seen?"

"She's a Tamerin girl," he said, as if that was a reasonable answer. His frown was back and his eyes turned hard.

I could feel my own eyes narrow as I finally understood what his frown meant. It wasn't from pain or worry—it was from pure, unadulterated hostility.

The familiar anger I had been working so hard to suppress boiled in response, but my mother placed a hand ever so casually on my leg. I forced my body to relax, but left the fire in my eyes as I gave a pleasant smile back to this prince. His eyes softened in surprise ever so slightly, and I enjoyed the moment of victory.

"But maybe she improves with acquaintance," Prince Trishton said, sitting down in the empty spot I now knew had been reserved for him. "Though her lack of appreciation of good food will be a sticking point." He looked down at my plate then back up at me, his smile with a hard edge to it.

I glared at him, but with a glance from my mother I tried to put on a mask of civility.

"I'd love to sample what is here," I said putting on my sweetest face. "But I'm afraid I am not familiar with the customs involved to do it properly."

Prince Trishton had already filled his plate and was about to put a large glob of something in his mouth, but with my declaration, he was honor bound to assist me. His eyes angry again, his own smile widened.

"Allow me to assist you."

He put several different items on my plate from various platters. "You use the bread to wrap around the food to eat, like this."

Then, from my plate he took a large helping of the only

thing that looked even remotely appetizing, and swallowed it, his eyes still locked on mine in a challenge.

I looked down at the plate, then, using the bread as he had shown me I picked up a long green vegetable. I felt triumphant, but the corner of Trishton's mouth perked up. I was just about to put it into my mouth when Your Honor reached across the table to grab my arm.

"My dear!" He exclaimed. "You mustn't eat that! We use it in cooking and for decoration, but it will burn your tongue off if you put it in your mouth!"

"Silly me," I said, my eyes burning flames at the boy across from me. He coughed a laugh into his hand before looking away, taking a long drink from his goblet.

"Here, Kailin," my mother said, "Let me help you."

My plate was cleared of anything else hazardous, which turned out to be half of what Prince Trishton had put on it, and I decided that to ignore him would be the best tactic. Show him that he was beneath my notice. The only problem was that he seemed to be doing the exact same thing.

And it was infuriating.

"Before I forget," Your Honor said, turning to my mother, "I thought you would like to know how Lady Kolish is, as I seem to remember you two were good friends."

"Oh we were, but I lost touch with her!" my mother said, her voice becoming animated. "How is she doing?"

"Very pregnant again when we left," Your Honor said with a chuckle.

"So she and Sir Alhol worked things out?"

They continued like that for the next hour and a half and through several courses, talking about people my mother had met when she had visited Richark—and it sounded like the entirety of the country had gotten married or had fifty kids in the last thirteen years. The other dignitaries attempted conversation around me, but nothing seemed to stick. Other than my mother and Your Honor, everyone else here seemed more than willing to just glare at each other.

I chanced a glance up at Prince Trishton over the pudding-like substance they had served for dessert, and he was watching me. His eyebrows were drawn together in a scowl, but it was more like he was confused than angry now. I tilted my head to the side ever so slightly, trying to figure out what he was thinking.

Curiosity.

It was no more than a faint echo, and if I had been doing anything but sitting around doing nothing I probably wouldn't have noticed it, but I did. I quickly looked around, suddenly afraid, but everything was as it should be. I turned back to Prince Trishton and his eyes were wide.

"I'm feeling tired, Uncle," he said, rising quickly out of his seat. "I think I'll go to bed early."

"Of course, if that's what you think you need." But Prince Trishton was already stalking back toward the Richark camp, his hands behind his back as his long legs took him away from us.

Or away from me.

I shook my head at my arrogance. I was nothing to him. Just like he was nothing to me.

"Perhaps it is time for us to retire as well," my mother said, rising. Your Honor rose too and extended his hands.

"May this feast be a sign of goodwill from our nation to yours," he said, his voice resonating in the night air.

"And may our acceptance of it be a sign of our goodwill in return," my mother replied, taking his hands briefly. Then they both bowed their heads slightly and my mother turned toward our camp, me at her heels. The air was still heavy with humidity, but now it simply felt like a hot summer's day back home, uncomfortable but not unbearably so.

"That was an interesting interaction you had with Prince Trishton," she said casually once we were a few yards from the stage.

"He's a shrub!" I spat, wishing I had taken that long, green vegetable and shoved it up his nose.

"Yes," she said, her mouth turning down. "A shrub that is a *prince* that you must not anger. I'm proud of how you behaved yourself today, refusing to be weak before him, but you must remember to play the game of diplomacy, even at personal cost."

I turned to look at her as we started moving again, her face fading into the setting moon directly behind her head. And I wondered, what had this game of diplomacy cost her?

THIRTY-NINE

I was sitting on the beach with the moonlight all around me. I realized now why the sand and waves were so familiar—I had seen them before. I had been on a beach much like the one we were now camped on the first time I had held the boy's hand.

I waited, listening to the wind move the branches of the tree above me, when he appeared sitting on the sand next to me.

We did nothing for a time, just sat next to each other watching the waves, his shadow hovering in the corner of my eye.

Then he moved his arm, but instead of reaching for my hand he put it around my shoulder.

This was new.

I hadn't dreamed about him in the week I was at sea and I found I missed our serial meetings more than I was willing to admit. My secret friend who knew me as well as I knew myself, and who I understood completely as well. Because it wasn't just that he was there for me.

Then his hand moved down my arm until he touched my skin right where the fabric ended under my elbow.

I closed my eyes and smiled at the crash of emotions that was now second nature to me.

Anticipation. Anxiety. Confusion.

Anticipation. Anxiety. Confusion.

Was he trying to say something to me? I focused and tried to sort the jumble of emotions he was sending.

Anticipation. Anxiety. Confusion

"Where were you? Like, why wasn't I in our dreams?" I guessed, in my own mind of course. I had no voice in these dreams, or else we would have solved a lot of questions a long time ago.

Trying to think of how I would tell him my guess, I made myself feel the same emotions back at him.

Unsatisfied.

At least I wasn't alone in my frustration at this extremely intimate yet potentially useless form of communication. I honestly didn't know why I hadn't seen him in my dreams while on the ship, let alone how to tell him that.

Confusion. Curiosity. Amusement. Frustration.

I sighed in my dream and leaned against his side, feeling how nice it was to be held for once in my life.

Then I frowned.

Was this the first time a boy had put his arm around me? That didn't feel right, but whoever would have wanted to...

My already distractible mind latched on to the echo of the memory I couldn't find, but I wasn't able to get more from it than just the feeling of being safe and wanted.

There was something important...or someone?

Confusion. Intrigue.

I stopped paying attention to what the strange boy was feeling, and more importantly, that he could feel what I was feeling.

The boy's arm pulled me a little closer, and I rested my head on his shoulder.

This *was real. That other memory probably had never happened, was only wishful thinking.*

I closed my eyes and sank against him a little more.

Attraction.

My eyes flew open when I felt a pair of lips on my forehead.

Curiosity. Relief. Excitement.

Alarm flew through me and I quickly pulled myself out of his arms, but like a drug addict instantly grabbed his hand.

Embarrassment. Confusion. Resentment.

But there wasn't any sort of self-abasement like he was worried about rejection. Those were feelings I never felt from him. Whoever he was, he was very self-assured.

I allowed myself to feel ashamed, trying to tell him that I was sorry I'd let my mind wander, knowing he probably felt my attraction for...someone and thought it was for him.

But then I realized what had just happened.

This boy had kissed me.

This boy had wanted *to kiss me.*

Me! Brown dress, frizzy-haired Kailin!

No one had ever wanted to kiss me before!

No...that wasn't true...was it?

Contrite. Fear. Longing. Loneliness.

Slowly, I inched my way back under his arm again.

Relief.

We sat there for a time, just letting our emotions ebb and flow back and forth like the waves we were watching, not really trying to say anything but at the same time saying everything.

Frustration. Anxiety. Sorrow. Rage.

He was trying to say something again, that something was happening in his life that had him frustrated and worried, with the familiar deep sorrow and, despite its purity, an anger that felt terribly irrational. I could almost hear him ranting and I smiled, recognizing the same irrationality in myself sometimes.

He paused.

Curiosity.

I knew he was asking about my life now. I tried to tell him about how I was feeling accepted and excited about how my mother was treating me, but still horribly lonely because I still couldn't tell her who I was. How I still felt nervous and overwhelmed by my task from The Great One—not even knowing what it was He wanted from me and afraid I would mess it up without realizing it. Then I thought about tonight and the kindle-brained prince, and a new fire burned in me that made him flinch back. I instantly felt sorry, and wished I could vent to him with more than just feelings.

Everything was quiet after that, with just a gentle humming of what we were feeling, and I thought the dream was about to end.

Apprehension. Curiosity. Determination.

I felt the shift in his emotions before he acted and shot out panic.

Desire.

His lips found my temple.

I froze at the contact, flooded by his feelings, as though the extra point of contact was amplifying the already heightened emotions. I didn't push him away, paralyzed by the way his emotions were over-shadowing and silencing my own.

Triumph. Excitement. Resolution. Longing.

I shivered as his lips moved down to my jawline right under my ear. I could feel everything he was feeling for me ten times stronger than anything I had ever felt before. He was telling me that our time of shared emotions had meant everything to him, that he didn't see me as just a comfortable friend but something stronger. Something deeper.

I closed my eyes and forgot my own name as the boy's mouth was now on my neck and the intensity of his emotions blinded any thought from forming in my mind. This was dangerous and raw, emotions unfiltered through the rationale of our brains and weighed against the consequences of experience. With each shift in his emotions mine shifted as well, until we were feeding back and forth into each other so seamlessly that I no longer knew which emotions were mine and which were his.

Curiosity.

The shift in emotion was what I needed to finally put my hands on the side of his head pulling his mouth off my skin before he could explore any further down my neck.

He froze.

Uncertainty.

Slowly, I pulled his face up toward mine. Determination flowed through me. I knew I needed to see his face, once and for all.

Shock. Apprehension.

But he didn't fight me.

I took a deep breath as I tilted his face up into the light.

All I could see was a shadowed outline with two dark eyes burning red fire.

Terror.

The dream shattered into blue flames.

FORTY

The next morning everything was quiet. Our soldiers had been on high alert all night, waiting for an attack from the Richark camp. I had spent a good long while staring at their slowly moving silhouettes after my nightmare had sent me back here—disoriented and longing for the boy I was now convinced was a demon. Why else would his eyes be made of red fire? Even so, I had kept gently touching my skin where he had kissed me, pushing away the maddening need to go running out into the night and find him until I finally passed out into dreamless exhaustion.

When I woke up to the sun shining through our thick fabric tent, I lay there for a minute, feeling sick at how warm the morning already was. Finally I turned my head, only to find my mother already dressed, sitting in front of a mirror propped up on one of our trunks, brushing her hair.

"Lady Cathrina!" I shouted, throwing off the covers and jumping to my feet. "Forgive me for oversleeping! I never oversleep! I don't know what happened!"

"Nonsense," my mother said, reaching for a green hair stick

to go with her gown. "I let you sleep on purpose. It takes some time to adjust to the climate here and I don't want to wear you out before you've been here a full day."

"That's kind of you," I said, sitting back down on my cot.

"I'm a Healer, remember?" She turned and smiled at me. "Your health is very important to me. Now." She stood and reached for her pouch to attach it to her sash. "The other ambassadors and I will be meeting in a few minutes to go over some final preparations for this afternoon's meetings. You won't be needed until the first official meeting, so I would suggest that you rest. If you can't sleep, only go for short walks today as you adjust to the heat."

"You're not insisting everyone else rest," I muttered. "I can go to the meeting too—"

"Kailin." She turned to look at me, and there was no humor in her eyes. "Please just do this for me."

She kept on staring until I nodded my head.

"Good," she said, turning to the door of our tent. "I'll come and find you in about two hours. Breakfast should be near the edge of the camp." And then she was gone, and I was left alone and unwanted.

I tried to lie back down, but the light was too bright and the air too warm. I finally got up, opened my trunk, and looked at my pink gown for today, dreading putting it on, even though it was the lightest fabric you could buy in Divlan. I suddenly envied the Richark women and their sleeveless gowns.

I put on the gown and tightened the ties, thinking about how I was going to ruin it with sweat before lunch, then turned to the mirror. I had filled out a little after two weeks of good eating, but my mother was right, my face did look flushed.

I sat down and did my best to put my hair up in the hair sticks as my mother had shown me, but after a few tries I gave up. So I cheated instead, braiding my hair and then wrapping it in a bun, using the hairsticks to secure it in place. I turned my head in the mirror, happy with the result. It wasn't exactly the style from home; instead it was my own version. I liked it; having my hair up made me look older as well as keeping the sticky strands off my neck.

Then I went out to find breakfast.

It wasn't hard. The smell of bacon wafting through all of camp would have been indication enough, but the flow of soldiers seemed to be gravitating in the right direction as well. As I approached the line of soldiers waiting for their food, one of them ran forward and gave me a bow.

I did a passable job of hiding my discomfort. This soldier was most likely from the outer rings like me—most of the army was, with only the officers being pulled from the inner rings.

"Miss Kailin," he said, his voice surprisingly deep for his skinny frame. "Allow me to escort you to the ambassadors' dining area."

I smiled and nodded my head, not trusting myself to speak.

He led me to a small open-walled tent with a table and chairs beneath it. I sat down and another soldier quickly brought me a plate of bacon, fruit, and a bowl of porridge with sugar in it.

I may have felt uncomfortable having other members of my ring unknowingly wait on me, but not enough to keep me from eating every bite.

I thanked the soldier who took away my dishes, only receiving a momentarily confused look at my acknowledgment.

Then I was left with the question of what to do with the rest of my morning. My breakfast had made me feel stronger, and I suddenly felt the need to explore this new place. I turned inland and looked at the forest, with its strange plants and trees, and shivered. Despite the radical difference in species, it reminded me far too much of the Holy Forest.

So my other option was the beach.

Curious, I looked over toward the large tent where the negotiations would later be held. It was already being raised over the platform where the banquet had been held the night before. I turned that way, strolling while watching the soldiers work.

Soldiers from both camps were supervising the raising of the tent, mistrust clear on both groups' faces. As I got closer I could hear shouts of directions from both sides, the people from Richark speaking with their intriguing accents.

"Miss Kailin," one of the soldiers said, seeing me approach. "This is dangerous territory! You shouldn't be so close to these doornails without a guard!"

"Then it's a good thing you are here," I said, trying to smile at him. He looked wearily at me, then turned back to his companions working on raising the tent. "Don't worry, I'll scream if I need help. You can go back."

He gave me a weak smile of gratitude that he wouldn't be stuck babysitting me, and I turned toward the ocean.

On either side of the bay the beach was made of soft stretches of sand with the occasional boulder, but here in the middle the waves were crashing against large outcroppings of rocks. They had fascinated me as we sailed in, and something inside me was itching to climb them.

I walked to them now, lifting my skirt hem as I stepped up onto the first jutting rock. I climbed my way up and over the large slabs of stone, stepping and hopping from one to another, until I finally reached the one farthest out in the water. I climbed down to where the water almost reached a ledge on the rock hidden from view of the beach. The waves were lapping just beneath me, and the breeze off the water was almost cool on my face.

I closed my eyes and breathed in the salty air, suddenly grateful for the solitude as I allowed myself to feel the sting of this morning's rejection. I knew she meant well, but my mother didn't know the pressure I was under.

What if I wasn't there when whatever it was I was supposed to do happened and then war started and it was all my fault?!

I reached out for the lights, but stopped short because the *pull* made my eyes snap open.

I turned, seeing about two rocks away another large one hidden from the beach with a young man sitting on top of it, watching me. If it had been anyone else I probably would have been embarrassed to be caught, but instead I just felt annoyed to have to share this moment with Prince Trishton. He was wearing blue today, with his matching head scarf flapping in his face.

"Were you there this whole time?" I tried to smooth down my skirt, but the ocean breeze kept whipping it tight to my legs.

"Yes," he said, and he actually had the nerve to smile.

"It's rude not to announce yourself, especially in the presence of ladies." I gave up on my skirt and shoved it under my legs so at least it wouldn't blow up over my face, and folded my arms in front of me.

"You didn't say anything either, and I think it is against the law not to address royalty immediately. At least it is in civilized countries." He smiled evilly at me, clearly looking for a reaction.

So I looked out at the ocean and ignored him.

I looked over again as he moved, sliding down from his

perch onto the next rock down, which was still higher than mine and I had to look up at him.

"Well, we're not in Richark," I said. "And why were you just sitting there anyway?"

"I wanted to see if you were going to go for a swim." He sat down again, his feet dangling right in front of me. "Though you wouldn't get very far in that gown, so you'd probably have to take it off. I might have had quite a show if I had just kept quiet."

"Why, you! You!"

"Yes?" He asked, and it was then I noticed that though his smile was there, his eyes were hard again.

"You shrub!"

Then he laughed at me, and the hardness went out of his eyes. It was a nice, full laugh, but I forced myself to glare at him.

"I have absolutely no idea what that means, but it sure does sound mean, if not pathetic," he said leaning forward. "Do you have any more insults you want to call me by?"

I stood up and tried to stomp off, but my foot slipped. I was suddenly falling through the air and into the cold water.

I flailed for only a second before I was pulled under by a wave and my head hit something hard. I tried to stay focused, to persuade myself to keep thrashing toward the surface, but I couldn't tell which way it was. All I could feel was panic as my lungs burned with water forcing itself into them.

Then there was a pair of arms around me, yanking me to the surface.

"Stop struggling!"

I couldn't help it. I was dying.

Then I was pulled up onto something hard while being turned on my side, my back being pounded as I coughed up mouthful after mouthful of burning water. Everything hurt.

My lungs, my nose, my eyes, but especially my head. I felt something being pressed against it.

"Ah!" I turned onto my back, but the pressure was still there against my head, as another hand held down my shoulder to keep me from turning away. I finally opened my eyes and found Prince Trishton's face above me, his wet hair falling down around him as he held his headscarf against my head.

"I said hold still!" His voice was hard, but his eyes were panicked.

"Trishton?" I whispered.

"Yes, it's me," he said, and I felt like his voice was saying more than just his words. He sounded just as shocked as I was feeling, but his eyes softened as he took me in. Everything seemed to slow down, as if the two of us had entered a bubble of time that existed only for the two of us. I stopped struggling and his hand let go of my shoulder, reaching down instead to brush my plastered hair away from my face. I instantly felt warm and safe, the gesture reminding me so much of something I couldn't remember. I knew it was important, but I didn't have time to figure it out.

I closed my eyes, the exhaustion winning in my fight to stay conscious. The bubble burst and I could feel time speed up around us. I felt panic replace the warmth and heard his voice from far away yelling at me to stay awake, but I couldn't stay afloat, and I let myself drift as I had beneath the waves.

When I woke up I was in a tent I did not know. Our tent was cream, but this one was in multiple shades of blue, casting everything in a welcome coolness. A lamp hung above me, made of beautiful iron work. I heard a noise and turned my head, only to see Prince Trishton with his back toward me, his shirt off.

"Put a shirt on!" I yelled, trying to sit up, disoriented. The room spun and I quickly fell back down.

Prince Trishton jumped, dropping the shirt he had just pulled out of a trunk as he turned around to face me, which only made me turn redder now that I knew what he looked like from the front as well.

"I save your life and *that's* the first thing you say to me?!" He was looking at me with the same level of hostility he had spent most of last night appraising me with. I must have hallucinated the look he had given me out on the rocks.

"How long was I out?" I asked, turning back to looking at the lamp, the ceiling, anywhere but the shirtless young man next to me.

"About fifteen minutes," he said, picking up his shirt and pulling it over his head. It was blue like the one he'd been wearing before. The one that now was hanging on the back of an ornate chair in the corner drying.

"I'm sorry," I sighed. "You're right, thank you for saving me."

"You're welcome," he muttered, reaching for a new head-scarf from a second chest. "You owe me a new one of these, by the way," he said waving it at me. "Your blood ruined the other one."

"I'm so sorry," I said, feeling my eyes narrow at him. "I'll try to bleed less next time I bash my head against a rock."

"How about you just avoid going places you're clearly not skilled enough to navigate," he said, wrapping it around his head forcefully, pulling it tight into a knot on the side. "You severely threw off my morning."

"I'm sorry for inconveniencing you," I said, my teeth clenching.

"It was more than an inconvenience!" He sat down across from me on the second cot, pulling out a pair of shoes from underneath. "You owe me another pair of these too! I lost them when I jumped in!"

"If you were going to regret saving me so much, why did you do it?!" I tried sitting up again, wanting more than anything to storm out of there, but my head yelled at me. I groaned as I leaned back, my hand flying to my now-throbbing head. It was only then that I realized it was still wrapped in Prince Trishton's headscarf.

Prince Trishton's face suddenly appeared above me, just as it had on the rocks, but this time his eyes were confused.

"It was an accident," he said, his voice flat. Then his eyes turned to the same level of hate I had seen the night before— an irrational fury that made me suddenly afraid that he was going to fix what he had saved me from right then and there. He leaned closer, putting his hands on either side of the cot, trapping me.

"I'm not going to do it again," he breathed down at me. "Next time I'll just stand there and watch you drown."

I glared up at him, and despite my anger and fear, my heart started beating like crazy from having him so near. He smelled like spices, but none I had ever smelled before. I didn't let that lessen my scowl, though, and waited until I could see the look in his eye lose conviction. I smiled a little in victory, and his eyes narrowed.

"I mean it," he said, still hovering over me, "I'll let you die next time."

"WHERE IS SHE?!"

Prince Trishton shot back up and he quickly put on his signature frown as the tent flap flew open.

"Kailin!" My mother ran to my side and instantly started checking my vitals. "Your heart rate is skyrocketing! Are you in shock at all?"

"No," I said, forcing myself to be calm. "I'm feeling fine, just a little lightheaded."

"I told you she was all right," Your Honor said, following her in. "Trishton carried her here himself."

I turned to look at him, but he was scowling again.

"You're heavy," he said, before brushing past Your Honor and out of the tent. I watched him go, confusion being just the surface of the emotions that were coursing through me.

"Thank the Great One that he was there," my mother said, pulling back Prince Trishton's headscarf as I turned to look up at her. "It doesn't look that bad," she muttered examining the wound. "It will be more of a bump than a scar. Do you remember what happened?"

"I had climbed on the rocks," I started, realizing now how foolish I had been. "Then I slipped and fell into the water. I hit my head and Prince Trishton pulled me out of the water. I blacked out, though, before he carried me here."

"Kailin," my mother sighed. "When I said I wanted you to get some rest this morning I didn't mean on a sickbed!"

"I know," I said, feeling terrible in more ways than one. "I'm sorry." I tried to sit up again, but my mother pushed me back. "If you don't mind staying with her," she said, turning to Your Honor who was still standing by the door, "I'd like to go fetch some things from my tent for that cut." And then her jaw tightened. "And maybe keep war from breaking out before negotiations have even begun."

"Of course!" Your Honor said, and I finally noticed that his attention had more than one motivation.

Oh no.

NO!

I was frantically trying to get up, to show Admiral Cress and whoever else that Prince Trishton hadn't *kidnapped me!*

But my vision swam and my mother all but shoved me back down.

"She'll be more than safe here," he continued. "Despite what that Admiral fellow of yours keeps shouting."

Then she turned to me and put her hand on my cheek. "I'll be right back."

Then she left.

Your Honor pulled a chair up to the side of the cot.

"You know," he started, giving me his dazzling smile. "When Trishton said he was going to go for a walk along the rocks this morning, I thought about telling him not to. Now I'm glad I didn't!"

"It was stupid of me," I sighed. "I've never been a very good swimmer."

"None of us are with a bashed head!" Your Honor laughed. I had to smile back up at him. Then I remembered Prince Trishton's promise and frowned.

"I don't think Prince Trishton was very happy about saving my life."

"Don't worry about him," he said looking at the door. "He's just going through a difficult time." Then he looked back at me, his smile still there but sadder. "But I honestly think that this little incident with you will be good for him in the end."

"What do you mean?" I asked, pushing myself up onto an elbow, happy to find that the room didn't spin.

"He may come off a bit antagonistic, but his bark is much worse than his bite. It's the result, I'm afraid, of some difficulties he hasn't quite worked through yet."

"He's a prince," I said, my voice flat with accusation. "How difficult can his life be?"

Then I thought of something Aiden had said in a darkened

stairwell during a night that should have been one of the best of my life.

"Oh yes, he's a prince—but, my dear, he is a *third* prince. His parents already had, what is the saying? An heir and a spare? His brothers were only a year apart and were almost twenty when his mother became pregnant with him. I believe the polite way to say it is that he was a 'surprise.'" He smiled kindly, sighing a little. "Trishton has been having trouble with direction his whole life since he doesn't really fit into any of the traditional roles for a prince in Richark. It was easier when he was younger, but now that he's older, and with the death of Prince Alek-"

"What?!" I said, sitting up a little more, but it was too much and leaned back down again.

"My dear," Your Honor said, sounding surprised. "You *do* know the reason that we're here, don't you?"

"Yes, because we sank a ship with..."

Oh.

"I guess I didn't really realize the prince that died must have been his brother."

"Puts things in a different perspective when there is a face to go with the name," he said, his smile now thin, as if I should have known before.

He was right. I *should* have known.

No wonder Prince Trishton hated me.

But enough to act on this threat and start a war? No, that wasn't what I saw in the young man whose first instinct was to jump into a dangerous surf after a kindle-brained girl. He was angry and wanted to lash out, not destroy a whole civilization.

At least I thought that was what I saw.

"So now Prince Trishton is the spare?" I said, turning back to Your Honor. "Is that why he's here with you?"

"I'm afraid not," Your Honor sighed again. "His presence

here has to do more with my nagging than any official duty. His older brother just announced that his wife is pregnant again with their second child, the first being a healthy boy of five years. I'm afraid that Trishton is just as directionless as he has always been."

"Then he should make his own path instead of just sitting around causing trouble," I said, feeling frustrated for some reason. But why should I care if he wasted his life doing nothing? What was he to me?

"I couldn't agree with you more," Your Honor said, his mouth turning up into a small smile. "Maybe he'd take it to heart if told by a beautiful young lady instead of a crotchety old man."

"That's not what I meant," I said, feeling my face turning red.

"Here we are!" My mother appeared at the tent door and walked over to a small table and started mixing together the familiar paste that would keep my cut from getting infected and help it heal cleanly. "I hope that Your Honor hasn't been boring you too much while I was gone."

"No," I said, leaning back down. "I just hope that the rest of the delegation from Richark is half as nice as he has been to me."

"Don't we all!" he laughed.

My mother came over and pulled off the headscarf, setting it down on the table before washing and treating the wound.

"Now this might—"

"Sting a little, I know," I said with a smile. She smiled back at me, but I still winced as she globbed the paste onto my head. Then she reached for some fresh bandages from her satchel and wrapped them around my forehead.

"Do you think you can walk?" she asked.

I sat up all the way, and nodded at her when I felt the ground stay where it was supposed to be.

"Good," she said; then she turned to Your Honor. "We are in great debt to you and your nephew."

"Not at all. If anything, I think I may be in debt to you. I believe I see in the Secret Realm much good coming from this."

"I can only hope so," my mother said as she smiled back. Your Honor opened the tent flap for her as she stepped out into the sun, then he turned to me.

Before I followed her, I grabbed Trishton's headscarf off the table. Your Honor gave me a questioning look, but I simply ducked my head as I hurried to follow my mother.

CHAPTER

FORTY-ONE

I had to change into the yellow gown as it was the only one that wasn't currently being washed from sweat and seawater.

I hated this gown; I thought it made me look like a bumblebee with my black hair.

"Remember to keep your eyes down during the prayers," my mother said, brushing my hair around the bandage. "The other ambassadors may or may not heed my advice, but I expect better from you."

"What else are you supposed to do during a prayer?" I asked.

My mother smiled at me as she handed me her satchel, freshly filled with notebooks, paper, and pens.

"Are you ready to go make history?" she asked, her eyes alive and excited.

"How about we *change* history? The first time negotiations actually save Tamerin and Richark from war!"

"Sounds good!" She laughed and pulled back the tent flap.

Gerald and Admiral Cress were waiting for us in the clearing between our tents.

"Let's get this over with," Gerald said as we approached him, his arms crossed and his foot tapping impatiently. Admiral Cress was already ahead of us giving directions to some soldiers. When he saw us he gave them a smart salute and came over.

"Nothing to worry about, My Lady," he said with a bow. "I was just finishing up preparations for our safe escape once the fighting starts." He gave me a look that was accusatory, like it was my fault I *hadn't* been kidnapped so he could start his little war.

"There will *be* no fighting!" my mother snapped. "How many times do I have to tell you that assuming that these talks are pointless will *make* them pointless!"

"It doesn't hurt to be prepared," Admiral Cress said, standing up straighter.

"Just don't order anything until you've talked to me first, all right?" she said, exasperated.

"As you wish, my lady," Admiral Cress said, his eyes narrowing at her.

Linken came out of her tent, looking slightly more frazzled than usual as she sorted through the papers in her arms, a concerned look on her face.

"Are you ready, Linken?" my mother asked, her voice shifting to one of encouragement.

"Yes," Linken said, not looking up as she stepped closer to us. "I just wanted to review our side of the evidence again."

"You'll be fine." Gerald had stepped up next to her and pulled down her papers. There was a pause, a beat where she looked up at him, and I would have sworn he loosened his hard demeanor. Then the wall was back up and he turned away from her.

"I'm ready to go whenever you are," Linken said, turning to my mother. Her cheeks seemed slightly flushed, but it might have just been the heat.

A whole platoon of soldiers was waiting for us at the edge of camp to escort us to the negotiation tent, and as one body they fell into step behind our small group. I could see Richark's delegation being similarly treated. Like two hordes bent on destruction, we slowly approached each other.

Your Honor was out in front, flanked on either side with the other dignitaries I had seen the night before.

There was no sign of Prince Trishton.

Good. I was glad. Wasn't I?

We stopped in front of the large, open tent door, with the ocean crashing against the rocks I had fallen off of just hours before. There was a pause as both sides seemed to measure each other. No one looked at me, and once again I was glad to be invisible. Then Your Honor took a step forward.

"The Nation of Richark welcomes the Nation of Tamerin to this tent of peace!" Your Honor said in a loud voice.

"The Nation of Tamerin welcomes the Nation of Richark to this tent of peace," my mother said, taking a step forward of her own.

"It is custom that all great endeavors are begun by invoking the blessing of the Secret Realms," Your Honor continued. Then he bowed his head and placed his hands on his heart, everyone on his side doing the same. I quickly followed Lady Cathrina's example and bowed my head as well, placing my hands on my heart because that was what *we* did, not because of what our enemies were doing.

"I see into the realm between this world and the next," Your Honor began, his voice clear and strong. "I seek wisdom of the darkness—I seek wisdom of the light—I seek power of the gray between, to lead my steps through this life. Lead us through these negotiations, as our path will one day take us from the darkness of this world to the light beyond—from the confusion, pain, and anger of this world to the peace and understanding once our mortal eyes are closed forever and our true eyes become open to the wonders held only within those realms. Guide our steps, we pray."

He raised his head and the rest of his dignitaries did the same.

"Do you have a prayer to offer to your Great One?" Your Honor asked, his voice solemn.

"We do not have a priest with us to offer such public prayers, but ours were said in the privacy of our tents and hearts before we began our journey here to meet you this day." My mother raised her hand toward the open tent. "Shall we begin?"

Your Honor only smiled in that jolly way I had come to expect of him. Then with a nod he and his delegation entered the tent, filling their side of the long dividing table while we filled ours.

I was only mildly surprised when my mother indicated I should sit next to her in the center, across from Your Honor and the empty chair. Your Honor caught me looking at it.

"Prince Trishton wasn't feeling well," he said, smiling softly at me, "but he still may join us later on." I blushed without knowing why and quickly started to take out the paper and books from my mother's satchel, arranging them on the table in front of us.

"If it becomes something serious, I hope you will not hesitate to send for me," my mother said, sitting down.

"I have a feeling it won't stay with him long," Your Honor said, but his eyes looked concerned. The dignitary sitting next to him snickered and Your Honor shot her a glare.

The woman instantly turned to his own set of notes.

"Now," Your Honor said, "According to the agreed-upon agenda, I believe our first order of business is to hear evidence from both sides concerning the sinking of The Black Raven. Since we were the side with the most loss of life, I believe that we are to go first, if that is acceptable to you."

"Of course," my mother said before Admiral Cress, who was sitting on her other side, could make a war-provoking objection.

Your Honor nodded to a woman two seats to his left, and she stood up, her eyes filled with almost as much hate as I had seen in Prince Trishton's last night. She was tall, with dark brown skin and a sleeveless purple gown that showed her shoulders, her hair draped in a matching sheer scarf so both flowed down her back.

"The Black Raven was in prescribed neutral waters," she began in a strong voice. "On its way from inspecting a section of our fleet performing training exercises in the Eastern Sea, when the Tamerin ship, The Rising Sun, appeared on the horizon. It was on the same path that The Black Raven was already traveling on its return to Richark, and since we were not at war, it seemed foolish to alter course. As The Black Raven approached, The Rising Sun changed course to chase The Black Raven—"

"That is outrageous!" Admiral Cress yelled.

"Within minutes," the woman continued, and I swore she looked excited by his outburst, "The Rising Sun opened fire and The Black Raven, along with almost her entire crew—"

Admiral Cress shot to his feet.

"Admiral!" my mother yelled, but not loud enough.

"We don't need to hear their 'evidence' when I have written testimony of every man on board The Rising Sun confirming that they did not change course to 'chase' it!"

"A worthless piece of paper!" The woman yelled back.

"What good is one witness or a hundred if they are made by your Peasants who will be executed for saying any differently?!"

"Ha!" Admiral Cress said, his face glowing in a victory. "Shows how little you know about our navy! We *never* execute our Peasants!"

"Admiral!" Lady Cathrina yelled again, a new desperation in her voice.

"We just throw them overboard—Peasants aren't worth the trouble of a proper execution."

There was silence. Or maybe they were still talking, I didn't know. I suddenly couldn't hear anything other than my own heart as I forgot how to breathe.

"Kailin," my mother said, her hand on my leg. "You look flushed—I think you should go rest."

"I can stay," I whispered, my voice weak.

She didn't say anything, only looked at me with her 'don't be a shrub' look, and I nodded my head as I stood up. I caught Your Honor's eye and he looked concerned, but everything was suddenly fuzzy around the edges.

Once I stepped outside the sun blinded me, making my head even lighter. I quickly moved around to the back of the tent into the shade facing the jungle. There I found a small bench and collapsed onto it, away from the prying eyes of the soldiers still at attention at the tent flap door.

Soldiers that were Peasants. Soldiers that wouldn't receive even a proper execution if they displeased their superiors.

My head sank into my hands, my entire body shaking.

I could see it all again—Healer Steverno slapping me, the Healer in the hospital that Healer Arios had saved me from, the way Lord Larsion had tried to break my ribs, the warning Aiden had given me of what was supposed to have happened to me if my mother hadn't intervened....

I was just like them. Death without notice, without ceremony. As if I hadn't existed at all.

I could hear the voices muted through the thick fabric, grateful that I couldn't hear any more of what they were saying.

I didn't notice I was crying until I felt someone appear next to me. I waited for him to grab my hand, desperate to share what I was feeling and to feel his strength and caring for me, but he didn't reach over.

Of course he didn't. This was the real world.

"You make horrible noises when you cry, did you know that?"

And Prince Trishton was most definitely *not* the boy in my dreams.

"Go away," I muttered, refusing to lift my face out of my hands.

"I don't think I will," he said, his voice light. "My uncle was very insistent that I attend today."

"So why aren't you in there representing your country like you're supposed to be!" I hissed, all too aware that we weren't alone on this beach, while lifting my face out of my hands. I was planning on banishing him with my eyes, but froze when I saw his.

Prince Trishton was sitting on the bench next to me, and though his mouth was in a hard little frown his eyes were soft as they took in my tear-stained face.

"Why aren't *you* in there?" he whispered back.

"I—" I started, not sure what to say. His constant flipping between being a shrub and someone I felt I could trust had my head spinning.

"I guess I'm still not feeling well," I said, wiping at my face with my hands and standing up. "I should go lie down."

"You seemed fine enough marching over here."

"And you would know this how? I didn't see you with the delegation."

"Just because I wasn't interested in being in the front lines for someone to stab didn't mean I wasn't watching the show from a safe distance." I glared, but all it did was raise the corner of his mouth slightly, making his hard face into a hand-some not-so-hard face. "Plus, I don't think you would be sitting here alone if your head were hurting bad enough to bring you to tears."

"Head injuries are finicky," I said, narrowing my eyes at him, but he wasn't looking at me anymore. He was looking into the jungle in front of us; or more precisely, he was looking somewhere that I wasn't.

I clenched my jaw and sat back down.

"Why do you care if it's still hurting?"

"I don't." He was rubbing his hands on his pants, and I wondered if he did in fact sweat in this climate. "I was just wondering why you were crying. Did someone insult your precious little Tamerin?"

"No, it was something Admiral Cress said..." I turned to look out into the jungle as well, not understanding why I was telling him this. "He was explaining that Richarkian intelligence gathering was faulty because your delegate didn't know that we didn't execute Peasants—that they're simply killed with less ceremony than pigs."

Prince Trishton didn't respond for a moment, and I could almost believe he was reacting to the news.

"I don't see how pointing out how barbarian your countrymen are would be that shocking. I'm sure you see Peasants slaughtered every day." He spat out that part, and I'm sure he thought he was insulting me by showing his disapproval.

But he wasn't.

I looked down at my hands, remembering the tone of

Admiral Cress's voice, how obvious and trivial it was to him. "Some of us live more sheltered lives than others—we know of the social norms but they've never touched us directly. I wasn't aware that was how Peasants in the Navy were treated until today."

"And that—how they were treated—bothered you?" He turned to look at me. I lifted my head and found his eyes boring into me.

I felt small under those eyes and prayed that he wouldn't guess the truth of my ring. I should have just kept my mouth shut, or lied. Everyone believed that Peasants were expendable—unless, of course, you were a Peasant.

"You didn't answer my question," I blurted out, "Why are you here?"

"Why am I here on The Islands?" he asked, his voice lightening again. "Or here on this bench torturing you? Or are you asking the greater question of why are any of us here on this planet floating amongst the stars."

I rolled my eyes, and was surprised to see his frown had transformed into a sad little smile.

"I'll answer your second question. I'm out here, on this bench, contemplating how ugly the color green is, because I don't like to be put on display." I looked over at him as he let out a breath, gazing into the jungle with troubled eyes.

"I thought as a prince you would have been used to it."

"You'd think that, wouldn't you," he laughed bitterly. "But for some reason I'm defective in that regard." Then he turned to me, a sarcastic smile on his lips. "Has my uncle told you yet what a poor prince I am?"

"He told me that you were directionless because you were born third—but I think that is just an excuse." His eyes narrowed, but I refused to be intimidated.

"Oh really?"

"Yes. I've lived for the past year with a girl who could make a living on excuses, and I think your problem is the same as hers."

"Only one problem?" His voice had gone flat again. "I've been making progress since coming here. Must be something in the climate."

"You're being lazy and childish. All because life didn't hand you your dreams on a silver platter you're throwing a fit and making as much trouble as you can instead of actually taking the initiative to do something with your life."

Prince Trishton's face didn't change, and neither did mine as we stared each other down.

Amusement.

My eyes grew wide but he had already turned back toward the jungle.

I must have imagined it.

"You're probably right," he said, his voice so light I was instantly suspicious.

"I am?"

"So here's the philosophical question: If I am fully aware of how childish I'm behaving, does that still make my behavior childish? Or am I simply a man using time-proven tactics to live as easy and carefree a life as I can."

"That's a kindle-brained question. Men can be more childish than children, but that's beside the point. You have so many opportunities, you could do so much good in the world!"

"Did my uncle set you up for this?" he said, suddenly angry while shooting to his feet. "Did he give you a script? Tell you to lean over and use your female charms to get me to finally change my life?"

I hadn't realized I was leaning toward him. I still was not used to the lower neckline on these gowns and I quickly sat up and pulled at my gown, turning bright red.

It wasn't lost on Prince Trishton as a smirk crossed his face.

"You're a terrible seductress if that was the plan."

"There was no *plan,*" I hissed back.

"You sure? Because a second ago you sounded like you wanted to fix me. Is that what it is—you're a girl who likes a project?"

"No! I don't want anything to do with you!"

"Then why are you bothering me?!"

"Why am *I* bothering *you*!? You're the one who came and found *me*!"

"Which is clearly as much a mistake as saving you!" he laughed.

I didn't like it. It was edged with something close to hysterical and I remembered the way he promised he would watch me die next time.

"You're crazy."

He laughed again.

"You have no idea." He waved his hand at the tent. "So is that it? Does my uncle think that you can cure me?"

Cure him?

Other than hate me for the very reasonable reason that my country killed his brother, I didn't see anything other than a spoiled child.

"I just think you should do something about yourself."

"I think I would rather do something about you."

A million thoughts flashed though my head of how he could do just that, and I was disgusted with myself that I was approving of all of them.

Which was probably why I didn't step away when he raised his hand—

Only to have him tap me on my bandage.

"How's your head really feeling?"

"Hurting!" I said, sinking onto the bench as a new wave of

dull throbbing started. I glared at him, the moment broken. "Thanks for that!"

"Sorry," he chuckled, sitting down next to me again, but this time he was so close that our legs were touching. "I just always assumed that Lady Cathrina was so amazing a Healer that you would have instantly been healed."

"No one is that good," I muttered. "Speaking of which, she would probably be furious that I'm still out in the sun and not lying down. She seems to think I'm about to melt at any second."

"Aren't you?" Prince Trishton asked, his tone still playful. "Isn't Tamerin a land of ice and snow, which is why, according to our great scholars, that your skin is so pale so you can blend in with it and hide from wild animals?"

"There are lots of people in Tamerin with darker skin. And I'm not pale."

"Compared to what people are *supposed* to look, you are sickly."

"You're really annoying, you know that, right?" I said.

He was smiling now. A real, genuine smile.

I liked it.

I hated that I liked it.

"I really do think I need to lie down," I said, standing up quickly.

"Do you need an escort?" He was standing now as well, just as close to me as he had been sitting down. Then he reached out and took my hand. "You're looking a little flushed," he said leaning closer, his voice softening. "I wouldn't want you to melt halfway back to your camp." My heart started beating a thousand beats a minute. His dark eyes were looking right into mine, and I could smell him again, that spicy scent that I could almost taste.

"I don't need an escort," I whispered.

"You sure?" His voice weaker than before. I could feel his other hand shake slightly as he lifted it to my face, brushing my hair back. Suddenly I was back on the rocks, lying in his arms with the waves crashing around us, his hand brushing away my hair, his face hovering above me brighter than the sun. I could feel my face turn red as the memory of his touch melded with his hand now lingering on my cheek. His eyes widened slightly as well, as if he could feel what I was feeling. He closed them for only a second, and when he opened them he was staring at my mouth.

Attraction.

"You should go in there and sit next to your uncle," I said. He paused, and then pulled back, eyeing me as if I had just slapped him. "If anything, it would make him happy to have you there."

"And it would make *me* happy to stay out here." He spat.

"Why are you so determined not to do your duty?!"

"It has nothing to do with duty, I just would rather skip this part of the talks!"

Pain.

Of course he didn't want to hear the details of how the Richarkian flagship was sunk.

"I'm sorry about your brother," I said quietly.

He dropped my hand.

"I don't need your pity," he said, his voice flat and dangerous.

"I wasn't—"

"And I don't need some Tamerin *whore* getting into my head!" He took a step back, looking at me with so much loathing I felt like I would crumble.

"I just said I was sorry!" I could feel tears starting to build, so I did what I always did.

I got angry.

He saw the shift inside me as soon as it happened, and his eyes went wide and wild at my challenge. He stepped close to me so quickly I didn't have time to react, leaning in so his mouth was right next to my ear.

"Not as sorry as you're going to be."

His chest was only an inch from mine, his face so close to mine I could feel his breath against my neck. I could sense the rage rolling off him, until it suddenly shifted into something else.

Something I had felt the night before, coming from another young man who may or may not exist.

But Prince Trishton existed.

Prince Trishton was very, *very* real.

I tried to hold still, but my chest started rising and falling out of control as I couldn't seem to get enough air. I saw his hand come up, reaching for the side of my face as his mouth turned from my ear.

I closed my eyes.

But then there was nothing but air next to me.

I opened my eyes just in time to see him turning the corner of the negotiation tent, heading back toward the Richark camp.

I fell back onto the bench and screamed quietly into my hands.

FORTY-TWO

"You can't be serious!" Admiral Cress shouted, leaning across the negotiation table. "A demand like that will disrupt our training exercises for months! We cannot allow such a disturbance!"

"Your training exercises," a diplomat from Richark replied, leaning over the table herself, "are much too close to Richark territory! They are frightening away trade!"

"Well maybe your trade partners shouldn't be crossing Tamerin waters in the first place!"

The room erupted and angry voices from both sides started yelling insults at each other. This was the fourth time it had happened this morning and the seventh since negotiations had started three days earlier, and instead of frightening me as it had the first few times, all it did now was irritate me. The only people who were not on the verge of leaping across the table were me, my mother next to me, Your Honor directly across from her, and his royal pain, Prince Trishton, next to him.

I was attempting to hold myself in the dignified way my

mother did, while Your Honor was lounging in his seat, his hands resting on his temples as if he couldn't get rid of a headache. Every now and then he would take a sip from his goblet, which was somehow still mostly full. The rest of us had finished off ours long before.

Prince Trishton was doodling on a piece of parchment, a bored look on his face. I had to remind myself that it was progress that he was even there, but watching him hour after hour with him doing nothing even to assist his uncle with notes, as I was doing for my mother...Ug, I had to restrain myself from adding my own voice to the shouts.

Didn't he care about his country?! That we were on the brink of war?!

He looked up at me as if sensing my attention, his eyes dark with questions. As they locked with mine, they seemed to soften slightly, the pull of his mouth turning down. Despite all the tumult, I thought it had become far too quiet and the air had suddenly become very heavy. I turned my head away.

"The training exercises are not set in stone, Admiral Cress," my mother said, breaking the chaos with her clear, commanding voice. "They can be moved if Richark can provide the necessary documentation showing that our military activity is hindering their trade. And besides that, may I remind you that Richark's trade partners are also *our* trade partners?"

She reached for her goblet, but frowned slightly, remembering that it was empty.

"Allow me," Your Honor said, pouring some of his into her cup. I heard a small gasp from Linken, probably from her thinking it would be better for my mother to die of heatstroke instead of sharing backwash with someone from Richark.

"Thank you," my mother said as she downed the liquid.

"But my lady," Admiral Cress began again, only to stop

when my mother turned her eye on him. "Of course, I will take another look at the exercise schedule."

Smart man.

"Well," Your Honor said, taking advantage of the brief pause in yelling, "I think we've had enough arguing for the morning. How about we call a recess and rejoin once the heat has let up some?"

I prayed a silent prayer to The Great One, thanking Him for the one man who seemed to have any sense in these talks. My face and hair were drenched in sweat. Somehow my mother did not have a speck of sweat on her. I wondered if they removed that ability in Nobles when they were children.

"I think that is a very good idea," my mother replied, rising from her seat. All the other dignitaries followed suit, and with a slight bow my mother turned and left the tent, followed by the rest of our delegation. As I followed behind, I thought a queen couldn't have made a more dramatic exit.

We had made it only halfway to our camp when my mother stopped, checking her pouch.

"Kailin," she said, digging around in it. "I left a vial of hand ointment in the negotiation tent. Could you please fetch it for me?"

"Yes My Lady," I said, trying to hide my annoyance at being delayed the joyous wonder that was stripping to my under-dress and letting my exhausted body have some relief from the heat. But my servant training kicked in and I kept my murmurings to myself.

When I arrived at the tent almost everyone was gone. There was only one person still sitting in his seat, his head bent over his doodles.

"If you wanted to improve your art skills, you should have stayed home."

Prince Trishton's head snapped up in surprise; then seeing

it was me, his eyes narrowed, his mouth turning down in a frown. I was too full of annoyance to notice how attractive it was.

"How do you know it isn't some sort of code for my spies to assassinate all of you?"

I could feel my eye twitch, and with the way he was looking at me I could almost imagine him giving such an order.

"I'd like to see them try."

He and I were silent for a moment longer, trying to murder each other with our glares. Like my mother and the other members of the deposition from Richark, he looked cool and comfortable, while I knew I looked like I had just jumped in a lake, sweat stains under my arms, my hair sticking to my neck. I should have felt self-conscious, but I couldn't feel anything. This was the first time we had spoken since he had called me a "Tamerin whore." I chose to focus on that part of our interaction, not the way he seemed to open up or make me smile. Or the kiss that most definitely did not almost happen. I could feel my face flush slightly and I turned away, walking toward where my mother had been sitting.

"Why are you still here?" I asked, moving a stack of law books to the side. "Don't you have some luncheon to attend?"

"I'm busy," he said, doodling again. I watched him for a few seconds, but he didn't acknowledge that I was there. Fine, if he was going to ignore me then I could ignore him. I looked down again at the mess of parchment, shifting through them.

"What are you doing?" he asked, not looking up.

"Nothing to concern your little royal head about."

"So you *do* remember that I'm a prince?" he said looking up, his mouth in a straight line. I could feel him looking at me, watching my path down the table toward him.

"How could I forget?"

"I wasn't sure anymore from all the glares you've been giving me during the negotiations. Aren't you afraid of what I could do to you?"

"Like annoy me to death?" He raised an eyebrow and I ducked down, looking at the planks under my mother's seat. "You could say I make it a habit of not judging someone by their position but rather from their strength of character." I looked up at him from the floor, hoping that he would understand that I found him lacking in that regard.

"Huh," he breathed, the corners of his mouth raising ever so slightly.

"Where are your servants?" I asked, standing up.

"My babysitters are not needed," he said, looking back down at his doodle, his voice rising flippantly just like it had when it was just the two of us on that bench. "Third prince, remember? I'm lucky they remember to feed me." Then the corners of his mouth rose a little more. "I like to think that I'm about the same status as you and the other Tamerin Nobles."

I stopped and looked at him, but I could see that he wasn't joking.

He really thought that I was a Noble.

"I'm not—"

"Lesser Noble, whatever. Your ring system has always bored me, along with everything else that has happened here so far."

I watched him, seeing if there was any recognition in the way he had spoken to me behind the negotiation tent that first day. He had certainly not looked bored then, but he had run from my eyes now and was intently doodling again.

"If you're so bored, why are you even here on the Islands?"

"Maybe I came on this mission for more than just the art lessons," he muttered.

"So you just wanted a vacation? Got tired of civilization and running water?"

"Or maybe I just wanted to be there to draw first blood when war was finally declared." I had moved right across from him now, and could see what he was drawing. It was a surprisingly accurate sketch of a ship on fire. A ship waving a flag that looked a lot like Tamerin's. Next to it was another sketch that looked like something a five-year-old would draw of a girl in a gown with "X"s for eyes and her tongue sticking out while an equally poorly drawn boy with a headscarf was stabbing her.

"Do you like it?" Trishton asked. "Uncle says that it's bad for inner spiritual peace, but I find sketching very soothing."

"You're better at drawing boats," I said flatly, trying to ignore the trail of blood he was scribbling from what I guessed was my chest.

He snorted, then with a flourish he signed his name at the bottom of the parchment.

"Here," he said holding it out for me. "A Royal Richark original! I'm sure you could get plenty for it back in Tamerin, or you could get it framed and hang it in your room."

I took it from him, glanced at it one more time, and promptly ripped it in half and threw the pieces behind me. Prince Trishton's eyes were livid, and I wondered how often since we had met he had fantasized about the war starting and using me as his first victim.

"If you didn't like it, you could have given it back."

"Why do you want a war?!"

"Lots of reasons. One of which being your country's apparent lack of respect for the arts." He reached over to a stack of parchment a few seats down and snatched another page, slamming it down in front of him, and began sketching again, looking up at me and down again while his hand quickly moved the pen across it.

"Doesn't it bother you at all the people who will *die* if we start fighting each other!?"

"No more than it usually bothers me that people are dying every day because of the decisions my father makes."

I didn't know how to respond, so I continued looking for my mother's vial among the piles of papers on the negotiation table. Prince Trishton was still sketching, looking up at me and back down again every few seconds, a hatred in his eyes that made me want to shy away in spite of my brave words.

"There!" he shouted, and practically threw his pen down.

"What—" but he had already turned the parchment to show me.

This one was not of a boat.

It was a beautiful sketch of a young woman lying on her side, her eyes closed peacefully, one arm draped under her head while the other one was draped across her chest. It was rough in its pen strokes, but it was still drawn with such skill that I couldn't believe that he had made it in only a few minutes.

Then I noticed two things.

The first was that the young woman was an almost perfect copy of the face I kept seeing in my mother's mirror.

The second was the thin trickle of blood falling from her slit throat.

"Do you like this one better?" Prince Trishton asked, smiling. "I tried to up the quality. I think it turned out pretty well, don't you?"

I stared at the picture and could feel my pulse increasing.

"You're insane," I whispered. "You don't even know who I am. How could you hate me so much?"

His smile disappeared.

"I don't hate you," he said, turning his picture back to face him again. "I just want to see you dead." He said the words, but they lacked the conviction he'd claimed only a minute earlier. He was looking down at the picture, one finger tracing the slit along my neck.

Heartbreak.

I slowly reached my hand forward and turned the picture back around toward me. He didn't protest, but looked up at me, curious.

He really had done a good job. The curve of my check, the light way my hair was falling around me, the delicate touch of my fingers brushing the sand. If I looked half as pretty as he was making me out to be, then my transformation from Peasant to whatever it was I had become really was remarkable.

I really did look like a Noble.

"I've never seen myself drawn before," I said. "It really is a beautiful picture—minus the whole throat being slit part."

I looked back up at him and he was watching me, confusion edging his eyes while his smug smile fell into a frown.

"But starting a war isn't going to bring your brother back."

The softness was gone as he snatched the picture back.

I started to search through more of the endless piles of papers, desperate now to get away from him, when suddenly he reached across the table and grabbed my hand, yanking me across the now-falling parchment and books as he pulled it close to his face. Shocked, I looked up at him, my face no longer brave. He held my hand so tight I didn't even think of trying to get it back.

"You have interesting hands," he said, his accent emphasizing *interesting* like it was his favorite word. "Small, careful." Then, looking up at me he smiled as if I were already dead on the ground in front of him. "And oh so very, *very* calloused."

I pulled my hand back and held it close to me, as realization dawned as to what he was saying. He leaned back in his chair, his smug smile splattered all over his face.

"So my question," he said, his voice turning sharp, "is why a Tamerin *Peasant* is parading as Lady Cathrina's assistant, dressed above her station, and speaking to a foreign prince as if she were his equal?"

I wanted to run, to hide, to scream at the sky, but I couldn't let him win. Not while I was here, on this island, having come so far and knowing I still had so far to go.

Slowly, I dropped my hand to my side, pulling myself up to my full height, willing my eyes to shine with the electric power I had seen my mother use so many times before against weaker individuals. And this *boy* was weaker than me—not because of any fault in him but because I wanted to be stronger.

"My name is Kailin of Valehaven," I stated, my voice sounding strange and not my own. "I am the daughter of a dead village whore and a passing tramp. I grew up an orphan Peasant raised by a dishonored Healer, only to become an unnoticed servant. In spite of all this, I have risen to become Lady Cathrina's trusted assistant."

I expected Trishton to be bored, to examine his fingernails and brush me off, or to grab a hidden dagger and kill me then and there, but instead his gaze became fixed on me, his eyes wide, his jaw slack. I leaned across the table, bringing my face close to his as I whispered, "You should fear what I may become."

Trishton grabbed my face and kissed me.

I felt like I was underwater again, drowning, and with a horrid thought I realized that I was enjoying it. His face smelled of a thousand different spices I'd never heard of, his mouth rough in a way that made me hungry and empty all at once.

Then it all changed.

I suddenly felt a warmth that wasn't coming from the kiss, but that I knew was pouring into me from his touch. His lips became gentle on mine, and I could feel myself falling into one of his hands on the side of my face, pulled toward him as if the tide had pulled me under the waves.

Right at the moment I thought I would become lost, he pulled his mouth away ever so slightly, keeping his lips from barely touching mine again. His thumb rubbed along my cheek, and my heart caught in my throat.

Longing.

I pulled away out of his reach just as he leaned forward again. I stood there looking at him, trying to force myself to turn away, but I couldn't. His dark eyes were huge, as though he had never seen me before.

"How dare you touch me," I breathed, forcing myself to feel angry. "Maybe in your country women can be used in such a manner, but I am not one of your subjects and Peasant or no, I will not be touched without permission!"

"So all I needed to do was ask and I could kiss you?" he said, forcing animation into his voice. "What other things could I do if I said 'please'?"

I could feel my face turn red and it wasn't from embarrassment.

"You can go jump in the ocean!" I hissed.

"What can I say," he said, crossing his arms while leaning back in his chair. "I'm attracted to powerful women."

I turned and marched up the beach. There was nothing else to be gained from staying other than, perhaps, my temper leading to a new reason to start a war because another one of Richark's princes had been murdered.

I threw open the flap of our tent, startling my mother, who was already lying down on her cot.

"I couldn't find the vial," I muttered, marching straight to my cot.

"What happened?" my mother was behind me, loosening my ties.

"I played the game," I said through gritted teeth.

And lost.

CHAPTER

FORTY-THREE

I was not looking forward to my nap that afternoon.

Even though each afternoon and night I was exhausted, I had stopped looking at sleep as a form of relief. In the evenings the boy was still there, but now we stayed on opposite ends of our strip of beach, both too afraid of the other to come any closer.

But even that shared, or rather *un*shared, terror, was preferable to what awaited me each afternoon.

The first afternoon I dreamed I was in that destroyed village I had seen on my way to Divlan, only this time it was filled with the corpses come back to life and praying around The Great One's broken shrine.

Yesterday I dreamed I was back at the Academy, only this time it was *me* feeding Lord Larsion's poison to the old man, forcing it down his throat while his body was thrashing wildly, all the while telling him to trust me when he could clearly see I was killing him.

My mother said it was the change of climate and the strain of our mission. Stress and heat—two worthy scapegoats. She

488

had rubbed a cooling ointment on my neck before lying down herself, but I didn't think it would help.

So instead I lay there, too tired to fight off thoughts about Aiden, until the promised nightmare would have been preferable and I gave up and closed my eyes.

I was falling through an endless blackness until my feet landed on stone.

Then I was running.

I was in the Academy, but it was not how I had left it. The carved faces in the stone pillars had become images of agony. The halls were deserted as if I were the first living thing to have ever entered. Where before there was life and the bustle of healing and learning, everything was dark and full of dust and dirt. The beautiful windows were shattered, but no light was let in.

I turned a corner and was suddenly in Aiden's room, looking out his window, but instead of the garden it was a full view of the city in flames, the screams of the innocent rising up with the smoke.

Then Aiden was behind me, and I instinctively turned and threw my arms around his neck. He was shirtless like I had found him the night before I had left, but instead of warm his skin felt ice cold under my touch. I shied away, but he pulled me to himself and was kissing me with a passion I had never felt from him before.

I kissed him back just as wildly.

He lifted me off my feet and pressed me against a wall, but it wasn't the stone of the Academy. It was the rough wood of my bed in my aunt's cottage. It was burning all around us, and I could feel the heat from the crumbling walls scorching the top of my skin while Aiden's touch was burning me from underneath as I drew him even closer.

"I love you," I whispered against his lips, knowing that it might be the last words I ever said.

He froze at my words, then slowly pulled his face back from mine.

I gasped.

It wasn't Aiden kissing me.

It was Prince Trishton.

He looked just as shocked as I was, his mouth hanging open slightly, and his eyes wide.

His eyes that destroyed all reason inside me. Instead of the dark, inky pools I had seen only an hour ago they were ablaze with an all-consuming, bright red fire.

"It's you," he whispered.

In that instant the link between us reforged, and this time I didn't shy away from the avalanche he poured into me. Knowing his face, his name, and that he was undoubtedly and completely real sealed my fate. I gasped as his arms tightened so I couldn't breathe, but I didn't care. I could feel the flames reach my bed and singe my skin as I grabbed his face and pulled his mouth toward mine.

I woke with a scream.

I was drenched in sweat, the usual disorientation I always felt after sharing with the boy in my dreams. It shot through my system as my eyes squinted from the sunlight that was still blinding even through the fabric of our tent. I quickly looked at my arms and saw, just as I expected, the marks of where he had held me. I could still smell the smoke and feel the heat, and my lips hurt from the kiss he had given me.

I breathed, forcing the crazed longing of our broken connection to the back of my mind, knowing there was some-thing earth-shatteringly important I needed to remember.

I closed my eyes as I raised my fingers to touch my lips, my entire frame trembling. Then I remembered.

Trishton?

I felt nothing but my own destroyed reality. I was a fool for thinking I could keep this boy separated from everything that was happening in my life. He was real—and he had now kissed me. Twice!

TRISHTON?!

The boy with whom I had shared my deepest emotions, who had given me a full view of everything that swirled inside his hopes, dreams, and fears. And the whole time it was the young man I had written off as a self-serving, arrogant shrub.

I have to find him.

I was almost to the door when I realized I was still in my underdress. I may have felt unstable, but I hadn't completely lost it. I quickly turned around to find my gown.

That's when I realized I was alone in the tent. My mother was gone, and so was her healing satchel.

That's when I heard the yelling. I must have been out of my mind not to have been woken up by it let alone not notice it until now.

I quickly dressed and stepped out of the tent. There were soldiers everywhere rushing about, forming ranks. None of the other ambassadors were around to explain what had happened, until the wind blew open Linken's tent flap and I saw her standing inside. I ran over to ask where my mother had gone, but stopped when I heard Gerald's voice.

"Why is this happening now?!"

"You wore your red vest today!" Linken sounded terrified.

"This isn't red! It's maroon!"

"But—"

Then the tent flap was yanked back and Gerald was standing there glaring down at me.

"How long were you standing there?!" he yelled in my face.

"What happened?!" I shouted above the chaos. "Where is Lady Cathrina?!"

"Get back into your tent, Kailin!" Gerald grabbed my arm, his fingers digging into my skin as he dragged me back across the clearing. "You need to stay out of the way while we handle this!" He threw me back into our tent and I knocked over my mother's cot in my fall. I heard him tell a soldier to make sure I didn't leave.

Angry now, I went to work untying the back of the tent until it was loose enough for me to slide under the bottom. Then I ran toward where I could see a large group of people on the negotiation platform. Soldiers from both sides had formed ranks, and the air was charged like lightning waiting to strike. Ships were moving on the horizon. No one noticed me as I wove my way around the onlookers, grateful for the training I had received from being an invisible servant.

When I reached the front I saw the ambassadors from Richark yelling and screaming at Admiral Cress, who was red in the face from screaming back. There was a slight parting of a circle of guards standing behind the Richark ambassadors and I saw a trace of the purple gown my mother had been wearing that day on the ground.

I tried to use my stealth to sneak around the guards, but these were not as easily fooled.

"Stop there!" one of them yelled, grabbing my arm. "Or are you on your way to kill someone else?!"

Kill someone?! What was my mother doing over there on the ground?! In a panic, I tried to pull myself free. "I'm Lady Cathrina's assistant! You have to let me through!"

"I'll escort her," said a voice behind me. Grabbing my arm harder than the guard did, Trishton propelled me forward. I turned to look up at him, but he wouldn't look at me. His hair was disheveled and missing his headscarf, and there were lines on his face from a pillow.

"It really was you," I whispered.

His face paled slightly, but he still refused to look at me.

We broke through the last line of guards and I saw my mother on the ground next to a body. I gasped as I recognized Your Honor.

"Is he—" I started, looking up at Trishton's grim face.

"Not yet," he cut in, finally looking at me, but instead of recognition all I saw was the rage I had felt so many times before. "You say you're so powerful, do something to save him!" With that he threw me on the ground next to where my mother was working.

"What happened?!" I whispered, the gravity of the situation crashing down on me. "What is wrong with him?!"

My mother looked up at me, and I saw something I had never seen on her face before.

Fear.

"It is some sort of poison," she whispered back, her breathing labored. "I've seen it once before a few months ago, but I have no idea how to treat it. If it is like the case before we have a couple of hours."

She was trying to hide the panic in her voice, but her hands were shaking, sweat beading on her forehead.

"Arios was always the expert on poisons," I heard her whisper to herself. "He would know what to do."

I looked back and saw the diplomats on the verge of strangling each other, and saw again in my mind the image from my dream of Divlan in flames and its citizens being murdered by the thousands. If this sweet man died, it would mean war. Tamerin would be blamed for the assassination, and from the way he was looking down at us, I had no doubt that Trishton would lead the charge, mystical connection or not.

"There has to be something we can do?" I whispered, quickly looking through her healing satchel hoping something, anything would give me an idea.

"I've given him something that will stabilize him, but I—" With a gasp, my mother doubled over, a sudden pain in her eyes as the pupils went wide. Then she toppled over on top of Your Honor's body.

My whole body went rigid with fear.

"Your prince has murdered Lady Cathrina!" Admiral Cress shouted. "MEN! TO ARMS!"

"NO!" I shouted, jumping to my feet! "She has been poisoned as well!" As soon as I said it I knew it was true.

Everyone had stopped moving and turned to me, all of them desperate enough for an answer to listen to an obscure, unknown girl. I knew I had to give them something. I had to buy myself more time. "Lady Cathrina had just finished giving me instructions on how this particular poisoning is to be treated. I can heal them."

It was a lie. The biggest lie I have ever told, and turning my head I locked eyes with Trishton. He had been here the whole time. He knew the truth. His hands were clenched into fists, and it took everything I had to stare him down. But then I changed. Instead of trying to fight him, to force him to bend to my will, I allowed the smallest amount of softness into my face.

Then I reached out to him with my soul, pouring my emotions into him with everything I had.

Please, I pleaded, *we have to save them. Help me.*

His eyes widened, then he turned and yelled, "move them to my personal tent! Lady Cathrina's assistant will treat them there!"

Relief overwhelmed me, only to be replaced by fear as Trishton grabbed Lady Cathrina's healing satchel with his other hand and dragged me off behind the servants carrying the bodies.

"You better have a plan, Peasant girl," he hissed low

enough for only me to hear. The connection was still there, though weak.

Panic. Fear. Hopelessness.

"I do," I replied, but a look up at his face made it clear he could feel my emotions as well—and they were not encouraging. "I'm going to heal them." I was my mother's daughter. She was unmovable, and so was I.

Trishton had stopped for only a moment outside his tent.

Apprehension.

Then we ducked inside.

This was the same tent I had woken up in that first morning and realized it must have been the one Trishton shared with his uncle. He and my mother were already on the cots there, servants ready.

I all but shoved them out the door, giving them instruction that *no one* was to be within hearing distance of this tent.

I couldn't do anything about what *I* could hear, though.

My mother and Your Honor might have a few hours, but Tamerin didn't!

"Quick," I said to Trishton. "Get all that ornate stuff off him."

Surprisingly he didn't question me and did it while I loosened my mother's ties and pulled her hair back.

And suddenly I was back almost a year ago the night of the fire with the smell of smoke in the air trying to think of what I was supposed to do next.

"Tell me what to do!" Trishton yelled.

I bit my lip and tried to fight down my panic.

"Seven doors and—"

He grabbed my hand.

Confidence.

I fell to my knees.

There were suddenly tears out of the corner of my eyes as I looked up at him.

"I was *not* telling you to fall over," he said, his voice weak and thin. I nodded as he pulled me up, not letting go of my hand once I was on my feet again.

Panic.

I yanked my hand out of his before I started falling apart again.

I dumped everything out of my mother's healing satchel onto a table against one wall, searching for something, *anything* that could be useful. I found all sorts of antivenom for snakes and spiders, and several for *food* poisoning, but nothing that said "will cure any and all unexplainable poisoning."

I fell down onto a bench.

There wasn't anything I could do.

I was just a Peasant orphan who was about to lose her mother and start a war.

The Great One was wrong, there wasn't anything special about me.

The Great One.

THE GREAT ONE!

I fell to my knees and grabbed my chest, head down but my eyes wouldn't shut.

"HELP ME!" I yelled.

"I'm trying!"

Trishton.

The boy from my dreams was *here!*

I wasn't alone.

"Pray with me!" I grabbed his hands and dragged him down with me.

Panic.

"Call on the lights!"

Terror.

"NO!"

He tried to jump up but I threw all my weight on him and he crashed back down.

"If we don't then *they will die!*"

He looked over at his uncle, and I could see real tears forming in his eyes.

He closed them and I closed mine.

And I called on the lights.

Even before I opened my eyes I knew what I would see. Your Honor and my mother aglow, though there were several holes of darkness and the lights were falling into them. That didn't surprise me.

What *did* surprise me was that I didn't see any lights at all in Trishton.

He was looking at me in shock.

"You don't hurt," he whispered.

"What?"

"You don't have them." Then he looked back at them. "And they don't hurt." He snapped his eyes down to our hands. Then he looked up at me, and my heart skipped a beat.

Salvation.

"FOCUS!" I said, "the blue lights are running out!"

"BLUE!?"

That's when I saw it, threads that were trailing out of the tent.

They looked like what I had seen from the lights in the old man, but those ones were connected to sunshine and the soft blanket and...

I ran out the back of the tent, not letting go of Trishton's hand as I crashed through the jungle, following the thread.

"Where are we going?!"

"I don't know!"

"What?!"

"I'm following the threads, you shrub!"

"But there aren't any threads here, they were all back there shooting out toward the soon-to-be war zone!"

I was about to tell him I had no idea what he was talking about when I tripped and fell hard, bringing him down with me.

I let go of his hand.

I screamed and grabbed my head, terrified of why I was surrounded by trees with hair.

Then I was pulled into someone's arms.

And the pain went away.

"Don't let go again," Trishton said, dragging me to my feet.

I nodded and started running again. I fell two more times, but each time I either brought Trishton down on top of me or just pulled him down in the mud as well, but we didn't let go of each other's hands again.

Then I tripped on a thick vine and landed on stone.

Trishton forgot to pull me up, and I couldn't blame him.

Because there in front of us were stone blocks raised on stone slabs, some broken and all worn, but were clearly man-made.

And there, in the middle of one wall, was a door carved with the image of a tree growing out of its base.

I stepped toward it, transfixed.

What was a Blessing Tree doing in the middle of the jungle in the middle of the ocean?

"Doors..." Trishton whispered. "What is this place?"

It didn't matter.

Because the threads were tangling themselves in the flowers of the vines as the base of the image.

"Those flowers!" I said. "We need them!"

"Yeah," he said, still staring wide-eyed at the image. "Sure, why not."

"You have to help me or let go of my hand."

That got him going and between us we collected all the flowers we could hold.

Without a look back we took off into the jungle again.

Somehow the trek back went faster, and before we knew it we were back in the tent.

When we got inside I looked at Trishton and he looked at me.

I was going to need both hands.

"Whatever you do," he said. "Don't call on the lights again."

"But I need—"

"If you don't want to be as crazy as the third Richarkian prince don't try to make the lights come again!"

Terror.

I nodded and closed my eyes.

And let go of his hand.

My head throbbed like crazy, but when I opened my eyes Trishton was sobbing in a corner.

"Trishton!"

"Save them!" He said into the heels of his hands.

I nodded and looked at the flowers.

They each had five purple petals with yellow, pollen-filled centers.

I didn't know which part to use, so I just mashed them whole in one of my mother's bowls. Then I added a little purified water she kept in a bottle and made a paste.

When I thought it was the right consistency I looked back at her.

I turned to Trishton to ask him to help open their mouths, but he was just staring dead ahead, as if he had cried out his soul instead of just his eyes.

I opened their mouths myself and spooned my mixture under their tongues.

Nothing happened and I began to panic.

There was no way I could tell if it was working. I would have to—

Your Honor turned and vomited, making me jump. I ran over and pounded his back until the black bile was all out. Then he did it again, and this time my mother turned and vomited as well. I was now running back and forth between them until Trishton suddenly appeared to help his uncle while I helped my mother.

When they were both done, their breathing and pulses were stronger. They weren't awake, but I ran out and grabbed a soldier, dragging him in with me.

"They just threw up the poison!" I yelled at him. "They aren't going to die! Now tell both sides to stand down!"

"But—" said the Tamerin soldier.

"Or you get to be the one to explain to Lady Cathrina why we're *at war when she wakes up!*"

He ran out of the tent.

Trishton had to practically drag one of the ambassadors to come to see Your Honor to prove that they were on the mend, but they left convinced afterwards.

The yelling died down.

I sat down on a bench and let the servants come and clean up the mess. At some point Trishton sat down next to me.

"I'm going to need another cot," I said. "I'm going to have to monitor them all night."

"You'll have whatever you need, dream girl."

Dream girl.

The girl from his dreams.

I laughed.

"What?" He said, narrowing his eyes at me.

"It is just, I *hated* you. And you kept saying that you wanted to kill me and then to have you be, to be—"

He laughed. No headscarf, mud-covered, and with some sort of vegetation in his hair and smudges on his cheek right next to—

I kissed him.

And oh, he tasted like a thousand spices.

His arms wrapped around me and I leaned into him.

My secret friend.

The boy from my dreams.

My best—

No.

NO!

AIDEN!

I pulled out of his arms, shocked.

Aiden was my best friend!

I didn't even know anything about this boy!

I slammed down every emotional wall I had.

Aiden may not have believed in my calling, and this boy, from everything I could tell, had the *same* calling—

But I couldn't do it.

I couldn't give up the man I loved to give my heart to someone else, no matter what this boy might mean to me.

"Kailin—"

"We should probably clean up ourselves," I said, turning from him toward the door. I pulled back the flap and told the servant there what I was going to need from my tent.

It was going to be a long time until I was going to be able to go there again.

CHAPTER
FORTY-FOUR

T had taken my shoes off, letting the wet sand slip between my toes. My skirt was pulled up so my calves were showing, but I didn't care as I let the shallow waves dance across the top of my feet.

Trishton was walking beside me, his shoes off as well. We weren't touching, but he was walking so close we might as well have been.

It seemed like we were together every moment, whether he was helping me nurse my mother and his uncle back to health or we were sitting across from each other during the final days of negotiations, trekking through the jungle trying to find that strange stone building, or like now, walking alone together along the beach.

And this would be our last walk.

The meetings were over, my mother and Your Honor were strong enough to travel, and both of our ships were leaving with the evening tide.

And I would never see him again.

His hand moved toward mine.

I smacked it.

"Hey!" he yelled, babying it, "I wasn't trying to hold your hand again, I just wanted to see if..."

He took my hand and like a shrub, I let him.

And felt nothing.

He gently dropped it and put his hands behind his back, not looking at me.

It had been like this since that night a week ago.

No sharing, no dreams.

It was as though whatever connection we had had was severed.

I was on my own again.

I tried to see that as proof I had accomplished what The Great One had set out for me to accomplish, but if that was so, why could I still feel the *pull* whenever I prayed?

I looked over at him and didn't need mystical insight to know that he was miserable.

Because now he was on his own again too, only being on his own meant much more to him than it did to me.

He had told me he couldn't remember a time in his life that he wasn't plagued by the lights and that they always gave him excruciating pain. He wouldn't say much more other than that his uncle and his dead older brother were the only ones who knew the truth about his "headaches." While his uncle had been trying to put everything into a "trials make you stronger" perspective, his brother had actually done the best thing he could have done.

He treated him like he was normal.

Not like an unwanted third prince. Not as an invalid who had to stay in his rooms for days at a time.

Just as a little brother.

Trishton had *worshiped* that brother.

And now he was gone.

Just like I was about to be.

I sighed, wishing that I had a few more days with him.

"Hey," I said, bumping his shoulder. "You should feel proud. You managed to stop a war; back home you'll be a hero!"

"Not likely," he snorted. "First, the assassin was never found, even though we figured out that it was my uncle's cup that had been poisoned and your mother, through that grand gesture of drinking from his, drank it as well. With no one to execute, neither side is very happy with the other, so I would say we didn't do much more than delay it. And remember, neither side actually thought anything was going to come of this trip except war." He let out a breath and looked over at me. "They'll have to continue negotiations, this time with a real plan for peace, either in Richark or Tamerin."

I knew what he was asking.

"I don't think my mother would bring me to Richark," I said, grateful that I could finally talk to someone about my newfound family. "She can play pretend for a few weeks, but a longer trip to Richark that would last potentially *months* is beyond even her." I looked down and let my feet sink into the mud. "When we get back I get a brown dress and a broom."

"I thought you were going to talk to her."

Ug. He was almost as bad as Aiden.

"And I will, when the time is right."

"So on the ship?"

What if she rejected me and I was trapped with her for a week?!

"No."

"So back at the Academy?"

I hesitated.

What if she rejected me and I didn't have Aiden there to protect me?

"When the time is right."

He snorted.

"You could always come back to Richark with me."

I glared at him.

"No thank you."

"Well then," he smiled. "I'll just have to come to Tamerin."

I laughed out loud.

"What," he said, "worried I'll meet your boyfriend?"

"For the last time I don't *have* a boyfriend!"

"Well you *could* have one," he muttered.

"Trishton!" I yelled, making him jump.

"How many times do I have to remind you that you are a *prince*! Even though no one thought enough of your safety to stop you from coming on this mission doesn't mean they'll be willing to deliver you to their sworn enemies on a silver platter!"

"Gold."

"What?"

"A gold platter," he gave me another stupid smile. "Silver is for delivering knights."

I kicked a wave at him, bringing a shout and a smile to his face. He responded by grabbing my arm to throw me in, but I held on to his hand and pulled him down with me. We laughed while sitting in the shallow water, our clothes now soaked.

Then Trishton leaned close to me, and for half a heartbeat I was afraid that he would try to kiss me again, but at the last second he plopped a pile of seaweed on my head.

"You shrub!" I yelled, trying to retaliate, but he was already on his feet.

"Come on," he said, helping me up. "Race you to that tree!"

I watched him run, his legs splashing in the water as he flew across the sand, as if all he wanted in the world was to run forever.

Smiling, I ran after him.

I sat on a bench in the Academy's garden in the late morning sun, stunned.

Because I was back here inside these walls and was not dressed in brown.

My gown was green.

And my hair sticks dangled an inch of colored beads.

As soon as we returned my mother had taken me back to her family home and instructed the servants to take care of me. When I panicked she said that if she really was my mistress, then I was supposed to obey her and pretend for a little bit more; then she left to go give her report to the Senate.

That night she returned after I had gone to bed, but in the morning Healer Clara was downstairs with her, waiting for me.

To take me shopping.

Apparently during her report the night before, she had spoken of how her Peasant servant girl had saved her life and our nation from war and asked for a reward for me.

To be given a scholarship.

I had stared at her in shock.

She then continued, as if I weren't already reeling, that she was so sorry she couldn't set me up with my stipend herself because she was leaving that morning to take a sabbatical for the summer.

I tried to protest, but I stopped short of giving her the real reason I didn't want her to go.

When put on the line, I acted like a true sapling and simply said good-bye to my still clueless mother.

Which led me to where I was now.

Sitting on a bench where anyone could see me.

Or know where to find me.

I pulled a strand of my hair over my shoulder and nervously started running it through my hands.

I didn't look at him when he opened the door.

I didn't look at him when he just stood there.

I didn't look at him when he came over.

And I most certainly kept my eyes forward when he sat down.

He didn't say anything for a long time.

"You came back."

"And I'm even alive," I spat, turning on him.

It was a mistake.

It was summer now, and the sky matched his eyes. And he looked exactly the opposite of the way I had left him, with a clean cream shirt and open green vest, hair combed and clean-shaven. The only thing that marred his appearance were deep shadows under his wide eyes.

Had he missed me at all? I thought that when he heard about my ring advancement he would come here to find me and he did so...

I saw the box of plants at his feet.

Of course, he was here to *garden,* and it had nothing to do with me at all.

"You are alive, aren't you?" he said, still immobile and staring.

"And I'm sure it is just eating you up that you, the great and mighty Lord Aiden, was proven wrong," I said standing, wanting to run away. I had thought I would want to see him, but to have him hear I was back and not come looking for me...

"Normally I would be bothered, but right now I'm more than happy that I was wrong."

"You are?"

"Of course I am! Did you really think I wanted you to die?!"

"Well you sure didn't show that much concern when you left me in the stairwell!"

"What are you talking about?! I tried to keep you from going!"

I turned.

"Wait!" he yelled, making me pause. "That's not what I meant to say!"

"And what did you mean to say?" I said turning back to him.

"I meant to say that I'm sorry! I shouldn't have yelled at you or blamed you, I should have trusted you that you weren't suicidal or kindle-brained or—"

My teeth ground at the thought of him thinking any of those things about me. I guess my face must have shown something about what I was feeling because he looked away and ran a hand through his hair.

"Look," he said, turning back to me, looking more miserable than I thought he was capable of looking. "I'm sorry, that's the important thing. And I have done nothing but regret what I said and did and fear what must have happened to you." He reached for my hand with both of his and I let him take it, his head down, as if he couldn't bear to look at me. "I thought it would be better than when you had disappeared because at least I knew where you were, but instead it has been worse, because now I knew that I would never see you again and I wasted what could have been our last night together." Then he looked up at me, and there was nothing but earnestness in his eyes now. "I kept listening every time I heard something about the negotiations, counting the days, wondering how scared you must be, what they would do to you, especially since you are a servant. But I kept hoping that maybe I was wrong, that maybe you would come back, that maybe you did have some sort of mystical powers—"

He froze, his words hanging heavy between us.

"And what do you think about my mystical powers now?" I whispered.

His face crumpled in on itself.

"I suppose I believe in them."

"And The Great One?" I said sitting back down, unbelieving.

"Now don't go crazy," he muttered.

"I think if you believe in one than you believe in both; it isn't that complicated."

"Maybe it isn't for you but for us mere mortals it is a little more nuanced than that!" Then he ran his hand through his hair again. "Look, isn't it enough that I believe in you even if I don't really believe the other stuff?"

"I suppose so," I said, letting him take my hand with both of his again. "For now."

Then he looked like he was trying to decide something.

"What, exactly, are your mystical powers?"

What were they? Did I even know what they were? I laughed.

"I think," I started, "that I can see into people's souls. Like I can see their life force or something in these blue lights, and then what will make those things brighter, healthier."

"That actually sounds like a very useful skill." I could see the wheels turning in his head...

"No," I said. "I'm not going to use them to diagnose people!"

"Why not? I thought you wanted me to believe you!"

"I do, I just, there are...side effects."

"What do you mean by side effects?" He asked, looking concerned.

"I mean, I have trouble remembering where I am and who people are and—"

"Maybe you just need to practice more," he said excitedly. How could he go from being convinced I was mentally lacking to becoming just as bad as Trishton? Because if I couldn't get it working for him, then—

"I mean, what do you have to lose?"

My eyes narrowed at him.

And I called on the lights.

And gasped.

He was beautiful. All his threads, all his reasons, all his—

His thread was a mooring line wrapped in gold cord and leading straight to my chest.

"Kailin?" he asked.

I let the lights go.

And found myself in a beautiful garden with a strange boy holding my hand.

I yelled and reeled back off the bench, scooting away from him on the grass, when he reached for me.

"Kailin! What is it?! What happened?!"

This strange young man tried to reach for me again, but I pulled away.

"Leave me alone!" I yelled.

"But Kailin—"

"Why do you keep calling me that!? I don't know who you are!"

"Kailin?" he asked, his eyes wide. "But it's me, Aiden."

"Aiden?" I whispered.

Then I remembered.

Crying, I threw myself into his arms.

"Ok, I get it," he said, his heart a horse's gallop under my hand. "You are never going to do that again."

"No," I said pulling back, drunk on what it felt like to be held by him again. "You're right, I need to figure this out, because even if you don't believe it, The Great One did give me these powers for a reason, and it can't just be to stop a war, because even though I used them to do that, they haven't gone away."

"You used them to stop the war?"

"Yes," I said, my eyes wide. "My mother and another delegate from Richark got poisoned, and I was able to find the antidote and heal them."

He stared at me.

And stared at me.

"It's all in my mother's report that she gave to the Senate; you can probably read it for yourself if you want."

It was at the moment one of my hair sticks came out and fell to the ground. He reached down to pick it up, then froze, staring at it.

"Kailin," he said, looking at me, and it was as though he were really getting a good look at me for the first time. "Why are you dressed like a Healer?"

I looked at him in shock. Did he really not know?

"I thought you knew I came back yesterday."

"I've been in the hospital and my room since yesterday morning, I haven't even been to the dining hall," he said, holding my stick limply in his hand, half of my hair hanging down around my neck.

"So you don't know?" I whispered. Without knowing, without realizing when he apologized that there was now a chance to be together—he said all that just for me?

"Know what?!"

"My mother asked the Senate for a reward for me for stopping the war." His eyes went wide. "I'm a scholarship student now."

He laughed, and his laughter spread to me.

Then he picked me up and spun me around the way he had when he found out about my nobility.

When he finally stopped he was still laughing.

"What's so funny?"

"I just, I thought I was losing you when you left, and then to have you come back not only alive but now with a ring advancement and able to take classes—"

"Classes!" I laughed at him, "I thought you would just be happy to be seen in public with me!"

"Well, there is that too." Then his already bright eyes turned even brighter. "How about you let me take you out for lunch?"

I froze in his arms and stared at him.

Because if Lord Aiden could now take me out to a restaurant in broad daylight, then everything else must have been true.

And if all that is true, then the last part was true too.

I was a student at the Healer Academy.

"What do you say, Tamerin's beautiful savior? Be my girlfriend out where everyone can see you?"

I thought I would float away from happiness.

"I say," I said, pulling away toward the door holding on to his hand. "That wherever you take me better have chocolate."

He gave me a smile as bright as the sun, but instead of following me he turned my hand over and pressed my palm against his lips.

I shivered.

"Forgive me?"

"Well," I said, putting my finger under his chin so he

looked up at me, "I suppose I will, but only if you promise never to leave me again."

"I'll do even better than that," he said, tucking my hand in his arm like a true gentleman. "I'll promise to protect you until my dying breath."

I laughed at such a ridiculous thing, but he had only honesty in his eyes. I stretched up on my tiptoes and brushed my lips against his.

"I accept, my gallant protector. Now," I said, pulling him forward, "protect me from starving."

"Yes, My Lady."

I looked at him in panic, but he just rolled his eyes.

"When you're ready. I now know better than to force you to do anything."

"Good," I said. "If that is how you feel now, then I'll consent to being your girlfriend."

He grinned and pulled me toward him and gave me a real kiss, one I could feel all the way down to my toes.

As we walked out of the garden, hand in hand, I realized that I wasn't just a Peasant, or a servant, and definitely not just a bastard child to be shunned. Now I was a student at the Healer Academy, and even more remarkably, I was The Great One's servant, for whatever that meant.

But most important of all, I was becoming what I was always meant to be—a Healer.

The End

SNEAK PEEK AT THE SECOND HEALER ACADEMY BOOK!

PROLOGUE

The wind was hot against my face. Not blistering hot like it would be in the desert on the other side of the Sacred Mountains, where you could get half your face scraped off if you didn't remember to cover your head.

But still. It was uncomfortable - and I hated being uncomfortable.

I was a prince, after all.

The familiar sight of the city sprawled out below my balcony, from the foot of the Sacred Mountains on my right, to the Scarlet Bay on my left, already choked with ships.

There were no servants bothering me, no curses from the guards on the walls below, no sounds at all..

That's how I knew it was a dream.

I reached my hand over, but she wasn't there.

That's how I knew that it wasn't going to be the type of dream I wanted.

The emptiness spread through me, the hollowness ripping my ribcage apart until I had to hug my chest. Not just a whiny

"I miss her," though I've done plenty of that over the past few months. No, this was a physical sensation of being apart from her, like having my leg cut off and trying to stand.

How had I become so weak? I had spent my life dealing with and containing the madness. By last spring when I would have an "episode" I could easily pass it off as a headache.

Then I met her.

And the pain had gone away.

I lifted my eyes to the bay and the ships that were there, hating myself for ever boarding my own vessel four months before.

I was a fool for not bringing her with me. But how was I to know that the dreams would never come back? That the sweet relief of her touch, her soul seeping into mine, bringing me a balm I hadn't dared imagine I needed until I had first dreamed of her violet eyes eight months ago.

I let my own eyes be drawn past the port and towards the open sea, knowing that Tamerin lay beyond its expanse. And just like it had before, my vision became clear and I could see the heathen city as if it was only an hour's journey away.

And it was burning.

A knock came from the sky.

My eyes cracked open, letting me see the wall of luggage tied down in front of me, the Richarkian Royal crest stamped on each one. The rocking of the ship was next, a reminder of where I was - or really where I wasn't. But most importantly it reminded me of where I was going to be.

The knock came again.

I sat up and swung my legs over the edge of the bed, trying to flatten my shoulder length hair into something a little more dignified.

"Enter!"

The door opened and a servant - Ralic was his name - stood in the doorway.

"You asked to be notified when land was in view," he said with a bow. Not a grovel of self-deprecation like I had seen the Tamerin servants use during the negotiations last spring. His was simply a slight bending of the waist to show respect. Or at least that's what I told myself he felt for me.

"Thank you," I said as I stood up, now used to catching my balance on the constantly swaying deck beneath me.

"Would you like help dressing?" Ralic asked, standing back up, his voice formal and distant. I thought that after two weeks of tending me he might have warmed up a little to something resembling a human being, but his young face could have been made of stone. I don't know why I expected anything different; every one of my servants had always treated me with such distance. Maybe because he was new - no, servants talked. No one wanted to be stuck serving a prince who wasn't supposed to be born.

But still, it would have been nice to know why-

I realized my mistake a fraction of a second too late, forgetting the one rule that dominated my life.

Never, never care!

My chest pulled as if a hand had reached inside my heart and pulled it out, my vision dimming of all natural light.

All except for the thousands of red lights now aglow beneath Ralic's skin.

And I could feel his pain.

All of it.

A brother that bullied him and left him insecure. His resentment at having to tend to me, his frustration at my moods, how the others taunted him. His fear of never becoming more, his emptiness when he found out that he was sent on this mission as well, being pulled away from his family and a rather pretty girl in the royal laundry.

And his fear and disgust of my 'headaches.'

It hurt so much - and none of it was mine.

I sank back down on my bed, covering my eyes, willing it to stop, but I could still feel him inside my head, a hammer cracking my skull open right between my eyes.

"Your highness?" Ralic asked and I could hear him stepping forward. "Are you unwell?"

"I'm fine," I said, taking a deep breath, then letting it out.

I opened my eyes, and the lights were gone.

I stared at Ralic, knowing that I should look away, but I couldn't. He was the only thing that made sense. Why was the ground moving? Why was my room so small? What was that awful smell?!

Ralic's eyes narrowed as I stared at him, and I could feel myself panic, though I didn't know why. All I knew was that it was important that he didn't know how lost I suddenly was.

"Just a light headache," I said with a flippant smile. One I knew he hated, thanks to those damned lights, though you never could have told by his calm face.

"Would you like me to bring your breakfast here?"

Breakfast?

I was suddenly hit with a wave of memories, of delicately spiced meats and cool sugared fruits. I had eaten them the night before, in a room, surrounded by other people who didn't want me there...

"No, I'll take it in the dining room with the other delegates." My smile broadened. That must have been one of the shortest memory lapses I've ever had, and I was feeling more than a little smug about it.

Not like I could gloat to anyone, but still, it felt good. I mean, my head still ached as though a rock had fallen on it, but at least I didn't ask any stupid questions this time or go wandering around lost in the palace.

"The other delegates have already eaten."

My moment of triumph disappeared in the face of reality.

Of course they had already eaten. Why would they wait for me? I was only, you know, their prince.

"Then I will eat it in the dining room alone," I said, trying my best to keep the bitterness out of my voice. Well, most of it, at least. "You may go now."

Ralic bowed again before closing my door.

I crashed back on my bed, breathing through my hands, trying to purge myself of what I had seen and felt, but it was no use. The specific memories would fade with time, but the feelings would stay sometimes for weeks.

I honestly didn't mind that most of the palace staff avoided me these days.

I stood up and went to the porthole above the head of my bed and looked out.

And there it was, just like in my dream. I had seen paintings of Tamerin's capitol, but I was not prepared for the sprawl of buildings, the endless creeping of brown and tan, the haze from the thousands of fires needed to keep the million inhabitants warm. Or maybe they were just cooking fires to keep them all fed. I would need to remember not to let on how door-stopping cold it was here.

I turned away to pull on the clothes I had set out the night before, but looked back out at the city as I tied my favorite head scarf, black as my hair.

I put a hand on the side of the window, and took a breath, reaching out with my thoughts...

Kailin.

Nothing.

KAILIN!

I could feel my call echo out, as if there was an infinitely long hallway I was shouting down, only to hear my own voice calling back.

She wasn't there.

ACKNOWLEDGMENTS

When I started writing *The Healer Academy* in the spring of 2011, I had no idea of the journey ahead of me, or of the people who would help take this book from a dream into a reality.

First, I would like to thank Anna Munger, my editor extraordinaire. Her amazing skills helped shape this story into the book it is. She was also my cheerleader when I was feeling discouraged and my therapist when I needed to rant. I love working with her and feel so blessed that she's a part of my writing life.

Next is my husband's not-cousin Rahul Mital. He was my doctor friend who would answer all my weird texts so I got the medical aspects of this book right. Disclaimer: if I still got something wrong it's not his fault.

Next is Beth Lowenstein, who is an angel and did all my proofreading. I legitimately feel like she saved my book. If you're amazed at how readable it is, it's because of her.

Next is Jess Campbell, my bestie who helped me in so many ways. From going through edits with me to listening to me spill my guts with ideas about how to get this book off the ground, she's exactly what I could want in a writing buddy.

Next is Megan Parson, my teenager who read my book and became my number one fan in my teenager fan club. She gave me confidence that my book will connect with the young adults who I wrote this book for in the first place.

And last of all to my wonderful, patient husband Amit. He's

the one who has encouraged me in every way possible, from introducing me as his "writer wife" to letting me write when I maybe should have been doing other things. Without his love and support none of this ever would have happened.

There are so many other people who helped to bring this book to life that I could be here all day listing them. If you weren't included, know that I love you and appreciate all you did for me.

I hope you, the reader, enjoyed reading *The Healer Academy* as much as I enjoyed writing it. Thank you for picking up my book and letting me share Kailin's story with you.

About the Author

Marinda Misra is an emerging author of young adult fantasy. Hailing from the Santa Cruz Mountains in California, she now lives in the Seattle area with her husband and three children. When she isn't writing she is volunteering with young girls, eating fresh kettle corn, and enjoying the water and mountains.

Follow her for updates, newsletter, and other links on her link tree at linktr.ee/marinda.misra.

marindamisra.substack.com

instagram.com/marinda_misra_author

facebook.com/marindamisraauthor

tiktok.com/@marindamisra

goodreads.com/marindamisra